[See p. 43

"HE SPOKE OUT FRANKLY, NOT COUNTING THE RISK"

THE TRUANTS

A Novel

BY

A. E. W. MASON

AUTHOR OF "FOUR FEATHERS"

ILLUSTRATED
BY WILLIAM HURD LAWRENCE

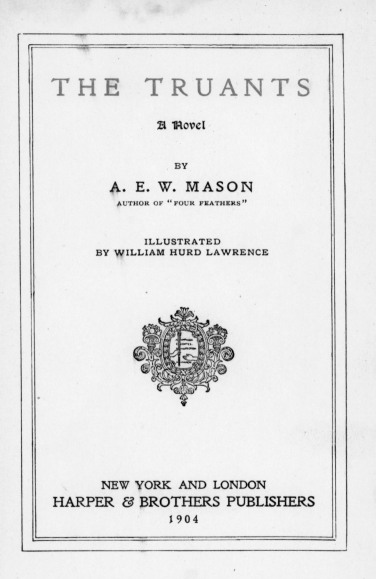

NEW YORK AND LONDON
HARPER & BROTHERS PUBLISHERS
1904

CONTENTS

CONTENTS

iv

ILLUSTRATIONS

V

THE TRUANTS

I

PAMELA MARDALE LEARNS A VERY LITTLE HISTORY

THERE were only two among all Pamela Mardale's friends who guessed that anything was wrong with her, and those two included neither her father nor her mother. Her mother, indeed, might have guessed had she been a different woman. But she was a woman of schemes and little plots, who watched with concentration their immediate developments, but had no eyes for any lasting consequence. And it was no doubt as well for her peace of mind that she never guessed. But of the others it was unlikely that any one would suspect the truth. For Pamela made no outward sign. She hunted through the winter from her home under the Croft Hill in Leicestershire; she went everywhere, as the saying is, during the season in London; she held her own in her own world, lacking neither good spirits nor the look of health. There were, perhaps, two small peculiarities which marked her off from her companions. She was interested in things rather than in persons, and she preferred to talk to old men rather than to youths. But such points, taken by themselves, were not of an importance to attract attention. Yet there were two among her friends who suspected—Alan Warrisden and the school-master of Roquebrune, the little village carved out of the hill-side to the east of Monte Carlo. The school-master was the nearer to the truth, for he not only knew that something was amiss, he suspected what the some-thing was. But then he had a certain advantage, since he had known Pamela Mardale when she was a child. Their acquaintance came about in the follow-ing way:

He was leaning, one evening of December, over the parapet of the tiny square beside the school-house, when a servant from the Villa Pontignard approached him.

"Could M. Giraud make it convenient to call at the villa at noon to-morrow?" the servant asked. "Madame Mardale is anxious to speak to him."

M. Giraud turned about with a glow of pleasure upon his face.

"Certainly," he replied. "But nothing could be more simple. I will be at the Villa Pontignard as the clock strikes."

The servant bowed and without another word paced away across the square and up the narrow, winding street of Roquebrune, leaving the school-master a little abashed at his display of eagerness. M. Giraud rec-ognized that in one man's mind, at all events, he was now set down for a snob, for a lackey disguised as a school-master. But the moment of shame passed. He had no doubt as to the reason of the summons, and he tingled with pride from head to foot. It was his little brochure upon the history of the village—written with what timidity and printed at what cost to his meagre purse!—which had brought him recognition from the lady of the villa upon the spur of the hill. Looking upward, he could just see the white walls of the villa glimmering through the dusk; he could imagine its garden of trim lawns and dark cypresses falling from bank to bank in ordered tiers down the hill-side.

"To-morrow at noon," he repeated to himself, and now he was seized with a shiver of fear at the thought of the mistakes in behavior which he was likely to make. What if Madame Mardale asked him to breakfast? There would be unfamiliar dishes to be eaten with particular forks. Sometimes a knife should be used and sometimes not. He turned back to the parapet with the thought that he had better, perhaps, send up a note in the morning pleading his duties at the school as a reason for breaking his engagement. But he was young, and, as he looked down the steep slope of rock on which the village is perched, anticipation again got the better of fear. He began to build up his life like a fairy palace from the foundation of this brief message.

A long lane of steps led winding down from the square, and his eyes followed it, as his feet had often done, to the little railway-station by the sea, through which people journeyed to and fro between the great cities — westward to France and Paris, eastward to Rome and Italy. His eyes followed the signal-lights towards another station of many lamps far away to the right, and as he looked there blazed out suddenly other lights of a great size and a glowing brilliancy, lights which had the look of amazing jewels discovered in an Eastern cave. These were the lights upon the terrace of Monte Carlo. The school-master had walked that terrace on his mornings of leisure, had sat unnoticed on the benches, all worship of the women and their daintiness, all envy of the men and the composure of their manner. He knew none of them, and yet one of them had actually sent for him, and had heard of his work. He was to speak with her at noon to-morrow.

Let it be said at once that there was nothing of the lackey under the school-master's shabby coat. The visit which he was bidden to pay was to him not so much a step upward as outward. Living always in this remote, high village, where the rock cropped out between the houses and the streets climbed through tunnels of rock, he was always tormented with visions of great cities and thoroughfares ablaze; he longed for the jostle of men, he craved for other companionship than he could get in the village wine-shop on the first floor, as a fainting man craves for air. The stars came out above his head; it was a clear night and they had never shone brighter. The Mediterranean, dark and noiseless, swept out at his feet beyond the woods of Cap Martin. But he saw neither the Mediterranean nor any star. His eyes turned to the glowing terrace upon his right and to the red signal-lamps below the terrace.

M. Giraud kept his engagement punctually. The clock chimed upon the mantel-piece a few seconds after he was standing in the drawing-room of the Villa Pontignard, and before the clock had stopped chiming Mrs. Mardale came in to him. She was a tall woman, who in spite of her years still retained the elegance of her youth, but her face was hard and a trifle querulous, and M. Giraud was utterly intimidated. On the other hand, she had good manners, and the friendly simplicity with which she greeted him began to set him at his ease.

4

"You are a native of Roquebrune, monsieur?" said she.

"No, madame; my father was a peasant at Aigues-Mortes. I was born there," he replied, frankly.

"Yet you write, if I may say so, with the love of a native for his village," she went on. M. Giraud was on the point of explaining. Mrs. Mardale, however, was not in the least interested in his explanation, and she asked him to sit down.

"My daughter, monsieur, has an English governess," she explained, "but it seems a pity that she should spend her winters here and lose the chance of becoming really proficient in French. The curé recommended me to apply to you, and I sent for you to see whether we could arrange that you should read history with her in French during your spare hours."

M. Giraud felt his head turning. Here was his opportunity so long dreamed of come at last. It might be the beginning of a career; it was, at all events, that first difficult step outward. He was to be the teacher in appearance; at the bottom of his heart he knew that he was to be the pupil. He accepted the offer with enthusiasm, and the arrangements were made. Three afternoons a week he was to spend an hour at the Villa Pontignard.

"Well, I hope the plan will succeed," said Mrs. Mardale, but she spoke in a voice which showed that she had no great hopes of success. And as M. Giraud replied that he would at all events do his best, she rejoined, plaintively:

"It is not of you, monsieur, that I have any doubts. But you do not know my daughter. She will learn nothing which she does not want to learn; she will not endure any governess who is not entirely her slave;

and she is fifteen, and she really must learn something."

Pamela Mardale, indeed, was at this time the despair
of her mother. Mrs. Mardale had mapped out for her
daughter an ideal career. She was to be a model of
decorum in the Early Victorian style, at once an
ornament for a drawing-room and an excellent housekeeper, and she was subsequently to make a brilliant
marriage. The weak point of the scheme was that
it left Pamela out of the reckoning. There was her
passion for horses, for one thing, and her distinct refusal, besides, to sit quietly in any drawing-room.
When she was a child, horses had been persons to
Pamela rather than animals, and, as her conduct
showed, persons preferable by far to human beings.
Visitors to the house under Croft Hill were at times
promised a sight of Pamela, and, indeed, they sometimes did see a girl in a white frock, with long, black
legs and her hair tumbled all over her forehead, neigh-
ing and prancing at them from behind the gate of the
stable-yard. But they did not see her at closer quarters than that, and it was certain that, if by any chance
her lessons were properly learned, they had been learned upon the corn - bin in the stables. Portraits of
Pamela at the age of nine remain, and they show a girl
who was very pretty, but who might quite well have
been a boy, with a mass of unruly dark hair, a pair of
active dark eyes, and a good - humored face alertly
watching for any mischief which might come its way.

Something of the troubles which M. Giraud was
likely to find ahead of him Mrs. Mardale disclosed that
morning, and the school-master returned to his house
filled with apprehensions. The apprehensions, however, were not justified. The little school-master was

so shy, so timid, that Pamela was disarmed. She could be gentle when she chose, and she chose now. She saw, too, M. Giraud's anxiety to justify her mother's choice of him, and she determined, with a sense of extreme virtue, to be a credit to his teaching. They became friends, and thus one afternoon when they had taken their books out into the garden of the villa, M. Giraud confided to her the history of the brochure which had made them acquainted.

"It was not love for Roquebrune which led me to write it," he said. "It was, on the contrary, my discontent. I was tortured with longings; I was not content with the children's lessons for my working hours and the wine-shop for my leisure. I took long walks over Cap Martin to Mentone, along the Corniche road to La Turbie, and up Mont Agel. But still I had my longings as my constant companions, and, since everywhere I saw traces of antiquity, I wrote this little history as a relief. It kept my thoughts away from the great world."

The garden ran here to a point at the extreme end of that outcropping spur of rock on which the villa was built. They were facing westward, and the sun was setting behind the hills. It lay red upon the Mediterranean on their left, but the ravine and front were already dark, and down the hill-side the shadows of the trees were lengthening. At their feet, a long way below, a stream tumbled and roared among the oleanders in the depths of the ravine. Pamela sat gazing downward, her lips parted in a smile.

"The great world," she said, in a low voice of eagerness. "I wonder what it's like."

That afternoon marked a distinct step in their friendship, and thereafter, in the intervals of their reading, they talked continually upon this one point they had in common — their curiosity as to the life of the world beyond their village. But it happened that Pamela did the greater part of the talking, and one afternoon that fact occurred to her.

"You always listen now, monsieur," she said. "Why have you grown so silent?"

"You know more than I do, mademoiselle."

"I?" she exclaimed, in surprise. "I only know about horses." Then she laughed. "Really, we both know nothing. We can only guess and guess."

And that was the truth. Pamela's ideas of the world were as visionary, as dreamlike as his, but they were not his, as he was quick to recognize. The instincts of her class, her traditions, the influence of her friends, were all audible in her voice as well as in her words. To her the world was a great flower-garden of pleasure with plenty of room for horses. To him it was a crowded place of ennobling strife.

"But it's pleasant work guessing," she continued. "Isn't it? Then why have you stopped?"

"I will tell you, mademoiselle. I am beginning to guess through your eyes."

The whistle of a train, the train from Paris, mounted through the still air to their ears.

"Well," said Pamela, with a shrug of impatience, "we shall both know the truth some time."

"You will, mademoiselle," said the school-master, suddenly falling out of his dream.

Pamela looked quickly at him. The idea that he would be left behind, that he would stay here all his life listening to the sing-song drone of the children in the school-room, teaching over and over again with an infinite weariness the same elementary lessons, until he became shabby and worn as the lesson-books he handled, had never struck her till this moment. The trouble which clouded his face was reflected by sympathy upon hers.

"But you won't stay here," she said, gently. "Oh no! Let me think!" And she thought with a child's oblivion of obstacles and a child's confidence. She imparted the wise result of her reflections to M. Giraud the next afternoon.

He came to the garden with his eyes fevered and his face drawn.

"You are ill?" said Pamela. "We will not work to-day."

"It's nothing," he replied.

"Tell me," said she.

M. Giraud looked out across the valley.

"Two travellers came up to Roquebrune yesterday. I met them as I walked home from here. I spoke to them and showed them the village, and took them by the short cut of the steps down to the railway-station. They were from London. They talked of London and of Paris. It's as well visitors come up to Roquebrune rarely. I have not slept all night," and he clasped and unclasped his hands.

"Hannibal crossed the Alps," said Pamela. "I read it in your book," and then she shook a finger at him, just as the school-master might have done to one of his refractory pupils.

"Listen," said she. "I have thought it all out."

The school-master composed himself into the attentive attitude of a pupil.

"You are to become a deputy."

That was the solution of the problem Pamela saw no difficulties. He would need a dress-suit, of course, for official occasions, which she understood were numerous. A horse, too, would be of use, but that didn't matter so much. The horse was regretfully given up. It might come later. He must get elected first, never mind how. In a word, he was as good as a deputy already. And from a deputy to the President of the French Republic, the step, after all, was not so very long. "Though I am not quite sure that I approve of republics," said Pamela, very seriously.

However, that was the best she could do in the way of mapping out his future, and the school-master listened, seeing the world through her eyes. Thus three winters passed, and Pamela learned a very little history.

Towards the end of the third winter the history books were put away. Pamela was now eighteen and looking eagerly forward to her first season in London. And no doubt frocks and hats occupied more of her thoughts than did the fortune of the school-master. Some remorse for her forgetfulness seized her the day before she went away. It was a morning of spring, and the school-master saw her coming down the dark, narrow streets towards him. She was tall beyond the average, but without ungainliness, long of limb and lightly built, and she walked with the very step of youth. Her dark hair swept in two heavy waves above her forehead and was coiled down behind on the back of her neck. Her throat rose straight and slim from the firm shoulders, and her eyes glowed with anticipation. Though her hair was dark, she was not sallow. Her face was no less fresh and clear than were her eyes, and a soft color like the bloom of a fruit brightened her cheeks. In that old, brown street she shone like a brilliant flower, and Giraud, as he watched

"IN THAT OLD, BROWN STREET SHE SHONE LIKE A BRILLIANT
FLOWER"

her, felt all at once that he could have no place in her life, and in his humility he turned aside. But she ran after him and caught him up.

"I am going to-morrow," she said, and she tried to keep the look of happiness out of her eyes, the thrill out of her voice. And she failed.

"It is good-bye, then," said he.

"For a little while. I shall come back to Roque-brune in December."

The school-master smiled.

"I shall look forward from to-day until that month comes. You will have much to tell me."

"Yes, sha'n't I?" she cried, and then, lest her eagerness should hurt her friend, she added, "But I shall not forget our quiet afternoons on the garden terrace."

The recollection of them, however, was not strong enough to check either her thoughts or their utterance. Later on perhaps, in after years, she might in her musings return to that terrace and the speculations they indulged in, and the fairy palaces they built, with an envy of the ignorance and the high thoughts of youth. To-day she was all alert to grasp the future in her hands. One can imagine her looking much as she looked in those portraits of her childhood.

"News of the great world," she cried. "I shall bring it back. We will talk it over in Roquebrune and correct our guesses. For I shall know."

As a fact they never did talk over her news, but that she could not foresee. She went on her way with a smile upon her face: all confidence and courage and expectation, a brilliant image of youth. Giraud, as he watched her, the proud poise of her head, the light, springing step, the thing of beauty and gentleness which she was, breathed a prayer that no harm might come to her and no grief ever sadden her face.

The next morning she went away, and the schoolmaster lost his one glimpse of the outer world. But he lived upon the recollections of it and took again to his long walks on the Corniche road. The time hung heavily upon his hands. He hungered for news, and no news came; and when in the month of December he noticed that the shutters were opened in the Villa Pontignard, and that there was a stir of servants about the house, he felt that the shutters were being opened after a long, dark time from his one window on the outside world. He frequented the little station from that moment. No "Rapide" passed from France on its way to Italy during his leisure hours but he was there to watch its passengers. Mrs. Mardale came first, and a fortnight afterwards Pamela descended from a carriage with her maid.

Giraud watched her with a thrill of longing. It was not merely his friend who had returned, but his instructor, with new and wonderful knowledge added to the old.

Then came his first chilling moment of disillusion. It was quite evident that she saw him as she was stepping onto the platform. Her eyes went straight to his—and yet she turned away without the slightest sign of recognition and busied herself about her luggage. The world had spoiled her. That was his first thought, but he came to a truer understanding afterwards. And, indeed, that thought had barely become definite in his mind, when she turned again, and, holding out her hand, came to him with a smile.

"You are well?" she said.

"Yes," said he.

And they walked up the long flight of steps to Roquebrune talking banalities. She gave him none of the news for which he longed, and they spoke not at all of the career which together they had mapped out for him. All their long talks upon the terrace, their plans and their speculations, seemed in an instant to Giraud to have become part of a pleasant, very foolish, and very distant past. He was aware of the vast gulf between them. With a girl's inimitable quickness to adapt herself to new surroundings, she had acquired in the few months of her absence the ease, the polish, and the armor of a woman of the world. He was still the village school-master, the peasant tortured with vain aspirations, feeding upon vain dreams; and in this moment he saw himself very clearly. Her silence upon their plan helped him to see himself thus. Had she still believed in that imagined career, surely she would have spoken of it. In a word, he was still looking at the world through her eyes.

"You must come up to the villa," she said. "I shall look forward to your coming."

They were in the little square by the school-house, and he took the words for his dismissal. She went up the hill alone, and slowly, like one that is tired. Giraud, watching her, could not but compare her with the girl who had come lightly down that street a few months ago. It dawned upon him that, though knowledge had been acquired, something had gone, something perhaps more valuable, the elasticity from her step, the eagerness from her eyes.

Giraud did not go up to the villa of his own accord, but he was asked to lunch in a week's time, and after lunch Pamela and he went out into the garden. Instinctively they walked down to that corner on the point of the bluff which overhung the ravine and the white torrent among the oleanders in its depths. They had come, indeed, to the bench on which they used to sit before Pamela was quite aware of the direction their steps had taken. She drew back suddenly as she raised her head.

"Oh no, not here," she cried, and she moved away quickly with a look of pain. Giraud suddenly understood why she had turned away at the railway-station. Here they had dreamed, and the reality had shown the dreams to be bitterly false, so false that the very place where they had dreamed had become by its associations a place of pain. She had needed for herself that first moment when she had stepped down from the carriage.

"The world must be the home of great troubles," said Giraud, sadly.

"And how do you know that?" Pamela asked, with a smile.

"From you," he replied, simply.

The answer was unexpected. Pamela stopped and looked at him with startled eyes.

"From me? I have said nothing—nothing at all."

"Yet I know. How else should I know except from you, since through you alone I see the world?"

"A home of great troubles?" she repeated, speaking lightly. "Not for all. You are serious, my friend, this afternoon, and you should not be, for have I not come back?"

The school-master was not deceived by her evasion. There had come a gravity into her manner, and a womanliness into her face, in a degree more than natural at her years.

14

"Let us talk of you for a change," said she.

"Well, and what shall we say?" asked Giraud, and a constraint fell upon them both.

"We must forget those fine plans," he continued, at length. "Is it not so? I think I have learned that, too, from you."

"I have said nothing," she interrupted, quickly.

"Precisely," said he, with a smile. "The school at Roquebrune will send no deputy to Paris."

"Oh! why not?" said Pamela, but there was no conviction in her voice. Giraud was not of the stern stuff

"To break his birth's invidious bar."

He had longings, but there was the end.

"At all events," she said, turning to him with a great earnestness, "we shall be friends always, whatever happens."

The words were the death-knell to the school-master's aspirations. They conveyed so much more than was actually said. He took them bravely enough.

"That is a good thing," he said, in all sincerity. "If I stay here all my life, I shall still have the memory of the years when I taught you history. I shall know, though I do not see you, that we are friends. It is a great thing for me."

"For me, too," said Pamela, looking straight into his eyes, and she meant her words no less than he had meant his. Yet to both they had the sound of a farewell. And in a way they were. They were the farewell to the afternoons upon the terrace; they closed the door upon their house of dreams.

Giraud leaned that evening over the parapet in the little square of Roquebrune. The Mediterranean lay dark and quiet far below, the terrace of Monte Carlo glowed, and the red signal-lamps pointed out the way to Paris. But he was no longer thinking of his fallen plans. He was thinking of the girl up there in the villa who had been struck by some blind blow of Destiny, who had grown a woman before her time. It was a pity, it was a loss in the general sum of things which make for joy.

He had, of course, only his suspicions to go upon. But they were soon strengthened. For Pamela fell into ill-health, and the period of ill-health lasted all that winter. After those two years had passed she disappeared for a while altogether out of Giraud's sight. She came no more to the Villa Pontignard, but stayed with her father and her horses at her home in Leicestershire. Her mother came alone to Roquebrune.

II

PAMELA LOOKS ON

ALAN WARRISDEN was one of the two men who had walked up to Roquebrune on that afternoon of which M. Giraud spoke. But it was not until Pamela had reached the age of twenty that he made her acquaintance at Lady Millingham's house in Berkeley Square. He took her down to dinner, and, to tell the truth, paid no particular attention either to her looks or her conversation. His neighbor upon the other side happened to be a friend whom he had not seen for some while, and for a good part of the dinner he talked to her. A few days afterwards, however, he called upon Lady Millingham, and she asked at once, quite eagerly:

"Well, what did you think of Pamela Mardale?"

Warrisden was rather at a loss. He was evidently expected to answer with enthusiasm, and he had not any very definite recollections on which enthusiasm could be based. He did his best, however; but he was unconvincing. Lady Millingham shrugged her shoulders and frowned. She had been married precisely a year and was engaged in plans for marrying off all her friends with the greatest possible despatch.

"I shall send you in with somebody quite old the next time you dine here," she said, severely, and she discoursed at some length upon Pamela's charms. "She loves horses and yet she's not a bit horsy," she

said, in conclusion, "and there's really nothing better
than that. And just heaps of men have wanted to
marry her." She leaned back against her sofa and
contemplated Warrisden with silent scorn. She had
set her heart upon this marriage more than upon any
other. Of all the possible marriages in London, there
was not one, to her mind, so suitable as this. Pamela
Mardale came of one of the oldest families of com-
moners in Leicestershire. The family was not well
off, the estate had shrunk year by year, and what was
left was mortgaged, owing in some degree to that villa
at Roquebrune upon which Mrs. Mardale insisted.
Warrisden, on the other hand, was more than well off,
his family was known, and at the age of twenty-eight
he was still dividing his life between the season in
London and shooting expeditions about the world.
And he had the look of a man who might do something
more.

That visit had its results. Warrisden met Pamela
Mardale again, and realized that Lady Millingham's
indignation had been justified. At the end of that
season he proposed and was gently refused. But if
he was slow to move he was also firm to persevere.
He hunted with the Quorn that winter, and during the
following season he was persistently but unobtrusive-
ly at her elbow; so that Pamela came, at all events, to
count upon him as a most reliable friend. Having
duly achieved that place in her thoughts, he disappeared for ten months and returned to town one afternoon in the last week of June. There were letters
waiting for him in his rooms, and among them a card
from Lady Millingham inviting him to a dance upon
that night. At eleven o'clock his coupé turned out
of Piccadilly and entered Berkeley Square. At the

bottom of the square the lighted windows of the house blazed out upon the night, the balconies were banked with flowers, and behind the flowers, silhouetted against the light, were visible the thronged faces of men and women. Warrisden leaned forward scrutinizing the shapes of the heads, the contours of the faces. His sight, sharpened by long practice over wide horizons, was of the keenest; he could see, even at that distance, the flash of jewels on neck and shoulder. But the face he looked for was not there.

Lady Millingham, however, set his mind at ease.

"You are back, then?" she cried.

"This afternoon."

"You will find friends here."

Warrisden passed on into the reception-rooms. It seemed to him, indeed, that all the friends he had ever made were gathered to this one house on this particular evening. He was a tall man, and his height made him noticeable upon most occasions. He was the more noticeable now by reason of his sunburn and a certain look of exhilaration upon his face. The season was drawing to its end, and brown faces were not so usual but that the eyes turned to them. He spoke, however, the fewest possible words to the men who greeted him, and he did not meet the eyes of any woman. Yet he saw the women, and was in definite quest of one of them. That might have been noticed by a careful observer, for whenever he saw a man older than the rest talking to a girl he quickened his pace that he might the sooner see that girl's face. He barely looked into the ballroom at all, but kept to the corridors, and at last, in a doorway, came face to face with Pamela Mardale. He saw her face light up, and the hand held out to him was even eagerly extended.

"Have you a dance to spare?"

Pamela looked quickly round upon her neighbors.

"Yes, this one," she answered. She bowed to her companion, a man, as Warrisden expected, much older than herself, and led the way at once towards the balcony. Warrisden saw a youth emerge from the throng and come towards them. Pamela was tall, and she used her height at this moment. She looked him in the face with so serene an indifference that the youth drew back disconcerted. Pamela was deliberately cutting her partners.

Another man might have built upon the act, but Warrisden was shrewd, and shrewdness had taught him long since to go warily in thought where Pamela Mardale was concerned. She might merely be angry. He walked by her side and said nothing. Even when they were seated on the balcony he left it for her to speak first. She was sitting upon the outside against the railing, so that the light from the windows streamed full upon her face. He watched it, looking for the change which he desired. But it had still the one fault he found with it. It was still too sedate, too womanly for her years.

"I heard of you," she said. "You were shooting woodcock in Dalmatia."

"That was at Christmas."

"Yes. You were hurt there."

"Not seriously," he replied. "A sheep-dog attacked me. They are savage brutes, and indeed they have to be, there are so many wolves. The worst of it is, if you are attacked you mustn't kill the dog or there's trouble."

"I heard of you again. You were at Quetta, getting together a caravan."

"That was in February. I crossed by the new trade-route from Quetta to Seistan."

She had spoken in an indefinite tone, which left him with no clew to her thoughts. Now, however, she turned her eyes upon him, and said in a lower voice, which was very gentle:

"Don't you think you might have told me that you were going away for a year?"

Warrisden had gone away deliberately, and as deliberately he had abstained from telling her of his intention. He had no answer to make to her question, and he did not attempt to invent one. He sat still and looked at her. She followed the question with another.

"Don't you think it would have been kinder if you had written to me once or twice, instead of letting me hear about you from any chance acquaintance?"

Again he made no answer. For he had deliberately abstained from writing. The gentleness with which she spoke was the most hopeful sign for him which she had made that evening. He had expected a harsher accusation. For Pamela made her claims upon her friends. They must put her first or there was likely to be a deal of trouble.

"Well," she said, with a shrug of her shoulders, "I hope you enjoyed it."

"Yes. I wish I could have thought you would have enjoyed it too. But you wouldn't have."

"No," she answered, listlessly.

Warrisden was silent. He had expected the answer, but he was none the less disappointed to receive it. To him there was no century in the history of the world comparable to that in which he lived. It had its faults, of course. It was ugly and a trifle feverish, but to men of his stamp, the men with means and energy, a new world with countless opportunities had been opened up. Asia and Africa were theirs, and the farthest islands of the sea. Pamela, however, turned her back on it. The new trade-route to Seistan had no message for her. She looked with envy upon an earlier century.

"Of course," he resumed, "it's pleasant to come back, if only as a preparation for going away again."

And then Pamela turned on him with her eyes wide open and a look of actual trouble upon her face.

"No," she said, with emphasis. She leaned forward and lowered her voice. "You have no right to work upon people and make them your friends, if you mean, when you have made them your friends, to go away without a word for ever so long. I have missed you very much."

"I wanted you to miss me," he replied.

"Yes, I thought so. But it wasn't fair," she said, gently. "You see, I have been quite fair with you. If you had gone away at once, if you had left me alone when I said 'no' to you two years ago, then I should have no right to complain, I should have no right to call you back. But it's different now, and you willed that it should be different. You stayed by me. Whenever I turned, there were you at my side. You taught me to count on you as I count on no one else. Yes, that's true. Well, then, you have lost the right to turn your back now just when it pleases you."

"It wasn't because it pleased me."

"No; I admit that," she agreed. "It was to make

22

an experiment on me, but the experiment was made at my expense. For, after all, you enjoyed yourself," she added, with a laugh.

Warrisden joined in the laugh.

"It's quite true," he said. "I did." Then his voice dropped to the same serious tone in which she had spoken. "Why not say the experiment succeeded? Couldn't you say that?"

Pamela shook her head.

"No. I can give you no more now than I gave you a year ago, two years ago, and that is not enough. Oh, I know," she continued, hurriedly, as she saw that he was about to interrupt. "Lots of women are content to begin with friendship. How they can puzzles me. But I know they do begin with nothing more than that, and very often it works out very well. The friendship becomes more than friendship. But I can't begin that way. I would if I could, but I can't."

She leaned back in her chair, and sat for a while with her hands upon her knees in an attitude extraordinarily still. The jingle of harness in the square rose to Warrisden's ears, the clamor of the town came muffled from the noisy streets. He looked upward to the tender blue of a summer sky, where the stars shone like silver; and he leaned back disheartened. He had returned to London and nothing was changed. There was the same busy life vociferous in its streets, and this girl still sat in the midst of it with the same lassitude and quiescence. She seemed to be waiting, not at all for something new to happen, but for the things which were happening to cease, waiting with the indifference of the very old. And she was quite young. She sat with the delicate profile of her face outlined against the darkness; the color of youth was in her cheeks; the slender column of her throat, the ripple of her dark hair, the grace of her attitude claimed her for youth; she was fragrant with it from head to foot. And yet it seemed that there was no youth in her blood.

"So nothing has changed for you during these months," he said, deeply disappointed.

She turned her face quietly to him and smiled. "No," she answered, "there has been no new road for me from Quetta to Seistan. I still look on."

There was the trouble. She just looked on, and to his thinking it was not right that at her age she should do no more. A girl nowadays had so many privileges, so many opportunities denied to her grandmother, she could do so much more, she had so much more freedom, and yet Pamela insisted upon looking on. If she had shown distress, it would have been better. But no. She lived without deep feeling of any kind, in a determined isolation. She had built up a fence about herself, and within it she sat untouched and alone.

It was likely that no one else in the wide circle of her acquaintances had noticed her detachment, and certainly to no one but Warrisden had she admitted it. And it was only acknowledged to him after he had found it out for himself. For she did not sit at home. On the contrary, hardly a night passed during the season but she went to some party. Only, wherever she went, she looked on.

"And you still prefer old men to young ones?" he cried, in a real exasperation.

"They talk more of things and less of persons," she explained.

THE TRUANTS

That was not right either. She ought to be interested in persons. Warrisden rose abruptly from his chair. He was completely baffled. Pamela was like the sleeping princess in the fairy tale—she lay girt about with an impassable thicket of thorns. She was in a worse case, indeed, for the princess in the story might have slept on till the end of time, a thing of beauty. But was it possible for Pamela so to sleep to the end of life? he asked himself. Let her go on in her indifference, and she might dwindle and grow narrow, her soul would be starved and all the good of her be lost. Somehow a way must be forced through the thicket, somehow she must be wakened. But he seemed no nearer to finding that way than he had been two years ago, and she was no nearer to her wakening.

"No, there has been no change," he said, and as he spoke his eye was caught by a bright light which suddenly flamed up in the window of a dark house upon his right. The house had perplexed him more than once. It took so little part in the life of the square, it so consistently effaced itself from the gayeties of the people who lived about. Its balconies were never banked with flowers; no visitors mounted its steps; and even in the daytime it had a look of mystery. It may have been that some dim analogy between that house and the question which so baffled him arrested Warrisden's attention. It may have been merely that he was by nature curious and observant. But he leaned forward upon the balcony-rail.

"Do you see that light?" he asked. "In the window on the second floor?"

"Yes."

He took out his watch and noticed the time. It

25

was just a quarter to twelve. He laughed softly to himself, and said:

"Wait a moment!"

He watched the house for a few minutes without saying a word. Pamela, with a smile at his eagerness, watched too. In a little while they saw the door open and a man and a woman both in evening dress appear upon the steps. Warrisden laughed again.

"Wait!" he said, as if he expected Pamela to interrupt. "You'll see they won't whistle up a cab. They'll walk beyond the house and take one quietly. Very likely they'll look up at the lighted window on the second floor, as though they were school-boys who had escaped from their dormitories and were afraid of being caught by the master before they had had their fun. There, do you see?"

For as he spoke, the man and the woman stopped and looked up. Had they heard Warrisden's voice and obeyed his directions they could not have more completely fulfilled his prediction. They had the very air of truants. Apparently they were reassured. They walked along the pavement until they were well past the house. Then they signalled to a passing hansom. The cab-driver did not see them, yet they did not call out, nor did the man whistle. They waited until another approached and they beckoned to that. Warrisden watched the whole scene with the keenest interest. As the two people got into the cab he laughed again and turned back to Pamela.

"Well?" she said, with a laugh of amusement, and the quiet monosyllable, falling as it were with a cold splash upon his enjoyment of the little scene, suddenly brought him back to the question which was always latent in his mind—how was Pamela to be awakened?

THE TRUANTS

"It's a strange place, London," he said. "No doubt it seems stranger to me, and more full of interesting people and interesting things, just because I have come back from very silent and very empty places. But that house always puzzled me. I used to have rooms overlooking this square, high up, over there," and he pointed to the eastern side of the square towards Berkeley Street; "and what we have seen tonight used to take place every night, and at the same hour. The light went up in the room on the second floor and the truants crept out. Guess where they go to! The Savoy. They go and sit there among the lights and the music for half an hour, then they come back to the dark house. They live in the most curious isolation with the most curious regularity. There are three of them altogether: an old man—it is his light, I suppose, which went up on the second floor—and those two. I know who they are. The old man is Sir John Stretton."

"Oh!" said Pamela, with interest.

"And the two people we saw are his son and his son's wife. I have never met them. In fact, no one meets them. I don't know any one who knows them."

"Yes, you do," said Pamela, "I know them." And in her knowledge, although Warrisden did not know it, lay the answer to the problem which so perplexed him.

III

THE TRUANTS

WARRISDEN turned quickly to Pamela.
"You never mentioned them."

"No," she replied, with a smile. "But there's no mystery in my silence. I simply haven't mentioned them because for two years I have lost sight of them altogether. I used to meet them about, and I have been to their house."

"There?" asked Warrisden, with a nod towards the lighted window.

"No; but to the house Millie and Mr. Stretton had in Deanery Street. They gave that up two years ago when old Lady Stretton died. I thought they had gone to live in the country."

"And all the while they have been living here," exclaimed Warrisden. He had spoken truthfully of himself. The events and the people with whom he came, however slightly, into contact always had interested and amused him. It was his pleasure to fit his observations together until he had constructed a little biography in his mind of each person with whom he was acquainted. And there was never an incident of any interest within his notice but he sought the reason for it and kept an eye open for its consequence.

"Don't you see how strange the story is?" he went on. "They give up their house upon Lady Stretton's death and they come to live here with Sir John.

28

That's natural enough. Sir John's an old man. But they live in such seclusion that even their friends think they have retired into the country."

"Yes, it is strange," Pamela admitted. And she added, "I was Millie Stretton's bridesmaid."

Upon Warrisden's request she told him what she knew of the couple who lived in the dark house and played truant. Millie Stretton was the daughter of a judge in Ceylon, who, when Millie had reached the age of seventeen, had married a second time. The step-mother had lacked discretion; from the very first she had claimed to exercise a complete and undisputed authority; she had been at no pains to secure the affections of her step-daughter. And very little trouble would have been needed, for Millie was naturally affectionate. A girl without any great depth of feeling, she responded easily to a show of kindness. She found it neither difficult to make intimate friends nor hard to lose them. She was of the imitative type besides. She took her thoughts and even her language from those who at the moment were by her side. Thus her step-mother had the easiest of tasks, but she did not possess the necessary tact. She demanded obedience and in return offered tolerance. The household at Colombo, therefore, became for Millie a roofstead rather than a home, and a year after this marriage she betook herself and the few thousands of pounds which her mother had bequeathed her to London. The ostensible reason for her departure was the invitation of Mrs. Charles Rawson, a friend of her mother's. But Millie had made up her mind that a return to Ceylon was not to be endured. Somehow she would manage to make a home for herself in England.

She found her path at once made easy. She was

pretty, with the prettiness of a child, she gave no trouble, she was fresh, she dressed a drawing-room gracefully, she fitted neatly into her surroundings, she picked up immediately the ways of thought and the jargon of her new companions. In a word, with the remarkable receptivity which was hers, she was very quickly at home in Mrs. Rawson's house. She became a favorite no less for her modest friendliness than on account of her looks. Mrs. Rawson, who was nearing middle age, but whose love of amusements was not assuaged, rejoiced to have so attractive a companion to take about with her. Millie, for her part, was very glad to be so taken about. She had fallen from the obscure clouds into a bright and wonderful world.

It was at this time that Pamela Mardale first met Millicent Stretton, or rather, one should say, Millicent Rundell, since Rundell was at that time her name. They became friends, although so far as character was concerned they had little in common. It may have been that the difference between them was the actual cause of their friendship. Certainly Millie came rather to lean upon her friend, admired her strength, made her the repository of her confidences, and if she received no confidences in return, she was content to believe that there were none to make. It was at this time, too, that Millie fell in with Lady Stretton.

Lady Stretton, a tall old woman with the head of a Grenadier, had the characteristic of Sir Anthony Absolute. There was no one so good-tempered so long as she had her own way; and she generally had it.

"Lady Stretton saw that Millie was easily led," Pamela continued. "She thought, for that reason, she would be a suitable wife for Tony, her son, who was then a subaltern in the Coldstreams. So she did all she could to throw them together. She invited Millie up to her house in Scotland, the house Lady Millingham now has, and Mr. Stretton fell in love. He was evidently very fond of Millie, and Millie on her side liked him quite as much as any one else. They were married. Lady Stretton hired them the house I told you of, close to Park Lane, and took a great deal of trouble to see that they were comfortable. You see, they were toys for her. There, that's all I know. Are you satisfied?"

She leaned back in her chair, smiling at Warrisden's serious face.

"And what about the old man, Sir John Stretton?" he asked.

"I never met him," replied Pamela. "He never went out to parties, and I never went to that house."

As she concluded the sentence a man looked on to the balcony, and, seeing them, withdrew. Pamela rose at once from her chair, and, with a sudden movement of jealousy, Warrisden swung round and looked into the room. The man was well past the middle age, stout of build, and with a heavy, careworn face with no pleasure in it at all. He was the man who had been with Pamela when Warrisden had arrived. Warrisden turned back to the girl with a smile of relief.

"You are engaged?"

"Yes, for this dance to Mr. Mudge," and she indicated the man who was retiring. "But we shall meet again—at Newmarket, at all events. Perhaps in Scotland, too."

She held out her hand to Warrisden, and as he took it her voice dropped to a plea.

"Please don't go away again without telling me first, without talking it over, so that I may know where you are from month to month. Please promise!"

Warrisden promised, and went away from the house with her prayer echoing in his ears. The very sound of her voice was audible to him, and he never doubted the sincerity of its appeal. But if she set such store on what she had, why was she content with just that and nothing more, he asked himself. Why did she not claim a little more and give a little more in return? Why did she come to a halt at friendship, a mere turnpike on the great road, instead of passing through the gate and going on down the appointed way. He did not know that she passed the turnpike once, and that if she refused to venture on that path again it was because, knowing herself, she dared not.

In the narrows of Berkeley Street, Warrisden was shaken out of these reflections. A hansom jingled past him, and by the light of the lamp which hung at the back within it he caught a glimpse of the truants. They were driving home to the dark house in the square, and they sat side by side silent and with troubled faces. Warrisden's thoughts went back to what Pamela had told him that night. She had told him the half, but not the perplexing, interesting half, of their history. That, indeed, Pamela could not tell, for she did not know Sir John Stretton, and the old man's warped and churlish character alone explained it.

It was by his doing that the truants gave up their cheery little house in Deanery Street and came to live in Berkeley Square. The old man was a miser, who during his wife's existence had not been allowed to gratify his instincts. He made all the more ample amends after she had died. The fine allowance on which the young couple had managed to keep a pair of horses and a little brougham was stripped from them.

"Why should I live alone?" said the old man. "I am old, Tony, and I need some attention. The house is big, much too big for me, and the servants are eating their heads off for the want of something to do." There were, indeed, more servants than were needed. Servants were the single luxury Sir John allowed himself. Their liveries were faded, they themselves were insolent and untidy, but they were there, in the great, bare dining-room at dinner-time, in the hall when Sir John came home of an afternoon. For the old man went out each day as the clock struck three; he came back each evening at half-past six. He went out alone, he returned alone, and he never went to his club. He took an omnibus from the corner of Berkeley Street and journeyed eastward as far as Ludgate Hill. There he took a drink in the refreshment bar, and, coming out, struck northward into Holborn, where he turned westward, and, walking as far as the inn at the corner of the Tottenham Court Road, stepped for an hour into the private bar. Thence he took another omnibus, and finally reached home, where his footmen received him solemnly in the hall. To this home he brought Tony and his wife.

"There, choose your own rooms, Tony," he said, magnanimously. "What's that? Money? But what for? You'll have it soon enough."

Tony Stretton suggested that it was hardly possible for any man, however careful, to retain a commission in the Coldstreams without an allowance. Sir John, a tall, thin man with a high, bald forehead and a prim, Puritanical face, looked at his son with a righteous severity.

"A very expensive regiment. Leave it, Tony, and live quietly at home. Look after your father, my boy, and you won't need money," and he stalked upstairs, leaving Tony aghast in the hall. Tony had to sit down and think it over before he could quite realize the fate which had overtaken him. Here he was, twenty-six years old, brought up to spend what he wanted and to ask for more when that was ended, and he was to live quietly on nothing at all. He had no longer any profession, he was not clever enough to enter upon a new one without some sort of start, and in addition he had a wife. His wife, it was true, had a few thousands; they had remained untouched ever since the marriage, and Tony shrank from touching them now. He sat on one of the hall chairs, twisting his mustache and staring with his blank, blue eyes at the opposite wall. What in the world was he to do? Old Sir John was quite aware of those few thousands. They might just as well be used now, he thought, and save him expense. Tony could pay them back after his father was dead. Such was Sir John's plan, and Tony had to fall in with it. The horses and the brougham and all the furniture, the prints, the pictures, and the mirrors which had decked out so gayly the little house in Deanery Street went to the hammer. Tony paid off his debts and found himself with a hundred pounds in hand at the end; and when that was gone he was forced to come to his wife.

"Of course," said she, "we'll share what I have, Tony."

"Yes, but we must go carefully," he replied. "Heaven knows how long we will have to drag on like this."

So the money question was settled, but that was in reality the least of their troubles. Sir John, for the first time in his life, was master in fact as well as in name. He had been no match for his wife, but he was more than a match for his son. He was the fifth baronet of his name, and yet there was no landed property. He was rich, and all the money was safely tucked away in the public funds, and he could bequeath it as he willed. He was in a position to put the screw on Tony and his wife, and he did not let the opportunity slip. The love of authority grew upon him. He became exacting and portentously severe. In his black, shabby coat, with his long, thin figure and his narrow face, he had the look of a cold, self-righteous fanatic. You would have believed that he was mortifying his son for the sake of his son's soul, unless, perchance, you had peeped into that private bar in the Tottenham Court Road and had seen him drinking gloomily alone.

He laid down rules to which the unfortunate couple must needs conform. They had to dine with him every night and to sit with him every evening until he went to bed. It followed that they lost sight of their friends, and every month isolated them more completely. The mere humiliation of the position in which they stood caused them to shrink more and more into their privacy. When they walked out in the afternoon they kept away from the park; when they played truant in the evening, at the Savoy, they chose a little table in an obscure corner. This was the real history of the truants with whose fortunes those of Warrisden and Pamela were to be so closely intermingled. For that life in the dark house was not to last. Even as Warrisden passed them in Berkeley Street, Tony Stretton was saying over and over again in his inactive mind:

"It can't go on! It can't go on!"

IV

TONY STRETTON MAKES A PROPOSAL

REGULAR as Warrisden had declared the lives of the truants to be, on the night following the dance at Lady Millingham's there came a break in the monotony of their habits. For once in a way they did not leave the house in their search for light and color as soon as they were free. They stayed on in their own sitting-room. But it seemed that they had nothing to speak about. Millie Stretton sat at the table, staring at the wall in front of her, moody and despairing. Tony Stretton leaned against the embrasure of the window, now and then glancing remorsefully at his wife, now and then looking angrily up to the ceiling where the heavy footsteps of a man treading up and down the room above sounded measured and unceasing.

Tony lifted a corner of the blind and looked out.

"There's a party next door," he said; "there was another at Lady Millingham's last night. You should have been at both, Millie, and you were at neither. Upon my word, it's rough."

He dropped the blind and came over to her side. He knew quite well what parties and entertainments meant to her. She loved them, and it seemed to him natural and right that she should. Light, admiration, laughter and gayety, and fine frocks — these things she was born to enjoy, and he himself had in

37

the old days taken a great pride in watching her enjoyment. But it was not merely the feeling that she had been stripped of what was her due through him which troubled him to-night. Other and deeper thoughts were vaguely stirring in his mind.

"We have quarrelled again to-night, Millie," he continued, remorsefully. "Here we are cooped up together with just ourselves to rely upon to pull through these bad years, and we have quarrelled again."

Millie shrugged her shoulders.

"How did it begin?" he asked. "Upon my word, I don't remember. Oh yes, I—" and Millie interrupted him.

"What does it matter, Tony, how the quarrel began? It did begin, and another will begin to-morrow. We can't help ourselves, and you have given the reason. Here we are cooped up by ourselves with nothing else to do."

Tony pulled thoughtfully at his mustache.

"And we swore off quarrelling, too. When was that?"

"Yesterday."

"Yesterday!" exclaimed Tony, with a start of surprise. "By George! so it was. Only yesterday."

Millie looked up at him, and the trouble upon his face brought a smile to hers. She laid a hand upon his arm.

"It's no use swearing off, Tony," she said. "We are both of us living all the time in a state of exasperation. I just—tingle with it; there's no other word. And the least, smallest thing which goes wrong sets us quarrelling. I don't think either of us is to blame. The house alone gets on our nerves, doesn't it? These great, empty, silent, dingy rooms, with their tarnished furniture. Oh, they are horrible! I wander through them sometimes, and it always seems to me that a long time ago people lived here who suddenly felt one morning that they couldn't stand it for a single moment longer, and ran out and locked the street door behind them; and I have almost done it myself. The very sunlight comes through the windows timidly, as if it knew it had no right here at all."

She leaned back in her chair, looking at Tony with eyes that were hopeless and almost haggard. As Tony listened to her outburst the remorse deepened on his face.

"If I could have foreseen all this I would have spared you it, Millie," he said. "I would, upon my word." He drew up a chair to the table, and, sitting down, said, in a more cheerful voice, "Let's talk it over and see if we can't find a remedy."

Millie shook her head.

"We talked it over yesterday."

"Yes, so we did."

"And quarrelled an hour after we had talked it over."

"We did that, too," Tony agreed, despondently. His little spark of hopefulness was put out, and he sat in silence. His wife, too, did not speak, and in a short while it occurred to him that the silence was more complete than it had been a few minutes ago. It seemed that a noise had ceased, and a noise which, unnoticed before, had become noticeable by its cessation. He looked up to the ceiling. The heavy footsteps no longer dragged upon the floor overhead. Tony sprang up.

"There! He is in bed!" he exclaimed. "Shall we go out?"

"Not to-night," replied Millie.

He could make no proposal that night which was welcomed, and as he walked over to the mantel-shelf and filled his pipe there was something in his attitude and bearing which showed to Millie that the quick rebuff had hurt.

"I can't pretend to-night, Tony, and that's the truth," she added, in a kinder voice. "For, after all, I do only pretend nowadays that I find the Savoy amusing."

Tony turned slowly round with the lighted match in his hand and stared at his wife. He was a man slow in thought, and, when his thoughts compelled expression, laborious in words. The deeper thoughts which had begun of late to take shape in his mind stirred again at her words.

"You have owned it," he said.

"It has been pretence with you, too, then?" she asked, looking up in surprise.

Tony puffed at his pipe.

"Of late, yes," he replied. "Perhaps, chiefly since I saw that you were pretending."

He came back to her side and looked for a long time steadily at her while he thought. It was a surprise to Millie that he had noticed her pretence, as much of a surprise as that he had been pretending, too. For she knew him to be at once slow to notice any change in others and quick to betray it in himself. But she was not aware how wide a place she filled in all his thoughts, partly because her own nature with its facile emotions made her unable to conceive a devotion which was engrossing, and partly because Tony himself had no aptitude for expressing such a devotion, and, indeed, would have shrunk from its expression had the aptitude been his. But she did fill that wide place. Very slowly he had begun to watch her, very slowly and dimly certain convictions were taking shape, very gradually he was drawing nearer and nearer to a knowledge that a great risk must be taken and a great sacrifice made, partly by him, partly, too, by her. Some part of his trouble he now spoke to her.

"It wasn't pretence a year ago, Millie," he said, wistfully. "That's what bothers me. We enjoyed slipping away quietly when the house was quiet, and snatching some of the light, some of the laughter the others have any time they want it. It made up for the days; it was fun then, Millie, wasn't it? Upon my word, I believe we enjoyed our life—yes, even this life —a year ago. Do you remember how we used to drive home laughing over what we had seen, talking about the few people we had spoken to? It wasn't until we had turned the latch-key in the door and crept into the hall—"

"And passed the library door," Millie interrupted, with a little shiver.

Tony Stretton stopped for a moment. Then he resumed, in a lower voice: "Yes, it wasn't until we had passed the library door that the gloom settled down again. But now the fun's all over, at the latest when the lights go down in the supper-room, and often before we have got to them at all. We were happy last year"—and he shook her affectionately by the arm— "that's what bothers me."

His wife responded to the gentleness of his voice and action.

"Never mind, Tony," she said. "Some day we shall look back on all of it—this house and the empty rooms and the quarrels—" She hesitated for a second. "Yes, and the library door; we shall look back on it all and laugh."

"Shall we?" said Tony, suddenly. His face was most serious, his voice most doubtful.

"Why, what do you mean?" asked Millie. Then she added, reassuringly: "It must end sometime. Oh yes, it can't last forever."

"No," replied Tony; "but it can last just long enough."

"Long enough for what?"

"Long enough to spoil both our lives altogether."

He was speaking with a manner which was quite strange to her. There was a certainty in his voice; there was a gravity, too. He had ceased to leave the remedy of their plight to time and chance, since, through two years, time and chance had failed them. He had been seriously thinking, and as the result of thought he had come to definite conclusions. Millie understood that there was much more behind the words he had spoken, and that he meant to say that much more to her to-night. She was suddenly aware that she was face to face with issues momentous to both of them. She began to be a little afraid. She looked at Tony almost as if he were a stranger.

"Tony," she said, faintly, in deprecation.

"We must face it, Millie," he went on, steadily. "This life of ours here in this house will come to an end, of course, but how will it leave us, you and me? Soured, embittered, quarrelsome, or no longer quarrelsome but just indifferent to each other, bored by each other?" He was speaking very slowly, choosing each word with difficulty.

"Oh no," Millie protested.

"It may be even worse than that. Suppose we passed beyond indifference to dislike—yes, active dislike. We are both of us young, we can both reasonably look forward to long lives, long lives of active dislike. There might, too, be contempt on your side."

Millie stared at her husband.

"Contempt?" she said, echoing his words in surprise.

"Yes. Here are you most unhappy, and I take it sitting down. Contempt might come from that."

"But what else can you do?" she said.

"Ah," said Tony, as though he had been waiting for that question, couched in just those words. "Ask yourself that question often enough and contempt will come."

This idea of contempt was a new one to Millie, and very likely her husband was indiscreet in suggesting its possibility. But he was not thinking at all of the unwisdom of his words. His thoughts were set on saving the cherished intimacy of their life from the ruin which he saw was likely to overtake it. He spoke out frankly, not counting the risk. Millie, for her part, was not in the mood to estimate the truth of what he said, although it remained in her memory. She was rather confused by the new aspect which her husband wore. She foresaw that he was working towards the disclosure of a plan; and the plan would involve changes, great changes, very likely a step altogether into the dark. And she hesitated.

"We sha'n't alter, Tony," she said. "You can be sure of me, can't you?"

"But we are altering," he replied. "Already the alteration has begun. Did we quarrel a year ago as we do now? We enjoyed those evenings when we played truant a year ago;" and then he indulged in a yet greater indiscretion than any which he had yet allowed himself to utter. But he was by nature simple and completely honest. Whatever occurred to him, that he spoke without reserve, and the larger it loomed in his thoughts the more strenuous was its utterance upon his lips. He took a seat at the table by her side.

"I know we are changing. I take myself, and I expect it is the same with you. I am—it is difficult to express it—I am deadening. I am getting insensible to the things which not very long ago moved me very much. I once had a friend who fell ill of a slow paralysis which crept up his limbs little by little, and he hardly noticed its advance. I think that's happening with me. I am losing the associations—that's the word I want—the associations which made one's recollections valuable and gave a color to one's life. For instance, you sang a song last night, Millie, one of those coon songs of yours—do you remember? You sang it once in Scotland on a summer's night. I was outside on the lawn, and past the islands across the water, which was dark and still, I saw the lights in Oban Bay. I thought I would never hear that song again without seeing those lights in my mind, far away across the water, clustered together like the lights of a distant town. Well, last night all those associations were somehow dead. I remembered all right, but without any sort of feeling, that that song was a landmark in one's life. It was merely you singing a song, or rather it was merely some one singing a song."

It was a labored speech, and Tony was very glad to have got it over.

"I am very sorry," replied Millie, in a low voice. She did not show him her face, and he had no notion whatever that his words could hardly have failed to hurt. He was too intent upon convincing her, and too anxious to put his belief before her with unmistakable clearness to reflect in what spirit she might receive the words. That her first thought would be, "He no longer cares," never occurred to him at all, and cheerfully misunderstanding her acquiescence, he went on:

"You see, that's bad. It mustn't go on, Millie. Let's keep what we've got. At all costs, let us keep that!"

"You mean we must go away?" said Millie, and Tony Stretton did not answer. He rose from his chair and walked back to the fireplace and knocked the ashes from his pipe. Millie was accustomed to long intervals between her questions and his replies, but she was on the alert now. Something in his movements and his attitude showed her that he was not thinking of what answer he should make. He was already sure upon that point. Only the particular answer he found difficult to speak. She guessed it on the instant and stood up erect, in alarm.

"You mean that you must go away and that I must remain?"

Tony turned round to her and nodded his head.

"Alone! Here?" she exclaimed, looking round her with a shiver.

"For a little while. Until I have made a home for you to come to. Only till then, Millie. It needn't be so very long."

"It will seem ages!" she cried, "however short it is. Tony, it's impossible."

The tedious days stretched before her in an endless and monotonous succession. The great rooms would be yet more silent and more empty than they were; there would be a chill throughout all the house; the old man's exactions would become yet more oppressive, since there would be only one to bear them. She thought of the long, dull evenings in the faded drawing-room. They were bad enough now, those long evenings during which she read the evening paper aloud and Sir John slept, yet not so soundly but that he woke the instant her voice stopped and bade her continue. What would they be if Tony were gone, if there were no hour or so at the end when they were free to play truant if they willed? What she had said was true. She had been merely pretending to enjoy their hour of truancy, but she would miss it none the less. And in the midst of these thoughts she heard Tony's voice.

"It sounds selfish, I know, but it isn't really. You see, I sha'n't enjoy myself. I have not been brought up to know anything well or to do anything well— anything, I mean, really useful — I'll have a pretty hard time, too." And then he described to her what he thought of doing. He proposed to go out to one of the colonies, spend some months on a farm as a hand, and when he had learned enough of the methods, and had saved a little money, to get hold of a small farm to which he could ask her to come. It was a pretty and a simple scheme, and it ignored the great difficulties in the way, such as his ignorance and his lack of capital. But he believed in it sincerely, and every word in his short and broken sentences proved his belief. He had his way that night with Millicent. She was capable of a quick fervor, though the fervor might as quickly flicker out. She saw that the sacrifice was really upon his side, for upon him would be the unaccustomed burden of labor, and the labor would be strange and difficult. She rose to his height, since he was with her and speaking to her with all the conviction of his soul.

"Well, then, go!" she cried. "I'll wait here, Tony, till you send for me."

And when she passed the library door that night she did not even shrink.

V

PAMELA MAKES A PROMISE

MILLIE'S enthusiasm for her husband's plan increased each day. The picture which his halting phrases evoked for her, of a little farm very far away under Southern skies, charmed her more by reason of its novelty than either she or Tony quite understood. In the evenings of the following week, long after the footsteps overhead had ceased, they sat choosing the site of their house and building it. It was to be the exact opposite of their house of bondage. The windows should look out over rolling country, the simple decorations should be bright of color, and through every cranny the sun should find its way. Millie's hopes, indeed, easily outran her husband's. She counted the house already built, and the door open for her coming. Color and light bathed it in beauty.

"There's my little fortune, Tony," she said, when once or twice he tried to check the leap of her anticipations; "that will provide the capital."

"I knew you would offer it," Tony replied, simply. "Your help will shorten our separation by a good deal. So I'll take half."

"All!" cried Millie.

"And what would you do when you wanted a new frock?" asked Tony, with a smile.

Millie shrugged her shoulders.

"I shall join you so soon," she said.

THE TRUANTS

It dawned upon Tony that she was making too little of the burden which she would be called upon to bear —the burden of dull, lonely months in that great, shabby house.

"It will be a little while before I can send for you, Millie," he protested. But she paid no heed to the protest. She fetched her bank-book and added up the figures.

"I have three thousand pounds," she said.

"I'll borrow half," he repeated. "Of course, I am only borrowing. Should things go wrong with me, you are sure to get it back in the end."

They drove down to Millie's bank the next morning, and fifteen hundred pounds were transferred to his account.

"Meanwhile," said Tony, as they came out of the door into Pall Mall, "we have not yet settled where our farm is to be. I think I will go and see Chase."

"The man in Stepney Green?" Millie asked.

"Yes. He's the man to help us."

Tony called a cab and drove off. It was late in the afternoon when he returned, and he had no opportunity to tell his wife the results of his visit before dinner was announced. Millie was in a fever to hear his news. Never, even in this house, had an evening seemed so long. Sir John sat upright in his high-backed chair, and, as was his custom, bade her read aloud the evening paper. But that task was beyond her. She pleaded a headache and escaped. It seemed to her that hours passed before Tony rejoined her. She had come to dread with an intense fear that some hindrance would, at any moment, stop their plan.

"Well?" she asked, eagerly, when Tony at last came into their sitting-room.

"It's to be horses in Kentucky," answered Tony. "Farming wants more knowledge and a long apprenticeship; but I know a little about horses."

"Splendid!" cried Millie. "You will go soon?"

"In a week. A week is all I need."

Millie was quiet for a little while. Then she asked, with an anxious look:

"When do you mean to tell your father?"

"To-morrow."

"Don't," said she. She saw his face cloud—she was well aware of his dislike of secrecies—but she was too much afraid that, somehow, at the last moment an insuperable obstacle would bar the way. "Don't tell him at all," she went on. "Leave a note for him. I will see that it is given to him after you have gone. Then he can't stop you. Please do this, I ask you."

"How can he stop me?"

"I don't know; but I am afraid that he will. He could threaten to disinherit you; if you disobeyed, he might carry out the threat. Give him no opportunity to threaten."

Very reluctantly Tony consented. He had all a man's objections to concealments, she all a woman's liking for them; but she prevailed, and, since the moment of separation was very near, they began to retrace their steps through the years of their married life, and back beyond them to the days of their first acquaintance. Thus it happened that Millie mentioned the name of Pamela Mardale, and suddenly Tony drew himself upright in his chair.

"Is she in town, I wonder?" he asked, rather of himself than of his wife.

"Most likely," Millie replied. "Why?"

"I think I must try to see her before I go," said

Tony, thoughtfully; and more than once during the evening he looked with anxiety towards his wife; but in his look there was some perplexity, too.

He tried next day; for he borrowed a horse from a friend, and rode out into the Row at eleven o'clock. As he passed through the gates of Hyde Park he saw Pamela turning her horse on the edge of the sand. She saw him at the same moment and waited.

"You are a stranger here," she said, with a smile, as he joined her.

"Here and everywhere," he replied. "I came out on purpose to find you."

Pamela glanced at Tony curiously. Only a few days had passed since Warrisden had pointed out the truants from the window of Lady Millingham's house and had speculated upon the seclusion of their lives. The memory of that evening was still fresh in her mind.

"I want to ask you a question."

"Ask it and I'll answer," she replied, carelessly.

"You were Millie's bridesmaid?"

"Yes."

"You saw a great deal of her before we were married?"

"Yes."

They were riding down the Row at a walk under the trees, Pamela wondering to what these questions were to lead, Tony slowly formulating the point which troubled him.

"Before Millie and I were engaged," he went on, "before, indeed, there was any likelihood of our being engaged, you once said to me something about her."

"I did?"

"Yes. I remembered it last night. And it rather

worries me. I should like you to explain what you meant. You said, 'The man who marries her should never leave her. If he goes away shooting big game, he should take her with him. On no account must she be left behind.'"

It was a day cloudless and bright. Over towards the Serpentine the heat filled the air with a soft screen of mist, and at the bottom of the Row the rhododendrons glowed. As Pamela and Tony went forward at a walk the sunlight slanting through the leaves now shone upon their faces, and now left them in shade. And when it fell bright upon Pamela it lit up a countenance which was greatly troubled. She did not, however, deny that she had used the words. She did not pretend that she had forgotten their application.

"You remember what I said?" she remarked. "It is a long while ago."

"Before that," he explained, "I had begun to notice all that was said of Millie."

"I spoke the words generally, perhaps too carelessly."

"Yet not without a reason," Tony insisted. "That's not your way."

Pamela made no reply for a moment or two. Then she patted her horse's head, and said softly:

"Not without a reason." She admitted his contention frankly. She did more, for she turned in her saddle towards him, and, looking straight into his face, said:

"I was not giving you advice at the time. But, had I been, I should have said just those words. I say them again now."

"Why?"

Tony put his question very earnestly. He held

Pamela in a great respect, believing her clear-sighted beyond her fellows. He was, indeed, a little timid in her presence as a rule, for she overawed him, though all unconsciously. Nothing of this timidity, however, showed now. "That was what I came out to ask you. Why?"

Again Pamela attempted no evasion.

"I can't tell you," she said, quietly.

"You promised."

"I break the promise."

Tony looked wistfully at his companion. That the perplexing words had been spoken with a definite meaning he had felt sure from the moment when he had remembered them. And her refusal to explain proved to him that the meaning was a very serious one—one, indeed, which he ought to know and take into account.

"I ask you to explain," he urged, "because I *am* going away, and I *am* leaving Millie behind."

Pamela was startled. She turned quickly towards him.

"Must you?" she said, and before he could answer she recovered from her surprise. "Never mind," she continued; "shall we ride on?" and she put her horse to a trot. It was not her business to advise or to interfere. She had said too much already. She meant to remain the looker-on.

Stretton, however, was not upon this occasion to be so easily suppressed. He kept level with her, and as they rode he told her something of the life which Millie and he had led in the big, lonely house in Berkeley Square; and in spite of herself Pamela was interested. She had a sudden wish that Alan Warrisden was riding with them, too, so that he might hear his mystery re-

solved; she had a sudden vision of his face, keen as a
boy's, as he listened.

"I saw Millie and you a few nights ago. I was at a
dance close by, and I was surprised to see you. I
thought you had left London," she said.

"No; but I am leaving," Stretton returned; and he
went on to describe that idyllic future which Millie
and he had allotted to themselves. The summer sunlight was golden in the air about them; already it
seemed that new, fresh life was beginning. "I shall
breed horses in Kentucky. I was recommended to it
by an East End parson called Chase, who runs a mission on Stepney Green. I used to keep order in a
billiard-room at his mission one night a week, when I
was quartered at the Tower. A queer sort of creature,
Chase; but his judgment's good, and, of course, he is
always meeting all sorts of people."

"Chase?" Pamela repeated; and she retained the
name in her memory.

"But he doesn't know Millie," said Stretton, "and
you do. And so what you said troubles me very
much. If I go away remembering your words and
not understanding them, I shall go away uneasy. I
shall remain uneasy."

"I am sorry," Pamela replied. "I broke a rule of
mine in saying what I did, a rule not to interfere. And
I see now that I did very wrong in breaking it. I will
not break it again. You must forget my words."

There was a quiet decision in her manner which
warned Tony that no persuasions would induce her
to explain. He gave up his attempt and turned to
another subject.

"I have something else to ask—not a question this
time, but a favor. You could be a very stanch

friend, Miss Mardale, if you chose. Millie will be lonely after I have gone. You were a great friend of hers once—be a friend of hers again."

Pamela hesitated. The promise which he sought on the face of it no doubt looked easy of fulfilment. But Tony Stretton had been right in one conjecture. She had spoken the words which troubled him from a definite reason, and that reason assured her now that this promise might lay upon her a burden, and a burden of a heavy kind. And she shrank from all burdens. On the other hand, there was no doubt that she had caused Tony much uneasiness. He would go away, on a task which, as she saw very clearly, would be more arduous by far than even he suspected—he would go away troubled and perplexed. That could not be helped. But she might lighten the trouble, and make the perplexity less insistent, if she granted the favor which he sought. It seemed churlish to refuse.

"Very well," she said, reluctantly. "I promise."

Already Tony's face showed his relief. She had given her promise reluctantly, but she would keep it now. Of that he felt assured, and, bidding her good-bye, he turned his horse and cantered back.

Pamela rode homeward more slowly. She had proposed to keep clear of entanglements and responsibilities, and, behold! the meshes were about her. She had undertaken a trust. In spite of herself she had ceased to be the looker-on.

VI

NEWS OF TONY

THE promise which Pamela had given was a great relief to Tony; he went about the work of preparing for his departure with an easier mind. It was even in his thoughts when he stood with his wife upon the platform of Euston station five minutes before his train started for Liverpool.

"She will be a good friend, Millie," he said. "Count on her till I send for you. I think I am right to go, even though I don't understand——"

He checked himself abruptly. Millie, however, paid heed only to the first clause of his sentence.

"Of course you are right," she said, with a confidence which brought an answering smile to his face.

She watched the red tail-light of the train until it disappeared, and drove home alone to the big, dreary house. It seemed ten times more dreary, ten times more silent than ever before. She was really alone now. But her confidence in herself and in Tony was still strong. "I can wait," she said, and the consciousness of her courage rejoiced her. She walked from room to room and sat for a few moments in each, realizing that the coldness, the dingy look of the furniture, and the empty silence had no longer the power to oppress her. She even hesitated at the library door with her fingers on the key. But it was not until the next day that she unlocked it and threw it open.

For Pamela, mindful of her promise, called in the afternoon. Millicent was still uplifted by her confidence.

"I can wait quite patiently," she said; and Pamela scrutinized her with some anxiety; for Millicent was speaking feverishly, as though she labored under an excitement. Was her courage the mere effervescence of that excitement, or was it a steady, durable thing? Pamela led her friend on to speak of the life which she and Tony had led in the big house, sounding her the while so that she might come upon some answer to that question. And thus it happened that, as they came down the stairs together, Millicent again stopped before the library door.

"Look!" she said. "This room always seemed to me typical of the whole house, typical too of the lives we led in it."

She unlocked the door suddenly and flung it open. The floor of the library was below the level of the hall, and a smooth plane of wood sloped down to it very gradually from the threshold.

"There used to be steps here once, but before my time," said Millicent. She went down into the room. Pamela followed her, and understood why those two steps had been removed. Although the book-shelves rose on every wall from floor to ceiling, it was not as a library that this room was used. Heavy black curtains draped it with a barbaric profusion. The centre of the room was clear of furniture, and upon the carpet in that clear space was laid a purple drugget; and on the drugget opposite to each other stood two strong wooden crutches. The room was a mortuary chamber—nothing less. On those two crutches the dead were to lie awaiting burial.

Millie Stretton shook her shoulders with a kind of shiver.

"Oh, how I used to hate this room, hate knowing that it was here, prepared and ready!"

Pamela could understand how the knowledge would work upon a woman of emotions, whose nerves were already strung to exasperation by the life she led. For even to her there was something eerie in the disposition of the room. It looked out upon a dull yard of stone at the back of the house; the light was very dim, and the noise of the streets hardly the faintest whisper; there were a chill and a dampness in the air.

"How I hated it!" Millie repeated. "I used to lie awake and think of it. I used to imagine it more silent than any other of the silent rooms, and emptier —emptier because day and night it seemed to claim an inhabitant, and to claim it as a right. That was the horrible thing. The room was waiting—waiting for us to be carried down that wooden bridge and laid on the crutches here, each in our turn. It became just a symbol of the whole house. For what is the house, Pamela? A place that should have been a place of life, and is a place merely expecting death. Look at the books reaching up to the ceiling, never taken down, never read, for the room's a room for coffins. It wasn't merely a symbol of the house—that wasn't the worst of it. It was a sort of image of our lives, the old man's up-stairs, Tony's and mine down here. We were all doing nothing, neither suffering nor enjoying, but just waiting—waiting for death. Nothing, you see, could happen in this house but death. Until it came there would only be silence and emptiness."

Millie Stretton finished her outburst, and stood dismayed as though the shadow of those past days were still about her. The words she had spoken must have seemed exaggerated and even theatrical, but for her aspect as she spoke them. Her whole frame shuddered, her face had the shrinking look of fear. She recovered herself, however, in a moment.

"But that time's past," she said. "Tony's gone, and I—I am waiting for life now. I am only a lodger, you see. A month or two, and I pack my boxes."

She turned towards the door and stopped. The hall door had just at that moment opened. Pamela heard a man's footsteps sound heavily upon the floor of the hall and then upon the stairs.

"My father-in-law," said Millie.

"This was his doing?" asked Pamela.

"Yes," replied Millie. "It's strange, isn't it? But there's something stranger still."

The footsteps had now ceased. Millie led the way back to her room.

"When I got home yesterday," she related, "I had Tony's letter announcing his departure taken up to Sir John. I waited for him to send for me. He did not. I am not sure that I expected he would. You see, he has never shown the least interest in us. However, when I went up to my room to dress for dinner, I saw that the candles were all lighted in Tony's room next door, and his clothes laid out upon the bed. I went in and put the candles out — rather quickly." Her voice shook a little upon those last two words. Pamela nodded her head as though she understood, and Millicent went on, after a short pause:

"It troubled me to see them burning—it troubled me very much. And when I came down-stairs I told the footman the candles were not to be lit again, since Tony had gone away. He answered that they had

been lit by Sir John's orders. At first I thought that
Sir John had not troubled to read the letter at all. I
thought that all the more because he never once, either
during dinner or afterwards, mentioned Tony's name
or seemed to remark his absence. But it was not so.
He has given orders that every night the room is to
be ready and the candles lit as though Tony were here
still, or might walk in at the door at any moment. I
suppose that, after all, in a queer way he cares."

Again her voice faltered; and again a question rose
up insistent in Pamela's mind. She knew her friend,
and it was out of her knowledge that she had spoken
long ago in Tony's presence when she had said, "Her
husband should never leave her." It was evident that
Tony's departure had caused his wife great suffering.

Millicent had let that fact escape in spite of her
exaltation. Pamela welcomed it, but she asked: "Was
that regret a steady and durable thing?"

Pamela left London the next day with her question
unanswered, and for two months there was no opportunity for her of discovering an answer. Often during
that August and September, on the moors in Scotland or at her own home in Leicestershire, she would
think of Millie Stretton, in the hot and dusty town
among the houses where the blinds were drawn. She
imagined her sitting over against the old, stern, impas-
sive man at dinner, or wearily reading to him his newspaper at night. Had the regret dwindled to irritation,
and the loneliness begotten petulance?

Indeed, those months were dull and wearisome
enough for Millicent. No change of significance came
in the routine of that monotonous household. Sir
John went to his room perhaps a little earlier than had
been his wont, his footsteps dragged along the floor

for a while longer, and his light burned in the window after the dawn had come. Finally he ceased to leave his room at all. But that was all. For Millicent, however, the weeks passed easily. Each day brought her a day nearer to the sunlit farm fronting the open plain. She marked the weeks off in her diary with a growing relief; for news kept coming from America, and the news was good.

Early in October, Pamela passed through London on her way to Sussex, and broke her journey that she might see her friend.

"Frances Millingham is writing to you," she said. "She wants you to stay with her in Leicestershire. I shall be there, too. I hope you will come."

"When?"

"At the beginning of the new year."

Millicent laughed.

"I shall have left England before then. Tony will have made his way," she said, with a joyous conviction.

"There might be delays," Pamela suggested, in a very gentle voice. For suddenly there had risen before her mind the picture of a terrace high above a gorge dark with cypresses. She saw again the Mediterranean, breaking in gold along the curving shore, and the gardens of the Casino at Monte Carlo. She heard a young girl prophesying success upon that terrace with no less certainty than Millicent had used. Her face softened and her eyes shone with a very wistful look. She took out her watch and glanced at it. It was five o'clock. The school - children had gone home by now from the little school-house in the square of Roquebrune. Was the school-master leaning over the parapet looking downward to the station or to the deserted walk in front of the Casino? Was a train passing along the sea's edge towards France and Paris?

"One must expect delays, Millie," she insisted; and again Millie laughed.

"I have had letters. I am expecting another. It should have come a fortnight since;" and she told Pamela what the letters had contained.

At first Tony had been a little bewildered by the activity of New York, after his quiescent years. But he had soon made an acquaintance, and the acquaintance had become a friend. The two men had determined to go into partnership; a farm in Kentucky was purchased, each man depositing an equal share of the purchase-money.

"Six weeks ago they left New York. Tony said I would not hear from him at once."

And while they were sitting together there came a knock upon the door, and two letters were brought in for Millicent. One she tossed upon the table; with the other in her hand she turned triumphantly to Pamela.

"Do you mind?" she asked. "I have been waiting so long."

"Read it, of course," said Pamela.

Millie tore the letter open, and at once the light died out of her eyes and the smile vanished from her lips.

"From New York," she said, half-way between perplexity and fear. "He writes from New York;" and with trembling fingers she turned over the sheets and read the letter through.

Pamela watched her, saw the blood ebb from her cheeks, and dejection overspread her face. A great pity welled up in Pamela's heart, not merely for the wife who read, but for the man who had penned that letter—with what difficulty, she wondered, with how much pain! Failure was the message which it carried. Millicent's trembling lips told her that. And again the village of Roquebrune rose up before her eyes as she gazed out of the window on the London square. What were the words the school-master had spoken, when, stripped of his dreams, he had confessed success was not for him? "We must forget these fine plans. The school at Roquebrune will send no deputy to Paris." Pamela's eyes grew dim.

She stood looking out of the window for some while, but hearing no movement she at length turned back again. The sheets of the letter had fallen upon the floor; they lay scattered, written over in a round, sprawling, school-boy's hand. Millicent sat very still, her face most weary and despairing.

"It's all over," she said. "The friend was a swindler. He left the train at a station on the way and disappeared. Tony went on, but there was no farm. He is back in New York."

"But the man can be found?"

"He belongs to a gang. There is little chance, and Tony has no money. He will take no more of mine."

"He is coming home, then?" said Pamela.

"No; he means to stay and retrieve his failures."

Pamela said nothing, and Millicent appealed to her. "He will do that, don't you think? Men have started badly before, and have succeeded, and have not taken so very long to succeed."

"No doubt," said Pamela, and she spoke with what hopefulness she could. But she remembered Tony Stretton. Simplicity and good-humor were among his chief qualities; he was a loyal friend, and he had pluck. Was that enough? On the other hand, he had little knowledge and little experience. The school-master of Roqueburne and Tony Stretton stood side by side in her thoughts. She was not, however, to be put to the task of inventing encouragements. For before she could open her lips again Millicent said, gently:

"Will you mind if I ask to be left alone? Come again as soon as you can. But this afternoon—" Her voice broke so that she could not finish her sentence, and she turned hastily away. However, she recovered her self-control and went down the stairs with Pamela, and as they came into the hall their eyes turned to the library door, and then they looked at each other. Both remembered the conversation they had had within that room.

"What if you told Sir John?" said Pamela. "It seems that he does, after all, care."

"It would be of no use," said Millicent, shaking her head. "He would only say, 'Let him come home,' and Tony will not. Besides, I never see him now."

"Never?" exclaimed Pamela.

"No; he does not leave his room." She lowered her voice. "I do not believe he ever will leave it again. It's not that he's really ill, his doctor tells me, but he's slowly letting himself go."

Pamela answered absently. Sir John Stretton and his ailments played a small part in her thoughts. It seemed that the library was again to become typical of the house, typical of the life its inhabitants led. Nothing was to happen then. There was to be a mere waiting for things to cease.

But a second letter was lying up-stairs unopened on the table, and that letter, harmless as it appeared, was strangely to influence Millicent Stretton's life. It was many hours afterwards when Millicent opened it, and, compared with the heavy tidings she had by the same post received, it seemed utterly trifling and unimportant. It was no more, indeed, than the invitation from Frances Millingham of which Pamela had spoken. Pamela forgot it altogether when she heard the news which Tony had sent, but she was to be affected by it, too. For she had made a promise to Tony Stretton, and, as he had foreseen, she would at any cost fulfil it.

5

VII

THE LADY ON THE STAIRS

WHITEWEBS, Frances Millingham's house in Leicestershire, was a long, white building with many level windows. The square main block of the building rose in the centre two stories high, and on each side a wing of one story projected. Behind the house a broad lawn sloped to the bank of a clear and shallow trout-stream, with an avenue of old elms upon its left and a rose-garden upon its right. In front of the house a paddock made a ring of green, and round this ring the carriage - drive circled from a white, five-barred gate. Whitewebs stood in a flat, grass country. From the upper windows you looked over a wide plain of meadows and old trees, so level that you had on a misty day almost an illusion of a smooth sea and the masts of ships; from the lower, you saw just as far as the nearest hedge-row, except in one quarter of the compass. For to the southwest the ground rose very far away, and at the limit of view three tall poplars, set in a tiny garden on the hill's crest, stood clearly out against the sky like sentinels upon a frontier. These three landmarks were visible for many miles around. Pamela, however, saw nothing of them as she was driven over the three miles from the station to Whitewebs.

It was late on a February evening, and already dark. The snow had fallen heavily during the last week, and as Pamela looked out through the carriage windows she saw that the ground glimmered white on every side; above the ground a mist thickened the night air, and the cold was piercing. When she reached the house she found that Frances Millingham was waiting for her alone in the big inner hall, with tea ready; and the first question which she asked of her hostess was:

"Is Millie Stretton here?"

"Yes," replied Frances Millingham. "She has been here a week."

"I couldn't come before," said Pamela, rather remorsefully. "My father was at home alone. How is Millie? I have not seen her for a long time. Is she enjoying herself?"

Pamela's conscience had been reproaching her all that afternoon. She could plead in her own behalf that after the arrival of Tony's letter with its message of failure she had deferred her visit into the country, and had stayed in London for a week. But she had not returned to London since, and, consequently, she had not seen her friend. She had heard regularly from her, it is true; she also knew that there was yet no likelihood of the hoped-for change in the life of that isolated household in Berkeley Square. But there had been certain omissions of late in Millicent's letters which began to make Pamela anxious.

"Yes," Frances Millingham replied; "she seems to be happy enough."

Lady Millingham related the names of her guests. There were twelve in all, but the first ten may be omitted, for they are in no way concerned with Pamela's history. The eleventh name, however, was that of a friend.

"John Mudge is here, too," said Frances Millingham; and Pamela said, with a smile:

"I like him."

John Mudge was that elderly man whom Alan Warrisden had seen with Pamela at Lady Millingham's
dance, the man with no pleasure in his face. "And
Mr. Lionel Callon," said Frances; "you know him."

"Do I?" asked Pamela.

"At all events, he knows you."

It was no doubt a consequence of Pamela's deliber-
ate plan never to be more than an on-looker, that
people who did not arouse her active interest passed
in and out of her acquaintanceship like shadows upon
a mirror. It might be that she had met Lionel Callon.
She could not remember.

"A quarter past seven," said Frances Millingham,
glancing at the clock. "We dine at eight."

Pamela dressed quickly, in the hope that she might
gain a few minutes before dinner wherein to talk to
Millicent. She came down the stairs with this object
a good quarter of an hour before eight, but she was to
be disappointed. The stairs descended into the big
inner hall of the house, and just below the roof of the
hall they took a bend. As Pamela came round this
bend the hall was exposed to her eyes, and she saw,
below her, not Millicent at all, but the figure of a man.
He was standing by the fireplace, on her left hand as
she descended, looking into the fire, indeed, so that
his back was towards her. But at the rustle of her
frock he swung round quickly and looked up. He
now moved a few steps towards the foot of the stairs
with a particular eagerness. Pamela at that moment
had just come round the bend, and was on the small
platform from which the final flight of steps began.

The staircase was dimly lit, and the panelling of the wall against which it rested dark. Pamela took a step or two downward, and the light of the hall struck upon her face. The man came instantly to a dead stop, and a passing disappointment was visible upon his upturned face. It was evident that he was expecting some one else. Pamela on her side was disappointed, too, for she had hoped to find Millicent. She went down the stairs and stopped on the third step from the bottom.

"How do you do, Miss Mardale?" said the man. "You have arrived at last."

The man was Lionel Callon. Pamela recognized him now that they stood face to face; she *had* met him, but she had retained no impression of him in her memory. For the future, however, she would retain a very distinct impression. For her instincts told her at once and clearly that she thoroughly disliked the man. He was thirty-three in years, and looked a trifle younger, although his hair was turning gray. He was clean shaven, handsome beyond most men, and while his features were of a classical regularity and of an almost feminine delicacy, they were still not without character. There was determination in his face, and his eyes were naturally watchful. It was his manner which prompted Pamela's instinct of dislike. Assurance gave to it a hint of arrogance; familiarity made it distasteful. He might have been her host from the warmth of his welcome. Pamela put on her sedatest air.

"I am quite well," she said, with just sufficient surprise to suggest the question, "What in the world has my health to do with you?" She came down the three steps, and added: "We are the first, I suppose."

"There may be others in the drawing-room," said Callon, with a glance towards the open door. But Pamela did not take the hint. For one thing, no sound of any voice was audible in that room; for another, Mr. Callon was plainly anxious to be rid of her. Even as he was speaking his glance strayed past her up the staircase. Pamela disliked him; she was, besides, disappointed by him of that private talk with Millicent, which she desired. She was in a mood for mischief. She changed her manner at once, and, crossing over to the fireplace, engaged Mr. Callon in conversation with the utmost cordiality, and as she talked she began to be amused. Callon became positively uneasy; he could not keep still, he answered her at random, For instance, she put to him a question about the number of guests in the house. He did not answer at all for a moment or two, and when he did speak, is was to say: "Will the frost hold, do you think?"

"There's no sign of a thaw to-night," replied Pamela; and the sounds for which both were listening became audible—the shutting of a door on the landing above, and then the rustle of a frock upon the stairs. Mr. Callon was evidently at his wit's end what to do; and Pamela, taking her elbow from the mantel-piece, said, with great sympathy:

"One feels a little in the way—"

"Oh, not at all, Miss Mardale," Callon answered, hurriedly, with a flustered air.

Pamela looked at her companion with the blankest stare of surprise.

"I was going to say, when you interrupted me," she went on, "that one feels a little in the way when one has brought a couple of horses, as I have, and the frost holds."

Callon grew red. He had fallen into a trap; his very hurry to interrupt what appeared to be almost an apology betrayed that the lady upon the stairs and Mr. Lionel Callon had arranged to come down early. He had protested overmuch. However, he looked Pamela steadily in the face, and said:

"I beg your pardon, Miss Mardale."

He spoke loudly, rather too loudly for the ears of any one so near to him as Pamela. The sentence, too, was uttered with a note of warning. There was even a suggestion of command. The command was obeyed by the lady on the stairs, for all at once the frock ceased to rustle and there was silence. Lionel Callon kept his eyes fixed upon Pamela's face, but she did not look towards the stairs, and in a little while again the sound was heard. But it diminished. The lady upon the stairs was ascending, and a few minutes afterwards a door closed overhead. She had beaten a retreat.

Callon could not quite keep the relief which he felt out of his eyes or the smile from his lips. Pamela noticed the change with amusement. She was not in the mind to spare him uneasiness, and she said, looking at the wall above the mantel-piece:

"This is an old mirror, don't you think? From what period would you date it?"

Callon's thoughts had been so intent upon the stairs that he had paid no heed to the ornaments above the mantel-shelf. Now, however, he took note of them with a face grown at once anxious. The mirror was of an oval shape and framed in gold. Under the pretence of admiring it, he moved and stood behind Pamela, looking into the mirror over her shoulder, seeing what she could see, and wondering how much she had seen. He was to some extent relieved. The stairs were ill-lighted, the panelling of the wall dark mahogany; moreover, the stairs bent round into the hall just below the level of the roof, and at the bend the lady on the stairs had stopped. Pamela could not have seen her face. Pamela, indeed, had seen nothing more than a black-satin slipper arrested in the act of taking a step, and a black gown with some touches of red at the waist. She had, however, noticed the attitude of the wearer of the dress when the warning voice had brought her to a stop. The lady had stooped down and had cautiously peered into the hall. In this attitude she had been able to see, and yet had avoided being seen.

Pamela, however, did not relieve Mr. Callon of his suspense. She walked into the drawing-room and waited, with an amused curiosity, for the appearance of the black dress. It was long in coming, however. Pamela had no doubt that it would come last, and in a hurry, as though its wearer had been late in dressing. But Pamela was wrong. Millicent Stretton came into the room dressed in a frock of white lace, and at once dinner was announced. Pamela turned to Frances Millingham with a startled face:

"Are we all here?"

Frances Millingham looked round.

"Yes;" and Lord Millingham at that moment offered his arm to Pamela. As she took it, she looked at Millicent, who was just rising from her chair. Millicent was wearing with her white dress black shoes and stockings. She might be wearing them deliberately, of course; on the other hand, she might be wearing them because she had not had time to change them. It was Millicent, certainly, who had come down last.

"I beg your pardon, Miss Mardale," Callon had said, and it was upon the "Miss Mardale" that his voice had risen. The emphasis of his warning had been laid upon the name.

As she placed her hand on her host's arm, Pamela said:

"It was very kind of Frances to ask Millie Stretton here."

"Oh no," Lord Millingham replied. "You see, Frances knew her. We all knew, besides, that she is a great friend of yours."

"Yes," said Pamela; "I suppose everybody here knows that?"

"Mrs. Stretton has talked of it," he answered, with a smile.

The "Miss Mardale" might be a warning, then, to Millicent that her friend had arrived—was actually then in the hall. There was certainly no one but Millicent in that house who could have been conscious of any need to shrink back at the warning, who would have changed her dress to prevent a recognition; and Millicent herself need not have feared the warning had there not been something to conceal—something to conceal especially from Pamela, who had said, "I have promised your husband I would be your friend." There was the heart of Pamela's trouble.

She gazed down the two lines of people at the dinner-table, hoping against hope that she had overlooked some one. There was no one wearing a black gown. All Pamela's amusement in outwitting Callon had long since vanished. If Tony had only taken her advice without question, she thought. "Millie's husband should never leave her. If he goes away he should take her with him." The words rang in her mind all through dinner like the refrain of a song of which one cannot get rid. And at the back of her thoughts there steadily grew and grew a great regret that she had ever promised Tony to befriend his wife.

That Millicent was the lady on the stairs she no longer dared to doubt. Had she doubted, her suspicions would have been confirmed immediately dinner was over. In the drawing-room Millicent avoided any chance of a private conversation, and since they had not met for so long, such avoidance was unnatural. Pamela, however, made no effort to separate her friend from the other women. She had a plan in her mind, and in pursuit of it she occupied a sofa, upon which there was just room for two. She sat in the middle of the sofa, so that no one else could sit on it, and just waited until the men came in. Some of them crossed at once to Pamela, but she did not budge an inch. They were compelled to stand. Finally, Mr. Mudge approached her, and immediately she moved into one corner and bade him take the other. Mr. Mudge accepted the position with alacrity. The others began to move away; a couple of card-tables were made up. Pamela and John Mudge were left alone.

"You know every one here?" she asked.

"No, very few."

"Mr. Callon, at all events?"

Mr. Mudge glanced shrewdly at his questioner.

"Yes, I know him slightly," he answered.

"Tell me what you know."

Mr. Mudge sat for a moment or two with his hands upon his knees and his eyes staring in front of him. Pamela knew his history, and esteemed his judgment. He had built up a great contracting business from the poorest beginnings, and he remained without bombast or arrogance. He was to be met nowadays in many houses, and, while he had acquired manners, he had lost nothing of his simplicity. The journey from the Seven Dials to Belgrave Square is a test of furnace heat, and John Mudge had betrayed no flaws. There was a certain forlornness, too, in his manner which appealed particularly to Pamela. She guessed that the apples, for which through a lifetime he had grasped, had crumbled into ashes between his fingers. Sympathy taught her that the man was lonely. He wandered through the world amid a throng of acquaintances; but how many friends had he, she wondered. She did not interrupt his reflections, and he turned to her at last, with an air of decision.

"I am on strange ground here," he said, "as you know. I am the outsider; and when I am on strange ground I go warily. If I am asked what I think of this man or that, I make it a rule to praise."

"Yes; but not to me," said Pamela, with a smile. "I want to know the truth to-night."

Mudge looked at her deliberately, and no less deliberately he spoke:

"And I think you ought to know the truth to-night."

Mudge, then, like the rest, knew that she was Millicent's friend. Was it for that reason that she ought to know the truth?

"I know Callon a little," he went on, "but I know a good deal about him. Like most of the men who know him I dislike him heartily. Women, on the other hand, like him, Miss Mardale—like him too well. Women make extraordinary mistakes over men, just as men do over women. They can be very blind— like your friend—"

Mudge paused for an appreciable time. Then he went on, steadily:

"Like your friend, Lady Millingham, who invites him here."

Pamela was grateful for the delicacy with which the warning was conveyed, but she did not misunderstand it. She had been told indirectly, but no less definitely on that account, that Millie was entangled.

"Callon has good looks, of course," continued Mudge; and Pamela uttered a little exclamation of contempt. Mudge smiled, but rather sadly.

"Oh, it's something. All people have not your haughty indifference to good looks. He is tall, he has a face which is a face and not a pudding. It's a good deal, Miss Mardale."

Pamela looked in surprise at the stout, heavily built bald man who spoke. That he should ever have given a thought to how he looked was a new idea to her. It struck her as pathetic.

"But he is not merely good-looking. He is clever, persistent besides, and, so far as I can judge, untroubled by a single scruple in the management of his life. Altogether, Miss Mardale, a dangerous man. How does he live?" he asked, suddenly.

"I neither know nor care," said Pamela.

"Ah, but you should care," replied Mudge. "The answer is instructive. He has a small income—two hundred a year, perhaps; a mere nothing compared with what he spends—and he never does an hour's work, as we understand work. Yet he pays his card debts at his club, and they are sometimes heavy, and he wants for nothing. How is it done? He has no prospect of an inheritance, so post-obits are not the explanation."

Mr. Mudge leaned back in his chair and waited. Pamela turned the question over in her mind.

"I can't guess how it's done," she said.

"And I can do no more than hint the answer," he replied. "He rides one woman's horses, he drives another woman's phaeton, he is always on hand to take a third to a theatre, or to make up a luncheon-party with a fourth. Shall we say he borrows money from a fifth? Shall we be wrong in saying it?" And suddenly Mr. Mudge exclaimed, with a heat and scorn which Pamela had never heard from him before: "A very contemptible existence, anyway, Miss Mardale. But the man's not to be despised, mind. No, that's the worst of it. Some day, perhaps, a strong man will rise up and set his foot on him. Till that time he is to be feared." And when Pamela by a gesture rejected the word, Mudge repeated it. "Yes, feared. He makes his plans, Miss Mardale. Take a purely imaginary case," and somehow, although he laid no ironic stress on the word imaginary, and accompanied it with no look, but sat gazing straight in front of him, Pamela was aware that it was a real case he was going to cite. "Imagine a young and pretty woman coming to a house where most of the guests were strangers to her; imagine her to be of a friendly, unsuspecting temperament, rather lonely, perhaps, and either unmarried or separated for a time from her husband. Add that she will one day be very rich, or that her husband will be. Such a woman might be his prey, unless—"

Pamela looked up inquiringly.

"Unless she had good friends to help her."

Pamela's face, distressed before, grew yet more troubled now. The burden of her promise was being forced upon her back. It seemed she was not for one moment to be allowed to forget it.

"I'll tell you my philosophy, Miss Mardale," Mudge continued, "and I have inferred it from what I have seen. I do not believe that any man really comes to good unless he has started in life with the ambition to make a career for himself, with no help other than his hands and his brains afford. Later on he will learn that women can be most helpful; later on, as he gets towards middle life, as the years shorten and shorten, he will see that he must use whatever extraneous assistance comes his way. But he will begin with a fearless ambition to suffice with his own hands and head." Mr. Mudge dropped from the high level of his earnestness. He looked towards Lionel Callon, who was seated at a card-table, and the contempt again crept into his voice. "Now that man began life meaning to use all people he met, and especially women. Women were to be his implements." Mr. Mudge smiled suddenly. "He's listening," he said.

"But he is too far away to hear," replied Pamela.

"No doubt; but he knows we are speaking of him. Look, his attitude shows it. This, you see, is his battle-ground, and he knows the arts of his particular warfare. A drawing-room! Mr. Lionel Callon fights among the teacups. Cajolery first, and God knows by what means afterwards. But he wins, Miss Mardale; don't close your eyes to that! Look, I told you he was listening. The rubber's over, and he's coming towards us. Oh, he's alert upon his battle-ground! He knows what men think of him. He's afraid lest I should tell what men think to you. But he comes too late."

Callon crossed to the sofa, and stood talking there

until Frances Millingham rose. Pamela turned to Mr. Mudge as she got up.

"I thank you very much," she said, gratefully.

Mr. Mudge smiled.

"No need for thanks," said he. "I am very glad you came to-night, for I go away to-morrow."

Pamela went to her room and sat down before the fire. What was to be done, she wondered. She could not get Lionel Callon sent away from the house. It would be no use even if she could, since Millie had an address in town. She could not say a word openly.

She raised her head and spoke to her maid.

"Which is Mrs. Stretton's room?" And when she had the answer she rose from her chair and stood, a figure of indecision. She did not plead that John Mudge had exaggerated the danger; for she had herself foreseen it long ago, before Millie's marriage—even before Millie's engagement. It was just because she had foreseen it that she had used the words which had so rankled in Tony's memory. Bitterly she regretted that she had ever used them; greatly she wished that she could doubt their wisdom. But she could not. Let Millie's husband leave her, she would grieve with all the strength of her nature; let him come back soon, she would welcome him with a joy as great. Yes; but he must come back *soon*. Otherwise she would grow used to his absence; she would find his return an embarrassment, for it would be the return of a stranger with the prerogative of a husband; she might even have given to another the place he once held in her thoughts. And the other might be a Lionel Callon. For this was Millicent's character. She yielded too easily to affection, and she did not readily distinguish between affection and the show of it. She paddled in the shallows of passion, and flattered herself that she was swimming in the depths. Grief she was capable of—yes; but a torrent of tears obliterated it. Joy she knew; but it was a thrill with her lasting an hour.

Pamela walked along the passage and knocked at Millicent's door, saying who she was. Millicent opened the door, and received her friend with some constraint.

"Can I come in?" said Pamela.

"Of course," said Millie.

They sat opposite to one another on each side of the fire.

"I wanted to see you before I went to bed," said Pamela. "You have not told me lately in your letters how Tony is getting on."

Millie raised her hand to shield her face from the blaze of the fire. She happened to shade it also from the eyes of Pamela; and she made no reply.

"Is he still in New York?" Pamela asked; and then Millie replied.

"I do not know," she answered, slowly. She let her hand fall, and looked straight and defiantly at her friend.

"I have not heard from him for a long while," she added; and as she spoke there crept into her face a look of disdain.

VIII

GIDEON'S FLEECE

MILLICENT was reluctant to add any word of explanation. She sat with her eyes upon the fire, waiting, it seemed, until Pamela should see fit to go. But Pamela remained, and of the two women she was the stronger in will and character. She sat, with her eyes quietly resting upon Millicent's face; and in a little while Millicent began reluctantly to speak. As she spoke the disdainful droop of her lips became more pronounced, and her words were uttered in a note of petulance.

"He *would* stay to retrieve his failure. You remember?" she said.

"Yes," replied Pamela.

"I wrote to him again and again to come home, but he would not. I couldn't make him see that he wasn't really a match for the people he must compete with."

Pamela nodded her head.

"You wrote that to him?"

Millicent lifted her face to Pamela's.

"I put it, of course, with less frankness. I offered him, besides, the rest of my money, so that he might try again; but he refused to take a farthing more. It was unreasonable, don't you think? I could have got on without it, but he couldn't. I was very sorry for him."

"And you expressed your pity, too?" asked Pamela.

"Yes, indeed," said Millicent, eagerly. "But he never would accept it. He replied cheerfully that something was sure to happen soon, that he would be sure to find an opening soon. But, of course, he never did. It was not likely that with his inexperience he ever would."

Tony's own words had recoiled upon him. On the evening when he had first broached his plan to Millicent in Berkeley Square, he had laid before her, among others, this very obstacle, thinking that she ought to be aware of it, and never doubting but that he would surmount it. The honesty of his nature had bidden him speak all that he had thought, and he had spoken without a suspicion that his very frankness might put in her mind an argument to belittle him. He had seemed strong then, because he knew the difficulties, and counted them up when she omitted them. His image was all the more pale and ineffectual now because, foreknowing them well, he had not mastered them.

"I wrote to him at last that it wasn't any use for him to go on with the struggle. He would not tell me how he lived, or even where. I had to send my letters to a post-office, and he called for them. He must be living in want, in misery. I wrote to him that I had guessed as much from his very reticence, and I said how sorry I was. Yet, in spite of what I wrote," and here her voice hardened a little; she showed herself as a woman really aggrieved—"in spite of what I wrote, he answered me in a quite short letter, saying that I must not expect to hear from him again until he had recovered from his defeat and was re-established in my eyes. I can't understand that, can you?"

"I think so," Pamela answered. She spoke gently, for there was something to be said upon Millicent's side. The sudden collapse of her exaggerated hopes, the dreary life she led, and her natural disappointment at the failure of the man whom she had married, when once he stepped down into the arena to combat with his fellow-men. These things could not fail to provoke, in a nature so easily swayed from extreme to extreme as Millicent's, impatience, anger, and a sense of grievance. Pamela could hold the balance fairly enough to understand that. But chiefly she was thinking of Tony—Tony hidden away in some lodging in New York, a lodging so squalid that he would not give the address, and vainly seeking for an opportunity whereby he would make a rapid fortune; very likely going short of food, and returning home at night to read over a letter from his wife of which every line cried out to him, with a contemptuous pity: "You are a failure. You are a failure. Come home." Pamela's heart went out in pity, too. But there was no contempt in her pity. She could not but admire the perseverance with which, on this, the first time that he had ever walked hand in hand with misery, he endured its companionship.

"I think I understand," she said. "You say he answered you in that short way in spite of what you wrote. I think it was not in spite of, but because—".

Millie Stretton shook her head.

"No, that's not the reason," she replied. She gave one herself, and it fairly startled Pamela. "Tony no longer cares for me. He means to go out of my life altogether."

Pamela remembered what store Tony had always set upon his wife, how he had spoken of her that July morning in the park, and how he had looked at the moment when he spoke. It was just because he cared so much that he had taken his wild leap into the dark. That, at all events, she believed, and in such a strain she replied. But Millicent would not be persuaded.

"Before Tony went away," she said, stubbornly, "he let me see that he no longer cared. He was losing the associations which used to be vivid in his memory. Our marriage had just become a dull, ordinary thing. He had lost the spirit in which he entered into it."

Again Tony's indiscreet frankness had done him wrong. The coon song, which was always to be associated in his mind with the summer night, and the islets in the sea, and the broad stretch of water trembling away in the moonlight across to the lights of the yachts in Oban Bay, had become a mere coon song "sung by some one." Millicent had often remembered and reflected upon that unfortunate sentence, and as her disappointment in Tony increased, and the pitying contempt gradually crept into her mind, she read into it more and more of what Tony had not meant.

"I am sure you are wrong," said Pamela, very earnestly. "He went away because he cared. He went away to keep your married life and his from fading away into the colorless, dull, ordinary thing it so frequently becomes. He has lost ground by his failure. No doubt your own letters have shown that; and he is silent now in order to keep what he has. You have said it yourself. He will not write until he is able to re-establish himself in your thoughts."

But would Tony succeed? *Could* he succeed? The questions forced themselves into her mind even while she was speaking, and she carried them back to her room. The chances were all against him. Even if he retrieved his failure, it would be a long time before that result was reached—too long, perhaps, when his wife was Millicent, and such creatures as Lionel Callon walked about the world. And he might never succeed at all, he was so badly handicapped.

Pamela was sorely tempted to leave the entanglement alone to unravel itself. There was something which she could do. She was too honest to close her eyes to that. But her own history rose up against her and shook a warning finger. It had a message to her ears never so loudly repeated as on this night. "Don't move a step. Look on! Look on!" She knew herself well. She was by nature a partisan. Let her take this trouble in hand and strive to set it right, her whole heart would soon be set upon success. She was fond of Millicent already; she would become fonder still in the effort to save her. She liked Tony very much. The thought of him stoutly persevering, clinging to his one ambition to keep his married life a bright and real thing in spite of want and poverty— and even his wife's contempt—appealed to her with a poignant strength. But she might fail. She had eaten of failure once, and, after all these years, the taste of it was still most bitter in her mouth.

She fought her battle out over her dying fire, and at the end two thoughts stood out clearly in her mind. She had given her promise to Tony to be a good friend to his wife, and there was one thing which she could do in fulfilment of her promise.

She walked over to her window and flung it open. She was of the women who look for signs; no story quite appealed to her like the story of Gideon's Fleece. She looked for a sign now quite seriously. If a thaw

85

had set in, why, the world was going a little better with her, and perhaps she might succeed. But the earth was iron-bound, and in the still night she could hear a dry twig here and there snapping in the frost. No, the world was not going well. She decided to wait until things improved.

But next day matters were worse. For one thing, John Mudge went away, and he was the only person in the house who interested her at all. Furthermore, Lionel Callon stayed, and he announced some news.

"I have been chosen to stand for Parliament at the next election," he said; and he named an important constituency. Pamela noticed the look of gratification, almost of pride, which shone at once on Millie's face, and her heart sank. She interpreted Millie's thought, and accurately. Here was a successful man, a man who had got on without opportunities or means, simply by his own abilities; and there, far away in New York, was her failure of a husband. Moreover, Callon and Millicent were much together; they had even small secrets, to which in conversation they referred. The world was not going well with Pamela, and she waited for the fleece to be wet with dew.

After four days, however, the frost showed signs of breaking. A thaw actually set in that evening, and on the next morning two pieces of good news arrived. In the first place, Pamela received a letter from Alan Warrisden. There was nothing of importance in it, but it gave her his actual address. In the second, Millie told Frances Millingham that she had received news that Sir John Stretton was really failing, and although there was no immediate danger, she must hold herself in readiness to return to town. This to Pamela was really the best news of all. This morning, at all events, Gideon's Fleece was wet.   She looked out some trains in the railway-guide, and then sent a telegram to Warrisden to come by a morning train.   She would meet him at the railway-station.   The one step in her power she was thus resolved to take.

IX

THE NEW ROAD

ON the crest of that hill which was visible from the upper windows of Whitewebs, a village straggled for a mile; and all day in the cottages the looms were heard. The sound of looms, indeed, was always associated with that village in the minds of Pamela Mardale and Alan Warrisden, though they drove along its broad street but once, and a few hours included all their visit. Those few hours, however, were rich with consequence. For Pamela asked for help that day, and, in the mere asking, gave, as women must; and she neither asked nor gave in ignorance of what she did. The request might be small, the gift small, too; but it set her and her friend in a new relation each to each, it linked them in a common effort, it brought a new and a sweet intimacy into both their lives. So that the noise of a loom was never heard by them in the after-times but there rose before their eyes, visible as a picture, that gray, chill day of February, the red-brick houses crowding on the broad street in a picturesque irregularity, and the three tall poplars tossing in the wind. The recollection brought always a smile of tenderness to their faces; and in their thoughts they had for the village a strange and fanciful name. It was just a little Leicestershire village perched upon a hill, the village of looms, the village of the three poplars. But they called it Quetta.

THE TRUANTS

At the very end of the street, and exactly opposite to the small house from whose garden the poplars rose, there stood an inn. It was on the edge of the hill, for just beyond the road dipped steeply down between high hedges of brambles and elder-trees, and, turning at the bottom of the incline, wound thence through woods and level meadows towards Leicester. It was the old coach road, and the great paved yard of the inn and the long line of disused stables had once been noisy with the shouts of ostlers and the crack of whips. Now only the carrier's cart drove twice a week down the steep road to Leicester, and a faint whistle from the low-lying land and a trail of smoke showed where now the traffic ran. On the platform of the little road-side station, three miles from the village, Pamela met Alan Warrisden on the morning after she had sent off her telegram. She had a trap waiting at the door, and as they mounted into it she said:

"I rode over to the village this morning and hired this dog-cart at the inn. I am not expected to be back at Whitewebs until the afternoon; so I thought we might lunch at the inn, and then a man can drive you back to the station, while I ride home again."

"It was bad going for a horse, wasn't it?" said Warrisden.

The thaw had fairly set in; the roads, still hard as cement, ran with water, and were most slippery. On each side patches of snow hung upon the banks half melted, and the air was raw.

"Yes, it was bad going," Pamela admitted. "But I could not wait. It was necessary that I should see you to-day."

She said no more at the moment, and Warrisden was

content to sit by her side as she drove, and wait. The road ran in a broad, straight line over the sloping ground. There was no vehicle, not even another person, moving along it. Warrisden could see the line of houses ahead, huddled against the sky, the spire of a church, and on his right the three sentinel poplars. He was to see them all that afternoon.

Pamela drove straight to the inn, where she had already ordered luncheon; and it was not until luncheon was over that she drew up her chair to the fire and spoke.

"Won't you smoke?" she said, first of all. "I want you to listen to me."

Warrisden lit a pipe and listened.

"It is right that I should be very frank with you," she went on, "for I am going to ask you to help me."

"You need me, then?" said Warrisden. There was a leap in his voice which brought the color to her cheeks.

"Very much," she said; and, with a smile, she asked: "Are you glad?"

"Yes," he answered, simply.

"Yet the help may be difficult for you to give. It may occupy a long time, besides. I am not asking you for a mere hour or a day."

The warning only brought a smile to Warrisden's face.

"I don't think you understand," he said, "how much one wants to be needed by those one needs."

Indeed, even when that simple truth was spoken to her, it took Pamela a little while to weigh it in her thoughts and give it credence. She had travelled a long distance during these last years down her solitary road. She began to understand that now. To need

—actually to need people, to feel a joy in being needed
—here were emotions, familiar to most, and no doubt
at one time familiar to her, which were, nevertheless,
now very new and strange. At present she only
needed. Would a time come when she would go
further still? When she would feel a joy in being
needed? The question flashed across her mind.

"Yes," she admitted, "no doubt that is true. But
none the less there must be no misunderstanding between you and me. I speak of myself, although it is
not for myself that I need your help; but I am not
blind. I know it will be for my sake that you give it,
and I do not want you to give it in any ignorance of
me, or, perhaps"—and she glanced at him almost
shyly—"or, perhaps, expecting too much."

Warrisden made no other answer than to lean forward in his chair, with his eyes upon Pamela's face.
She was going to explain that isolation of hers which
had so baffled him. He would not for worlds have
interrupted her lest he should check the utterance on
her lips. He saw clearly enough that she was taking
a great step for her, a step, too, which meant much to
him. The actual explanation was not the important
thing. That she should confide it of her own accord—
there was the real and valuable sign. As she began
to speak again, diffidence was even audible in her voice.
She almost awaited his judgment.

"I must tell you something which I thought never
to tell to any one," she said. "I meant to carry it as
my secret out with me at the end of my life. I have
been looking on all these last years. You noticed that;
you thought perhaps I was just obeying my nature.
But I wasn't. I did not begin life looking on. I began it as eager, as expectant of what life could give

me as any girl that was ever born. And I had just my first season, that was all." She smiled rather wistfully as her thoughts went back to it. "I enjoyed my first season. I had hardly ever been in London before. I was eighteen; and everybody was very nice to me. At the end of July I went to stay for a month with some friends of mine on the coast of Devonshire, and—some one else stayed there, too. His name does not matter. I had met him during the season a good deal, but until he came down to Devonshire I had not thought of him more than as a friend. He was a little older than myself, not very much, and just as poor. He had no prospects, and his profession was diplomacy. . . . So that there was no possibility from the first. He meant never to say anything; but there came an hour, and the truth was out between us."

She stopped and gazed into the fire. The waters of the Channel ran in sunlit ripples before her eyes; the red rocks of Bigbury Bay curved warmly out on her right and her left; farther away the towering headlands loomed misty in the hot, still August air. A white yacht, her sails hardly drawing, moved slowly westward; the black smoke of a steamer stained the sky far out; and on the beach there were just two figures visible—herself and the man who had not meant to speak.

"We parted at once," she went on; and it seemed there was the whole story told. But Pamela had not told it all, and never did; for her mother had played a part in its unfolding. It was Mrs. Mardale's ambition that her daughter should make a great marriage; it was her daughter's misfortune that she knew little of her daughter's character. Mrs. Mardale had remarked the growing friendship between Pamela and the man, she had realized that marriage was quite impossible, and she had thought, with her short-sighted ingenuity, that if Pamela fell in love and found love to be a thing of fruitless trouble, she would come the sooner to take a sensible view of the world, and marry where marriage was to her worldly advantage. She thus had encouraged the couple to a greater friend-liness, throwing them together when she could have hindered their companionship; she had even urged Pamela to accept that invitation to Devonshire, know-ing who would be the other guests. She was disap-pointed afterwards when Pamela did not take the sensible view; but she did not blame herself at all. For she knew nothing of the suffering which her plan had brought about. Pamela had kept her secret. Even the months of ill-health which followed upon that first season had not opened the mother's eyes, and certainly she never suspected the weary nights of sleeplessness and aching misery which Pamela endured. Some hint of the pain of that bad past time, however, Pamela now gave to Warrisden.

"I stayed as much at home in Leicestershire as pos-sible," she said. "You see, there were my horses there; but even with them I was very lonely. The time was long in passing, and it wasn't pleasant to think that there would be so much of it yet, before it passed altogether. I went up to London for the season each year, and I went out a great deal. It helped me to keep from thinking."

The very simplicity with which she spoke gave an intensity to her words. There was no affectation in Pamela Mardale. Warrisden was able to fill out her hints, to understand her distress.

"All this is a great surprise to me," he said. "I have thought of you always as one who had never known either great troubles or great joys. I have hoped that some day you would wake, that I should find you looking out on the world with the eagerness of youth. But I believed eagerness would be a new thing to you."

He looked at her as she sat. The firelight was bright upon her face, and touched her hair with light; her dark eyes shone; and his thought was that which the school-master at Roquebrune had once sadly pondered. It seemed needlessly cruel, needlessly wanton, that a girl so equipped for happiness should, in her very first season, when the world was opening like a fairy-land, have been blindly struck down. There were so many others who would have felt the blow less poignantly. She might surely have been spared.

"You can guess, now," said Pamela, "why I have so persistently looked on. I determined that I would never go through such distress again. I felt that I would not dare to face it again." She suddenly covered her face with her hands. "I don't think I could," she cried, in a low, piteous voice. "I don't know what I would do," as though once more the misery of that time were closing upon her, so vivid were her recollections.

And once more Warrisden felt, as he watched her, the shock of a surprise. He had thought her too sedate, too womanly for her years, and here she sat shrinking in a positive terror, like any child, from the imagined recurrence of her years of trouble. Warrisden was moved as he had seldom been. But he sat quite still, saying no word; and in a little while she took her hands from her face and went on;

"My life was over, you see, at the very beginning, and I was resolved it should be over. For the future I would get interested only in trifling, unimportant things; no one should ever be more to me than a friend whom I could relinquish; I would merely look on. I should grow narrow, no doubt, and selfish." And, as Warrisden started, a smile came onto her face. "Yes, you have been thinking that, too, and you were right. But I didn't mind. I meant to take no risks. Nothing serious should ever come near me. If I saw it coming, I would push it away; and I have pushed it away."

"Until to-day, when you need my help," Warrisden interrupted.

"Yes, until to-day," Pamela repeated, softly.

Warrisden walked over to the window, and stood with his back towards her. The three tall poplars stood leafless up in front of him; the sky was heavy with gray clouds; the wind was roaring about the chimneys; and the roads ran with water. It was as cheerless a day as February can produce, but to Warrisden it had something of a summer brightness. The change for which he had hoped so long in vain had actually come to pass.

"What do you want me to do?" he asked, turning again to the room.

"I want you to find Millie Stretton's husband?" she replied; "and, at all costs, to bring him home again."

"Millie Stretton's husband?" he repeated, in perplexity.

"Yes. Don't you remember the couple who stepped out of the dark house in Berkeley Square, and dared not whistle for a hansom—the truants?"

Warrisden was startled. "Those two!" he exclaimed. "Well, that's strange. On the very night when we saw them, you were saying that there was no road for you, no new road from Quetta to Seistan. I was puzzling my brains, too, as to how in the world you were to be roused out of your detachment; and there were the means visible all the time, perhaps—who knows?—ordained." He sat down again in his chair. "Where shall I look for Mr. Stretton?" he asked.

"I don't know. He went away to New York, six months ago, to make a home for Millie and himself. He did not succeed, and he has disappeared."

"Disappeared?" cried Warrisden.

"Oh, but of his own accord," said Pamela. "I can't tell you why; it wouldn't be fair. I have no right to tell you. But he must be found, and he must be brought back. Again I can't tell you why; but it is most urgent."

"Is there any clew to help us?" Warrisden asked. "Had he friends in New York?"

"No; but he has a friend in England," said Pamela, "and I think it's just possible that the friend may know where he is to be found, for it was upon his advice that Mr. Stretton went to New York."

"Tell me his name."

"Mr. Chase," Pamela replied. "He is head of a mission in Stepney Green. Tony Stretton told me of him one morning in Hyde Park, just before he went away. He seemed to rely very much upon his judgment."

Warrisden wrote the name down in his pocket-book.

"Will he tell me, do you think, where Stretton is, even if he knows? You say Stretton has disappeared of his own accord."

"I have thought of that difficulty," Pamela answered. "There is an argument which you can use.

Sir John Stretton, Tony's father, is ill, and in all prob-
ability dying."

"I see. I can use the same argument to Stretton
himself, I suppose, when I find him?"

"I can give you no other," said Pamela; "but you
can add to it. Mr. Stretton will tell you that his
father does not care whether he comes back in time or
not. He is sure to say that. But you can answer
that every night since he went away the candles have
been lit in his dressing-room, and his clothes laid out
by his father's orders, on the chance that some evening he might walk in at the door."

That Sir John Stretton's illness was merely the pretext for Tony's return both understood. The real
reason why he must come home Pamela did not tell.
To her thinking Millie was not yet so deeply entangled
with Lionel Callon but that Tony's home-coming might
set the tangle right. A few weeks of companionship,
and surely he would resume his due place in his wife's
thoughts. Pamela, besides, was loyal to her sex. She
had promised to safeguard Millicent; she was in no
mind to betray her.

"But bring him back," she cried, with a real passion. "So much depends on his return, for Millie, for
him, and for me, too. Yes, for me! If you fail,
it is I who fail; and I don't want failure. Save me
from it!"

"I'll try," Warrisden answered, simply, and Pamela
was satisfied.

Much depended, for Warrisden, too, upon the success of his adventure. If he failed, Pamela would retire again behind her barrier; she would again resume
the passive, indifferent attitude of the very old; she
would merely look on as before and wait for things to

cease. If, however, he succeeded, she would be encouraged to move forward still; the common sympathies would have her in their grasp again; she might even pass that turnpike gate of friendship, and go boldly down the appointed road of life. Thus success meant much for him. The fortunes of the four people—Millicent, Tony, Pamela, and Warrisden—were knotted together at this one point.

"Indeed, I'll try," he repeated.

Pamela's horse was brought round to the inn door. The dusk was coming on.

"Which way do you go?" asked Warrisden.

"Down the hill."

"I will walk to the bottom with you. The road will be dangerous."

They went slowly down between the high elder hedges, Pamela seated on her horse, Warrisden walking by her side. The wide level lowlands opened out beneath them—fields of brown and green, black woods with swinging boughs, and the broad high-road with its white wood rails. A thin mist swirled across the face of the country in the wind, so that its every feature was softened and magnified. It loomed dim and strangely distant, with a glamour upon it like a place of old romance. To Pamela and Warrisden, as the mists wove and unwove above it, it had a look of dream-land.

They reached the end of the incline, and Pamela stopped her horse.

"This is my way," said she, pointing along the highway with her whip.

"Yes," answered Warrisden. The road ran straight for some distance, then crossed a wooden bridge and curved out of sight round the edge of a clump of trees.

"The new road," he said, softly. "The new road from Quetta to Seistan!"

Pamela smiled.

"This is Quetta," said she.

Warrisden laid his hand upon her horse's neck and looked suddenly up into her face.

"Where will be Seistan?" he asked, in a low voice.

Pamela returned the look frankly. There came a softness into her dark eyes. For a moment she let her hand rest lightly upon his sleeve and did not speak. She herself was wondering how far she was to travel upon this new road.

"I cannot tell," she said, very gently; "nor, my friend, can you. Only"—and her voice took on a lighter and a whimsical tone—"only I start alone on my new road."

And she went forward into the level country. Warrisden climbed the hill again, and turned when he had reached the top; but Pamela was out of sight. The dusk and the mists had enclosed her.

X

MR. CHASE

THE night had come when Warrisden stepped from the platform of the station into the train. Pamela was by this time back at Whitewebs; he himself was travelling to London; their day was over. He looked out of the window. Somewhere, three miles away, the village of the three poplars crowned the hill, but a thick wall of darkness and fog hid it from his eyes. It seemed almost as if Pamela and he had met that day only in thought at some village which existed only in a dream. The train, however, rattled upon its way. Gradually he became conscious of a familiar exhilaration. The day had been real. Not merely had it signalled the change in Pamela, for which for so long he had wished, not merely had it borne a blossom of promise for himself, but something was to be done immediately, and the thing to be done was of all things that which most chimed with his own desires. He was to take the road again, and the craving for the road was seldom stilled for long within his heart. He heard its call sung like a song to the rhythm of the wheels. The very uncertainty of its direction tantalized his thoughts.

Warrisden lodged upon the Embankment, and his rooms overlooked the Thames. The mist lay heavy upon London, and all that night the steamboats hooted as they passed from bridge to bridge. Warrisden lay long awake listening to them; each blast had its message for him, each was like the greeting of a friend; each one summoned him, and to each he answered with a rising joy, "I shall follow, I shall follow." The boats passed down to the sea through the night mist. Many a time he had heard them before, picturing the dark deck and the side-lights, red and green, and the yellow light upon the mast, and the man silent at the wheel, with the light from the binnacle striking up upon the lines of his face. They were little river or coasting boats for the most part, but he had never failed to be stirred by the long-drawn melancholy of their whistles. They talked of distant lands and an alien foliage.

He spent the following morning and the afternoon in the arrangement of his affairs, and in the evening drove down to the mission-house. It stood in a dull by-street close to Stepney Green, a rambling building with five rooms upon the ground-floor panelled with varnished deal and furnished with forms and rough tables, and, on the floor above, a big billiard-room, a bagatelle-room, and a carpenter's workshop. Mr. Chase was superintending a boxing-class in one of the lower rooms, and Warrisden, when he was led up to him, received a shock of surprise. He had never seen a man to the outward eye so unfitted for his work. He had expected a strong, burly person, cheery of manner and confident of voice; he saw, however, a tall young man with a long, pale face and a fragile body. Mr. Chase was clothed in a clerical frock-coat of unusual length, he wore bands of an irreproachable whiteness, and his hands were fine and delicate as a woman's. He seemed, indeed, the typical High

Church curate fresh that very instant from the tea-cups of a drawing-room.

"A gentleman to see you, sir," said the ex-army-sergeant, who had brought forward Warrisden. He handed Warrisden's card to Chase, who turned about and showed Warrisden his full face. Surprise had been Warrisden's first sentiment, but it gave place in an instant to distaste. The face which he saw was not ugly, but he disliked it. It almost repelled him. There was no light in the eyes at all; they were veiled and sunken; and the features repelled by reason of a queer antagonism. Mr. Chase had the high, narrow forehead of an ascetic, the loose mouth of a sensualist, and a thin crop of pale and almost colorless hair. Warrisden wondered why any should come to this man for advice, most of all a Tony Stretton. What could they have in common, the simple, good-humored, unintellectual subaltern of the Coldstream and this clerical exquisite? The problem was perplexing.

"You wish to see me?" asked Chase.

"If you please."

"Now? As you see, I am busy."

"I can wait."

"Thank you. The mission closes at eleven. If you can wait till then, you might come home with me and we could talk in comfort."

It was nine o'clock. For two hours Warrisden followed Chase about the mission, and with each half-hour his interest increased. However irreconcilable with his surroundings Chase might appear to be, neither he nor any of the members of the mission were aware of it. He was at ease alike with the boys and the men; and the boys and the men were at ease with him. Moreover, he was absolute master, although there were rough men enough among his subjects. The fiercest boxing-contest was stopped in a second by a motion of that delicate hand.

"I used to have a little trouble," he said to Warrisden, "before I had those wire frames fixed over the gas-jets. You see they cover the gas-taps. Before that was done, if there was any trouble, the first thing which happened was that the room was in darkness. It took some time to restore order"; and he passed on to the swimming-bath.

Mr. Chase was certainly indefatigable. Now he was giving a lesson in wood-carving to a boy, now he was arranging for an apprenticeship with another in the carpenter's shop. Finally he led the way into the great billiard-room where only the older men were allowed.

"It is here that Stretton used to keep order?" said Warrisden, and Chase at once turned quickly towards him.

"Oh," he said, slowly, in a voice of comprehension. "I was wondering what brought you here. Yes, this was the room."

Chase moved carelessly away and spoke to some of the men about the tables. But for the rest of the evening he was on his guard. More than once his eyes turned curiously and furtively towards Warrisden. His face grew stubborn and wore a look of weariness. Warrisden began to fear lest he should get no answer to the question he had to put. No appeal would be of any use—of that he felt sure. His argument must serve—and would it serve?

Chase, at all events, made no attempt to avoid the interview. As the hands of the clock marked eleven and the rooms emptied, he came at once to Warrisden.

"We can go now," he said, and unlocking a drawer, to Warrisden's perplexity, he filled his pockets with racket-balls. The motive for that proceeding became apparent as they walked to the house where Chase lodged. Their way led through alleys, and as they walked the children clustered about them, and Chase's pockets were emptied.

"We keep this house because men from the universities come down and put in a week now and then at the mission. My rooms are up-stairs."

Chase's sitting-room was in the strangest contrast to the bareness of the mission and the squalor of the streets. It was furnished with luxury, but the luxury was that of a man of taste and knowledge. There was hardly a piece of furniture which had not an interesting history; the engravings and the brass ornaments upon the walls had been picked up here and there in Italy. A bright fire blazed upon the hearth.

"What will you drink?" Chase asked, and brought from a cupboard bottle after bottle of liqueurs. It seemed to Warrisden that the procession of bottles would never end; some held liqueurs of which he had never even heard the name; but concerning all of them Mr. Chase discoursed with great knowledge and infinite appreciation.

"I can recommend this," he said, tentatively, as he took up one fat, round bottle and held it up to the light. "It is difficult, perhaps, to say definitely which is the best, but—yes, I can recommend this."

"Can't I have a whiskey-and-soda?" asked Warrisden, plaintively.

Mr. Chase looked at his companion with a stare.

"Of course you can," he replied; but his voice

was one of disappointment, and with an almost imperceptible shrug of the shoulders he fetched a Tantalus and a siphon of seltzer.

"Help yourself," he said, and lighting a gold-tipped cigarette he drew up a chair and began to talk. And so Warrisden came at last to understand how Tony Stretton had gained his great faith in Mr. Chase. Chase was a talker of a rare quality. He sat stooping over the fire with his thin hands outspread to the blaze, and for half an hour Warrisden was enchained. All that had repelled him in the man, all that had aroused his curiosity, was soon lost to sight. He yielded himself up as if to some magician. Chase talked not at all of his work or of the many strange incidents which he must needs have witnessed in its discharge. He spoke of other climates and bright towns with a scholarship which had nothing of pedantry, and an observation human as it was keen. Chase with the help of his Livy had traced Hannibal's road across the Alps, and had followed it on foot; he spoke of another march across snow-mountains of which Warrisden had never till this moment heard— the hundred days of a dead Sultan of Morocco on the passes of the Atlas, during which he led his forces back from Tafilet to Rabat. Chase knew nothing of this retreat but what he had read. Yet he made it real to Warrisden, so vividly did his imagination fill up the outlines of the written history. He knew his Paris, his Constantinople. He had bathed from the Lido and dreamed on the Grand Canal. He spoke of the peeling frescos in the villa of the Countess Guiccioli above Leghorn, of the outlook from the terrace over the vines and the olive-trees to the sea where Shelley was drowned; and where Byron's brig used to round into the wind, and with its sails flapping drop anchor under the hill. For half an hour Warrisden wandered through Europe in the pleasantest companionship, and then Chase stopped abruptly and leaned back in his chair.

"I was forgetting," he said, "that you had come upon a particular errand. It sometimes happens that I see no one outside the mission people for a good while, and during those periods, when I get an occasion, I am apt to talk too much. What can I do for you?"

The spirit had gone from his voice, his face. He leaned back in his chair, a man tired out. Warrisden looked at the liqueur bottles crowded on the table, with Chase's conversation still fresh in his mind. Was Chase a man at war with himself, he wondered, who was living a life for which he had no taste, that he might the more completely escape a life which his conscience disapproved? Or was he deliberately both hedonist and Puritan, giving to each side of his strange nature in turn its outlet and gratification?

"You have something to say to me," Chase continued. "I know quite well what it is about."

"Stretton," said Warrisden.

"Yes, you mentioned him in the billiard-room. Well?"

Chase was not looking at Warrisden. He sat with his eyes half-closed, his elbows on the arms of his chair, his finger-tips joined under his chin, and his head thrown back. There was no expression upon his face but one of weariness. Would he answer? Could he answer? Warrisden was in doubt—indeed, in fear. He led up to his question warily.

"It was you who recommended Stretton to try horse-breeding in Kentucky."

"Yes," said Chase, and he added: "After he had decided of his own accord to go away."

"He failed."

"Yes."

"And he has disappeared."

Chase opened his eyes but did not turn them to his companion.

"I did not advise his disappearance," he said. "That, like his departure, was his own doing."

"No doubt," Warrisden agreed. "But it is thought that you might have heard from him since his disappearance."

Chase nodded his head.

"I have."

"It is thought that you might know where he is now."

"I do," said Mr. Chase. Warrisden was sensibly relieved. One-half of his fear was taken from him. Chase knew, at all events, where Stretton was to be found. Now he must disclose his knowledge. But before he could put a question, Chase said, languidly:

"You say 'it is thought,' Mr. Warrisden. By whom is it thought? By his wife?"

"No. But by a friend of hers and his."

"Oh," said Chase, "by Miss Pamela Mardale, then." Warrisden started forward.

"You know her?" he asked.

"No. But Stretton mentioned her to me in a letter. She has sent you to me in fulfilment of a promise. I understand."

The words were not very intelligible to Warrisden. He knew nothing of Pamela's promise to Tony Stretton. But, on the other hand, he saw that Mr. Chase was giving a more attentive ear to what he said. He betrayed no ignorance of the promise.

"I am sent to fetch Stretton home," he said. "I want you to tell me where he is."

Chase shook his head.

"No," he said, gently.

"It is absolutely necessary that Stretton should come back," Warrisden declared, with great deliberation, and with no less deliberation Chase replied:

"In Stretton's view it is absolutely necessary that he should stay away."

"His father's dying."

Chase started forward in his chair and stared at Warrisden for a long time.

"Is that an excuse?" he said, at length.

It was, as Warrisden was aware. He did not answer the question.

"It is the truth," he replied; and he replied truthfully.

Chase rose from his chair and walked once or twice across the room. He came back to the fire, and, leaning an elbow on the mantel-piece, stared into the coals. Warrisden sat very still. He had used his one argument; he could add nothing to it; he could only wait for the answer in a great anxiety. So much hung upon that answer for Stretton and his wife, for Pamela, for himself! The fortunes of all four were knotted together. At last the answer came.

"I promised Tony that I would keep his secret," said Chase. "But when he asked for the promise and when I gave it, the possibility of his father dying was not in either his mind or mine. We considered—in letters, of course—other possibilities, but not this one. I don't think I have the right to remain silent. Even in the face of this possibility I should have kept my promise, I think, if you had come from his wife—for I know why he disappeared. But as things are, I will tell you. Tony Stretton is in the North Sea on a trawler."

"In the North Sea!" exclaimed Warrisden, and he smiled. After all, the steamboats on the river had last night called to him with a particular summons.

"Yes," continued Chase, and he fetched from his writing-desk a letter in Tony's hand. "He came back to England two months ago. He drifted across the country. He found himself at Yarmouth with a few shillings in his pocket. He knew something of the sea. He had sailed his own yacht in happier times. He was in great trouble. He needed time to think out a new course of life. He hung about on Gorleston pier for a day or two and then was taken on by a skipper who was starting out short of hands. He signed for eight weeks, and he wrote to me the day before he started. That's four weeks ago."

"Can I reach him?" Warrisden asked.

"Yes. The boat's the *Perseverance* and belongs to the Blue Fleet. A steam-cutter goes out every day from Billingsgate to fetch the fish. I know one of the owners. His son comes down to the mission. I can get you a passage. When can you start?"

"At any time," replied Warrisden. "The sooner the better."

"To-morrow, then," said Chase. "Meet me at the entrance to Billingsgate Market at half-past eleven. It will take you forty-eight hours with ordinary luck to reach the Doggerbank. Of course if there's a fog in the Thames the time will be longer. And, I warn you, the living's rough on a fish-carrier."

"I don't mind that," said Warrisden, with a smile. He went away with a light heart, and that night wrote a letter to Pamela, telling her of his interview with Mr. Chase. The new road seemed, after all, likely to prove a smooth one. As he wrote, every now and then a steamboat hooted from the river, and the rain pattered upon his window. He flung it up and looked out. There was no fog to-night, only the rain fell, and fell gently. He prayed that there might be no fog upon the Thames to-morrow.

Mr. Chase, too, heard the rain that night. He sat in his arm-chair listening to it, with a decanter at his elbow half-filled with a liquid like brown sherry. At times he poured a little into his glass and drank it slowly, crouching over his fire. Somewhere in the darkness of the North Sea, Tony Stretton was hidden. Very likely at this moment he was standing upon the deck of his trawler with his hands upon the spokes of the wheel and his eyes peering forward through the rain, keeping his long night-watch while the light from the binnacle struck upward upon the lines of his face. Mr. Chase sat late in a muse; but before he went to bed he locked the decanter and the glass away in a private cupboard and took the key with him into his bedroom.

XI

ON THE DOGGERBANK

THE *City of Bristol* swung out of the huddle of boats off Billingsgate wharf at one o'clock on the next afternoon. Mr. Chase, who stood on the quay among the porters and white-jacketed salesmen, turned away with an Episcopal wave of the hand. Warrisden leaned over the rail of the steamer's bridge, between the captain and the pilot, and shouted a reply. The *City of Bristol*, fish-cutter, of three hundred tons, was a boat built for speed, long and narrow, setting low on the water, with an upstanding forecastle forward, a small saloon in the stern, and a tiny cabin for the captain under the bridge on deck. She sidled out into the fairway, and went forward upon her slow, intricate journey to the sea. Below the Tower she took her place in the long, single file of ships winding between the mud-banks, and changed it as occasion served; now she edged up by a string of barges, now in a clear broad space she made a spurt and took the lead of a barkentine, which swam in indolence with bare masts behind a tug, and at times she stopped altogether, like a carriage blocked in Piccadilly. The screw thrashed the water, ceased, and struck again with a suggestion of petulance at the obstacles which barred the boat's way. Warrisden, too, chafed upon the bridge. A question pressed continually upon his mind— "Would Stretton return?" He had discovered where

Stretton was to be found. The tall gray spire of
Stepney Church rose from behind an inlet thick with
masts upon the left; he was already on his way to find
him. But the critical moment was yet to come. He
had still to use his arguments, and as he stood watching the shipping with indifferent eyes the arguments
appeared most weak and unpersuasive. Stretton's
father was dying, it was true. The son's return was
no doubt a natural obligation. But would the natural
obligation hold when the father was unnatural?
Those months in New York had revealed one quality
in Tony Stretton, at all events; he could persist. The
very name of the trawler in which he was at work
seemed to Warrisden of a bad augury for his success
—the *Perseverance!*

Greenwich, with its hill of grass, slipped behind on
the right; at the Albert Docks, a huge Peninsula and
Oriental steamer, deck towering above deck, swung
into the line; the high chimneys of the cement-works
on the Essex Flats began to stand out against the pale
gray sky, each one crowned with white smoke like a
tuft of wool; the barges, under their big brown sprit-
sails, now tacked this way and that, across a wider
stream; the village of Greenhithe and the white port-
holes of the *Worcester* showed upon the right.

"Would Stretton return?" The question revolved
in Warrisden's mind as the propeller revolved in the
thick, brown water. The fortunes of four people hung
upon the answer, and no answer could be given until
a night and a day and another night had passed, until
he saw the Blue Fleet tossing far away upon the
Doggerbank. Suppose that the answer were "No!"
He imagined Pamela sinking back into lassitude, nar-
rowing to that selfishness which she no less than he

foresaw, looking on again at the world's show with the lack-lustre indifference of the very old.

At Gravesend the *City of Bristol* dropped her pilot, a little, white-bearded, wizened man, who, all the way down the river, balancing himself upon the top-rail of the bridge like some nautical Blondin, had run from side to side, the while he exchanged greetings with the anchored ships; and just opposite to Tilbury Fort, with its scanty fringe of trees, ran alongside of a hulk and she took in a load of coal.

"We'll go down and have tea while they are loading her," said the captain.

The dusk was falling when Warrisden came again on deck, and a cold wind was blowing from the northwest. The sharp stem of the boat was cutting swiftly through the quiet water; the lift of the sea under her forefoot gave to her a buoyancy of motion; she seemed to have become a thing alive. The propeller cleft the surface regularly; there was no longer any sound of petulance in its revolutions; rather there was a throb of joy as it did its work unhindered. Throughout the ship a steady hum, a steady vibration, ran. The *City of Bristol* was not merely a thing alive, it was a thing satisfied.

Upon Warrisden, too, there descended a sense of peace. He was *en rapport* with the ship. The fever of his questioning left him. On either side the arms of the shore melted into the gathering night. Far away upon his right the lights of Margate shone brightly, like a chain of gold stretched out upon the sea; in front of him there lay a wide and misty bay, into which the boat drove steadily. All the unknown seemed hidden there; all the secret, unrevealed, beyond. There came whispers out of that illimitable bay to Warrisden's ears; whispers breathed upon the north wind, and all the whispers were whispers of promise, bidding him take heart. Warrisden listened and believed, uplifted by the grave quiet of the sea and its mysterious width.

The *City of Bristol* turned northward into the great channel of the Swin, keeping close to the light-ships on the left, so close that Warrisden from the bridge could look straight down upon their decks. The night had altogether come—a night of stars. Clusters of lights low down upon the left showed where the towns of Essex stood; upon the right hand the homeward-bound ships loomed up ghostlike and passed by; on the right, too, shone out the great green globes of the Mouse light like Neptune's reading-lamps. Sheltered behind the canvas screen at the corner of the bridge, Warrisden looked along the rake of the unlighted deck below. He thought of Pamela waiting for his return at Whitewebs, but without impatience. The great peace and silence of the night were the most impressive things he had ever known. The captain's voice complaining of the sea jarred upon him.

"It's no bobby's job," said the captain, in a low voice. "It's home once in three weeks from Saturday to Monday if you are in luck, and the rest of your time you're in carpet slippers on the bridge. You'll sleep in my chatoo to-night. I sha'n't turn in until we have passed the Outer Gabbard and come to the open sea. That won't be till four in the morning."

Warrisden understood that he was being offered the captain's cabin.

"No, thanks," said he, "the bench of the saloon will do very well for me."

The captain did not press his offer.

"Yes, there's more company in the saloon," he said. "I often sleep there myself. You are bound for the mission ship, I suppose."

"No. I want to find a man on the trawler *Perseverance*."

The captain turned. Warrisden could not see his face, but he knew from his attitude that he was staring at him in amazement.

"Then you must want to see him pretty badly," he commented. "The No'th Sea in February and March is not a bobby's job."

"Bad weather is to be expected?" asked Warrisden.

"It has been known," said the captain, dryly; and before the lights of the Outer Gabbard winked good-bye on the starboard quarter at four o'clock in the morning the *City of Bristol* was taking the water over her deck.

Warrisden rolled on the floor of the saloon—for he could not keep his balance on the narrow bench—and tried in vain to sleep. But the strong light of a lamp glared upon his eyes. Moreover, the heat was intolerable. Five men slept in the bunks; Warrisden made a sixth; at four in the morning the captain joined the party through his love of company. The skylight and the door were both tightly closed; a big fire burned in the stove, and a boiling kettle of tea perpetually puffed from its spout a column of warm, moist steam. Warrisden felt his skin prickly beneath his clothes; he gasped for fresh air.

Living would be rough upon the fish-carrier, Chase had told him, and rough Warrisden found it. In the morning the steward rose, and made tea by the simple process of dropping a handful of tea into the kettle and filling it up with water. A few minutes later he brought a dish of ham and eggs from the galley and slapped it down on the table.

"Breakfast!" he cried, and the five men opened their eyes, rubbed them, and without any other preparation sat down and ate. Warrisden slipped up the companion, unscrewed the skylight, and opened it for the space of an inch. Then he returned.

The *City of Bristol* was rolling heavily, and Warrisden noticed with surprise that all of the five men gave signs of discomfort. Surely, he thought, they must be used to heavy weather. But, nevertheless, something was wrong, They did not talk; finally the captain looked upward and brought his hand down upon the table.

"I felt something was wrong," said he, "the skylight's open."

All stared up to the roof.

"So it is!" they exclaimed, blankly.

"I did that," Warrisden said, humbly.

At once all the faces were turned on him in great anxiety.

"Now why?" asked the captain. "Don't you like it nice and snug?"

"Yes, oh yes," Warrisden said, hurriedly.

"Well, then," said the captain, and the steward went on deck and screwed the skylight down.

"After all, it's only for thirty-six hours," thought Warrisden, as he subsequiently bathed in a pail on deck. But he was wrong. For the Blue Fleet had gone a hundred miles north to the Fisher Bank, and thither the *City of Bristol* followed it.

The *City of Bristol* sailed on to the Fisher Bank and found an empty sea. It hunted the Blue Fleet for half a dozen hours, and as night fell it came upon a single trawler with a great flare-light suspended from its yard.

"They're getting in their trawl," said the captain, and he edged up within earshot.

"Where's the Blue Fleet?" he cried.

"Gone back to the Dogger," came the answer.

The captain swore and turned southward. For four days and nights Warrisden pitched about on the fish-carrier and learned many things, such as the real meaning of tannin in tea and the innumerable medical uses to which "Friar's Balsam" can be put. On the morning of the fifth day the *City of Bristol* steamed into the middle of the fleet and her engines stopped.

These were the days before the steam-trawler. The sailing-ships were not as yet laid up, two by two, alongside Gorleston Quay, and knocked down for a song to any purchaser. Warrisden looked over a gray, savage sea. The air was thick with spin-drift. The waves leaped exultingly up from windward and roared away to leeward from under the cutter's keel in a steep, uprising hill of foam. All about him the sailing-boats headed to the wind, sinking and rising in the furrows, so that Warrisden would just see a brown top-sail over the edge of a steep roller like a shark's fin, and the next instant the dripping hull of the boat flung out upon a breaking crest.

"You will have to look slippy when the punt from the *Perseverance* comes alongside with her fish," the captain shouted. "The punt will give you a passage back to the *Perseverance*, but I don't think you will be able to return here. There's a northwesterly gale blowing up and the sea is increasing every moment. However, there will be another cutter up to-morrow, and if it's not too rough you could be put on board of her."

It took Warrisden a full minute to realize the meaning of the captain's words. He looked at the tumbling, breaking waves; he listened to the roar of the wind through the rigging.

"The boats won't come alongside to-day!" he cried.

"Won't they?" the skipper replied. "Look!"

Certainly some manœuvre was in progress. The trawlers were all forming to windward in a rough semicircle about the cutter. Warrisden could see boat tackle being rigged to the main-yards and men standing about the boats capsized on deck. They were actually intending to put their fish on board in the face of the storm.

"You see, with the gale blowing up, they mayn't get a chance to put their fish on board for three or four days after this," the captain explained. "Oh, you can take it from me. The No'th Sea is not a bobby's job."

As Warrisden watched, one by one the trawlers dropped their boats and loaded them with fish-boxes. The boats pushed off, three men to each, with their life-belts about their oil-skins, and came down with the wind towards the fish-carrier. The trawlers bore away, circled round the *City of Bristol*, and took up their formation to leeward, so that, having discharged their fish, the boats might go down again with the wind to their respective ships. Warrisden watched the boats piled up with fish-boxes coming through the welter of the sea. It seemed some desperate race was being rowed.

"Can you tell me which is the boat from the *Perseverance*?" he asked.

"I think it's the fifth," said the captain.

The boats came down, each one the kernel of a globe

of spray. Warrisden watched, admiring how cleverly they chose the little gaps and valleys in the crests
of the waves. Each moment he looked to see a boat
tossed upward and overturned; each moment he
dreaded that boat would be the fifth. But no boat
was overturned. One by one they passed under the
stern of the *City of Bristol* and came alongside under
the shelter of its wall.

The fifth boat ranged up. A man stood up in the
stern.

"The *Perseverance!*" he cried. "Fourteen boxes!"
and as he spoke a great sea leaped up against the
windward bow of the cutter. The cutter rolled from
it suddenly, her low bulwarks dipped under water on
the leeward side, close by the *Perseverance's* boat.

"Shove off!" the man cried, who was standing up,
and as he shouted he lurched and fell into the bottom
of the boat. The two men in the bow pushed off
with their oars, but they were too late. The cutter's
bulwark caught the boat under the keel; it seemed she
must be upset and men and boxes whelmed in the sea
unless a miracle happened. But the miracle did happen. As the fish - cutter righted she scooped onto
her deck the boat with its boxes and its crew. The
incident all seemed to happen within the fraction of a
second. Not a man upon the fish-cutter had the
time to throw out a rope. Warrisden saw the cutter's
bulwarks dip, the sailor falling in the boat, and the
boat upon the deck of the cutter in so swift a succession that he had not yet realized disaster was inevitable
before disaster was avoided.

The sailor rose from the bottom of the boat and
stepped on deck, a stalwart, dripping figure.

"From the *Perseverance*, sir. Fourteen boxes," he

said, looking up to the captain on the bridge. And Warrisden, leaning by the captain's side upon the rail, knew the sailor to be Tony Stretton. The accent of the voice would have been enough to assure him, but Warrisden knew the face too.

"This is the man I want," he said to the captain.

"You must be quick then," the captain replied. "Speak to him while the boat is being unloaded."

Warrisden descended onto the deck.

"Mr. Stretton," said he.

The sailor swung round quickly. There was a look of annoyance upon his face.

"You are surely making a mistake," said he, abruptly. "We are not acquainted," and he turned back to the fish-boxes.

"I'm not making a mistake," replied Warrisden. "I have come out to the North Sea in order to find you."

Stretton ceased from his work and stood up. He led the way to the stern of the cutter, where the two men were out of earshot.

"Now," he said. He stood in front of Warrisden in his sea-boots and his oil-skins, firmly planted, yet swaying to the motion of the ship. There was not merely annoyance in his face, but he had the stubborn and resolute look of a man not lightly to be persuaded. Standing there on the cutter's deck, backed by the swinging seas, there was even an air of mastery about him which Warrisden had not expected. His attitude seemed, somehow, not quite consistent with his record of failure.

"Now," said Stretton, "we must be quick. The sea is getting worse each minute, and I have to get back to the *Perseverance*. You are—?"

"HE STOOD IN FRONT OF WARRISDEN, FIRMLY PLANTED"

"Alan Warrisden," said Warrisden, "a stranger to you."

"Yes," Stretton interrupted; "how did you find me out?"

"Chase told me."

Stretton's face flushed, angrily.

"He had no right to tell you. I wished for these few weeks to be alone. He gave me his word he would tell no one."

"He had to break his word," said Warrisden, firmly. "It is necessary that you should come home at once."

Stretton laughed. Warrisden was clinging to a wire stay from the cutter's mizzen-mast, and even so could hardly keep his feet. He had a sense of coming failure from the very ease with which Stretton stood resting his hands upon his hips, unsupported, on the unsteady deck.

"I cannot come," said Stretton, abruptly, and he turned away. As he turned, Warrisden shouted, for in that high wind words carried in no other way:

"Your father, Sir John Stretton, is dying."

Stretton stopped. He looked for a time thoughtfully into Warrisden's face. But there was no change in his expression by which Warrisden could gather whether the argument would prevail or no. And when at last he spoke it was to say:

"But he has not sent for me?"

It was the weak point in Warrisden's argument, and Stretton had, in his direct way, come to it at once. Warrisden was silent.

"Well?" asked Stretton. "He has not sent for me?"

"No," Warrisden admitted, "that is true."

"Then I will not come."

"But though he has not sent for you, it is very certain that he wishes for your return," Warrisden urged. "Every night since you have been away the candles have been lighted in your dressing-room and your clothes laid out in the hope that on one evening you will walk in at the door. On the very first night, the night of the day on which you went, that was done. It was done by Sir John Stretton's orders, and by his orders it has always since been done."

Just for a moment Warrisden thought that his argument would prevail. Stretton's face softened, then came a smile which was almost wistful about his lips, his eyes had a kindlier look; and the kindlier look remained. Kindliness, too, was the first tone audible in his voice as he replied. But the reply itself yielded nothing.

"He has not sent for me?"

He looked curiously at Warrisden, as if for the first time he became aware of him as a man acting from motives, not a mere instrument of persuasion.

"After all, who did send you?" he asked. "My wife?"

"No."

"Who, then?"

"Miss Pamela Mardale.'

Stretton was startled by the name. It was really the strongest argument Warrisden had in his armory. Only he was not aware of its strength.

"Oh!" said Stretton, doubtfully. "So Miss Mardale sent you!"

He thought of that morning in the Row, of Pamela's words: "I still give the same advice. Do not leave your wife." He recalled the promise she had given, although it was seldom long absent from his thoughts.

It might be that she sent this message in fulfilment of that promise. It might be that, for some unknown reason, he was now needed at his wife's side. But he had no thought of distrust, he had great faith in Millicent. She despised him, yes; but he did not distrust her. And, again, it might be that Pamela was merely sending him this news, thinking he would wish to hear of it in time. After all, Pamela was his friend. He looked out on the wild sea. Already the boats were heading back through the foam, each to its trawler.

"One must take one's risks," he said. "So much I have learned here in the North Sea. Look!" and he pointed to the boats. "Those boats are taking theirs. Yes, one must take one's risks. I will not come."

He went back to the middle of the ship. The punt of the *Perseverance* was already launched, the two fishermen waiting in it. As it rose on a swell, Stretton climbed over the bulwarks and dropped into the stern.

"Good-bye," he said. "I have signed on for eight weeks, and only four have passed. I cannot run away and leave the ship short-handed. Thank you for coming, but one must take one's risks."

The boat was pushed off and headed towards the *Perseverance*. The waves had increased, the crests toppled down the green slopes in foam. Slowly the boat was rowed down to the trawler, the men now stopping and backing water, now dashing on. Warrisden saw them reach the ship's side and climb on board; he saw the boat slung upward and brought in onto the deck. Then the screw of the *City of Bristol* struck the water again. Lurching through the heavy sea she steamed southward. In a few minutes the Blue Fleet was lost to sight.

XII

WARRISDEN TELLS OF HIS VOYAGE

WARRISDEN had failed. This was the account
of his mission which he had to give to Pamela
Mardale, and he gave it without excuses. He landed
at Billingsgate wharf at eleven o'clock on the second
day after the sails of the Blue Fleet had dropped out
of sight behind the screen of breaking waves. That
afternoon he travelled down to the village of the three
poplars. It was night when he stepped out of the
train onto the platform of the little station. One can
imagine what bitter and humiliating thoughts occupied his mind. Away on the crest of the hill the lights
of the village shone brightly through the clear night
air, just as the lights of Margate had shone across the
bay when the steam-cutter had sprung like a thing alive
to the lift of the sea beneath her bows. Then all the
breeze had whispered promises; now the high hopes
were fallen. "Do not fail!" Pamela had cried, with a
veritable passion, hating failure as an indignity. He
could hear the words in the very accent of her voice.
Once she had suffered failure, but it was not to be
endured again. That was what she had meant; and
he had failed. He drove along that straight road
which he had traversed with Pamela at his side; he
slept under the roof of the inn where Pamela had
claimed his help. The help had been fruitless, and
the next morning he rode down the hill and along the

road with the white wood rails—"the new road"—to
tell her so. The sun was bright; there was a sparkle
of spring in the air; on the black, leafless boughs birds
sang. He looked back to the three poplars pointing
to the sky from the tiny garden on the crest of the
hill. Quetta—yes! But it seemed there was to be
no Seistan.

He had started early, fearing that there might be a
meet that day; and he had acted wisely, for in the
hall there were one or two men lounging by the fire in
scarlet, and Pamela was wearing her riding-habit when
she received him. He was shown into a little room
which opened onto the garden behind the house, and
thither Pamela came.

"You are alone!" she said.

"Yes; Stretton would not come."

"None the less, I am very grateful."

She smiled as she spoke, and sat down, with her
eyes upon him, waiting for his story. The disappointment was visible upon his face, but not upon hers.
Pamela's, indeed, was to him at this moment rather
inscrutable. It was not indifferent, however. He
recognized that, and was, in a way, consoled. It had
been his fear that at the first word she would dismiss
the subject and turn her back on it for good. On the
contrary, she was interested, attentive.

"You found him, then?" she asked.

"Yes. You would like to hear what passed?"

"Of course."

"Even though I failed?"

She looked at him with some surprise at his insist-
ence.

"Yes, yes," she said, a little impatiently.

"We were nearly three days longer in reaching the

Blue Fleet than we anticipated," he began. "Stretton came on board the fish-cutter—" And Pamela interrupted him:

"Why were you nearly three days longer? Tell me about your own journey out to the fleet from the beginning."

She was, in fact, as much interested in her messenger as in the errand upon which she had sent him. Warrisden began to see that his journey, after all, was not entirely a defeat. The alliance to which they had set their hands up there in the village on the hill was bearing its fruit. It had set them in a new relationship to each other, and in a closer intimacy.

He told the story of his voyage, making light of his hardships on the steam-cutter. She, on the other hand, made much of them.

"To quote your captain," she remarked, with a smile, "it was not a bobby's job."

Warrisden laughed, and told her of Stretton's arrival in the punt of the *Perseverance*. He described the way in which he had come on board; he related the conversation which had passed between them at the stern of the cutter.

"He hadn't the look of a man who had failed," Warrisden continued. "He stood there on the swinging deck with his legs firmly planted apart, as easily as if he were standing on a stone pavement. I, on the other hand, was clinging desperately to a stay. He stood there, with the seas swinging up behind him, and stubbornly refused to come."

"You told him of his father's illness?" asked Pamela.

"He replied that his father had not sent for him."

"You spoke of the candles lit every night?"

"His answer was the same. His father had not sent

for him. Besides, he had his time to serve. He had signed on for eight weeks. There was only one moment when I thought that there was a chance I might persuade him; and, indeed, my persuasions had really nothing to do with it at all. It was just the mention of your name."

"My name?" asked Pamela, in surprise.

"Yes. In answer to a question of his I told him that I had been sent out by you, and for a moment he faltered."

Pamela nodded her head in comprehension.

"I understand; but he refused in the end?"

"Yes. He said: 'One must take one's risks.'"

Pamela repeated the sentence softly to herself; and Warrisden crossed over to her side. His voice took a gentler note, and one still more serious than that which he had used.

"Do you know what I think?" he asked. "You sent me out with a message to Stretton. I think that he has sent me back with a message for you—'One must take one's risks.' He said that he had learned that in the North Sea. He pointed to the little boats carrying the fish-boxes to the steamer through the heavy, breaking seas. Each man in each of the boats was taking his risks. 'Whether it's lacing your topsail or taking in a reef,' he said, 'one must take one's risks.'"

Pamela was silent for a while after he had spoken. She sat with her hands folded in her lap, and her face most serious. Then she looked up at her companion with a very friendly smile; but she did not answer him at all. And when she spoke, she spoke words which utterly surprised him. All the time since the ketches had disappeared behind the waves he had been plagued with the thought of the distress which defeat would cause her; and here she was saying:

"I am very glad that you went out to the North Sea for me, even though the journey proved fruitless. It makes us so much the better friends, doesn't it? And that is a gain for me. Think of it that way, and you will not mind the hardships and the waste of time."

She held out her hand—rather a rare act with her—and Warrisden took it. Then came the explanation why defeat meant so little just at this time.

"I need not have sent you at all," she continued, "could I have foreseen. Sir John Stretton died yesterday afternoon, suddenly. I received a telegram last night from Millie. So Tony will naturally come home when his four weeks are up. I wrote last night to Millie telling her where Tony was." She added, "I am glad that I did not foresee."

She rose from her chair, and they walked out through the hall to the front of the house. Warrisden helped her into the saddle, and she rode away.

Sir John had died, and Stretton would now naturally come home. That explained to Warrisden how it was that Pamela made so little of the defeat. But it was not the whole explanation. Pamela was waking from her long sleep, like the princess in the fairy-tale, and the mere act of waking was a pleasure. In the stir of emotions, hitherto rigorously suppressed, in the exercise of sympathies, she found a delight such as one may find in the mere stretching of one's muscles after a deep rest. The consciousness of life as a thing enjoyable began to tingle in her. She was learning again lessons which she remembered once to have learned before. The joy of being needed by those one needs—there was one of them. She had learned a new one to-day—"One must take one's risks." She repeated the sentence over to herself as she rode between the hedge-rows on this morning which had the sparkle of spring. A few days ago she would have put that view of life away from her. Now, old as it was, simple as it was, she pondered upon it as though it were a view quite novel. She found it, moreover, pleasant. She had travelled, indeed, farther along the new road than she was aware. The truth is that she had rather hugged to herself the great trouble which had overshadowed her life. She had done so unwittingly. She had allowed it to dominate her after it had lost its power to dominate, and from force of habit. She began to be aware of it now that she had stepped out from her isolation and was gathering again the strings of her life into her hands.

Pamela was wrong in her supposition that since Sir John's death the danger for Millicent was at an end. Tony Stretton would now return home, she thought; and nothing was further from Tony's thoughts. At the time when Pamela was riding through the lanes of Leicestershire on that morning of early spring, Tony was lying in his bunk in the cabin of the *Perseverance* reading over, for the thousandth time, certain letters which he kept beneath his pillow. This week he kept the long night watch from midnight until eight of the morning; it was now eleven, and he had the cabin to himself. The great gale had blown itself out. The trawl, which for three days had remained safely stowed under the lee bulwarks, was now dragging behind the boat; with her topsails set the ketch was sailing full and by the wind; and down the open companion the sunlight streamed into the cabin and played like water upon the floor. The letters Tony Stretton was reading were those which Millie had sent him. Disappointment was plain in every line; they were sown with galling expressions of pity; here and there contempt peeped out. Yet he was glad to have them; they were his monitors, and he found a stimulus in their very cruelty. Though he knew them by heart, he continually read them on mornings like this, when the sun shone down the companion, and the voices of his fellow-sailors called cheerily overhead; at night, leaning upon his elbow, and spelling them out by the dim light of the swinging lamp, while the crew slept about him in their bunks.

To his companions he was rather a mystery. To some of them he was just down on his luck; to others he was a man "who had done something."

"I suppose you have come out here to lie doggo," said the skipper to him, shouting out the words in the height of the gale, when both were standing by the lashed wheel one night. "I ask no questions. All I say is, you do your work. I have had no call to slap a haddick across your face. I say that fair and square. Water!"

He concluded his speech with a yell. Stretton saw a ragged line of white suddenly flash out in the darkness high up by the weather bow and descend with a roar. It was a wave breaking down upon the deck. Both men flung themselves down the companion, and the water sluiced after them and washed them struggling about the floor of the cabin. The wave saved Stretton from the need to reply, and the skipper did not refer to the subject again.

Stretton had signed on for this cruise on the *Perseverance* because he wanted a time during which he could be quite sure of his livelihood. So far he had failed. He must map out a new course for himself upon his life's chart. But for that work he needed time for thought, and that time, up till now, he had not enjoyed. The precarious existence which he had led since he had lost the half of Millie's small fortune—now a clerk in a store, and a failure; now a commercial traveller, and again a failure—had left him little breathing-space wherein to gather up his slow thoughts and originate a new plan. That breathing-space, however, the *Perseverance* had afforded him. During the long watches on fine nights, when the dark sails, swinging up and down to the motion of the boat, revealed and obscured the stars, he wrestled with the difficult problem of his life.

He could go back when his cruise was over if he chose. His father was dying; he faced the fact quite frankly. The object with which he set out would be, after all, accomplished, though not accomplished by himself. There would be a house for Millie and himself independent of the old man's caprice; their life would be freed from the shadow of his tyranny; their seclusion would come to an end; they could let the sunlight in upon their lives. Yes! But there were the letters down in the cabin there, underneath his pillow. Did not they alter the position? He had gone away to keep his wife—just, in a word, to prevent that very contempt of which the letters gave him proof. Must he not now stay away in order to regain her? His wife was at the bottom of all his thoughts. He had no blame for her, however much her written words might hurt. He looked back upon their life together, its pleasant beginnings when they were not merely lovers, but very good friends into the bargain.

For it is possible to be the one and yet not the other. They were good days, the days in the little house in Deanery Street, days full of fun and good temper and amusement. He recalled their two seasons in London — London bright with summer — and making of each long day a too-short holiday. Then had come the change, sudden, dark, and complete. In the place of freedom, subjection; in the place of company, isolation; in the place of friends, a sour old man, querulous and exacting. Then had come the great hope of another home; and swiftly upon that hope its failure through his incapacity. He could not blame her for the letters underneath his pillow. He was no less set upon regaining her than he had been before on keeping her. His love for her had been the chief motive of his life when he left the house in Berkeley Square. It remained so still. Could he go back? he asked himself.

There was one inducement persuading him always to answer "Yes"—the sentence which Pamela had spoken, and which she had refused to explain. " He should be at his wife's side." He had never understood that saying; it remained fixed in his memory, plaguing him. " He should be at his wife's side." So Pamela Mardale had said, and for what Pamela said he had the greatest respect. Well, he could be in a few weeks at his wife's side. But would it not be at too great a cost unless he had first redeemed himself from her contempt?

Thus he turned and turned, and saw no issue anywhere. The days slipped by, and one morning the fish-cutter brought to him a letter which told him that four days ago his father had died. He could not reach home in time for the funeral, even if he started at once. And he could not start at once; he had signed on for eight weeks.

But the letter left him face to face with the old problem. Should he go back or should he stay away? And if he stayed away, what should he do?

He came on deck one morning, and his skipper said:

"There's a fog on land, Stretton."

"How do you know that?" asked Stretton.

The captain pointed to some birds hovering over the masts of the ketch.

"Those are land birds," said he. "Look, there's a thrush and there's a blackbird. You won't find them so far from land without a reason. There has been a fog, and very likely a storm. They have lost their bearings in the fog."

The birds hovered about the ships of the fleet, calling plaintively. Stretton, watching them, felt very much like one of those birds. He, too, had lost his way in a fog, and, though he made no outcry, his need of guidance was no less great than theirs.

Then came a morning at last when the trawl was hauled in for the last time, and the boat's head pointed towards Yarmouth.

"When shall we reach harbor?" Stretton asked, anxiously.

"If this breeze holds, in twenty-four hours," replied the skipper.

Twenty-four hours! Just a day and a night, and Stretton would step from the deck onto Gorleston Quay; and he was no nearer to the solution of his problem than when he had stepped from the quay onto the deck eight weeks ago. Those eight weeks were to have resolved all his perplexities, and lo! the eight weeks had passed.

133

THE TRUANTS

He was in a fever of restlessness. He paced the deck all the day when he was not standing at the wheel; at night he could not sleep, but stood leaning over the bulwarks, watching the stars trembling in the quiet water. At one o'clock in the morning the *Perseverance* passed a light-ship. Already the boat was so near home! And in the hour which followed, his eight weeks of solitary communing, forced, as it were, by immediate necessity, bore their fruit. His inspiration—he counted the idea no less than an inspiration — came to him suddenly. He saw all at once his course marked out for him upon the chart of life. He would not suffer a doubt of it to enter his mind; he welcomed it with passion, and the great load was lifted from his mind. The idea had come. It was water in a dry land.

A fisherman leaning over the bulwark by Stretton's side heard him suddenly begin to sing over to himself a verse or two of a song:

"'Oh, come out, mah love! I'm a-waiting foh you heah!
    Doan' you keep yuh window closed to-night.'"

It was a coon song, which Stretton was humming over to himself. His voice dropped to a murmur. He stopped and laughed softly to himself, as though the song had very dear associations in his thoughts. Then his voice rose again, and there was now a kind of triumph in the lilt of the song which had nothing to do with the words:

"'De stars all a-gwine put dey little ones to bed
    Wid dey "hush now, sing a lullaby,"
De man in de moon nod his sleepy, sleepy head,
    And de sandman put a little in his eye.'"

The words went lilting out over the quiet sea. It seemed to Stretton that they came from a lighted window just behind him, and were sung in a woman's voice. He was standing on a lawn surrounded by high, dark trees in the warmth of a summer night. He was looking out past the islets over eight miles of quiet water to the clustered lights of the yachts in Oban Bay. The coon song was that which his wife had sung to him on one evening he was never to forget; and this night he had recovered its associations. It was no longer "a mere song sung by somebody." It seemed to him, so quickly did his anticipations for once outrun his judgment, that he had already recovered his wife.

The *Perseverance* was moored alongside of the quay at eight o'clock in the morning, and just at that time Millie was reading a letter of condolence from Lionel Callon.

XIII

TONY STRETTON RETURNS TO STEPNEY

MR. CHASE left the mission quite early in the evening and walked towards his lodging. That side of his nature which clamored for enjoyments and a life of luxury was urgent with him to-night. As he turned into his street he began to debate with himself whether he should go in search of a cab and drive westward out of the squalor. A church clock had just struck nine; he would find his club open and his friends about the fire. Thus debating, he came to his own door, and had unconsciously taken his latch-key from his pocket before he had decided upon his course. The latch-key decided him. He opened the door and went quickly up to his sitting-room. The gas was low, and what light there was came from the fire. Chase shut the door gently, and his face underwent a change. There came a glitter into his eyes, a smile to his lips. He crossed to the little cupboard in the corner and unlocked it, stealthily, even though he was alone. As he put his hand into it and grasped the decanter, something stirred in his arm-chair. The back of the chair was towards him. He remained for a second or two motionless, listening. But the sound was not repeated. Chase noiselessly locked the cupboard again and came back to the fire. A man was sitting asleep in the chair.

Chase laid a hand upon his shoulder and shook him.

"Stretton," he said; and Tony Stretton opened his eyes.

"I fell asleep waiting for you," he said.

"When did you get back?" asked Chase.

"I landed at Yarmouth this morning. I came up to London this afternoon."

Chase turned up the gas and lit a cigarette.

"You have not been home, then?" he said. "There is news waiting for you there. Your father is dead!"

"I know," Stretton replied. "He died a month ago."

Mr. Chase was perplexed. He drew up a chair to the fire and sat down.

"You know that?" he asked, slowly; "and yet you have not gone home?"

"No," replied Stretton. "And I do not mean to go."

Stretton was speaking in the quietest and most natural way. There was no trace in his manner of that anxiety which during the last few days had kept him restless and uneasy. He had come to his decision. Chase was aware of the stubborn persistence of his friend, and it was rather to acquire knowledge than to persuade that he put his questions.

"But why? You went away to make an independent home, free from the restrictions under which you and your wife were living. Well, you have got that home now. The reason for your absence has gone."

Stretton shook his head.

"The reason remains. Indeed, it is stronger now than it was when I first left England," he answered. He leaned forward with his elbows upon his knees, gazing into the fire. The light played upon his face, and Chase could not but notice the change which these few months had brought to him. He had grown thin,

137

and rather worn; he had lost the comfortable look of prosperity; his face was tanned. But there was more. It might have been expected that the rough surroundings amid which Stretton had lived would leave their marks. He might have become rather coarse, rather gross to the eye. On the contrary, there was a look of refinement. It was the long battle with his own thoughts which had left the marks. The mind was showing through the flesh. The face had become spiritualized.

"Yes, the reason remains," said Stretton. "I left home to keep my wife. We lived a life of quarrels. All the little memories, the associations, the thousand and one small private things—ideas, thoughts, words, jokes even, which two people who care very much for each other have in common—we were losing, and so quickly, so very quickly. I can't express half what I mean. But haven't you seen a man and a woman at a dinner-table, when some chance sentence is spoken, suddenly look at each other just for a second, smile perhaps, at all events speak though no word is spoken? Well, that kind of intimacy was going. I saw indifference coming, perhaps dislike, perhaps contempt; yes, contempt, just because I sat there and looked on. So I went away. But the contempt has come. Oh, don't think I believe that I made a mistake in going away. It would have come none the less had I stayed. But I have to reckon with the fact that it has come."

Mr. Chase sat following Stretton's words with a very close attention. Never had Stretton spoken to him with so much frankness before.

"Go on," said Chase. "What you are saying is— much of it—news to me."

"Well, suppose that I were to go back now," Stret-

ton resumed, "at once—do you see?—that contempt
is doubled."

"No," cried Chase.

"Yes, yes," Stretton insisted. "Look at it from
Millie's point of view, not from yours, not even from
mine. Look at the history of the incident from the
beginning! Work it out as she would; nay," he corrected himself, remembering the letters, "as she has.
I leave her when things are at their worst. That's not
all. I take half Millie's fortune and am fool enough
to lose it right away. And that's not all. I stay
away in the endeavor to recover the lost ground, and
I continually fail. Meanwhile Millie has the dreary,
irksome, exacting, unrequited life, which I left behind,
to get through as best she can alone; without pleasure,
and she likes pleasure—" He suddenly looked at
Chase, with a challenge in his eyes. "Why shouldn't
she?" he asked, abruptly. Chase agreed.

"Why shouldn't she?" he said, with a smile. "I
am not disapproving."

Stretton resumed his former attitude, his former
tone.

"Without friends, and she is fond of having friends
about her; without any chance of gratifying her spirits
or her youth! To make her life still more dishearten-
ing, every mail which reaches her from New York
brings her only another instalment of my disastrous
record. Work it out from her point of view, Chase;
then add this to crown it all." He leaned forward
towards Chase and emphasized his words with a gesture of his hand. "The first moment when her life
suddenly becomes easy, and does so through no help
of mine, I—the failure—come scurrying back to share
it. No, Chase, no!"

He uttered his refusal to accept that position with a positive violence, and flung himself back in his chair. Chase answered, quietly:

"Surely you are forgetting that it is your father's wealth which makes her life easy."

"I am not forgetting it at all."

"It's your father's wealth," Chase repeated. "You have a right to share in it."

"Yes," Stretton admitted; "but what have rights to do with the question at all? If my wife thinks me no good, will my rights save me from her contempt?"

And before that blunt question Mr. Chase was silent. It was too direct, too unanswerable. Stretton rose from his chair and stood looking down at his companion.

"Just consider the story I should have to tell Millie to-night—by George!" he exclaimed, suddenly—"if I went back to-night. I start out with fifteen hundred pounds of hers to make a home and a competence, and within a few months I am working as a hand on a North Sea trawler at nineteen shillings a week."

"A story of hardships undergone for her sake," said Chase; "for that's the truth of your story, Stretton. And don't you think the hardships would count for ever so much more than any success you could have won?"

"Hardships!" exclaimed Stretton, with a laugh. "I think I would find it difficult to make a moving tale out of my hardships. And I wouldn't if I could—no!"

As a fact, although it was unknown to Tony, Chase was wrong. Had Stretton told his story never so vividly, it would have made no difference. Millie Stretton had not the imagination to realize what those hardships had been. Tony's story would have been to her just a story, calling, no doubt, for exclamations of tenderness and pity. But she could not have understood what he had felt, what he had thought, what he had endured. Deeper feelings and a wider sympathy than Millie Stretton was dowered with would have been needed for comprehension.

Stretton walked across the room and came back to the fire. He looked down at Chase with a smile. "Very likely you think I am a great fool," he said, in a gentler voice than he had used till now. "No doubt nine men out of ten would say: 'Take the gifts the gods send you, and let the rest slide. What if you and your wife drift apart? You won't be the only couple.' But, frankly, Chase, that is not good enough. I have seen a good deal of it—the boredom, the gradual ossification. Oh no; I'm not content with that! You see, Chase "—he stopped for a moment and gazed steadily into the fire; then he went on quite simply, "you see, I care for Millie very much."

Chase knew well what weight to give to that short sentence. Had it been more elaborate it would have meant less. It needed no other commentary than the quiet sincerity with which it was uttered.

"Yes, I understand," he said.

Stretton seated himself again in his chair and took out a brier pipe from his pocket. The pipe had an open metal covering over the bowl.

"I need that no longer," Stretton said, with a laugh, as he removed it. Then he took out a pouch, filled his pipe, and lighted it.

"Have a whiskey-and-soda?" said Chase.

"No, thanks."

Chase lighted a cigarette and looked at his friend

with curiosity. The change which he had noticed in Stretton's looks had been just as noticeable in his words. This man sitting opposite to him was no longer the Tony Stretton who had once come to him for advice. That man had been slow of thought, halting of speech, good-humored, friendly; but a man with whom it was difficult to get at close quarters. Talk with him a hundred times, and you seemed to know him no better than you did at the moment when first you were introduced to him. Here, however, was a man who had thought out his problem— was, moreover, able lucidly to express it.

"Well," said Chase, "you are determined not to go back?"

"Not yet," Stretton corrected.

"What do you propose to do?"

The question showed how great the change had been, begun by the hard times in New York, completed by the eight weeks in the North Sea. For Chase put the question. He no longer offered advice, understanding that Stretton had not come to ask for it.

"I propose to enlist in the French Foreign Legion."

Stretton spoke with the most matter-of-fact air imaginable; he might have been naming the house at which he was to dine the next night. Nevertheless, Chase started out of his chair; he stared at his companion in a stupefaction.

"No," said Stretton, calmly; "I am not off my head, and I have not been drinking. Sit down again, and think it over."

Chase obeyed, and Stretton proceeded to expound that inspiration which had come to him the night before.

"What else should I do? You know my object,

now. I have to re-establish myself in my wife's thoughts. How else can I do it? What professions are open to me in which I could gain, I don't say distinction, but mere recognition? I am not a moneymaker; that, at all events, is evident. I have had experience enough during the last months to know that if I lived to a thousand I should never make money."

"I think that's true," Chase agreed, thoughtfully.

"Luckily there's no longer any need that I should try. What then? Run through the professions, Chase, and find one, if you can, in which a man at my age—twenty-nine—with my ignorance, my want of intellect, has a single chance of success. The bar? It's laughable. The sea? I am too old. The army? I resigned my commission years ago. So what then?"

He waited for Chase to speak, and Chase was silent. He waited with a smile, knowing that Chase could not speak.

"There must be an alternative," Chase said, doubtfully, at last.

"Name it, then."

That was just what Chase could not do. He turned in his mind from this calling to that. There was not one which did not need a particular education; there was not one in which Stretton was likely to succeed. Soldiering or the sea. These were the two callings for which he was fitted. From the sea his age debarred him; from soldiering, too, except in this one way. No, certainly, Stretton was not off his head.

"How in the world did you think of the Foreign Legion?" he asked.

Stretton shrugged his shoulders.

"I thought of most other courses first, and, one by one, rejected them as impossible. This plan came to me last of all, and only last night. We were passing a light-ship. In a way, you see, we were within sight of home. I was in despair; and suddenly the idea flashed upon me, like the revolving blaze from the light-ship. It is a sound one, I think. At all events, it is the only one."

"Yes," answered Chase, slowly; "I suppose there will be chances, for there's always something stirring on the Algerian frontier."

"There or in Siam," said Stretton.

"What arrangements are you making here?"

"I have written to my lawyers. Millie can do as she pleases with the income. She has power, too, to sell the house in Berkeley Square. I made my will, you know, before I left England."

Chase nodded, and for a while there fell a silence upon the two friends. A look of envy crept into the face of the clergyman as he looked at Stretton. He could appreciate a motive which set a man aiming high. He admired the persistence with which Stretton nursed it. The plan it had prompted might be quixotic and quite fruitless, but, at all events, it was definite; and a definite scheme of life, based upon a simple and definite motive, was not so common but that it was enviable. Stretton was so sure of its wisdom, too. He had no doubts. He sat in his chair not asking for approval, not caring for censure; he had made up his mind. The image of Stretton, indeed, as he sat in that chair on that evening, with the firelight playing upon his face, was often to come to Chase's thoughts.

"There will be great risks," he said. "Risks of death, of trouble in the battalion."

"I have counted them," Stretton replied; and he

leaned forward again, with his hands upon his knees. "Oh yes; there will be great risks! But there's a prize, too, proportionate to the risks. Risks! Every one speaks of them," he went on, with a laugh of impatience. "But I have been eight weeks on the Dogger-bank, Chase, and I know—yes, I know—how to estimate risks. Out there men risk their lives daily to put a few boxes of fish on board a fish-cutter. Take the risk half-heartedly and your boat's swamped for a sure thing, but take it with all your heart and there are the fish-boxes to your credit. Well, Millie is my fish-boxes."

He ended with a laugh, and, rising, took his hat.

"Shall I put you up for the night?" Chase asked.

"No, thanks," said Stretton. "I have got a bed at a hotel. I have something else to do to-night;" and a smile, rather wistful and tender, played about his lips. "Good-bye!" He held out his hand, and as Chase took it he went on: "I am looking forward to the day when I come back. My word, how I am looking forward to it! and I will look forward each day until it actually, at the long last, comes. It will have been worth waiting for, Chase—well worth waiting for, both to Millie and to me."

With that he went away. Chase heard him close the street-door behind him and his footsteps sound for a moment or two on the pavement. After all, he thought, a life under those Algerian skies, a life in the open air, of activity—there were many worse things, even though it should prove a second failure.

Chase stood for a little before the fire. He crossed slowly over to that cupboard in the corner at which Stretton's movement in the chair had stayed his hand. Chase looked back to the arm-chair, as though he half expected still to see Stretton sitting there. Then he slowly walked back to the fire and left the cupboard locked. Stretton had gone, but he had left behind him memories which were not to be effaced— the memory of a great motive and of a sturdy determination to fulfil it. The two men were never to meet again; but, in the after-time, more than once, of an evening, Chase's hand was stayed upon that cupboard door. More than once he looked back towards the chair as if he expected that again his friend was waiting for him by the fire.

XIV

TONY STRETTON PAYS A VISIT TO BERKE-
LEY SQUARE

WHILE Tony Stretton was thus stating the problem of his life to Mr. Chase in Stepney Green,
Lady Millingham was entertaining her friends in Berkeley Square. She began the evening with a dinner-
party, at which Pamela Mardale and John Mudge were
present, and she held a reception afterwards. Many
people came, for Frances Millingham was popular.
By half-past ten the rooms were already overhot and
overcrowded, and Lady Millingham was enjoying herself to her heart's content. Mr. Mudge, who stood
by himself at the end of a big drawing-room close to
one of the windows, saw the tall figure of Warrisden
come in at the door and steadily push towards Pamela. A few moments later M. de Marnay, a youthful
attaché of the French Embassy, approached Mr. Mudge.
M. de Marnay wiped his forehead and looked round
the crowded room.

"A little is a good thing," said he, "but too much
is enough." And he unlatched and pushed open the
window. As he spoke Mr. Mudge saw Callon appear
in the doorway.

"Yes," he answered, with a laugh; "too much is
enough."

Mudge watched Callon's movements with his usual
interest. He saw him pass, a supple creature of

smiles and small talk, from woman to woman. How long would he last in his ignoble career? Mudge wondered. Would he marry in the end some rich and elderly widow? Or would the crash come, and parties know Mr. Lionel Callon no more? Mudge never saw the man but he had a wish that he might get a glimpse of him alone in his own rooms, with the smile dropped from his face, and the unpaid bills piled upon his mantel-shelf, and his landlord very likely clamoring for the rent. He imagined the face grown all at once haggard and tired and afraid—afraid with a great fear of what must happen in a few years at the latest, when, with middle-age heavy upon his shoulders, he should see his coevals prospering and himself bankrupt of his stock-in-trade of good looks, and without one penny to rub against another. No presage of mind weighed upon Callon to-night, however, during his short stay in Frances Millingham's house. For his stay was short.

As the clock upon the mantel-piece struck eleven his eyes were at once lifted to the clock-face, and almost at once he moved from the lady to whom he was talking and made his way to the door.

Mr. Mudge turned back to the window and pushed it still more open. It was a clear night of April, and April had brought with it the warmth of summer. Mr. Mudge stood at the open window facing the coolness and the quiet of the square; and thus by the accident of an overcrowded room he became the witness of a little episode which might almost have figured in some by-gone comedy of intrigue.

Callon passed through the line of carriages in the roadway beneath, and crossed the corner of the square to the pavement on the right-hand side. When he reached the pavement he walked for twenty yards or so in the direction of Piccadilly until he came to a large and gloomy house. There a few shallow steps led from the pavement to the front door. Callon mounted the steps, rang the bell, and was admitted.

There were a few lights in the upper windows and on the ground floor; but it was evident that there was no party at the house. Callon had run in to pay a visit. Mr. Mudge, who had watched this, as it were, the first scene in the comedy, distinctly heard the door close, and the sound somehow suggested to him that the time had come for him to go home to bed. He looked at his watch. It was exactly a quarter past eleven — exactly, in a word, three-quarters of an hour since Tony Stretton, who "had something else to do," had taken his leave of his friend Chase in Stepney.

Mr. Mudge turned from the window to make his way to the door, and came face to face with Pamela and Alan Warrisden. Pamela spoke to him. He had never yet met Warrisden, and he was now introduced. All three stood and talked together for a few minutes by the open window. Then Mudge, in that spirit of curiosity which Callon always provoked in him, asked, abruptly,

"By-the-way, Miss Mardale, do you happen to know who lives in that house?" and he pointed across the corner of the square to the house into which Callon had disappeared.

Pamela and Warrisden looked quickly at each other. Then Pamela turned with great interest to Mr. Mudge.

"Yes, we both know," she answered. "Why do you ask?"

"Well, I don't know," said Mudge; "I think that I should like to know."

The glance which his two companions had exchanged, and Pamela's rather eager question, had quickened his curiosity. But he got no answer for a few moments. Both Pamela and Warrisden were looking out towards the house. They were standing side by side. Mr. Mudge had an intuition that the same thought was passing through both their minds.

"That is where the truants lived last July," said Warrisden, in a low voice. He spoke to Pamela, not to Mr. Mudge at all, whose existence seemed for the moment to have been clean forgotten.

"Yes," Pamela replied, softly. "The dark house, where the truants lived and where"—she looked at Warrisden and smiled with a great friendliness— "where the new road began. For it was there really. It's from the steps of the dark house, not from the three poplars, that the new road runs out."

"Yes, that is true," said Warrisden.

And again both were silent.

Mr. Mudge broke in upon the silence. "I have no doubt that the truants lived there, and that the new road begins at the foot of the steps," he said, plaintively; "but neither statement adds materially to my knowledge."

Pamela and Warrisden turned to him and laughed. It was true that they had for a moment forgotten Mr. Mudge. The memory of the starlit night, in last July, when from this balcony they had watched the truants slip down the steps and furtively call a cab was busy in their thoughts. From that night their alliance had dated, although no suspicion of it had crossed their minds. It seemed

strange to them now that there had been no pre-
monition.

"Well, who lives there?" asked Mudge.

But even now he received no answer; for Warrisden
suddenly exclaimed, in a low, startled voice,

"Look!" and with an instinctive movement he
drew back into the room.

A man was standing in the road looking up at the
windows of the dark house. His face could not be
seen under the shadow of his hat. Pamela peered
forward.

"Do you think it's he?" she asked, in a whisper.

"I am not sure," replied Warrisden.

"Oh, I hope so! I hope so!"

"I am not sure. Wait! Wait and look!" said
Warrisden.

In a few moments the man moved. He crossed
the road and stepped onto the pavement. Again he
stopped, again he looked up to the house; then he
walked slowly on. But he walked northward, that
is, towards the watchers at the window.

"There's a lamp-post," said Warrisden; "he will
come within the light of it. We shall know."

And the next moment the light fell white and clear
upon Tony Stretton's face.

"He has come back," exclaimed Pamela, joyfully.

"Who?" asked Mr. Mudge; "who has come back?"

This time he was answered.

"Why, Tony Stretton, of course," said Pamela, impatiently. She was hardly aware of Mr. Mudge, even
while she answered him; she was too intent upon Tony
Stretton in the square below. She did not therefore
notice that Mudge was startled by her reply. She did
not remark the anxiety in his voice as he went on.

"And that is Stretton's house?"

"Yes."

"And his wife, Lady Stretton, is she in London? Is she there—now?"

Mr. Mudge spoke with an excitement of manner which at any other time must have caused surprise. It passed now unremarked; for Warrisden, too, had his preoccupation. He was neither overjoyed, like Pamela, nor troubled, like Mr. Mudge; but as he looked down into the square he was perplexed.

"Yes," replied Pamela, "Millie Stretton is at home. Could anything be more fortunate?"

To Mudge's way of thinking, nothing could be more unfortunate. Pamela had come late to the play; Mr. Mudge, on the other hand, had seen the curtain rise and had a clearer knowledge of the plot's development. The husband outside the house, quite unexpected, quite unsuspicious, and about to enter; the wife and the interloper within: here were the formulas of a comedy of intrigue. Only, Mr. Mudge doubtfully wondered, after the husband had entered and when the great scene took place, would the decorous accent of the comedy be maintained? Nature was, after all, a violent dramatist, with little care for the rules and methods. Of one thing, at all events, he was quite sure, as he looked at Pamela: she would find no amusement in the climax. There was, however, to be an element of novelty, which Mr. Mudge had not foreseen.

"What puzzles me," said Warrisden, "is that Stretton does not go in."

Stretton walked up to the corner of the square, turned, and retraced his steps. Again he approached the steps of the house. "Now," thought Mr. Mudge, with a good deal of suspense—"now he will ascend them." Pamela had the same conviction, but in her case hope inspired it. Tony, however, merely cast a glance upward and walked on. They heard his foot-steps for a little while upon the pavement; then that sound ceased.

"He has gone," cried Pamela, blankly; "he has gone away again."

Mr. Mudge turned to her very seriously.

"Believe me," said he, "nothing better could have happened."

Tony, in fact, had never had a thought of entering the house. Having this one night in London, he had yielded to a natural impulse to revisit again the spot where he and Millie had lived—where she still lived. The bad days of the quarrels and the indifference and the weariness were forgotten by him to-night. His thoughts went back to the early days when they played truant, and truancy was good fun. The escapes from the house, the little suppers at the Savoy, the stealthy home-comings, the stumbling up the stairs in the dark, laughing and hushing their laughter—upon these incidents his mind dwelt wistfully, yet with a great pleasure and a great hopefulness. Those days were gone, but in others to come all that was good in them might be repeated. The good-humor, the in-timacy, the sufficiency of the two, each to the other, might be recovered if only he persisted. To return now, to go in at the door and say, "I have come home," that would be the mistake which there would be no retrieving. He was at the cross-ways, and if he took the wrong road life would not give him the time to retrace his steps. He walked away, dreaming of the good days to come.

Meanwhile Lionel Callon was talking to Millie in that little sitting-room which had once been hers and Tony's.

Millie was surprised at the lateness of his visit, and when he was shown into the room she rose at once.

"Something has happened?" she said.

"No," Callon replied. "I was at Lady Millingham's party. I suddenly thought of you sitting here alone. I am tired besides, and overworked. I knew it would be a rest for me if I could see you and talk to you for a few minutes. You see, I am selfish."

Millie smiled at him.

"No, kind," said she.

She asked him to sit down.

"You look tired," she added. "How does your election work go on?"

Callon related the progress of his campaign, and with an air of making particular confidences. He could speak without any reserve to her, he said. He conveyed the impression that he was making headway against almost insuperable obstacles. He flattered her, moreover, by a suggestion that she herself was a great factor in his successes. The mere knowledge that she wished him well, that perhaps once or twice in the day she gave him a spare thought, helped him much more than she could imagine. Millie was induced to believe that, although she sat quietly in London, she · was thus exercising power through Callon in his constituency.

"Of course, I am a poor man," said Callon. "Poverty hampers one."

"Oh, but you will win," cried Millie Stretton, with a delighted conviction; "yes, you will win."

She felt strong, confident—just, in a word, as she

had felt when she had agreed with Tony that he must go away.

"With your help, yes," he answered; and the sound of his voice violated her like a caress. Millie rose from her chair.

At once Callon rose, too, and altered his tone.

"You have heard from Sir Anthony Stretton?" he said. "Tell me of yourself."

"Yes, I have heard. He will not return yet."

There came a light into Callon's eyes. He raised his hand to his mouth to hide a smile.

"Few men," he said, with the utmost sympathy, "would have left you to bear these last weeks alone."

He was standing just behind her, speaking over her shoulder. He was very still, the house was very silent. Millie was suddenly aware of danger.

"You must not say that, Mr. Callon," she said, rather sharply.

And immediately he answered: "I beg your pardon. I had no idea my sympathy would have seemed to you an insult."

He spoke with a sudden bitterness. Millicent turned round in surprise. She saw that his face was stern and cold.

"An insult?" she said, and her voice was troubled. "No, you and I are friends."

But Callon would have none of these excuses. He had come to the house deliberately to quarrel. He had a great faith in the efficacy of quarrels, given the right type of woman. As Mudge had told Pamela, he knew the tactics of the particular kind of warfare which he waged. To cause a woman some pain, to make her think with regret that in him she had lost a friend, that would fix him in her thoughts. So Callon quarrelled. Millie Stretton could not say a word but he misinterpreted it. Every sentence he cleverly twisted into an offence.

"I will say good-bye," he said, at length, as though he had reached the limits of endurance.

Millie Stretton looked at him with troubled eyes.

"I am so sorry it should end like this," she said, piteously. "I don't know why it has."

Callon went out of the room and closed the door behind him. Then he let himself into the street. Millie Stretton would miss him, he felt sure. Her looks, her last words assured him of that. He would wait now without a movement towards a reconciliation. That must come from her; it would give him in her eyes a reputation for strength. He knew the value of that reputation. He had no doubt, besides, that she would suggest a reconciliation. Other women might not, but Millie—yes. On the whole, Mr. Callon was very well content with his night's work. He had taken, in his way of thinking, a long step. The square was empty except for the carriages outside Lady Millingham's door. Lionel Callon walked briskly home.

XV

MR. MUDGE COMES TO THE RESCUE

LIONEL CALLON'S visit to Millie Stretton bore, however, consequences which had not at all entered into his calculations. He was unaware of the watchers at Lady Millingham's window; he had no knowledge of Pamela's promise to Tony Stretton; no suspicion, therefore, that she was now passionately resolved to keep it in the spirit and the letter. He was even without a thought that his advances towards Millie had at all been remarked upon or their motive discovered. Ignorance lulled him into security. But within a short while a counter-plot was set in train.

The occasion was the first summer meeting on Newmarket Heath. Pamela Mardale seldom missed a race meeting at Newmarket during the spring and summer. There were the horses, in the first place; she met her friends besides; the heath itself, with its broad expanse and its downs, had for her eyes a beauty of its own; and in addition the private enclosure was separated by the width of the course from the crowd and clamor of the ring. She attended this particular meeting, and after the second race was over she happened to be standing amid a group of friends within the grove of trees at the back of the paddock. Outside, upon the heath, the air was clear and bright; a light wind blew pleasantly. Here the trees were in bud, and the sunlight, split by the boughs, dappled with light and

157

shadow the glossy coats of the horses as they were led in and out among the boles. A mare was led past Pamela, and one of her friends said:

"Semiramis. I think she will win this race."

Pamela looked towards the mare, and saw, just beyond her, Mr. Mudge. He was alone, as he usually was; and though he stopped in his walk, now here, now there, to exchange a word with some acquaintance, he moved on again, invariably alone. Gradually he drew nearer to the group in which Pamela was standing, and his face brightened. He quickened his step; Pamela, on her side, advanced rather quickly towards him.

"You are here?" she said, with a smile. "I am glad, though I did not think to meet you."

Mr. Mudge, to tell the truth, though he carried a race-card in his hand and glasses slung across his shoulder, had the disconsolate air of a man conscious that he was out of place. He answered Pamela, indeed, almost apologetically.

"It is better, after all, to be here than in London on a day of summer," he said; and he added, with a shrewd glance at her, "You have something to say to me—a question to ask."

Pamela looked up at him in surprise.

"Yes, I have. Let us go out."

They walked into the paddock and thence through the gate into the enclosure. The enclosure was at this moment rather empty. Pamela led the way to the rails alongside the course, and chose a place where they were out of the hearing of any by-stander.

"You remember the evening at Frances Millingham's?" she asked. She had not seen Mr. Mudge since that date.

Mr. Mudge replied immediately.

"Yes; Sir Anthony Stretton"—and the name struck so oddly upon Pamela's ears that, serious as at this moment she was, she laughed—"Sir Anthony Stretton turned away from the steps of his house. You were distressed, Miss Mardale; I, on the contrary, said that nothing better could have happened. You wish to ask me why I said that?"

"Yes," said Pamela, "I am very anxious to know. Millie is my friend. I am, in a sort of way, too, responsible for her;" and, as Mr. Mudge looked surprised, she repeated the word—"Yes, responsible. And I am rather troubled." She spoke with a little hesitation. There was a frown upon her forehead, a look of perplexity in her dark eyes. She was reluctant to admit that her friend was in any danger or needed any protection from her own weakness. The freemasonry of her sex impelled her to silence. On the other hand, she was at her wits' end what to do. And she had confidence in her companion's discretion; she determined to speak frankly.

"It is not only your remark which troubles me," she said, "but I called on Millie the next afternoon."

"Oh, you did?" exclaimed Mr. Mudge.

"Yes; I asked after Tony. Millie had not seen him and did not expect him. She showed me letters from his solicitors empowering her to do what she liked with the house and income, and a short letter from Tony himself, written on the *Perseverance*, to the same effect."

She did not explain to Mr. Mudge what the *Perseverance* was, and he asked no questions.

"I told Millie," she continued, "that Tony had returned, but she refused to believe it. I told her when and where I had seen him."

"You did that?" said Mr. Mudge. "Wait a moment." He saw and understood Pamela's reluctance to speak. He determined to help her out. "Let me describe to you what followed. She stared blankly at you and asked you to repeat what you had said?"

"Yes," replied Millie, in surprise; "that is just what she did."

"And when you had repeated it she turned a little pale, perhaps was disconcerted, perhaps a little—afraid."

"Yes, it is that which troubles me," Pamela cried, in a low voice. "She was afraid. I would have given much to have doubted it. I could not; her eyes betrayed it, her face, her whole attitude. She was afraid."

Mr. Mudge nodded his head and went quietly on.

"And when she had recovered a little from her fear she questioned you closely as to the time when you first saw Stretton outside the house and the time when he went away."

He spoke with so much certitude that he might have been present at the interview.

"I told her that it was some little time after eleven when he came, and that he only stayed a few minutes," answered Pamela.

"And at that," rejoined Mr. Mudge, "Lady Stretton's anxiety diminished."

"Yes, that is true, too," Pamela admitted; and she turned her face to him with its troubled appeal. "Why was she afraid? For, since you have guessed that she was, you must know the reason which she had for fear. Why was it so fortunate that Tony Stretton did not mount the steps of the house and ring the bell?"

Mr. Mudge answered her immediately, and very quietly.

"Because Lionel Callon was inside the house."

A great sympathy made his voice gentle—sympathy for Pamela. None the less the words hurt her cruelly. She turned away from him so that he might not see her face, and stood gazing down the course through a mist. Bitter disappointment was hers at that moment. She was by nature a partisan. The thing which she did crept closer to her heart by the mere act of doing it. She knew it, and it was just her knowledge which had so long kept her to inaction. Now her thoughts were passionately set on saving Millie, and here came news to her which brought her to the brink of despair. She blamed Tony. "Why did he ever go away?" she cried. "Why, when he had come back, did he not stay?" And at once she saw the futility of her outcry. Tony, Millie, Lionel Callon — what was the use of blaming them? They acted as their characters impelled them. She had to do her best to remedy the evil which the clash of these three characters had produced. "What can be done?" she asked of herself. There was one course open certainly. She could summon Warrisden again, send him out a second time in search of Tony Stretton, and make him the bearer, not of an excuse, but of the whole truth. Only she dreaded the outcome; she shrank from telling Tony the truth, fearing that he would exaggerate it. "Can nothing be done?" she asked again, in despair, and this time she asked the question aloud, and turned to Mr. Mudge.

Mudge had been quietly waiting for it.

"Yes," he answered, "something can be done. I should not have told you, Miss Mardale, what I knew unless I had already hit upon a means to avert the peril; for I am aware how much my news must grieve you."

Pamela looked at Mr. Mudge in surprise. It had not occurred to her at all that he could have solved the problem.

"What can I do?" she asked.

"You can leave the whole trouble in my hands for a few days."

Pamela was silent for a little while; then she answered, doubtfully,

"It is most kind of you to offer me your help."

Mr. Mudge shook his head at Pamela with a certain sadness.

"There's no kindness in it at all," he said; "but I quite understand your hesitation, Miss Mardale. You were surprised that I should offer you help, just as you were surprised to see me here. Although I move in your world I am not of it. Its traditions, its instincts, even its methods of thought—to all of these I am a stranger. I am just a passing visitor who, for the time of his stay, is made an honorary member of your club. He meets with every civility, every kindness; but he is not inside, so that when he suddenly comes forward and offers you help in a matter where other members of your club are concerned you naturally pause."

Pamela made a gesture of dissent, but Mr. Mudge gently insisted:

"Let me finish. I want you to understand equally well why I offer you help which may very likely seem to you an impertinence."

"No, indeed," said Pamela; "on the contrary, I am very grateful."

Others were approaching the spot where they stood. They turned and walked slowly over the grass away from the paddock.

"There is no need that you should be," Mudge continued; "you will see that, if you listen." And in a few words he told her at last something of his own career. "I sprang from a Deptford gutter, with one thought—to get on, and get on, and get on. I moved from Deptford to Peckham. There I married. I moved from Peckham to a residential suburb in the southwest. There my wife died. Looking back now, I am afraid that in my haste to get on I rather neglected my wife's happiness. You see, I am frank with you. From the residential suburb I moved into the Cromwell Road, from the Cromwell Road to Grosvenor Square. I do not think that I was just a snob; but I wanted to have the very best of what was going. There is a difference. A few years ago I found myself at the point which I had aimed to reach, and, as I have told you, it is a position of many acquaintances and much loneliness. You might say that I could give it up and retire into the country. But I have too many undertakings on my hands; besides, I am too tired to start again, so I remain. But I think you will understand that it will be a real pleasure to me to help you. I have not so many friends that I can afford to lose the opportunity of doing one of them a service."

Pamela heard him to the end without any interruption; but when he had finished she said, with a smile:

"You are quite wrong about the reason for my hesitation. I asked a friend of mine a few weeks ago to help me, and he gave me the best of help at once. Even the best of help fails at times, and my friend did. I was wondering merely whether it would not be a little disloyal to him if I now accepted yours, for I know he would be grieved if I went to any one but him."

"I see," said Mr. Mudge; "but I think that I can give you help which no one else can."

It was clear from his quiet persistence that he had a definite plan. Pamela stopped and faced him.

"Very well," she said. "I leave the whole matter for a little while in your hands."

"Thank you," said Mr. Mudge; and he looked up towards the course. "There are the horses going down."

A sudden thought occurred to Pamela. She opened the purse she carried on her wrist, and took out a couple of pounds.

"Put this on Semiramis for me, please," she said, with a laugh. "Be quick, if you will, and come back."

Though she laughed she was still most urgent he should go. Mr. Mudge hurried across the course, made the bet, and returned. Pamela watched the race with an eagerness which astonished Mr. Mudge, so completely did she seem to have forgotten all that had troubled her a minute ago. But he did not understand Pamela. She was, after her custom, seeking for a sign, and when Semiramis galloped in a winner by a neck, she turned with a hopeful smile to her companion.

"We shall win, too."

"I think so," Mudge replied, and he laughed. "Do you know what I think of Lionel Callon, Miss Mardale? The words are not mine, but the sentiment is unexceptionable. A little may be a good thing, but too much is enough."

XVI

THE FOREIGN LEGION

IT was mid-day at Sidi-Bel-Abbés in Algeria. Two French officers were sitting in front of a café at the wide cross-roads in the centre of the town. One of them was Captain Tavernay, a man of forty-seven, tall, thin, with a brown face worn and tired with the campaigns of thirty years, the other a young lieutenant, M. Laurent, fresh and pink, who seemed to have been passed out but yesterday from the school of St.-Cyr. Captain Tavernay picked up his cap from the iron table in front of him and settled it upon his grizzled head. Outside the town trees clustered thickly, farms were half-hidden among groves of fig-trees and hedges of aloes. Here there was no foliage. The streets were very quiet, the sunlight lay in dazzling pools of gold upon the sand of the roads, the white houses glittered under a blue, cloudless sky. In front of the two officers, some miles away, the bare cone of Jebel-Tessalah sprang upward from a range of hills dominating the town, and a speck of white upon its shoulder showed where a village perched. Captain Tavernay sat looking out towards the mountain with the lids half-closed upon his eyes. Then he rose deliberately from his chair.

"If we walk to the station," he said, "we shall just meet the train from Oran. A batch of thirty recruits is coming in by it. Let us walk to the station, Laurent."

Lieutenant Laurent dropped the end of his cigarette onto the ground, and stood up reluctantly.

"As you will, captain," he answered. "But we should see the animals soon enough at the barracks."

The words were spoken in a voice which was almost, and with a shrug of the shoulders was, quite contemptuous. The day was hot, and Lieutenant Laurent unwilling to move from his coffee and the shade into that burning sunlight. Captain Tavernay gazed mildly at his youthful junior. Long experience had taught him to leave much to time and little to argument. For himself he loved his legionaries. He had a smile of indulgence for their faults even while he punished them; and though his face seldom showed the smile and his punishments were not unjustly light, the culprits none the less knew it was there hidden somewhere close to his heart. But then he had seen his men in action, and Lieutenant Laurent had not. That made all the difference. The Foreign Legion certainly did not show at its best in a cantonment. Among that motley assemblage — twelve thousand men distinct in nationality as in character, flung together pell-mell, negroes and whites, criminals, adventurers, silent unknown men haunted by memories of other days or tortured by remorse—a garrison town with its monotony and its absinthe played havoc. An Abyssinian rubbed shoulders in the ranks with a scholar who spoke nine languages, a tenor from the Théâtre de la Monnaie at Brussels with an unfrocked priest. Often enough Captain Tavernay had seen one of his legionaries sitting alone hour after hour at his little table outside the café, steadily drinking glass after glass of absinthe, rising mechanically to salute his officer, and sinking back among his impenetrable secrets.

Was he dreaming of the other days, the laughter and the flowers, the white shoulders of women? Was he again placing that last stake upon the red which had sent him straight from the table to the nearest French depot? Was he living again some tragic crisis of love in which all at once he had learned that he had been befooled and derided? Captain Tavernay never passed such a man but he longed to sit down by his side and say: "My friend, share your secret with me, so it will be easier to bear." But the etiquette of the Foreign Legion forbade. Captain Tavernay merely returned the salute and passed on, knowing that very likely his legionary would pass the night in the guard-room, and the next week in the cells. No, the town of Sidi-Bel-Abbés was not the place wherein to learn the mettle of the legionary. Away to the south there, beyond the forest of trees on the horizon's line, things were different. Let Lieutenant Laurent see them in their bivouacs at night under the stars, and witness their prowess under arms, *ces animaux* would soon become *mes enfants*.

Therefore he answered Lieutenant Laurent in the mildest voice.

"We shall see them at the barracks, it is true. But you are wrong when you say that it will be soon enough. At the barracks they will be prepared for us; they will have their little stories ready for us; they will be armed with discretion. But let us see them descend from the train; let us watch their first look round at their new home, their new fatherland. We may learn a little, and if it is ever so little it will help us to know them the better afterwards. And, at the worst, it will be an amusing little exercise in psychology."

THE TRUANTS

They walked away from the café and strolled down the Rue de Mascara under the shady avenue of trees, Tavernay moving with a long, indolent stride, which covered a deal of ground with a surprising rapidity, Laurent fidgeting discontentedly at his side. M. Laurent was beginning, in fact, to regret the hurry with which he had sought a commision in the Foreign Legion. M. Laurent had, a few months ago, in Paris, imagined himself to be irrevocably in love with the wife of one of his friends, a lady at once beautiful and mature; M. Laurent had declared his passion upon a suitable occasion; M. Laurent had been snubbed for his pains; M. Laurent in a fit of pique had sought the consolation of another climate and foreign service; and M. Laurent was now quickly realizing that he was not nearly so heart-broken as he had fancied himself to be. Even now while he walked to the station he was thinking that, after all, Paris was endurable, even though one particular woman could not refrain from a little smile of amusement when he crossed her path.

Captain Tavernay had timed their walk accurately. For as they reached the station the train was signalled. "Let us stand here, behind these cases," said Tavernay. "We shall see and not be seen."

In a few moments the train moved slowly in and stopped. From the farthermost carriage the detachment descended, and, following a sous-officier in the uniform of the Legion, walked towards the cases behind which Tavernay and his companion were concealed. In front came two youths, fair of complexion and of hair, dressed neatly, well shod, who walked with a timidity of manner as though they expected to be questioned and sent packing.

"Who can they be?" asked Laurent. "They are boys."

"Yet they will give their age as eighteen," replied Tavernay, and his voice trembled ever so slightly. "And we shall ask no questions."

"But they bear no marks of misery. They are not poor. Where can they come from?" Laurent repeated.

"I can tell you that," said Tavernay. He was much moved. He spoke with a deep note of reverence. "They come from Alsace or Lorraine. We get many such. They will not serve Germany. At all costs they *will* serve France."

Lieutenant Laurent was humbled. Here was a higher motive than pique, here was a devotion which would not so quickly tire of discipline and service. He gazed with a momentary feeling of envy at these two youths who insisted at so high a price on being his compatriots.

"You see," said Tavernay, with a smile, "it was worth while to come to the station and see the recruits arrive even on so hot a day as this."

"Yes," replied Laurent; and then, "Look!"

Following the two youths walked a man, tall and powerful, with the long, loose stride of one well versed in sports. He held his head erect and walked defiantly, daring you to question him. His hands were long and slender, well kept, unused to labor, his face aquiline and refined. He looked about thirty-five years old. He wore a light overcoat of fine material which hung open, and underneath the overcoat he was attired in evening dress. It was his dress which had riveted Laurent's attention; and certainly nothing could have seemed more bizarre, more strangely out of place. The hot African sun poured down out of a cloudless sky; and a new recruit for the Foreign Legion stepped out of a railway-carriage as though he had come straight from a ballroom. What sudden disaster could have overtaken him? In what tragedy had he borne a part? Even Laurent's imagination was stimulated into speculation. As the man passed him, Laurent saw that his tie was creased and dusty, his shirt-front rumpled and soiled. That must needs have been. At some early hour on a spring morning some four or five days ago this man must have rushed into the guard-room of a barrack-square in some town of France. Laurent turned to Tavernay eagerly.

"What do you make of him?"

Tavernay shrugged his shoulders.

"A man of fashion who has made a fool of himself. They make good soldiers as a rule."

"But he will repent."

"He has already had the time and he has not. There is no escort for recruits until they reach Marseilles. Suppose that he enlisted in Paris. He is given the fare. At any station between Paris and Marseilles he could have got out and returned."

The man in evening dress walked on. There were dark shadows under his eyes, the eyes themselves were sombre and alert.

"We shall know something of him soon," said Tavernay. He watched his recruit with so composed an air that Laurent cried out:

"Can nothing astonish you?"

"Very little," answered Tavernay, phlegmatically. "Listen, my friend. One day some years ago a captain of Hussars landed at Oran. He came to Bel-Abbés with a letter of introduction to me. He stayed with me. He expressed a wish to see my men upon parade. I turned them out. He came to the parade-ground and inspected them. As he passed along the ranks he suddenly stopped in front of an old soldier with fifteen years' service in the Legion, much of which fifteen years had been passed in the cells. The old soldier was a drunkard — oh, but a confirmed drunkard. Well, in front of this man my young captain with the curled mustaches stopped—stopped and turned very pale, but he did not speak. My soldier looked at him respectfully, and the captain continued his inspection. Well, they were father and son—that is all. Why should anything astonish me?" and Captain Tavernay struck a match and lighted a cigarette.

The match, however, attracted attention to the presence of the officers. Four men who marched, keeping time with their feet and holding their hands stiffly at their sides, saw the flame and remarked the uniforms. Their hands rose at once to the salute.

"Ah! German deserters," said Tavernay. "They fight well."

Others followed—men in rags and out of shoe-leather; outcasts and fugitives; and behind them came one who was different. He was tall and well knit, with a frank, open face, not particularly intellectual; on the other hand, not irretrievably stupid. He was dressed in a double-breasted blue serge suit, and as he walked he now and then gave a twist to his fair mustache, as though he were uneasy and embarrassed. Captain Tavernay ran his eyes over him with the look of a connoisseur.

"Aha!" said he, with a chuckle of satisfaction. "The true legionary! Hard, finely trained; he has done work, too. Yes! You see, Laurent, he is a little ashamed, a little self-conscious. He feels that he is looking a fool. I wonder what nationality he will claim."

"He comes from the North," said Laurent. "Possibly from Normandy."

"Oh, I know what he is," returned Tavernay. "I am wondering only what he will claim to be. Let us go outside and see."

Tavernay led the way to the platform. Outside, in front of the station, the sous-officier marshalled his men in a line. They looked a strange body of men as they stood there, blinking in the strong sunlight. The man in the ruffled silk hat and the dress suit toed the line beside a bundle of rags, the German deserters rubbed elbows with the "true legionary" in the blue serge. Those thirty men represented types of almost all the social grades, and to a man they were seeking the shelter of anonymity in that monastery of action— the Foreign Legion.

"Answer to your names," said the sous-officier, and from a paper in his hand he began to read. The answers came back, ludicrous in their untruth. A French name would be called:

"Montaubon."

And a German voice replied:

"Present."

"Ohlsen," cried the sous-officier, and no answer was given. "Ohlsen," he repeated, sharply. "Is not Ohlsen here?"

And suddenly the face of the man in the serge suit flushed, and he answered, hurriedly:

"Present."

Even the sous-officier burst into a laugh. The reason for the pause was too obvious; "Ohlsen" had forgotten that Ohlsen was now his name.

"My lad, you must keep your ears open," said the sous-officier. "Now, attention. Fours right. March!"

And the detachment marched off towards the barracks.

"Ohlsen," said Tavernay, and he shrugged his shoulders. "Well, what does it matter? Come!"

"Ohlsen" was Tony Stretton, and all the way along the Rue Daya to the barracks he was longing for the moment when he would put on the uniform and cease to figure ridiculously in this grotesque procession. None the less he had to wait with the others drawn up in the barrack square until Captain Tavernay returned. The captain went to his office, and thither the recruits were marched. One by one they entered in at the door, answered his questions, and were sent off to the regimental tailor. Tony Stretton was the last.

"Name?" asked Tavernay.

"Hans Ohlsen."

"Town of enlistment?"

"Marseilles."

Tavernay compared the answers with some writing on a sheet of paper.

"Yes, Marseilles. Passed by Dr. Paul as sound of body. Yes," and he resumed his questions.

"Nationality?"

"Swede."

Captain Tavernay had a smattering of most languages, and he was greatly inclined to try his new recruit with a few questions in the Swedish tongue. But the etiquette of the Legion forbade. He went on without a smile.

"Age?"

"Thirty."

"Vocation?"

"Fisherman."

Captain Tavernay looked up. This time he could not help smiling.

"Well, it is as good as any other," said he, and suddenly there was a sound of cries, and three soldiers burst out of a narrow entrance on the farther side of the parade-ground and came running across the square to the captain's quarters. Both Tavernay and Stretton looked through the door. There was not a tree in that great square; the sunlight poured down upon the bare ground with a blinding fierceness; all the recruits but Stretton had marched off; a second ago it had been quite empty and very silent. Now these three men were hurrying across it shouting, gesticulating with their hands. Stretton looked at them with surprise. Then he noticed that one of them, the man running in the middle and a little ahead of the others, carried a revolver in his hand and brandished it. Moreover, from the look of his inflamed face, he was shouting threats; the others were undoubtedly shouting warnings. Scraps of their warnings came to Stretton's ears. "Mon capitaine!" "Il veut vous tuer!" "Rentrez!" They were straining every muscle to catch the threatening soldier up.

Stretton strode to the door, and a voice behind him cried:

"Halt!"

It was Tavernay who was speaking.

"But he is already half-way across the square."

"Halt!"

And there was no disobeying the command. Captain Tavernay walked to the door.

"A Spanish corporal whom yesterday I degraded

"SUDDENLY THERE WAS A SOUND OF CRIES"

to the ranks," said he. "Half a pint of aguardiente and here's the result."

Captain Tavernay stepped out of the door and leisurely advanced towards the running men. He gave an order, he raised his hand, and the two soldiers who warned him fell back and halted. Certainly Captain Tavernay was accustomed to obedience. The Spanish ex-corporal ran on alone, straight towards Tavernay, but as he ran, as he saw the officer standing there alone, quietly waiting his onslaught, his threats weakened, his pace slackened. He came to a stop in front of Tavernay.

"I must kill you," he cried, waving his revolver.

"You shall kill me from behind, then," said Tavernay, calmly. "Follow me!" And he turned round and with the same leisurely deliberation walked back to his room. The ex-corporal hesitated and—obeyed. He followed Captain Tavernay into the room where Stretton stood.

"Place your revolver on the table."

The Spaniard again obeyed. Tavernay pushed open the door of an inner room.

"You are drunk," he said. "You must not be seen in this condition by your fellow-soldiers. Go in and lie down!"

The Spaniard stared at his officer stupidly, tottering upon his limbs. Then he staggered into the captain's room. Tavernay turned back to Stretton, and a ghost of a smile crept into his face.

"It is theatrical," he said, with a little shrug of the shoulders. "But what would you have, monsieur?" and he spoke to Stretton as to an equal. "You are astonished. It is very likely not your way in your—fishing-boats," he continued, with a chuckle. Stretton

knew very well that he meant "army." "But there
is no Foreign Legion among your—fishermen." He
laughed again, and gathering up his papers dismissed
Stretton to the tailor's. But after Stretton had taken
a few steps across the parade, Tavernay called him
back again. He looked at him with a very friendly
smile.

"I, too, enlisted at Marseilles," he said. "One can
rise in the Foreign Legion by means of these," and he
touched lightly the medals upon his breast. This was
Tony Stretton's introducton to the Foreign Legion.

XVII

CALLON LEAVES ENGLAND

SPRING that year drew summer quickly after it. The lilac was early in flower, the days bright and hot. At nine o'clock on a May morning Callon's servant drew up the blinds in his master's room and let the sunlight in. Lionel Callon stretched himself in bed and asked for his letters and his tea. As he drank his tea he picked up his letters one by one, and the first at which he looked brought a smile of satisfaction to his face. The superscription told him that it was from Millie Stretton. That little device of a quarrel had proved successful, then. He tore open the envelope and read the letter. Millie wrote at no great length, but what was written satisfied Callon. She could not understand how the quarrel had arisen. She had been thinking it over many times since it happened, and she was still baffled. She had not had a thought of hurting him. How could she, since they were friends? She had been hoping to hear from him, but since some time had passed and no word had reached her, she must write and say that she thought it sad their friendship should have ended as it had.

It was a wistful little letter, and as Callon laid it down he said to himself, "Poor little girl!" but he said the words with a smile rather than with any contrition. She had been the first to write—that was the main point. Had he given in, had he been the one to make the advance, to save her the troubled speculations, the sorrow at this abrupt close to their friendship, Millie Stretton would have been glad, no doubt, but she would have thought him weak. Now he was the strong man. He had caused her suffering and abased her to seek a reconciliation. Therefore he was the strong man. Well, women would have it so, he thought, with a chuckle, and why should he complain?

He wrote a note to Millie Stretton announcing that he would call that afternoon, and despatched the note by a messenger. Then he turned to his other letters, and among them he found one which drove all the satisfaction from his thoughts. It came from a firm of solicitors, and was couched in a style with which he was not altogether unfamiliar.

"SIR,—Messrs. Deacon & Sons (Livery Stables, Montgomery Street), having placed their books in our hands for the collection of their outstanding debts, we must ask you to send us a check in settlement of your account by return of post, and thus save further proceedings. We are, yours, etc.,
"HUMPHREYS & NEILL."

Callon allowed the letter to slip from his fingers, and lay for a while very still, feeling rather helpless, rather afraid. It was not merely the amount of the bill which troubled him, although that was inconveniently large. But there were other reasons. His eyes wandered to a drawer in his dressing-table. He got out of bed and unlocked it. At the bottom of that drawer lay the other reasons, piled one upon the other—letters couched in just the same words as that which he had received this morning, and—still worse!—signed by this same firm of Humphreys & Neill. Moreover, every one of those letters had reached him

within the last ten days. It seemed that all his trades-
men had suddenly placed their books in the hands of
Messrs. Humphreys & Neill.

Callon took the letters back to his bed. There were
quite an astonishing number of them. Callon himself was surprised to see how deep he was in debt.
They littered the bed—tailor's bills, bills for expensive little presents of jewelry, bills run up at restaurants
for dinners and suppers, bills for the hire of horses
and carriages, bills of all kinds—and there were just
Mr. Callon's election expenses in Mr. Callon's ex-
chequer that morning. Even if he parted with them
they would not pay a fifth part of the sum claimed.
Fear invaded him; he saw no way out of his troubles.
Given time, he could borrow enough, no doubt, scrape
enough money together one way or another to tide
himself over the difficulty. His hand searched for
Millie Stretton's letter and found it and rejected it.
He needed time there; he must walk warily or he
would spoil all. And looking at the bills he knew
that he had not the time.

It was improbable, nay, more than improbable, that
all these bills were in the hands of one firm by mere
chance. No, somewhere he had an enemy. A man
—or it might be a woman—was striking at him out of
the dark, striking with knowledge, too. For the blow
fell where he could least parry it. Mr. Mudge would
have been quite satisfied could he have seen Callon as
he lay that morning with the summer sunlight pouring into his bedroom. He looked more than his age,
and his face was haggard. He felt that a hand was
at his throat, a hand which gripped and gripped with
an ever-increasing pressure.

He tried to guess who his enemy might be. But

there were so many who might be glad to do him an ill turn. Name after name occurred to him, but among those names was not the name of Mr. Mudge. That shy and inoffensive man was the last whom he would have suspected to be meddling with his life.

Callon sprang out of bed. He must go down to Lincoln's Inn Fields and interview Messrs. Humphreys & Neill. Summonses would never do with a general election so near. He dressed quickly, and soon after ten was in the office of that firm. He was received by a bald and smiling gentleman in spectacles.

"Mr. Callon?" said the smiling gentleman, who announced himself as Humphreys. "Oh yes. You have come in reference to the letters which our clients have desired us to send you?"

"Yes," replied Callon. "There are a good number of letters."

The smiling gentleman laughed genially.

"A man of fashion, Mr. Callon, has, of course, many expenses which we humdrum business people are spared. Let me see. The total amount due is—" and Mr. Humphreys made a calculation with his pen.

"I came to ask for an extension of time," Callon blurted out, and the smiling gentleman ceased to smile. He gazed through his spectacles with a look of the utmost astonishment. "You see, Mr. Humphreys, all these bills, each one accompanied with a peremptory demand for payment, have been presented together almost, as it were, by the same post."

"They are all, however, to account rendered," said Mr. Humphreys, as he removed and breathed upon his spectacles.

"It would, I frankly confess, seriously embarrass me to settle them all at once."

"Dear, dear!" said Mr. Humphreys, in a voice of regret. "I am very sorry. These duties are very painful to me, Mr. Callon. But I have the strictest instructions," and he rose from his chair to conclude the interview.

"One moment," said Callon, bluntly, "I want to ask you how it is that all my bills have come into your hands? Who is it who has bought them up?"

"Really, really, Mr. Callon," the lawyer protested, "I cannot listen to such suggestions," and then the smile came back to his face. "Why not pay them in full?" His eyes beamed through his spectacles. He had an air of making a perfectly original and delightful suggestion. "Sit down in this comfortable chair now and write me out a little check for—let me see—" and he went back to his table.

"I must have some time," said Callon.

Mr. Humphreys was gradually persuaded that a period of time was reasonable.

"A day, then," he said. "We will say a day, Mr. Callon. This is Wednesday. Some time to-morrow we shall hear from you." And he bowed Callon from his office. Then he wrote a little note and despatched it by a messenger into the city. The message was received by Mr. Mudge, who read it, took up his hat, and, jumping into a hansom-cab, drove westward with all speed.

Lionel Callon, on the contrary, walked back to his rooms. He had been in tight places before, but never in a place quite so tight. Before it was really the money which had been needed. Now what was needed was his ruin. And, to make matters worse, he had no idea of the particular person who wished to ruin him. He walked gloomily back to his club and lunched in solitude. A day remained to him, but what could he do in a day unless?— There was a certain letter in the breast-pocket of Callon's coat to which more than once, as he lunched, his fingers strayed. He took it out and read it again. It was too soon to borrow in that quarter, but his back was against the wall. He saw no other chance of escape. He drove to Millie Stretton's house in Berkeley Square at the appointed time that afternoon.

But Mr. Mudge had foreseen. When he jumped into his hansom-cab he had driven straight to the house in Audley Square where Pamela Mardale was staying with some friends.

"Are you lunching anywhere?" he asked. "No? Then lunch with Lady Stretton, please! And don't go away too soon! See as much as you can of her during the next two days."

As a consequence, when Lionel Callon was shown into the drawing-room he found Pamela Mardale in her most talkative mood and Millie Stretton sitting before the tea-table silent and helpless. Callon stayed late. Pamela stayed later. Callon returned to his club, having said not a single word upon the momentous subject of his debts.

At his club Callon ordered a stiff brandy-and-soda. Somehow he must manage to see Millie Stretton alone. He thought for a moment of writing; he, indeed, actually began to write. But the proposal looked too crude when written down. Callon knew the tactics of his game. There must, in a word, be an offer from Millie, not a request from him. He tore up his letter, and while he was tearing it up Mr. Mudge entered the smoking-room. Mudge nodded carelessly to Callon, and then seemed to be struck by an idea. He came across to the writing-table and said:

"Do I interrupt you? I wonder whether you could help me? You know so many people that you might be able to lay your finger at once on the kind of man I want."

Callon looked up carelessly at Mudge.

"No. You are not interrupting me. What kind of man do you want?"

"I want a man to superintend an important undertaking which I have in hand."

Callon swung round in his chair. All his carelessness had gone. He looked at Mr. Mudge, who stood drumming with his fingers on the writing-table.

"Oh," said Callon. "Tell me about it."

He walked over to a corner of the room which was unoccupied and sat down. Mudge sat beside him and lighted a cigar.

"I want a man to supervise, you understand. I don't want an expert, for I have engineers and technical men enough on the spot. And I don't want any one out of my office. I need some one on whom I can rely, to keep me in touch with what is going on, some one quite outside my business and its associations."

"I see," said Callon. "The appointment would be for how long?"

"Two years."

"And the salary would be good?"

Callon leaned back on the lounge as he put the question, and he put it without any show of eagerness. Two years would be all the time he needed wherein to set himself straight; and it seemed the work would not be arduous.

"I think so," replied Mudge. "You shall judge for yourself. It would be four thousand a year."

Callon did not answer for a little while, simply because he could not trust himself to speak. His heart was beating fast. Four thousand a year for two years! He would be able to laugh at that unknown enemy who was striking at him from the dark.

"Should I do?" he asked, at length, and even then his voice shook. Mr. Mudge appeared, however, not to notice his agitation. He was looking down at the carpet and tracing the pattern with the ferrule of his walking-stick.

"Of course," he said, with a smile, as though Callon had been merely uttering a joke. He did not even lift his eyes to Callon's face. "Of course; I only wish you were serious."

"But I am," cried Callon.

Mr. Mudge looked at his companion now and with surprise.

"Are you? But you wouldn't have the time to spare. You are standing for a constituency."

Callon shrugged his shoulders.

"Oh, I am not so very keen about Parliament. And there are reasons why I would welcome the work."

Mr. Mudge answered with alacrity.

"Then we will consider it settled. Dine with me to-night at my house and we will talk the details over."

Callon accepted the invitation, and Mudge rose from his seat. Callon, however, detained him.

"There's one difficulty in the way," and Mr. Mudge's face became clouded with anxiety. "The truth is, I am rather embarrassed at the present moment. I

184

owe a great deal of money, and I am threatened with proceedings unless it is immediately paid."

Mudge's face cleared at once.

"Oh, is that all?" he exclaimed, cheerily. "How much do you owe?"

"Pretty nearly my first year's salary."

"Well, I will advance you half at once. Offer them two thousand on account, and they will stay proceedings."

"I don't know that they will," replied Callon.

"You can try them, at all events. If they won't accept half, send them to me, and we will make some other arrangement. But they are sure to. They are pressing for immediate payment because they are afraid they will get nothing at all by any other way. But offer them two thousand down, and see the pleasant faces with which they will greet you." Mr. Mudge was quite gay now that he understood how small was the obstacle which hindered him from gaining Lionel Callon's invaluable help. "I will write you a check," he said, and sitting down at a writing-table he filled out a check and brought it back. He stood in front of Callon with the check in his hand. He did not give it to Callon at once. He had not blotted it, and he held it by a corner and gently waved it to and fro so that the ink might dry. It followed that those tantalizing "naughts," three of them, one behind the other, and preceded by a two, like a file of soldiers with a sergeant at the head, and that excellent signature "John Mudge," were constantly before Callon's eyes, now approaching him like some shy maiden in a flutter of agitation, now coyly receding. But to no shy maiden had Lionel Callon ever said "I love you" with so glowing an ardor as he felt for that most tantalizing check.

"I ought to have told you," said Mr. Mudge, "that the undertaking is a railway abroad."

Callon had been so blinded by the dazzle of the check that he had not dreamed of that possibility. Two years abroad, even at four thousand a year, did not at all fit in with his scheme of life.

"Abroad?" he repeated, doubtfully. "Where?"

"Chile," said Mr. Mudge; and he looked at the check to see that the ink was quite dry. Perhaps Mr. Mudge's voice was a trifle too unconcerned. Perhaps there was something a little too suggestive in his examination of his check. Perhaps he kept his eyes too deliberately from Callon's face. At all events, Callon became suddenly suspicious. There flashed into his mind by some trick of memory a picture—a picture of Mr. Mudge and Pamela Mardale talking earnestly together upon a couch in a drawing-room and of himself sitting at a card-table—fixed there till the game was over, though he knew well that the earnest conversation was aimed against himself. He started, he looked at Mudge in perplexity.

"Well?" said Mudge.

"Wait a moment!"

Pamela Mardale was Millie Stretton's friend. There was that incident in the hall—Millie Stretton coming down the stairs and Pamela in front of the mirror over the mantel-piece. Finally there was Pamela's persistent presence at Millie Stretton's house this afternoon. One by one the incidents gathered in his recollections and fitted themselves together and explained one another. Was this offer a pretext to get him out of the way? Callon, after all, was not a fool, and he asked himself why in the world Mr. Mudge should, just at this moment when he was in desperate straits, offer him £4000 a year to superintend a railway in Chile?

"Well?" said Mudge again.

"I must have time to think over the proposition," replied Callon. He meant that he must have time to obtain an interview with Millie Stretton. But Mudge was ready for him.

"Certainly," said he. "That is only reasonable. It is seven o'clock now. You dine with me at eight. Give me your answer then."

"I should like till to-morrow morning," said Callon.

Mr. Mudge shook his head.

"That, I am afraid, is impossible. We shall need all to-morrow to make the necessary arrangements and to talk over your duties. For if you undertake the work you must leave England on the day after."

Callon started up in protest. "On the day after!" he exclaimed.

"It gives very little time, I know," said Mudge. Then he looked Callon quietly and deliberately in the eyes. "But, you see, I want to get you out of the country at once."

Callon no longer doubted. He had thought, through Mr. Mudge's help, to laugh at his enemy, and lo! the enemy was Mudge himself. It was Mudge who had bought up his debts, who now held him in so secure a grip that he did not think it worth while to practise any concealment. Callon was humiliated to the verge of endurance. Two years in Chile pretending to supervise a railway! He understood the position which he would occupy; he was within an ace of flinging the offer back. But he dared not.

"Very well," he said. "I will give you my answer at eight."

"Thanks. Be punctual." Mr. Mudge sauntered away. There could only be the one answer. Mr. Lionel Callon might twist and turn as he pleased, he would spend two years in Chile. It was five minutes past seven. Callon could hardly call at the house in Berkeley Square with any chance of seeing Lady Stretton between now and eight. Mudge was contented with his afternoon.

At eight o'clock Callon gave in his submission and pocketed the check. At eleven he proposed to go, but Mudge, mindful of an evening visit which he had witnessed from a balcony, could not part from his new manager so soon. There was so little time for discussion even with every minute of Callon's stay in England. He kept Callon with him until two o'clock in the morning; he made an appointment with him at ten, and there was a note of warning in his voice which bade Callon punctually keep it. By one shift and another he kept him busy all that day, and in the evening Callon had to pack, to write his letters, and to make his arrangements for his departure. Moreover, Pamela Mardale dined quietly with Millie Stretton and stayed late. It thus happened that Callon left England without seeing Millie Stretton again. He could write, of course, but he could do no more.

XVIII

SOUTH OF OUARGL'A

"HALT!" cried Captain Tavernay.
The bugler at his side raised his bugle to his
lips and blew. The dozen chasseurs d'Afrique and
the ten native scouts who formed the advance-guard
stopped upon the signal. A couple of hundred yards
behind them the two companies of the Foreign Legion
came to a stand-still. The convoy of baggage mules
upon the right flank, the hospital equipment, the ar-
tillery section, the herd of oxen which was driven along
in the rear—in a word, the whole expedition halted in
a wood of dwarf oaks and junipers at three o'clock in
the afternoon.

The order was given to gather wood for the night's
camp-fires and the companies were dismissed. Each
soldier made his little bundle and fixed it upon his
shoulders. Again the bugle rang out, sounding the
"fall in." And the tiny force marched out from the
trees of the High Plateaux into the open desert. It
was extraordinary with what abruptness that tran-
sition was made. One minute the companies were
treading upon turf under rustling leaves, the next they
were descending a slope carpeted with halfa - grass
which stretched away to the horizon's rim, with hardly
a bush to break its bare monotony. At the limit of
vision a great arc like a mirror of silver glittered out of
the plain.

"Water," said a tall, bearded soldier who marched in the front rank of the first company. It was he who had stepped from the train at Bel-Abbés with a light dust-coat over his evening dress suit. He passed now as fusilier Barbier, an ex-engineer of Lyons.

"No," replied Sergeant Ohlsen, who marched at his side. "The crystals of a dry salt lake."

In the autumn of last year Ohlsen—or rather, to give him his right name, Tony Stretton—had marched upon an expedition from Mesheria to the Chott Tigri, and knew therefore the look of those tantalizing salt lakes. That expedition, which had conducted a survey for a road to the Tiguig oasis, had brought him his promotion.

"But we camp by the lake to-night," he added. "The wells of El-Guethifa are close."

The companies went forward, and above that salt lake they saw the mirages begin to shimmer, citadels and hanging gardens, tall towers and waving woods and majestic galleons, topsail over topsail, floating upon summer seas. At the wells the sheikh of the district was waiting upon a mule.

"I want fifty camels with their saddles and their drivers at five o'clock to-morrow morning," said Tavernay; and although as far as the eye could reach there was no moving thing upon that vast plain except the small group of Arabs and soldiers about the well, by five o'clock the camels were squatting upon the sand with their drivers beside them. The mules were sent back from El-Guethifa that morning, the baggage was packed upon the camels, and the little force, insufficient in numbers and supplies, went forward on its long and untoward march.

It passed through the oases of El-Maia and Methlili

to Ouargla, at that time the last outpost of French
authority. At Ouargla it rested for a week; and there,
renewing its supplies, penetrated southward to survey the desert country of the Touaregs for the con-
struction of the oft - mooted trans - Saharan railway.
South of Ouargla all the difficulties of the advance
were doubled. The companies went down through the
archipelago of oases in the dangerous Touat country
among a sullen people who had little food to supply,
and would hardly supply it. Tavernay led his men
with care, neither practising a discipline needlessly
strict nor relaxing into carelessness. But he was un-
der-officered, and his officers even so were inexperi-
enced. Lieutenant Laurent, a man irritable and un-
just, was his second in command, and there were but
two sous-lieutenants besides. In spite of all Tavernay's care, the convoy diminshed. One day a camel
would stumble on the slippery bottom of a salt marsh,
fall and break its limbs; the next, another would fail
and die through a long-untended wound caused by the
rough saddle upon its back. In the ranks of the soldiers, too, there was trouble, and Laurent was not the
man to deal with it. There was hardly a company of
the legion, recruited as it largely was from the outcasts and the men of sorrows, in which there were not
some of disordered minds, some whom absinthe had
brought to the edges of insanity. Upon these the
severity of the expedition worked havoc. Tents had
been perforce discarded. The men slept under the
stars. They woke from freezing nights to the bitter
winds of dawn, and two hours after dawn they were
parched by a burning sun, and all the day they suffered under its pitiless and blinding glare. Storms
whelmed them in lofty spirals of whirling, choking sand.

For a week they would toil over high, red, mountainous ground of loose stones; then would follow the monotony of bare, round plains, piled here and there with black rocks quivering and glittering in the heat when the sun rose day after day upon their left hand in scarlet, and set in scarlet upon their right, and they themselves were still the tiny centre of the same empty, inhospitable space; so that only the difference of the ground they trod, the feel of soft sand beneath their feet, where a minute before they had marched on gravel, told them that they progressed at all. The worst of the men became prone to disobedience, eager for change; and every now and then a soldier would rise upon his elbow in the night-time, gaze furtively about over his sleeping comrades, watch the sentries until their backs were turned, and then crawl past them into the darkness. Of these men none ever returned. Or some mania would seize upon them and fix a strange idea in their brains, such as that which besieged Barbier, the fusilier, who had once stepped out of the railway-carriage in his evening dress. He leaned over towards Stretton one evening, and said, in a hoarse, trembling voice,

"I can stand it no longer."

Both men were sitting by a tiny fire which Barbier was feeding with handfuls of halfa-grass and sticks. He was kneeling up in front of it, and by the red, waving light Stretton saw that his face was quivering with excitement.

"What can't you stand?" he asked.

"It is Captain Tavernay," replied Barbier. He suddenly laughed in a pitiful fashion and cast a glance over his shoulder. "There is a man put on to watch me. Night and day I am watched by Captain Tavernay's orders. He wants to fix a crime on me! I know. He wants to trap me. But let him take care!"

Stretton fetched the doctor, who listened for a while to Barbier's rambling, minatory talk and then shrugged his shoulders.

"Hallucinations," said he. "Ideas of persecution. The commonest form," and having fixed Barbier into his proper category he walked away. There was nothing to be done for Barbier upon this expedition. He had to be watched; that was all. Thus for seven hundred miles the force pushed southward from Ouargla, and thus from within it disintegrated as it went. Tavernay could not but notice the change, but he said nothing to any subordinate. The men would fight well if fighting happened. That he knew, and meanwhile he marched on.

It was just when the seven hundred miles had been completed that Tavernay realized fighting was likely to happen. He went the round of the camp as the sun was setting, when the rifles were piled and the fires crackling. Stretton was at his side, and saw his commander stop and shade his eyes. Tavernay was looking westward. Far away against the glowing ball of the sun, which was just dipping down behind the plain, the figure of an Arab mounted upon a camel stood motionless and black. Tavernay swung round and looked behind him. On the crest of a sand-hill to the north a second rider stood distinct against the sky.

Tavernay watched the men for a long time through his glasses.

"Touaregs," said he, gravely. "Masked Touaregs," and that night the sentinels were doubled; and in the morning the bugle did not sound the reveille.

Moreover, when the force advanced, it advanced in the formation of a square, with the baggage camels in the centre, one gun in the front line and the other in the rear. They had marched into the country where the Senoussa sect prevailed. The monasteries of that body sent out their missionaries eastward to Khordofan, westward to Tafilet, preaching the purification of the Mohammedan religion and the enlargement of Mohammedan countries now subject to the infidels. But nowhere had the missionaries raised their standard with more success than in this Touat country of the Sahara. The companies marched that day alert and cheerful. They were consolidated by the knowledge of danger. Captain Tavernay led them with pride.

"An insufficient force, ill-found, inadequately officered," he thought. "But the men are of the legion." They were "mes enfants" to him all that day.

But the attack was not yet to be delivered. During the night the two scouts had ridden on their swift Maharis northwestward to the town of Lasalah. They knocked upon the gates of the great mud fortress of Abd-el-Kader, the sheikh, and were instantly admitted to the dark room where he sat upon a pile of rugs. When the eyes of the scouts became accustomed to the gloom they saw there was yet another in the room, a tall man robed in black with a black mask of cotton wound about his face so that only his eyes were visible. This was the chieftain of the Hoggar Touaregs.

"Well?" said Abd-el-Kader, and the scouts told him roughly the number of the force and the direction of the journey.

Then Abd-el-Kader turned to the Touareg chieftain. "We will let them go farther south, since southward they are marching," he said, in his suave, gentle voice. "A hundred miles more and they will be among the sand-dunes. Since they have cannon, the attack must be sudden. Let it be at the wells of Bir-el-Gharamo."

The Touareg chieftain rode out that day towards his hills; and, unmolested, Captain Tavernay's expedition went down to the dunes. Great waves of yellow sand, sometimes three hundred feet from crest to base, intersected the face of the desert; the winds had given to their summits the overhang of a breaking sea; they ran this way and that as though the currents of an ocean had directed their course; they had the very look of motion; so that Stretton could not but remember the roaring combers of the cold North Sea as he gazed upon these silent and arrested copies. They made of that country a maze of intricate valleys. Led by a local guide commandeered from the last oasis, the companies of the legion marched into the maze, and on the second day saw, as they came over a hill, just below them in a narrow hollow, a mud parapet built about the mouth of a well. This was Bir-el-Gharamo, and here they camped. Sentries were posted on the neighboring crests; suddenly the darkness came and overhead the stars rushed down towards the earth. There was no moon that night, nor was there any sound of danger heard. Three times Tavernay went the round of the sentries—at eight and at ten and at twelve. But at three o'clock, just as the dawn was breaking, a shot was heard. Tavernay sprang up from the ground, the alarm rang out clear from the bugle over the infinite waste, the companies of the legion seized their piled rifles and fell into battle order with an incredible neatness and expedition.

There was no confusion, no noise. The square was

formed about the well—-the camels were knee-haltered in the middle, the guns placed at the corners. But it was still dark. A few shots were fired on the dunes, and the sentries came running back.

"Steady," cried Captain Tavernay. "They are coming. Fire low!"

The first volley rang out, and immediately afterwards on every side of that doomed square the impact of the Touaregs' charge fell like the blow of some monstrous hammer. All night they had been gathering noise-lessly in the surrounding valleys. Now they had charged with lance and sword from the surrounding crests. Three sides of the square held their ground. The fourth wavered, crumpled in like a piece of broken card-board, and the Arabs were within the square stab-bing at the backs of the soldiers, loosing and stamped-ing the camels. And at once where deep silence had reigned a minute ago the air was torn with shrill cries and oaths and the clamor of weapons. The square was broken; but here a group of men stood back to back and with cartridge and bayonet held its ground; there another formed; and about each gun the men fought desperately. Meanwhile the morning came, a gray, clear light spread over the desert. Tavernay himself was with one of the machine-guns. It was dragged clear of the mêlée and up a slope of sand. The soldiers parted in front of it, and its charge began to sweep the Touaregs down like swaths, and to pit the sand-hills like a fall of rain. About the second gun the fight still raged.

"Come, my children," said Tavernay. "Fight well. The Touaregs give no quarter."

Followed by Stretton he led the charge. The Touaregs gave way before their furious onslaught.

"'STEADY,' CRIED CAPTAIN TAVERNAY. 'THEY ARE COMING. FIRE LOW!'"

The soldiers reached the gun, faced about, and firing
steadily kept off the enemy while the gun was run
back. As soon as that was saved the battle was over.
All over the hollow, wherever the Touaregs were
massed, the two guns rattled out their canister. No
Arab could approach them. The sun rose over the
earth, and while it was rising the Touaregs broke and
fled. When it shone out in its full round there was
no one left of them in that hollow except the wounded
and the dead. But the victory had been dearly bought.
All about the well, lying pell-mell among the Arabs
and the dead camels, were the French Legionaries,
some quite still and others writhing in pain and crying
for water. Stretton drew his hand across his forehead. He was stunned and dazed. It seemed to him
that years had passed, that he had grown very old.
Yet there was the sun new-risen. There was a dull
pain in his head. He raised his hand and drew it
away wet with blood. How or when he had received
the blow he was quite unaware. He stood staring
stupidly about him. So very little while ago men
were lying here sleeping in their cloaks, quite strong,
living people; now they were lying dead or in pain; it
was all incomprehensible.

"Why?" he asked, aloud, of no one. "Now, why?"

Gradually, however, custom resumed its power.
There was a man hanging limp over the parapet of
the well. He looked as though he had knelt down
and stooped over to drink, and in that attitude had
fallen asleep. But he might so easily be pushed into
the well, and custom had made the preservation of
wells from impurity an instinct. He removed the
body and went in search of Tavernay. Tavernay was
sitting propped up against a camel's saddle; the doctor

was by his side; a blood-stained bandage was about his thigh. He spoke in a weak voice.

"Lieutenant Laurent?"

Stretton went in search. He came across an old, gray-headed soldier rolling methodically a cigarette.

"He is dead, over there," said the soldier. "Have you a light?"

Laurent was lying clasped in the arms of a dead Touareg. He had been stabbed by a lance in the back. One of the sous-lieutenants was killed, the other dangerously wounded. A sergeant-major lay with a broken shoulder beside one of the guns. Stretton went back to Tavernay.

"You must take command, then," said Tavernay. "I think you have learned something about it on your fishing-boats." And in spite of his pain he smiled.

Stretton mustered the men and called over the names. Of the two hundred and thirty men who had made up the two companies of the legion only forty-seven could stand in the ranks and answer to their names. For those forty-seven there was herculean work to do. Officers were appointed, the dead bodies were roughly buried, the camels collected, litters improvised for the wounded, the goat-skins filled with water. Late in the afternoon Stretton came again to Tavernay.

"We are ready, sir."

Tavernay nodded, and asked for a sheet of paper, an envelope, and ink. They were fetched from his portfolio, and very slowly and laboriously he wrote a letter and handed it to Stretton.

"Seal it," he said; "now, in front of me."

Stretton obeyed.

"Keep that letter. If you get back to Ouargla without me give it to the commandant there."

Tavernay was lifted in a litter onto the back of a camel, and the remnant of the geographical expedition began its terrible homeward march. Eight hundred miles lay between Bir-el-Gharamo and the safety of Ouargla. The Touaregs hung upon the rear of the force, but they did not attack again. They preferred another way. One evening a solitary Arab drove a laden camel into the bivouac. He was conducted to Stretton, and said:

"The Touaregs ask pardon and pray for peace. They will molest you no more. Indeed, they will help you, and as an earnest of their true desire for your welfare they send you a camel-load of dates."

Stretton accepted the present and carried the message to Tavernay, who cried at once, "Let no one eat those dates." But two soldiers had already eaten of them and died of poison before the morning. Short of food, short of sentinels, the broken force crept back across the stretches of soft sand, the grayish-green plains of halfa-grass, the ridges of red hill. One by one the injured succumbed; their wounds gangrened; they were tortured by the burning sun and the motion of the camels. A halt would be made, a camel made to kneel, and a rough grave dug.

"Pelissier!" cried Stretton, and a soldier stepped out from the ranks who had once conducted mass in the church of the Madeleine in Paris. Pelissier would recite such prayers as he remembered, and the force would move on again, leaving one more soldier's grave behind it in the desert to protest unnoticed against the economy of governments. Then came a morning when Stretton was summoned to Captain Tavernay's side.

For two days Tavernay had tossed in a delirium. He now lay in a rough shelter of cloaks, in his right senses, but so weak that he could not lift a hand and with a face so pinched and drawn that his years seemed to have been doubled. His eyes shone out from big, black circles. Stretton knelt down beside him.

"You have the letter?"

"Yes."

"Do not forget."

He lay for a while in a sort of contentment; then he said:

"Do not think this expedition has been waste. A small force first and disaster . . . the big force afterwards to retrieve the disaster, and with it victory, and government, and peace, and a new country won for France. That is the law of the legion. . . . *My* legion." He smiled, and Stretton muttered a few insincere words.

"You will recover, my captain. You will lead your companies again."

"No," said Tavernay, in a whisper. "I do not want to. I am very happy. Yes, I say that who joined the legion twenty years ago. And the legion, my friend, is the nation of the unhappy. For twenty years I have been a citizen of that nation. . . . I pity women who have no such nation to welcome them and find them work. . . . For us there is no need of pity."

And in a few moments he fell asleep, and two hours later, sleeping, died. A pile of stone was built above his grave, and the force marched on. Gaunt, starved, and ragged, the men marched northward, leaving the Touat country upon their left hand. It struck the caravan route from Tidikelt to Ouargla; it stumbled at last through the gates of the town. Silently it marched through the streets to the French fortress. On no survivor's face was there any sign of joy that at last their hardships were over, their safety assured. All were too tired, too dispirited. The very people who crowded to see them pass seemed part of an uninteresting show. Stretton went at once to the commandant and told him the story of their disaster. Then he handed him the letter. The commandant broke the seal and read it through.

"Tell me how and when this was written."

Stretton obeyed, and after he had heard the commandant sat with his hand shading his eyes. When he spoke, his voice showed that he was deeply moved.

"You know what the letter contains, Sergeant Ohlsen?"

"No, my commandant."

"Read, then, for yourself," and he passed the letter across his office table. Stretton took it and read. There were a few lines written, only a few, but those few lines recommended Sergeant Ohlsen for promotion to the rank of officer. The commandant held out his hand.

"That is like our Tavernay," he said. "He thought always of his soldiers. He wrote it at once, you see, after the battle was over lest he should die and justice not be done. Have no fear, my friend. It is you who have brought back to Ouargla the survivors of the legion."

XIX

THE TURNPIKE GATE

IT was not, however, only Millie Stretton whose fortunes were touched by Tony's absence. Warrisden, whom Stretton had met but the once on board the *City of Bristol*, was no less affected. On a day of that summer during which Tony camped far away on the edge of the Sahara, Warrisden rode down the steep hill from the village of the three poplars on his way to Whitewebs. Once Pamela had ridden along this road between the white wood rails and the black bare stems of trees on a winter's evening of mist. That was more than fifteen months ago. The brown furrows in the fields were now acres of waving yellow; each black clump was now an ambuscade of green, noisy with birds. The branches creaked in a light wind and rippled and shook the sunlight from their leaves, the road glistened like chalk. It was ten o'clock on an August morning, very clear and light. Voices from far away among the corn sounded tiny and distinct, like voices heard through a telephone. Round this bend at the thicket corner Pamela had disappeared on that dim, gray evening. How far had she since travelled on the new road, Warrisden wondered. She was at Whitewebs now. He was riding thither to find out.

When he inquired for her at the door, he was at once led through the house into the big garden at the back. Pamela was sitting in a chair at the edge of the lawn under the shade of the great avenue of elms which ran straight from the back of the house to the shallow stream at the garden's boundary. She saw him at once as he came out from the glass door on to the gravel, and she rose from her chair. She did not advance to him, but just stood where she was, watching him approach; and in her eyes there was a great perplexity. Warrisden came straight to her over the lawn. There was no hesitation in his manner, at all events. On the other hand, there was no air of assurance. He came with a definite object; so much was evident, but no more. He stopped in front of her and raised his hat. Pamela looked at him and said nothing. She did not even give him her hand. She stood and waited almost submissively, with her troubled eyes resting quietly on his.

"You expected me?" he said.

"Yes. I received your letter this morning."

"You have guessed why I have come?"

"Yes."

"And you are troubled," said Warrisden.

They turned and walked under the branches into the avenue. Overhead there was a bustle of blackbirds and thrushes; a gardener sharpening his scythe in the rose-garden made a little rasping sound. Over all the lawn the August sunlight lay warm and golden like a benediction.

"I have come to ask you the old question," said Warrisden. "Will you marry me?"

Pamela gazed steadily ahead as she walked, and she walked very slowly. She was prepared for the question, yet she took her time to answer it. And the answer when at last she gave it was no answer at all.

"I do not know," she said, in a low, clear voice.

Warrisden looked at her. The profile of her face was towards him. He wondered for the thousandth time at its· beauty and its gentleness. The broad, white forehead under the sweep of her dark hair, the big, dark eyes shining beneath her brows, the delicate color upon her cheeks, the curve of the lips. He wondered and longed. But he spoke simply and without extravagance, knowing that he would be understood.

"I have done nothing for you of the things men often do when a woman comes into their lives. I have tried to make no career. I think there are enough people making careers. They make the world very noisy, and they raise a deal of dust. I have just gone on living quietly as I did before, believing you would need no such proof."

"I do not," said Pamela.

"There might be much happiness for both of us," he continued. And again she answered, without looking at him,

"I do not know."

She was not evading him. Evasions, indeed, were never to her liking; and here, she was aware, were very serious issues.

"I have been thinking about you a great deal," she said. "I will tell you this. There is no one else. But that is not all. I can say, too, I think, quite certainly, that there will be no one else. Only that is not enough, is it? Not enough, at all events, for you and me."

Warrisden nodded his head.

"No, that is not enough," he said, gravely.

They walked on side by side in silence for a little while.

"It is only fair that I should be very frank with you," she went on. "I have been thinking so much about you in order that when you came again with this old question, as I knew you would, I might be quite clear and frank. Do you remember that you once spoke to me about the turnpike gate—the gate which I was to open and through which I was to go, like other men and women, down the appointed road?"

"Yes, I remember."

"You meant, as I understand it, the gate between friendship and the ever so much more which lies beyond?"

"Yes."

And Pamela repeated his word. "Yes," she said. "But one cannot open that gate at will. It opens of itself at a touch, or it stays shut."

"And it stays shut now?"

Pamela answered him at once.

"Say, rather, that I have raised a hand towards the gate, but that I am afraid to try." And she turned her face to him at last. Her eyes were very wistful.

They stopped upon the grass bank of the stream at the end of the avenue. Pamela looked down into the dark, swiftly running water, and went on choosing each word, testing it, as it were, before she uttered it.

"You see, that new road beyond the gate is no new road to me. I have trodden it before and crept back —broken. Therefore, I am afraid." She paused. Warrisden was aware from her attitude that she had not finished. He did not stir lest he should check what more remained to say, and that remnant never be spoken at all. And it was well for him that he did not stir; for she said, in the same clear, low voice which she had hitherto used, and just as steadily,

"I am the more afraid because I think that if I did touch that gate it might open of itself."

She had begun, in a word, to feel premonitions of that suspense and of that glowing life in which for a few brief months she had once been steeped. Did she expect a letter from Warrisden, there was an eagerness in her anticipation with which she was well familiar. Was the letter delayed, there was a keenness in her disappointment which was like the pang of an old wound. And this recognition that the good days might come again, as in a cycle, brought to her very vividly the memory of the bad, black days which had followed. Fear of those latter days, and the contrast of their number with the number of those which had gone before, drove her back. For those latter days in their turn might come round again.

Warrisden looked at her and his heart filled with pity for the great trouble which had overwhelmed her. She stood by his side with the sunlight playing upon her face and her hair—a girl brilliant with life, ripe to turn its possibilities into facts; and she shrank from the ordeal, so hardly had she been hit! She was by nature fearless, yet was she desperately afraid.

"Will nothing make you touch the gate and try?" he asked, gently. And then, quietly as he spoke, the greatness of his longing made itself heard. "My dear, my dear," he said, "will nothing make you take your risks?"

The words struck sharply upon her memories. She turned her eyes to him.

"It is strange that you should use those words," she said. "For there is one thing which might make me take my risks. The return of the man who used them to you in the North Sea."

"Tony Stretton?" exclaimed Warrisden.

"Yes. He is still away. It is said that he is on a long shooting expedition somewhere in Central Africa, and out of reach. But that is not the truth. We do not know where he is, or when he will come back."

"Shall I try to find him again?" said Warrisden. "This time I might succeed in bringing him home."

Pamela shook her head.

"No," she answered. "I think I know why he stays away. And there would be only one way of persuading him to return. Well—that means I must not use, unless things have come to an extremity."

The one means of persuasion was the truth. If she sent for Tony Stretton again she must explain what that saying of hers spoken so long ago had meant. She must write why he should not have left his wife. She must relate the sordid story, which rendered his return imperative. That she was prepared to do, if all else failed, in the last resort, but not till then.

"But the extremity has not been reached," she continued, "and I hope it never will. I hope Tony Stretton will come back soon of his own accord. That would be the best thing which could happen, ever so much the best." She did not blame Tony for his absence, for she understood the motive which caused it. In a way she was inclined to approve of it in itself, just as a motive—that is to say. It was the character of Millie Stretton and his ignorance of it which made his experiment so hazardous. Complete confidence in his wife's honor, indeed, was to her thinking, and rightly, an essential part of his motive. She wished him to return of his own accord and keep that confidence.

"There is not the same necessity," she continued, choosing her words, "that he should return immediately as there was when I sent you out to the North Sea; but it is possible that the necessity might recur." For she knew that, though Callon was far away in Chile, letters came from him to Millie. Only lately a careless remark of Millie's with reference to that state had assured her of this. And if the letters still came, though Callon had been away a year, it followed that they were answered.

"In that case you would send for me?" said Warrisden.

"Yes. I should rely on you."

And Warrisden answered, quietly, "Thank you."

He asked no questions. He seemed to understand that Pamela must use him, and, while using him, not fail of loyalty to her sex. A feeling of self-reproach suddenly troubled Pamela. She had never told him that she had used another's help and not his. She wondered whether it was quite fair not to tell him. But she kept silent. After all, she thought, the news would only hurt him; and Mr. Mudge's help had been help which he could not have given. She went back to the matter of their relationship to each other.

"So you understand what I think," she said. "I am afraid. I look for signs. I cannot help doing that. I have set my heart on keeping a promise which I made to Tony Stretton. If he returns, whether of his own accord or by my persuasion, and things go well— why, then"—and she turned her face from him and said, looking steadily in front of her—"why, then, perhaps."

As she spoke her face changed wonderfully. The mere utterance of the word aloud conjured up dreams. A wistful smile made her lips beautiful; her eyes grew dim. Just for a moment she gave those dreams their way. She looked across the garden through a mist, seeing nothing of the trees or the colored flowers, but gazing into a vision of other and golden days—of days perhaps to come. Warrisden stood at her side and did not speak. But something of those dreams he guessed, her face had grown so young.

She shook her dreams from her in a few moments.

"So you see, at present," she resumed, "marriage is impossible. It will always be impossible to me unless I can bring—everything, not merely companionship, not merely liking; but the ever so much more which there is. I cannot contemplate it at all under any other conditions"—and now she looked at her companion—"and I believe it is the same with you."

"Yes," Warrisden replied, "I ask for everything."

He had his convictions, and since there was complete confidence between these two, he spoke them now.

"It is unsafe, of course, to generalize on the subject of women. But I do think this. If a man asks little from a woman, she will give him even less than he asks, and she will give it grudgingly, sparingly, counting what she gives. And that little, to my mind, is worth rather less than nothing. Better have no ties than weak ones. If, on the other hand, a man asks a great deal, and continually asks it, why, the woman may get bored, and he may get nothing. In which case he is no worse off than he was before. But if, on the other hand, the woman does give in return—"

"Well?" asked Pamela.

"Well, then, she gives ever so much more than he asks, and gives it willingly, with open hands."

Pamela thought the theory over.

"Yes, I think that is generally true," she said. "But, after all, I am giving you very little."

Warrisden laughed.

"That's true," he replied. "But then you are not bored, and I have not done asking."

Pamela laughed, too, and their talk thus ended in a lighter note. They walked towards the house, and as they did so a woman came out onto the lawn.

"This is Millie Stretton," said Pamela.

"She is staying here?" cried Warrisden.

"Yes," replied Pamela. "Before she comes I want to ask you to do something for me. Oh, it is quite a small thing. But I should like you very much to do it. Where do you go to from here?"

"To London," said Warrisden. "I have business there."

The business which called him to town had, indeed, only occurred to him during the last half-hour. It had arisen from their conversation. It seemed to Warrisden immediate and imperative.

"Will you be in London to-morrow?" asked Pamela.

"Yes."

"Then I want you to write to me. Just a little letter —nothing much, a line or two. And I want you to post it, not by the country post, but afterwards, so that it will reach me in the evening. Don't write here, for I am going home. And please don't forget."

Millie Stretton joined them a moment afterwards, and Warrisden was introduced to her.

"I have had an offer for the house in Berkeley Square," she said to Pamela. "I think I will take it. I shall be glad to be rid of it."

They went back into the house. Warrisden wondered at Pamela's request for a letter, and at her urgency that it should arrive at a particular time. He was not discontented with the walk which they had taken under the avenue of elms. It seemed to him that Pamela was coming slowly towards him. There was a great difference between her "No" of last year and her "I do not know" of to-day. Even that "I do not know" while they talked had become "perhaps." Had she not owned even more, since she was afraid the gate would open of itself did she but touch and try? His hopes, therefore, rode high that day, and would have ridden yet higher could he have guessed why she so desired a few lines in his handwriting in the evening of the day after to-morrow.

The reason was this. Repairs, long needed, had at last been undertaken in the house of Pamela's father, a few miles away, and those repairs involved the rooms reserved for Pamela. There were certain drawers in that room which had not been unlocked for years, and of which Pamela sedulously guarded the keys. They held letters, a few small presents, one or two photographs, and some insignificant trifles which could not be valued, since their value depended only on their associations. There were, for instance, some cheap red beads, and the history of those beads tells all that need be said of the contents of those locked drawers.

Two hundred years before a great, full-rigged ship, bound with a general cargo for the Guinea coast, sailed down the Channel out of Portsmouth. Among the cargo was a great store of these red beads. The beads were to buy slaves for the plantations. But the great ship got no farther on her voyage than Bigbury Bay in Devonshire. She damaged her rudder in a storm, and the storm swept her onto the bleak rocks of Bolt Tail, dragged her back again into the welter of the sea, drove her into Bigbury Bay, and flung her up there against the low, red cliffs, where all her crew perished,

The cargo was spilled among the breakers, and the shores of that bay were littered with red beads. You may pick them up to this day among the pebbles. There Pamela had picked them up on a hot August morning, very like to that which now dreamed over this green, quiet garden of Leicestershire; and when she had picked them up she had not been alone. The locked cabinets held all the relics which remained to her from those few bright weeks in Devon; and the mere touch of any one, however trifling, would have magic to quicken her memories. Yet now the cabinets must be unlocked and all that was in them removed. There was a bad hour waiting for Pamela when she would remove these relics one by one—the faded letters in the handwriting which she would never see again on any envelope; the photograph of the face which could exchange no look with her; the little presents from the hand which could touch hers no more. It would be a relief, she thought, to come down-stairs when that necessary work was done, that bad hour over, and find a letter from Warrisden upon the table. Just a few lines. She needed nothing more.

XX

MR. CHASE DOES NOT ANSWER

BOTH Pamela and Millie Stretton walked with Warrisden through the hall to the front door. Upon the hall table letters were lying. Pamela glanced at them as she passed, and caught one up rather suddenly. Then she looked at Warrisden, and there was something of appeal in her look. It was as though she turned to a confederate on whom she could surely rely. But she said nothing, since Millie Stretton was at her side. For the letter was in the handwriting of Mr. Mudge, who wrote but rarely, and never without a reason. She read the letter in the garden as soon as Warrisden had ridden off, and the news which it contained was bad news. Callon had lived frugally in South America—by Christmas he would have discharged his debts; and he had announced to Mudge that he intended at that date to resign his appointment. There were still four months, Pamela reflected —nay, counting the journey home, five months; and within that time Tony Stretton might reappear. If he did not, why, she could summon Warrisden to her aid. She looked at Millie, who was reading a book in a garden chair close by. Did she know, Pamela wondered? But Millie gave no sign.

Meanwhile, Warrisden travelled to London upon that particular business which made a visit there in August so imperative. It had come upon him while he had been talking with Pamela that it would be as well for him to know the whereabouts of Tony Stretton at once; so that if the need came he should be ready to set out upon the instant. On the following evening, accordingly, he drove down to Stepney. It was very likely that Chase would be away upon a holiday. But there was a chance that he might find him clinging to his work through this hot August, a chance worth the trouble of his journey. He drove to the house where Chase lodged, thinking to catch him before he set out for his evening's work at the mission. The door of the house stood open to the street. Warrisden dismissed his cab, and walked up the steps into the narrow hall. A door upon his right hand was opened, and a young man politely asked Warrisden to step in. He was a fair-haired youth, with glasses upon his nose, and he carried a napkin in his hand. He had evidently been interrupted at his dinner by Warrisden's arrival. He was not dining alone, for a youth of the same standing, but of a more athletic mould, sat at the table. There was a third place laid, but not occupied.

Warrisden looked at the third chair.

"I came to see Mr. Chase," he said. "I suppose that he has gone early to the mission?"

"No," said the youth who had opened the door. "He has not been well of late. The hot weather in these close streets is trying. But he certainly should have something to eat by now, even if he does not intend to get up."

He spoke in a pedantic, self-satisfied voice, and introduced himself as Mr. Raphael Princkley and his companion as Mr. Jonas Stiles, both undergraduates of Queen's College, Oxford.

"We are helping Chase in his work," continued Mr. Princkley. "It is little we can do, but you are no doubt acquainted with the poetry of Robert Browning—

 "'The little more, and how much it is.'

In that line we find our justification."

The fair-haired youth rang the bell for the housekeeper. She was an old woman, fat and slow, and she took her time in answering the summons.

"Mrs. Wither, have you called Mr. Chase?" he asked, when the old lady appeared at the door.

"No, Mr. Princkley, sir!" she replied. "You told me yesterday evening not to disturb him on any account until he rang."

Mr. Princkley turned to Warrisden.

"Mr. Chase was unwell all yesterday," he said, "and at dinner-time he told us that he felt unequal to his duties. He was sitting in that empty place, and we both advised him not to overtax his strength."

He appealed with a look to Mr. Stiles for corroboration.

"Yes; we both advised him," said Stiles, between two mouthfuls, "and, very wisely, he took our advice."

"He rose from his chair," continued Princkley. "There was some fruit upon the table. He took an apple from the dish. I think, Stiles, that it was an apple which he took?"

Mr. Stiles agreed and went on with his dinner.

"It was certainly an apple which he took. He took it in his hand."

"You hardly expected him to take it with his foot!" rejoined Warrisden, politely. Warrisden was growing a little restive under this detailed account of Chase's indisposition.

"No," replied Princkley, with gravity. "He took it in quite a natural way, and went up-stairs to his sitting-room. I gave orders to Mrs. Wither that he must not be disturbed until he rang. That is so, Mrs. Wither, is it not? Yes. I thank you."

"That was yesterday evening!" cried Warrisden.

"Yesterday evening," replied Mr. Princkley.

"And no one has been near him since?"

Then Mrs. Wither intervened.

"Oh yes. I went into Mr. Chase's room an hour afterwards. He was sitting in his arm-chair before the grate—"

"Holding the apple in his hand, I think, Mrs. Wither, you said?" continued Stiles.

"Yes, sir," said Mrs. Wither. "He had his arm out resting on the arm of the chair, and the apple was in his hand."

"Well, well!" exclaimed Warrisden.

"I told him that I would not call him in the morning until he rang, as he wanted a good rest."

"What did he say?" asked Warrisden.

"Nothing, sir. As often as not he does not answer when he is spoken to."

A sudden fear seized upon Warrisden. He ran out of the room and up the stairs to Chase's sitting-room. He knocked on the door; there was no answer. He turned the handle and entered. Chase had not gone to bed last night. He was still sitting in his arm-chair before the grate. One arm was extended along the arm of the chair, with the palm turned upward, and in the palm lay an apple. Chase was sitting huddled up, with his head fallen forward upon his breast like a man asleep. Warrisden crossed the room and touched the hand which held the apple. It was quite cold.

The apple rolled onto the floor. Warrisden turned to the housekeeper. She was standing in the doorway, and staring over her shoulder were the two undergraduates.

"He was dead," said Warrisden, "when you looked into the room an hour afterwards!"

The three people in the doorway stood stupidly aghast. Warrisden pushed them out, locked the door on the outside, and removed the key.

"Mr. Princkley, will you run for a doctor?" he asked.

Princkley nodded his head and went off upon his errand.

Warrisden and Stiles descended the stairs into the dining-room.

"I think you had better take the news to the mission," said Warrisden; and Stiles in his turn went off without a word. Mrs. Wither, for her part, had run out of the house as quickly as she could. She hardly knew what she was doing. She had served as housekeeper to Mr. Chase ever since he had come to Stepney, and she was dazed by the sudden calamity. She was aware of a need to talk, to find the neighbors and talk.

Warrisden was thus left alone in the house. It had come about without any premeditation upon his part. He was the oldest man of the three who had been present, and the only one who had kept his wits clear. Both Princkley and Stiles had looked to him to decide what must be done. They regarded him as Chase's friend, whereas they were mere acquaintances. It did not even occur to Warrisden at first that he was alone in the house, that he held in his hand the key to Chase's room. He was thinking of the strange, perplexing life which had now so strangely ended. He thought of his first meeting with Chase in the mission,

and of the distaste which he had felt; he remembered
the array of liqueur bottles on the table, and the half-
hour during which Chase had talked. A man of morbid pleasures, that had been Warrisden's impression.
Yet there were the years of work, here, among these
squalid streets. Even August had seen him clinging
to — nay, dying at — his work. As Warrisden looked
out of the window he saw a group of men and women
and children gather outside the house. There was not
a face but wore a look of consternation. If they spoke
they spoke in whispers, like people overawed. A very
strange life! Warrisden knew many — as who does
not?—who saw the high-road distinctly, and could not
for the life of them but walk upon the low one. But
to use both deliberately, as it seemed Chase had done;
to dip from the high road onto the low, and then pain-
fully to scramble up again, and again willingly to drop,
as though the air of those stern heights were too rig-
orous for continuous walking; to live the double life
because he could not entirely live the one and would
not entirely live the other. Thus Warrisden solved
the problem of the *dilettante* curate and his devotion
to his work, and his solution was correct.

But he held the key of Chase's room in his hand;
and there was no one but himself in the house. His
thoughts came back to Pamela and the object of his
journey up to town. He was sorely tempted to use
the key, since now the means by which he had hoped
to discover in what quarter of the world Stretton
wandered and was hid were tragically closed to him.
Chase could no longer speak, even if he would. Very
likely there were letters up-stairs lying on the table.
There might be one from Tony Stretton. Warrisden
did not want to read it—a mere glance at the post-

mark and at the foreign stamp upon the envelope. Was that so great a crime? Warrisden was sorely tempted. If only he could be sure that Chase would a second time have revealed what he was bidden to keep hid, why, then, would it not be just the same thing as if Chase were actually speaking with his lips? Warrisden played with the key. He went to the door and listened. There was not a sound in the house except the ticking of a clock. The front door still stood open. He must be quick if he meant to act. Warrisden turned to the stairs. The thought of the dead man huddled in the chair, a silent guardian of the secret, weighted his steps. Slowly he mounted. Such serious issues hung upon his gaining this one piece of knowledge! The fortunes of four people—Pamela and himself, Tony Stretton and his wife—might all be straightened out if he only did this one thing, which he had no right to do. He would not pry among Chase's papers; he would merely glance at the table, that was all. He heard voices in the hall while he was still upon the stairs. He turned back with a feeling of relief.

At the foot of the stairs stood Mr. Princkley and the doctor. Warrisden handed the key of the room to the latter, and the three men went up. The doctor opened the door and crossed to the arm-chair. Then he looked about the room.

"Nothing has been touched, of course?"

"Nothing," replied Warrisden.

The doctor looked again at the dead man. Then he turned to Warrisden, mistaking him, as the others had done, for some relation or near friend.

"I can give no certificate," said he.

"There must be an inquest?"

"Yes."

Then the doctor moved suddenly to the table, which stood a few feet from the arm-chair. There was a decanter upon it half filled with a liquid like brown sherry, only a little darker. The doctor removed the stopper and raised the decanter to his nose.

"Ah!" said he, in a voice of comprehension. He turned again to Warrisden.

"Did you know?" he asked.

"No."

The doctor held the decanter towards Warrisden. Warrisden took it, moistened the tip of a finger with the liquid, and tasted it. It had a bitter flavor.

"What is it?" he asked.

"Laudanum," said the doctor. "An overdose of it."

"Where is the glass, then, in which it was taken?"

A tumbler stood upon the table close to the decanter stopper. The doctor took it up.

"Yes, I noticed that," said Warrisden; "I noticed that it is clean."

The doctor took the glass to the window, turned it upsidedown, and held it to the light. It was quite dry, quite clean.

"Surely it's evident what happened," said Warrisden. "Chase came into the room, opened that cupboard door in the corner there. His keys are still dangling in the lock. He took the decanter and the tumbler out, placed them on the table at his side, sat down in his chair with the apple in his hand, leaned back and quietly died."

"Yes, no doubt," said the doctor. "But I think here will be found the reason why he leaned back and quietly died," and he touched the decanter. "Opium poisoning. It may not have been an overdose, but a regular practice." He went to the door and called for Mrs. Wither. Mrs. Wither had now returned to the house. When she came up-stairs into the room, he pointed to the decanter.

"Did you ever see this before?"

"No, sir," she answered.

"Or that cupboard open?"

"No, it was always locked."

"Quite so," said the doctor. "You had better get some women to help you here," he went on; and, with Warrisden's assistance, he lifted Chase from the chair and carried him into his bedroom.

"I must give notice to the police," he went on, and again he appealed to Warrisden. "Do you mind staying in the house till I come back?"

"Not at all."

The doctor locked the door of the room and took the key away with him. Warrisden waited with Princkley in the dining-room. The doctor had taken away the key. It seemed that his chance of discovering the secret which was of so much importance to Pamela and Millie Stretton and himself had vanished. If only he had come yesterday, or the day before! He sat down by the window and gazed out upon the street. A group of men and women were gathered in the roadway looking up at the windows and talking quietly together. Then Princkley from behind said:

"Some letters came for Chase this morning. They were not taken up to his room. You had better look at them."

Every one took him for a close friend. Princkley brought him the letters, and he glanced at the superscriptions lest any one should wear a look of immediate importance. He held the letters in his hand and turned them over one by one, and half-way through the file he stopped. He had come to a letter written upon thin paper, in a man's handwriting, with a foreign stamp upon the envelope. The stamp was a French one, and there was printed upon it, "Poste d'Algérie."

Warrisden examined the post-mark. The letter came from Ain-Sefra. Warrisden went on with his examination without a word. But his heart quickened. He wondered whether he had found the clew. Ain-Sefra, in Algeria. Warrisden had never heard of the place before. It might be a health resort, a wintering-place. But this was the month of August. There would be no visitors at this time to a health resort in Algeria. He handed the letters back to Princkley.

"I cannot tell whether they are important or not," he said. "I knew Chase very slightly. His relations must be informed. I suppose Mrs. Wither knows where they live."

He took his departure as soon as the doctor had returned with the police, and drove back to his rooms. A search through the encyclopædia told him nothing of Ain-Sefra; but, on the other hand, he could not look at the article on Algeria without the Foreign Legion leaping to his eyes at once—so great and magnificent a part it played in the modern history of that colony. The Foreign Legion! Warrisden jumped to the conviction that there was the secret of Tony Stretton's disappearance. Every reason he could imagine came to his aid. Let a man wish to disappear, as, from whatsoever reason, Tony Stretton did, where else could he so completely bury himself and yet live? Hardships? Dangers? Yes. But Tony Stretton had braved hardships and dangers in the North Sea and had made light of them. A detachment of the Foreign Legion might well be stationed at this oasis of Ain-Sefra of which his encyclopædia knew nothing. He had no doubt there was a trooper there, serving under some false name, who would start if the name of "Stretton" were suddenly shouted to him behind his back.

Warrisden wrote no word of his conjecture to Pamela; he wished to raise no hopes which he could not fulfil. Convinced as he was, he wished for certain proof. But in fulfilment of his promise he wrote to Pamela that night. Just a few lines—nothing more, as she had asked. But in those few lines he wrote that he would like her to procure for him a scrap of Tony Stretton's handwriting. Could she do it? In a week the scrap of handwriting arrived. Warrisden, looking at it, knew that the same hand had addressed the envelope at Ain-Sefra to Mr. Chase.

Warrisden was ready now, if the summons to service should come once more from Pamela.

XXI

CALLON REDIVIVUS

ALL through that autumn Pamela watched for Tony's return, and watched in vain. Winter came, and with the winter a letter from Mr. Mudge. Lionel Callon had booked his passage home on a steamer which sailed on Christmas eve from the port of Valparaiso. Pamela received the news one morning of December. She hunted that day with the Quorn, and for once her thoughts were set on other matters than this immediate business. The long grass meadows slipped away under her horse's feet the while she pondered how once more the danger of Callon's presence was to be averted. At times she hoped it would not need averting. Callon had been eighteen months away, and Millie was quick to forget. But she was no less quick to respond to a show of affection. Let Callon lay siege again persistently, and the danger at once was close. Besides, there were the letters. That he should have continued to write during the months of his absence was a sign that he had not foregone his plan of conquest.

Pamela returned home with a scheme floating in her mind. Some words which her mother had spoken at the breakfast-table had recurred to her, and at tea Pamela revived the subject.

"Did you say that you would not go to Roquebrune this winter, mother?" she asked.

"Yes," Mrs. Mardale replied; "I have been for so many winters now. I shall stay in England, for a change. We can let the Villa Pontignard, no doubt."

"Oh, there is no hurry," said Pamela. She added: "I shall be going to London to-morrow, but I shall be back in the evening."

She thought over her plan that evening. Its execution would cost her something, she realized. For many years she had not been out of England during the winter. She must leave her horses behind, and that was no small sacrifice for Pamela. She had one horse in particular, a big Irish horse, which had carried her in the days when her troubles were at their worst. He would follow her about the paddock or the yard nuzzling against her arm; a horse of blood and courage, yet gentle with her, thoughtful and kind for her as only a horse among the animals can be. She must leave him. On the other hand, her thoughts of late had been turning to Roquebrune for a particular reason. She had a feeling that she would rather like to tread again those hill-paths, to see once more those capes and headlands of which every one was a landmark of past pain—just as an experiment. She travelled to London the next day and drove from St. Pancras into Regent's Park.

Millie Stretton had taken a house on the west side of the park. It looked east across the water and through the glades of trees, and in front of it were the open spaces of which Tony and she had dreamed; and the sunlight streamed through the windows and lay in golden splashes on the floors when there was sunlight in London anywhere at all. When she looked from her window on the first morning, she could not but remember the plans which Tony and she had de-

bated long ago. They had been so certain of realizing
them. Well, they were realized now, for her at all
events. There was the sunlight piercing through
every cranny; there were the wide expanses of green,
and trees. Only the windows looked on Regent's Park,
and on no wide prairie; and of the two who, with so
much enthusiasm, had marked out their imaginary
site and built their house, there was only one to enjoy
the fulfilment. Millie Stretton thought of Tony that
morning, but with an effort. What Pamela had foreseen had come to pass. He had grown elusive to her
thoughts, she could hardly visualize his person to herself; he was almost unreal. Had he walked in at that
moment he would have been irksome to her as a
stranger.

It was, however, Pamela Mardale who walked in.
She was shown over the house, and until that ceremony
was over she did not broach the reason for her visit.
Then, however, Millie said with delight:

"It is what I have always wanted—sunlight."

"I came to suggest more sunlight," said Pamela.
"There is our villa at Roquebrune in the south of
France. It will be empty this winter. And I thought
that perhaps you and I might go out there together
as soon as Christmas is past."

Millie was standing at the window with her back to
Pamela. She turned round quickly.

"But you hate the place," she said.

Pamela answered with sincerity.

"None the less I want to go this winter. I want to
go very much. I won't tell you why. But I do want
to go. And I should like you to come with me."

Pamela was anxious to discover whether that villa
and its grounds, and the view from its windows, had

still the power to revive the grief with which they had been so completely associated in her mind. Hitherto she had shrunk from the very idea of ever revisiting Roquebrune; of late, however, since Warrisden, in a word, had occupied so large a place in her thoughts, she had wished to put herself to the test, to understand whether her distress was really and truly dead, or whether it merely slumbered and could wake again. It was necessary for Warrisden's sake, as much as her own, that she should come to a true knowledge. And nowhere else could she so certainly acquire it. If the sight of Roquebrune, the familiar look of the villa's rooms, the familiar paths whereon she had carried so overcharged a heart, had no longer power to hurt and pain her, then she would be sure that she could start her life afresh. It was only fair—so she phrased it in her thoughts—that she should make the experiment.

Millie turned back to the window.

"I do not think that I shall leave London this winter," she said. "You see, I have only just got into the house."

"It might spare you some annoyance," Pamela suggested.

"I don't understand," said Millie.

"The annoyance of having to explain Tony's absence. He will very likely have returned by the spring."

Millie shrugged her shoulders.

"I have borne that annoyance for two years," she replied. "I do not think I shall go away this winter."

Was Millie thinking of Callon's return? Pamela wondered. Was it on his account that she decided to remain? Pamela could not ask the question. Her plan had come to naught, and she returned that afternoon to Leicestershire.

Christmas passed, and half-way through the month of January Callon called, on a dark afternoon, at Millie Stretton's house. Millie was alone; she was, indeed, expecting him. When Callon entered the room he found her standing with her back to the window, her face to the door, and so she stood, without speaking, for a few moments.

"You have been a long time away," she said, and she looked at him with curiosity, but with yet more anxiety to mark any changes which had come in his face.

"Yes," said he, "a long time."

Millie rang the bell and ordered tea to be brought.

"You have not changed," said she.

"Nor you."

Millie had spoken with a noticeable distance in her manner; and she had not given him her hand. With her back towards the light she had allowed very little of her expression to be visible to her visitor. When tea was brought in, however, she sat between the fireplace and the window, and the light fell upon her. Callon sat opposite to her.

"At last I know that I am at home again," he said, with a smile. Then he leaned forward and lowered his voice, although there was no third person in the room. He knew the value of such tricks. "I have looked forward during these eighteen months so very much to seeing you again."

Millie's face colored, but it was with anger rather than pleasure. There was a hard look upon her face; her eyes blamed him.

"Yet you went away without a word to me," she said. "You did not come to see me before you went, you never hinted you were going."

"You thought it unkind?"

"It was unkind," said Millie.

"But I wrote to you. I have written often."

"In no letter have you told me why you went away," said Millie.

"You missed me when I went, then?"

Millie shrugged her shoulders.

"Well, I had seen a good deal of you. I missed—I missed—something," she said. Callon drank his tea and set down his cup.

"I have come to tell you why I went away without a word. I never mentioned the reason in my letters; I meant to tell you it with my lips. I did not *go* away; I was *sent* away."

Millie was perplexed. "Sent away?" she repeated. "I understood, from what you wrote, that you accepted a post from Mr. Mudge?"

"I had to accept it," said Callon. "It was forced on me Mudge was only the instrument to get me out of the way."

"Who sent you away, then?" asked Millie.

"A friend of yours—Miss Pamela Mardale."

Millie Stretton leaned back in her chair. "Pamela!" she cried, incredulously. "Pamela sent you away! Why?"

"Because she thought that I was seeing too much of you."

Callon watched for the effect which his words would produce. He saw the change come in Millie's face. There was a new light in her eyes, her face flushed, she was angry; and anger was just the feeling he had meant to arouse, anger against Pamela, anger which would drive Millie towards him. He had kept his explanation back deliberately until he could speak it

himself. From the moment when he had started from
England he had nursed his determination to tell it to
Millie Stretton. He had been hoodwinked, outwitted
by Pamela and her friend; he had been banished to
Chile for two years. Very well. But the game was
not over yet. His vanity was hurt as nothing had
ever hurt it before. He was stung to a thirst for re-
venge. He would live frugally, clear off his debts,
return to England, and prove to his enemies the futility
of their plan. He thought of Pamela Mardale; he
imagined her hearing of his departure and dismissing
him straightway contemptuously from her thoughts.
For eighteen months he nursed his anger, and waited
for the moment when he could return. There should
be a surprise for Pamela Mardale. She should understand that he was a dangerous fellow to attack. Already within a day of his landing he had begun to
retaliate. The anger in Millie Stretton's face was of
good augury for him.

"Pamela!" cried Millie, clinching her hands together
suddenly. "Yes, it was Pamela."

She bethought her of that pressing invitation to the
south of France, an invitation from Pamela, who looked
on the shires as the only wintering-place. That was
explained now. Mr. Mudge had informed Pamela, no
doubt, that Lionel Callon was returning. Millie was
furious. She looked on this interference as a gross impertinence.

Callon rose from his chair.

"You can imagine it was humiliating to me to be
tricked and sent away. But I was helpless. I am a
poor man; I was in debt. Miss Mardale had an old, rich
man devoted to her in Mr. Mudge. He bought up my
debts, his lawyer demanded an immediate settlement

of them all, and I could not immediately settle them. I was threatened with proceedings, with bankruptcy."

"You should have come to me," cried Millie.

Callon raised a protesting hand.

"Oh, Lady Stretton, how could I?" he exclaimed in reproach. "Think for a moment! Oh, you would have offered help at a hint. I know you. You are most kind, most generous. But think, you are a woman. I am a man. Oh no!"

Callon did not mention that Mr. Mudge had compelled him to accept or refuse the post in Chile with only an hour's deliberation, and that hour between seven and eight in the evening. He had thought of calling upon Millie to suggest in her mind the offer which she had now made, but he had not had the time. He was glad now. His position was thereby so much the stronger.

"I had to accept Mudge's offer. Even the acceptance was made as humiliating as it possibly could be. For Mudge deliberately let me see that his only motive was to get me out of the country. He did not care whether I knew his motive or not. I did not count," he cried, bitterly. "I was a mere pawn upon a chessboard. I had to withdraw from my candidature. My career was spoiled. What did they care—Mr. Mudge and your friend? I was got out of your way."

"Oh, oh!" cried Millie, and Callon stepped quickly to her side.

"Imagine what these months have been to me," he went on. "I was out there in Chile, without friends. I had nothing to do. Every one else upon the railway had his work, his definite work, his definite position. I was nothing at all, a mere prisoner, in everybody's way, a man utterly befooled. But that was not the worst of it. Shall I be frank?" He made a pretence of hesitation. "I will. I will take the risk of frankness. I was sent away just when I had begun to think a great deal about you." Millie Stretton, who had been gazing into her companion's face with the utmost sympathy, lowered her eyes to the floor. But she was silent.

"That was the worst," he continued, softly. "I was angry, of course. I knew that I was losing the better part of two years—"

And Millie interrupted him: "How did she know?" she exclaimed.

"Who? Oh, Miss Mardale. Do you remember the evening she came to Whitewebs? I was waiting for you in the hall. You came down the stairs and ran up again. There was a mirror on the mantel-piece. She guessed then. Afterwards she and Mudge discussed us in the drawing-room. I saw them."

Millie got up from her chair and moved to the fireplace.

"It was on my account that you have lost two years, that your career has been hindered," she said, in a low voice. She was really hurt, really troubled. "I am so very sorry. What return can I ever make to you? I will never speak to Pamela again."

Callon crossed and stood beside her.

"No, don't do that," he said; "it would be—unwise."

Her eyes flashed up to his quickly, and as quickly fell. The color slowly deepened in her cheeks.

"What does it matter about my career?" he continued, with a smile. "I see you again. If you wish to make me a return, let me see you very often!"

He spoke with tenderness, and he was not pretend-

ing. What space did Millie Stretton fill in his thoughts?
She was pretty, she was sympathetic, she was ready to
catch the mood of her companion. It was not merely
an act of retaliation which Callon projected. Such
love as he had to give was hers. It was not durable, it
was intertwined with meanness, it knew no high aims;
yet, such as it was, it was hers. It gained, too, a fictitious
strength from the mere fact that he had been deliberately kept from her. The eighteen months of bondage
had given her an importance in his eyes, had made her
more desirable through the very difficulty of attaining
her. Millie allowed him to come again and again.
She had a natural taste for secrecies, and practised
them now, as he bade her do, without any perception
of the humiliation which they involved. If he called
at her house, it was after the dusk had fallen, and when
she was at home to no other visitors. They dined together in the restaurants of unfashionable hotels, and
if she drove to them in her brougham, she sent it away,
and was escorted to her door in a cab. Callon was a
past-master in concealment; he knew the public places
where the public never is, and rumor did not couple their
names. But secrecy is not for the secret when the
secret ones are a man and a woman. It needs too
much calculation in making appointments, too much
punctuality in keeping them, too close a dependence
upon the probable thing happening at the probable
time. Sooner or later an accident, which could not be
foreseen, occurs. It may be no more than the colli-
sion of a cab and the summons of the driver. Or some
one takes, one morning, a walk in an unaccustomed
spot. Or the intriguers fall in quite unexpectedly
with another, who has a secret too, of which they were
not aware. Sooner or later some one knows.

THE TRUANTS

It was the last of these contingencies which brought about the disclosure in the case of Callon and Millie Stretton. Six weeks had passed since Callon's return. It was just a month from Easter. Millie dined with some friends, and went with them afterwards to a theatre in the Haymarket. At the door she sent her carriage home, and when the performance was over she took a hansom-cab. She declined any escort, and was driven up Regent Street towards her home. At the corner of Devonshire Street, in Portland Place, a man loitered upon the pavement with a white scarf showing above his coat-collar. Millie opened the trap and spoke to the driver. The cab stopped by the loiterer at the street corner, who opened the doors and stepped in. The loiterer was Lionel Callon.

"Drive round Regent's Park," he said.

The cab drove northward through Park Place and along the broad road towards Alexandra Gate. The air was warm, the stars bright overhead, the dark trees lined the roadway on the left, the road under the wheels was very white. There was a great peace in the park. It was quite deserted. In a second it seemed they had come out of the glare and the roar of streets into a land of quiet and cool gloom. Millie leaned back while Callon talked, and this was the burden of his talk.

"Let us go to the south of France. I will go first. Do you follow! You go for Easter. It will be quite natural. You stay at Eze, I at the little Réserve by the sea a mile away. There is a suite of rooms there. No one need know." Three times the cab drove round the park while Callon urged, and Millie more and more faintly declined. The driver sat perched upon his box, certain of a good fare, indifferent. Inside his cab, on this quiet night, the great issues of life and honor were debated. Millie had just her life in her hands. One way or the other, by a "Yes" or a "No," she must decide what she would do with it, and, to whatever decision she came, it must reach out momentous with consequences and touch other lives beyond hers, and, beyond those others, others still. Her husband, her relations, her friends—not one of them but was concerned in this midnight drive. It seemed to Millie almost that she heard them hurrying about the cab, calling to her, reaching out their hands. So vivid was her thought that she could count them, and could recognize their faces. She looked among them for her husband. But Tony was not there. She could not see him, she could not hear his voice. Round and round past the trees, on the white road, the cab went jingling on, the driver, indifferent, upon his perch, the tempter and the tempted within.

"Your husband does not care," said Callon. "If he did, would he stay so long away?"

"No, he does not care," said Millie. If he cared, would he not be among that suppliant throng which ran about the cab? And all at once it seemed that the hurrying footsteps lagged behind. The voices called more faintly; she could not see the outstretching hands.

"No one need know," said Callon.

"*Some one always* knows," replied Millie.

"What then?" cried Callon. "If you love you will not mind. If you love you will abandon every-thing—every one. If you love!"

He had taken the right way to persuade her. Call upon Millie for a great sacrifice, she would make it, she would glory in making it, just for the moment. Disenchantment would come later; but nothing of it would

235

she foresee. As she had matched herself with Tony, when first he had proposed to leave her behind in his father's house, so now she matched herself with Callon; she felt strong.

"Very well," she said. "I will follow."

Callon stopped the cab and got out. As he closed the doors and told the cabman where to drive, a man, wretchedly clad, slouched past and turned into the Marylebone Road. That was all. Sooner or later some one was sure to discover their secret. It happened that the some one passed them by to-night.

XXII

MR. MUDGE'S CONFESSION

ON the following morning a telegram was brought to Pamela at her father's house in Leicestershire. It came from Mr. Mudge, and contained these words:

"Important that I should see you. Coming down. Please be at home at two."

Punctually Mr. Mudge arrived. Pamela received him in her own sitting-room. She was waiting with a restless anxiety, and hardly waited for the door to be closed.

"You have bad news for me," she said. "Oh, I know! You are a busy man. You would not have come down to me had you not bad news. I am very grateful for your coming, but you have bad news."

"Yes," said Mr. Mudge, gravely; "news so bad that you must ask your other friend to help you. I can do nothing here."

It cost Mr. Mudge a little to acknowledge that he was of no avail in this particular instance. He would rather have served Pamela himself, had it been possible. He was fully aware of his age and his looks and his limitations. He was quite willing to stand aside for the other friend; indeed, he wished, with all his heart, that she should be happy with some mate of her own people. But at the same time he wished her to owe as much as possible of her happiness to him. He was her friend, but there was just that element of jealousy in his friendship which springs up when the friends are man and woman. Pamela understood that it meant some abnegation on his part to bid her call upon another than himself. She was still more impressed, in consequence, with the gravity of the news he had to convey.

"Is it Mr. Callon?" she asked.

"Yes," he replied. "It is imperative that Sir Anthony Stretton should return, and return at once. Of that I am very sure."

"You have seen Mr. Callon?" asked Pamela.

"And Lady Stretton. They were together."

"When?"

"Last night. In Regent's Park."

Pamela hesitated. She was doubtful how to put her questions. She said,

"And you are sure the trouble is urgent?"

Mr. Mudge nodded his head.

"Very sure. I saw them together. I saw the look on Lady Stretton's face. It was a clear night. There was a lamp, too, in the cab. I passed them as Callon got out and said 'Good-night.'"

Pamela sat down in a chair and fixed her troubled eyes on her companion.

"Did they see you?"

Mr. Mudge smiled.

"No."

"Let me have the whole truth," cried Pamela. "Tell me the story from the beginning. How you came to see them—everything."

Mr. Mudge sat down in his turn. He presented to her a side of his character which she had not hitherto suspected. She listened, and was moved to sympathy as no complaint could ever have moved her; and Mr.

Mudge was the last man to complain. Yet the truth came out clearly. Outwardly prosperous and enviable, he had yet inwardly missed all. A man of so wide a business, so many undertakings, so occupied a life, it was natural to dissociate him from the ordinary human sympathies and desires. It seemed that he could have neither time nor inclination to indulge them. But here he was, as he had once done before, not merely admitting their existence within him, but confessing that they were far the greater part of him, and that because they had been thwarted the prosperous external life of business to which he seemed so ardently enchained was really of little account. He spoke very simply. Pamela lost sight of the business machine altogether. Here was a man, like another, telling her that through his vain ambitions his life had gone astray. She found a pathos in the dull and unimpressive look of him—his bald, uncomely head, his ungraceful figure. There was a strange contrast between his appearance and the fanciful antidote for disappointment which had brought him into Regent's Park when Callon and Lady Stretton were discussing their future course.

"I told you something of my history at Newmarket," he said. "You must remember what I told you or you will not understand."

"I remember very well," said Pamela, gently. "I think that I shall understand."

Pamela of late, indeed, had gained much understanding. Two years ago the other point of view was to her always without interest. As often as not she was unaware that it existed; when she was aware, she dismissed it without consideration. But of late her eyes had learned to soften at the troubles of others, her mind to be perplexed with their perplexities.

"Yes," said Mudge, nodding his head, with a smile, towards her. "You will understand now."

And he laid so much emphasis upon the word that Pamela looked up in surprise.

"Why now?" she asked.

"Because, recently, imagination has come to you. I have seen, I have noticed. Imagination, the power to see clearly, the power to understand—perhaps the greatest gift which love has in all his big box of gifts."

Pamela colored at his words. She neither admitted nor denied the suggestion they contained.

"I have, therefore, no fear that you will misunderstand," Mr. Mudge insisted. "I told you that my career, such as it is, has left me a very lonely man among a crowd of acquaintances who are no more in sympathy with me than I myself am in sympathy with them. I did not tell you that I had found a way of alleviation."

"No," said Pamela. She was at a loss to understand how this statement of her companion was connected with his detection of Callon and Lady Stretton; but she had no doubt there was a connection. Mudge was not of those who take a pride in disclosing the details of their life and character in and out of season. If he spoke of himself, he did so with a definite reason, which bore upon the business in hand. "No; on the contrary, you said that you could not go back and start afresh. You had too much upon your hands. You were fixed in your isolation."

"I did not even then tell you all the truth. I could not go back half-way, that is true. I do not think I would find any comfort in that course even if I could; but I can and I do go back all the way at times. I reconstruct the days when I was very, very poor, and yet full of hope, full of confidence. I do not mean that I sit in front of my fire and tell myself the story. I do much more. I actually live them over again, so far as I can. That puzzles you," he said, with a laugh.

Pamela, indeed, was looking at him with a frown of perplexity upon her forehead.

"How do you live them again?" she asked. "I don't understand."

"In this way," said Mudge. "I keep an old, worn-out suit of clothes locked up in a cupboard. Well, when I find the house too lonely, and my servants, with their noiseless tread, get on to my nerves, I just put on that suit of clothes and revisit the old haunts where I used to live forty and fifty years ago. Often I have come back from a dinner-party, let myself in at my front door, and slipped out of a side entrance half an hour later on one of my pilgrimages. You would never know me; you might toss me a shilling, that's all. Of course, I have to be careful. I am always expecting to be taken up as a thief as I slink away from the house. I would look rather a fool if that happened, wouldn't I?" and he laughed. "But it never has yet." He suddenly turned to her. "I enjoy myself upon those jaunts, you know; I really enjoy myself. I like the secrecy. To slip out of the great, silent house, to get clear away from the pictures and the furniture and the obedience, and to tramp down into the glare and the noise of the big streets, and to turn into some pothouse where once, years ago, I used to take my supper and dream of the future. It's a sort of hide-and-seek in itself." He laughed again, and then suddenly became serious. "But it's much more than that—ever so much more."

"Where do you go?" asked Pamela.

"It depends upon the time I have. If it's early I go down to Deptford, very often. I get into a tram and ride down a street where I once wandered all night because I hadn't the price of a lodging. I look at the old cookshop where I used to flatten my nose against the glass and dream that I had the run of my teeth. I get down and go into a public-house, say, with a sanded floor, and have a sausage and mash and a pot of beer, just as I was doing forty years ago when this or that scheme, which turned out well, first came into my head. But don't misunderstand," Mudge exclaimed. "I don't set off upon these visits for the satisfaction of comparing what I was then with what I have become. It is to get back to what I was then, as nearly as I can; to recapture, just for a moment, some of the high hopes, some of the anticipations of happiness to be won which I felt in those days; to forget that the happiness has never been won, that the high hopes were for things not worth the trouble spent in acquiring them. I was wet, very often hungry, always ill-clothed; but I was happy in those days, Miss Mardale, though very likely I didn't know it. I was young, the future was mine, a solid reality; and the present—why, that was a time of work and dreams. There's nothing much better than that combination, Miss Mardale—work and dreams!"

He repeated the words wistfully, and was silent for a moment. No doubt those early struggles had not been so pleasant as they appeared in the retrospect; but time had stripped them of their bitterness and left to Mr. Mudge just that part of them which was worth remembering.

"I had friends in those days," he went on. "I

wonder what has become of them all? In all my
jaunts I have never seen one."

"And where else do you go?" asked Pamela.

"Oh, many places. There's a little narrow market
between Shaftesbury Avenue and Oxford Street, where
the gas-jets flare over the barrows on a Saturday night,
and all the poor people go marketing. That's a haunt
of mine. I was some time, too, when I was young, at
work near the Marylebone Road. There's a tavern
near Madame Tussaud's where I used to go and have
supper at the counter in the public bar. Do you remember the night of Lady Millingham's reception,
when we looked out of the window and saw Sir Anthony Stretton? Well, I supped at that tavern in
the Marylebone Road on that particular night. I
was hard put to it, too, when I used to work in Marylebone. I slept for three nights in Regent's Park.
There's a coffee-stall close to the bridge, just outside
the park, on the north side."

Pamela started and Mudge nodded his head.

"Yes; that is how I came to see Lady Stretton and
Mr. Callon. A hansom-cab drove past me just as I
crossed the road to go out of the gate to the coffee-stall.
I noticed it enough to see that it held a man and a
woman in evening dress, but no more. I stayed at
the coffee-stall for a little while talking with the cab-
men and the others who were about it, and drinking
my coffee. As I returned into the park the cab drove
past me again. I thought it was the same cab, from
the casual glance I gave, and with the same people inside it. They had driven round, were still driving
round. It was a fine night, a night of spring, fresh
and cool and very pleasant. I did not wonder; I
rather sympathized with them," he said, with a smile.

"You see, I have never driven round Regent's Park at night with a woman I cared for beside me"; and again the wistful note was very audible in his voice; and he added, in a low voice, "That was not for me."

He shook the wistfulness from him and resumed.

"Well, as I reached the south side of the park, and was close by Park Place, the cab came towards me again and pulled up. Callon got out. I saw him clearly. I saw quite clearly, too, who was within the cab. So you see there is danger. Mere friends do not drive round and round Regent's Park at night."

Mr. Mudge rose and held out his hand.

"I must get back to town. I have a fly waiting to take me to the station," he said.

Pamela walked with him to the door of the house. As they stood in the hall she said:

"I thanked you, before you spoke at all, for putting your business aside for my sake and coming down to me. I thank you still more now, and for another reason. I thank you for telling me what you have told me about yourself. Such confessions "—and she smiled upon the word—"cannot be made without great confidence in the one they are made to."

"I have that confidence," said Mudge.

"I know. I am glad," replied Pamela; and she resumed: "They cannot be made, either, without creating a difference. We no longer stand where we did before they were made. I always looked upon you as my friend; but we are far greater friends now: is not that so?"

She spoke with great simplicity and feeling, her eyes glistened a little, and she added, "You are not living now with merely acquaintances around you."

Mr. Mudge took her hand.

"I am very glad that I came," he said, and, mounting into the fly, he drove away.

Pamela went back to the house and wrote out a telegram to Warrisden. She asked him to come at once to—and then she paused. Should he come here? No; there was another place, with associations for her which had now grown very pleasant and sweet to her thoughts. She asked him to meet her at the place where they had once kept tryst before—the parlor of the inn upon the hill in the village of the three poplars.

XXIII

ROQUEBRUNE REVISITED

THERE, accordingly, they met on the following afternoon. Pamela rode across the level country between the Croft Hill, which overhung her house, and the village. In front of her the three poplars pointed skyward from the ridge. She was anxious and troubled. It seemed to her that Millie Stretton was slipping beyond her reach; but the sight of those trees lightened her of some portion of her distress. She was turning more and more in her thoughts towards Warrisden whenever trouble knocked upon her door. In the moment of greatest perplexity his companionship, or even the thought of it, rested her like sleep. As she came round the bend of the road at the foot of the hill, she saw him coming down the slope towards her. She quickened her horse and trotted up to him.

"You are here already?" she said. "I am very glad. I was not sure that I had allowed you time enough."

"Oh yes," said Warrisden. "I came at once. I guessed why you wanted me from the choice of our meeting-place. We meet at Quetta on the same business which brought us together at Quetta before. Is not that so?"

"Yes," said Pamela.

They walked to the door of the inn at the top of the hill. A hostler took charge of Pamela's horse, and they went within to the parlor.

"You want me to find Stretton again?" said Warrisden.

Pamela looked at him remorsefully.

"Well, I do," she answered; and there was compunction in the tone of her voice. "I would not ask you unless the matter was very urgent. I have used you for my needs, I know, with too little consideration for you, and you very generously and willingly have allowed me to use you. So I am a little ashamed to come to you again."

Here were strange words from Pamela. They were spoken with hesitation, too, and the color burned in her cheeks. Warrisden was surprised to hear them. He laid his hand upon her arm and gave it a little affectionate shake.

"My dear, I am serving myself," he said, "just as much as I am serving you. Don't you understand that? Have you forgotten our walk under the elms in Lady Millingham's garden? If Tony returned, and returned in time, why, then you might lay your finger on the turnpike gate and let it swing open of its own accord. I remember what you said. Tony's return helps me, so I help myself in securing his return."

Pamela's face softened into a smile.

"Then you really do not mind going?" she went on. "I am remorseful, in a way, because I asked you to go once before in this very room, and nothing came of all your trouble. I want you to believe now that I could not ask you again to undergo the same trouble, or even more, as it may prove, were not the need ever so much more urgent than it was then."

"I am sorry to hear that the need is more urgent," Warrisden replied; "but, on the other hand, the trouble I shall have to bear is much less, for I know where Stretton is."

Pamela felt that half of the load of anxiety was taken from her shoulders.

"You do?" she exclaimed.

Warrisden nodded.

"And what he is doing. He is serving with the Foreign Legion in Algeria. I thought you might want to lay your hands on him again, and I wished to be ready. Chance gave me a clew—an envelope with a post-mark. I followed up the clew by securing an example of Stretton's handwriting. It was the same handwriting as that which directed the envelope, so I was sure."

"Thank you," said Pamela. "Indeed, you do not fail me," and her voice was musical with gratitude.

"He was at Ain-Sefra, a little town on the frontier of Algeria," Warrisden resumed.

And Pamela interrupted him.

"Then I need not make so heavy a demand upon you, after all," she said. "It was only a letter which I was going to ask you to carry to Tony. Now there is no necessity that you should go at all, for I can post it."

She produced the letter from a pocket of her coat as she spoke.

"Ah, but will it reach Stretton if you do?" said Warrisden.

Pamela had already seated herself at the table and was drawing the inkstand towards her. She paused at Warrisden's question and looked up.

"Surely Ain-Sefra, Algeria, will find him?"

"Will it?" Warrisden repeated. He sat down at the table opposite to her. "Even if it does, will it reach him in time? You say the need is urgent. Well, it was last summer when I saw the post-mark on the envelope, two days after we talked together in Lady Millingham's garden. I had business in London."

"I remember," said Pamela.

"My business was just to find out where Stretton was hiding himself. He was at Ain-Sefra then; he may be at Ain-Sefra now. But it is a small post, and he may not. The headquarters of the Legion are at Sidi Bel-Abbès, in the north. He may be there, or he may be altogether out of reach on some Saharan expedition."

There was yet another possibility which occurred to both their minds at this moment. It was possible that no letter would ever reach Stretton again; that Warrisden, searched he never so thoroughly, would not be able to find the man he searched for. There are so many graves in the Sahara. But neither of them spoke of this possibility, though a quick look they interchanged revealed to each its presence in the other's thoughts.

"Besides, he wanted to lie hidden. So much I know, who know nothing of his story. Would he have enlisted under his own name, do you think? Or even under his own nationality? It is not the common practice in the Foreign Legion. And that's not all. Even were he soldiering openly under his own name, how will you address your letter with any likelihood that it will reach him? Just 'La Légion Étrangère'? We want to know to what section of La Légion Étrangère he belongs. Is he chasseur, artilleryman, sapper? Perhaps he serves in the cavalry. Then which is his squadron? Is he a plain foot-soldier? Then in what battalion, and what rank does he occupy? We cannot answer any of these questions, and, unanswered, they certainly delay your letter; they may prevent it ever reaching him at all."

Pamela laid down her pen and stared blankly at Warrisden. He piled up the objections one by one in front of her until it seemed she would lose Tony once more from her sight after she had got him for a moment within her vision.

"So you had better intrust your letter to me," he concluded. "Address it to Stretton under his own name. I will find him if he is to be found, never fear. I will find him very quickly."

Pamela addressed the letter. Yet she held it for a little time in her hand after it was addressed. All the while Warrisden had been speaking she had felt an impulse strong within her to keep him back; and it was because of that impulse, rather than with any thought of Millie Stretton and the danger in which she stood, that Pamela asked, doubtfully,

"How long will you be?"

"I should find him within ten days."

Pamela smiled suddenly.

"It is not so very long," said she, and she handed the letter across to Warrisden. "Well, go!" she cried, with a certain effort. "Telegraph to me when you have found Tony. Bring him back, and come back yourself." She added, in a voice which was very low and wistful, "Please come back soon!" Then she rose from the table, and Warrisden put the letter in his pocket and rose too.

"You will be at home, I suppose, in ten days?" he said.

And Pamela said quickly, as though some new idea had just been suggested to her mind,

"Oh, wait a moment!"

She stood quite still and thoughtful. There was a certain test by which she had meant to find the soundings of her heart. Here was a good opportunity to apply the test. Warrisden would be away upon his journey; she could not help Millie Stretton now by remaining in England. She determined to apply the test.

"No," she said, slowly. "Telegraph to me at the Villa Pontignard, Roquebrune, Alpes Maritimes, France. I shall be travelling thither immediately."

Her decision was taken upon an instant. It was the logical outcome of her thoughts and of Warrisden's departure; and since Warrisden went because of Millie Stretton, Pamela's journey to the south of France was due, in a measure, to that lady, too. Yet no one would have been more astonished than Millie Stretton had she learned of Pamela's visit at this time. She would have been quick to change her own plans; but she had no knowledge of whither Pamela's thoughts were leading her. When Callon in the hansom-cab had said to her, "Come south," her first swift reflection had been, "Pamela will be safe in England." She herself had refused to go south with Pamela. Pamela's desire to go was to her mind a mere false pretext to get her away from her one friend. If she did not go south, she was very sure that Pamela would not. There had seemed to her no safer place than the Riviera. But she was wrong. Here, in the village of the three poplars, Pamela had made her decision.

"I shall go to Roquebrune as soon as I can make arrangements for a servant or two," she said.

"Roquebrune," said Warrisden, as he wrote down the address. "I once walked up a long flight of steps to that village many years ago. Perhaps you were at the villa then. I wonder. You must have been a little girl. It was one February. I came over from Monte Carlo, and we walked up from the station. We met the school-master."

"M. Giraud!" exclaimed Pamela.

"Was that his name? He had written a little history of the village and the Corniche road. He took me under his wing. We went into a wine-shop on the first floor of a house in the middle of the village, and we sat there quite a long time. He asked us about Paris and London with an eagerness which was quite pathetic. He came down with us to the station, and his questions never ceased. I suppose he was lonely there."

Pamela nodded her head.

"Very. He did not sleep all night for thinking of what you had told him."

"You were there, then?" cried Warrisden.

"Yes; M. Giraud used to read French with me. He came to me one afternoon quite feverish. Two Englishmen had come up to Roquebrune, and had talked to him about the great towns and the lighted streets. He was always dreaming of them. Poor man, he is at Roquebrune still, no doubt."

She spoke with a great tenderness and pity, looking out of the window, and for the moment altogether lost to her surroundings. Warrisden roused her from her reverie.

"I must be going away."

Pamela's horse was brought to the door and she mounted.

"Walk down the hill beside my horse," she said; "just as you did on that other day, when the hill was slippery, your hand upon his neck—so."

Very slowly they walked down the hill. There were no driving mists to-day, the evening was coming with a great peace, the fields and woods lay spread beneath them toned to a tranquil gray. The white road glimmered. At the bottom of the hill Pamela stopped.

"Good-bye," she said, and there was more tenderness in her voice and in her face than he had ever known. She laid her hand upon his arm and bent down to him.

"Come back to me," she said, wistfully. "I do not like letting you go; and yet I am rather proud to know that you are doing something for me which I could not do for myself, and that you do it so very willingly."

She did not wait to hear any answer, but took her hand from his arm and rode quickly away. That turnpike gate of friendship had already swung open of its own accord. As she rode from Quetta that evening, she passed beyond it and went gratefully and hopefully, with the other men and women, down the appointed road.

She knew it while she was riding homeward to the Croft Hill. She knew it and was very glad. She rode home very slowly through the tranquil evening and gave herself up to joy. It was warm, and there was a freshness in the air as though the world renewed itself. Darkness came; only the road glimmered ahead of her—the new road, which was the old road. Even that glimmer of white had almost vanished when at last she saw the lighted windows of her father's house. The footman told her that dinner was already served, but she ran past him very quickly up the stairs, and coming to her own room locked the door and sat for a long while in the darkness, her blood throbbing in her veins, her whole heart uplifted, not thinking at all, but just living, and living most joyfully. She sat so still that she might have been in a swoon; but it was the stillness of perfect happiness. She knew the truth that night.

But, none the less, she travelled south towards the end of the week, since there a telegram would come to her. She reached the Villa Pontignard in the afternoon, and walked through the familiar rooms which she had so dreaded ever to revisit. She went out to the narrow point of the garden where so often she had dreamed with M. Giraud of the outside world, its roaring cities and its jostle of people. She sat down upon the parapet. Below her the cliff fell sheer, and far below, in the darkness at the bottom of the gorge, the water tumbled in foam with a distant hum. On the opposite hill the cypresses stood out black from the brown and green. Here she had suffered greatly, but the wounds were healed. These dreaded places had no longer power to hurt. She knew that very surely. She was emancipated from sorrow, and as she sat there in the still, golden afternoon, the sense of freedom ran riot in her blood. She looked back over the years to the dragging days of misery, the sleepless nights. She felt a pity for the young girl who had then looked down from this parapet and prayed for death; who had counted the many years of life in front of her; who had bewailed her very strength and health. But ever her eyes turned towards the Mediterranean and searched the horizon. For beyond that blue, calm sea stretched the coasts of Algeria.

There was but one cloud to darken Pamela's happiness during these days while she waited for Warrisden's telegram. On the morning after she had arrived, the old curé climbed from the village to visit her. Almost Pamela's first question was of M. Giraud.

"He is still here?"

"Yes, he is still here," replied the curé, but he pursed up his lips and shook his head.

"I must send for him," said Pamela.

The curé said nothing. He was standing by the window, and almost imperceptibly he shrugged his shoulders as though he doubted her wisdom. In a moment Pamela was at his side.

"What is it?" she asked, gently. "Tell me."

"Oh, mademoiselle, there is little to tell! He is not the school-master you once knew. That is all. The wine-shop has made the difference—the wine-shop and discontent. He was always dissatisfied, you know. It is a pity."

"I am so sorry," said Pamela, gravely, "so very sorry."

She was silent for a while, and greatly troubled by the curé's news.

"Has he married?" she asked.

"No."

"It would have been better if he had."

"No doubt, mademoiselle," said the curé, "but he has not, and I think it is now too late."

Pamela did not send for M. Giraud. It seemed to her that she could do no good even if at her request he came to her. She would be going away in a few days. She would only hurt him and put him to shame before her. She took no step towards a renewal of their friendship, and, though she did not avoid him, she never came across him in her walks.

For ten days she walked the old hill-paths, and dreams came to her with the sunlight. They gave her company in the evenings, too, when she looked from her garden upon the quiet sea and saw, away upon the right, the lights, like great jewels, burning on the terrace of Monte Carlo. She went down one morning onto that terrace, and, while seated upon a bench, suddenly saw, at a little distance, the back of a man which was familiar to her.

She was not sure, but she was chilled with apprehension. She watched from behind her newspaper, and in a little while she was sure, for the man turned and showed his face. It was Lionel Callon. What was he doing here, she asked herself. And another question trod fast upon the heels of the first — "Was he alone?"

Callon was alone on this morning, at all events. Pamela saw him speak to one or two people and then mount the terrace steps towards the town. She gave him a little time, and then, walking through the gardens, bought a visitors' list at the kiosk in front of the rooms. She found Callon's name. He was the only visitor at a reserve, on the Corniche road, which was rather a restaurant than a hotel. She searched through the list, fearing to find the name of Millie Stretton under the heading of some other hotel. To her relief it was not there. It was possible, of course, that Callon was merely taking a holiday by himself. She wished to believe that, and yet there was a fear speaking loudly at her heart. "Suppose that Tony should return too late just by a few days!" She was still holding the paper in her hands when she heard her name called, and, turning about, saw some friends. She lunched with them at Ciro's, and asked, carelessly, during luncheon,

"You have not seen Millie Stretton, I suppose?"

"THE MAN TURNED AND SHOWED HIS FACE. IT WAS LIONEL
CALLON"

"No," they all replied. And one asked: "Is she expected?"

"I don't know whether she will come or not," Pamela replied. "I asked her to come with me, but she could not do that, and she was not sure that she would come at all."

This she said, thinking that if Millie did arrive it might seem that she came because Pamela herself was there. Pamela went back to Roquebrune that afternoon, and, after she had walked through the village and had come out on the slope of hill above, she met the postman coming down from the Villa Pontignard.

"You have a telegram for me?" she said, anxiously.

"Mademoiselle," he replied, "I have just left it at the house."

Pamela hurried on, and found the telegram in the *salon*. She tore it open. It was from Warrisden. It told her that Tony Stretton was found, and would return. It gave the news in vague and guarded language, mentioning no names. But Pamela understood the message. Tony Stretton was actually coming back. "Would he come too late?" she asked, gazing out in fear across the sea. Of any trouble, out there in Algeria, which might delay his return, she did not think at all. If it was true that he had enlisted in the Legion, there might be obstacles to a quick return. But such matters were not in her thoughts. She thought only of Callon upon the terrace of Monte Carlo. "Would Tony come too late?" she asked; and she prayed that he might come in time.

17

XXIV

THE END OF THE EXPERIMENT

THE village of Ain - Sefra stands upon a high and fertile oasis on the very borders of Morocco. The oasis is well watered, and the date-palm grows thickly there. It lies far to the south. The railway, in the days when Tony Stretton served in the Foreign Legion, did not reach to it; the barracks were newly built, the parade-ground newly enclosed; and if one looked southward from any open space, one saw a tawny belt of sand in the extreme distance streak across the horizon from east to west. That is the beginning of the great Sahara. Tony Stretton could never see that belt of sand but his thoughts went back to the terrible homeward march from Bir-el-Gharamo to Ouargla. From east to west the Sahara stretched across Africa, breaking the soldiers who dared to violate its privacy, thrusting them back maimed and famine-stricken, jealously guarding its secrets, and speaking, by its very silence, its terrible "thus far and no farther," no less audibly and a thousand times more truthfully than ever did the waves of the sea.

On one noonday Stretton mounted the steps onto the veranda of the hospital. He looked across open country to the great yellow line. He thought of the Touaregs hanging persistently upon the flanks of his tiny force, the long, laborious days of thirst and hunger, the lengthening trail of graves which he left be-

hind — those mile-stones of invasion. He felt as
though the desert gripped him again and would not
loose its hold, clinging to his feet with each step he
took in the soft, yielding sand. He had brought back
his handful of men, it was true; they had stumbled
into Ouargla at the last, but there were few of them
who were men as good as they had been when they had
set out. Even the best, it almost seemed to him, had
lost something of vitality which they would never recover; had a look fixed in their eyes which set them
apart from their fellows—the look of those who have
endured too much, who gazed for too long a time upon
horrors; while the others were for the most part only
fit to squat in the shade and to wait for things to cease.
There was one whom Stretton had passed only a minute before sitting on the ground under the shadow of
the barrack-wall. Stretton was haunted by the picture of that man, for he was the only white man he had
ever seen who did not trouble to raise a hand to brush
away the flies from his face, but allowed them to settle
and cluster about the corners of his mouth.

There was another in the hospital behind him. Him
the Sahara definitely claimed. Stretton turned and
walked into the building.

He passed down the line of beds, and stopped where a
man lay tossing in a fever. Stretton leaned over the bed.

"Barbier," he said.

Fusilier Barbier had grown very gaunt and thin during these latter weeks. He turned his eyes upon
Stretton, and muttered incoherently. But there was
recognition neither in his eyes nor in his voice. An
orderly approached the bed as Stretton stood beside it;
and, in a low voice, lest, haply, Barbier should hear
and understand, Tony asked:

"What did the doctor say?"

"Nothing good, my sergeant," the orderly replied, with an expressive shrug of the shoulders.

"I am very sorry," said Stretton, gravely.

Certainly Barbier looked to be lying at death's door. One hand and arm, emaciated and the color of wax, lay outside upon the coverlet of the bed. His eyes, unnaturally lustrous, unnaturally large, shone deep-sunken in dark, purple rings. His eyelids were red, as though with much weeping, and, below the eyes, his face was drawn with fever and very white. Stretton laid his hand gently upon Barbier's forehead. It was burning hot. Stretton dismissed the orderly with a nod. There was a haggard nobility in Barbier's appearance—his long, finely shaped hands, his lithe, well-knit figure, all betrayed the man of race. Yet he had once sunk to babbling about persecution at a fire in the desert, like any morbid child.

A heavy step sounded in the ward, and Stretton's colonel stood beside him, a stoutly built man, with a white mustache and imperial, and a stern yet not unkindly face. It expressed a deal of solicitude at this moment.

"I have seen the doctor this morning," said the colonel, "and he has given up hope. Barbier will hardly live out the night. They should never have sent him to us here. They should not have discharged him from the asylum as cured."

The idea of persecution had become fixed in Barbier's brain. It had never left him since the evening when he first gave utterance to it in the desert. The homeward march, indeed, had aggravated his mania. On his return he had been sent to the asylum at Bel-Abbès, but there he had developed cunning enough to conceal his hallucination. He had ceased to complain that his officers were in a conspiracy to entrap and ruin him, no more threats were heard, no more dangerous, stealthy glances detected. He was sent back to his battalion at Ain-Sefra. A few weeks and again his malady was manifest, and on the top of that had come fever.

"I am very sorry," Stretton said again; and then, after looking about him and perceiving that the orderly was out of earshot, he bent down towards Barbier, lower than he had bent before, and he called upon him in a still lower voice.

But Barbier was no longer the name he used.

"Monsieur le Comte," he said, first of all, and then "Monsieur de—" He uttered a name which the generation before had made illustrious in French diplomacy.

At the sound of the name Barbier's face contracted. He started up in his bed upon one arm.

"Hush!" he cried. A most extraordinary change had come over him in a second. His eyes protruded, his mouth hung half open, his face was frozen into immobility by horror. "There is some one on the stairs," he whispered, "coming up—some one treading very lightly—but coming up—coming up." He inclined his head in the strained attitude of one listening with a great concentration and intentness, an image of terror and suspense. "Yes, coming up—coming up! Don't lock the door! That betrays all. Turn out the lights! Quickly! So. Oh, will this night ever pass!"

He ended with a groan of despair. Very gently Stretton laid him down again in the bed and covered him over with the clothes. The sweat rolled in drops from Barbier's forehead.

"He never tells us more, my colonel," said Stretton.
"His real name—yes!—he betrayed that once to me.
But of this night nothing more than the dread that it
will never pass. Always he ends with those words.
Yet it was that night, no doubt, which tossed him be-
yond the circle of his friends and dropped him down
here, a man without a name, among the soldiers of the
Legion."

Often Stretton's imagination had sought to pierce the
mystery. What thing of horror had been done upon
that night? In what town of France? Had the some
one on the stairs turned the handle and entered the
room when all the lights were out? Had he heard Barbier's breathing in the silent darkness of the room?
Stretton could only reconstruct the scene. The
stealthy footsteps on the stairs, the cautious turning
of the door handle, the opening of the door, and the
impenetrable blackness, with one man, perhaps more
than one, holding his breath somewhere and crouching by the wall. But no hint escaped the sick man's
lips of what there was which must needs be hidden,
nor whether the thing which must needs be hidden
was discovered by the one who trod so lightly on the
stairs. Was it a dead man? Was it a dead woman?
Or a woman alive? There was no answer. There
was no knowledge to be gained, it seemed, but this—
that because of that night a man in evening dress,
who bore an illustrious name, had fled at daybreak
on a summer morning to the nearest barracks, and
had buried his name and all of his past life in the Foreign Legion.

As it happened, there was just a little more knowledge to be gained by Stretton. He learned it that
morning from his colonel.

"When you told me who 'Barbier' really was, sergeant," said the colonel, "I made inquiries. Barbier's father died two years ago; but an uncle and a sister lived. I wrote to both, offering to send their relation back to them. Well, the mail has this morning come in from France.

"There is an answer, sir?" asked Stretton.

"From the uncle," replied the colonel. "Not a word from the sister; she does not mean to write. The uncle's letter makes that clear, I think. Read!" He handed the letter to Stretton. A check was enclosed, and a few words were added.

"See, if you please, that Barbier wants for nothing which can minister to body and soul."

That was all. There was no word of kindliness or affection. Barbier was dying. Let him, therefore, have medicine and prayers. Love, wishes for recovery, a desire that he should return to his friends, forgiveness for the thing which he had done, pity for the sufferings which had fallen to him—these things Fusilier Barbier must not expect. Stretton, reading the letter by the sick man's bed, thought it heartless and callous as no letter written by a human hand had ever been. Yet—yet, after all, who knew what had happened on that night? The uncle, evidently. It might be something which dishonored the family beyond all reparation; which, if known, would have disgraced a great name, so that those who bore it in pride must now change it for very shame. Perhaps the father had died because of it, perhaps the sister had been stricken down. Stretton handed the letter back to his colonel.

"It is very sad, sir," he said.

"Yes, it is very sad," returned the colonel. "But

for us this letter means nothing at all. Never speak of it; obliterate it from your memory." He tore the paper into the tiniest shreds. "We have no reproaches, no accusations for what Barbier did before Barbier got out of the train at Sidi Bel-Abbès. That is not our affair. For us the soldier of the Legion is only born on the day when he enlists."

Thus, in one sentence, the colonel epitomized the character of the Foreign Legion. It was a fine saying, Stretton thought. He knew it to be a true one.

"I will say nothing," said Stretton, "and I will forget."

"That is well. Come with me, for there is another letter which concerns you."

He turned upon his heel and left the hospital. Stretton followed him to his quarters.

"There is a letter from the War Office which concerns you, Sergeant Ohlsen," said the colonel, with a smile. "You will be gazetted, under your own name, to the first lieutenancy which falls vacant. There is the notification."

He handed the paper over to Stretton and shook hands with him. Stretton was not a demonstrative man. He took the notification with no more show of emotion than if it had been some unimportant order of the day.

"Thank you, sir," he said, quietly, and for a moment his eyes rested on the paper.

But, none the less, the announcement, so abruptly made, caused him a shock. The words danced before his eyes so that he could not read them. He saluted his colonel and went out onto the great open parade-ground, and stood there in the middle of that space, alone, under the hot noonday sun.

THE TRUANTS

The thing for which he had striven had come to pass, then. He held the assurance of it in his hand. Hoped for and half expected as that proof had been ever since he had led the survivors of the geographical expedition under the gate of Ouargla, its actual coming was to him most wonderful. He looked southward to where the streak of yellow shone far away. The long marches, the harassing anxiety, the haunting figures of the Touaregs, with their faces veiled in their black masks and their eyes shining between the upper and the lower strip — yes, even those figures which appalled the imagination in the retrospect by a suggestion of inhuman ferocity—what were they all but contributories to this event? His ordeal was over. He had done enough. He could go home.

Stretton did not want for modesty. He had won a commission from the ranks, it is true; but he realized that others had done this before, and under harder conditions. He himself had started with an advantage—the advantage of previous service in the English army. His knowledge of the manual exercise, of company and battalion drill, had been of the greatest use at the first. He had had luck, too—the luck to be sent on the expedition to the Figuig oasis, the luck to find himself sergeant with Captain Tavernay's force. His heart went out in gratitude to that true friend who lay in his bed of sand so far away. Undoubtedly, he realized, his luck had been exceptional.

He turned away from the parade-ground and walked through the village, and out of it towards a grove of palm-trees. Under the shade of those trees he laid himself down on the ground and made out his plans. He would obtain his commission, secure his release, and so go home. A few months and he would be home!

THE TRUANTS

It seemed hardly credible; yet it was true, miraculously true. He would write home that very day. It was not any great success which he had achieved, but, at all events, he was no longer the man who was no good. He could write with confidence; he could write to Millie.

He lay under the shadow of the palms looking across to the village. There rose a little mosque with a white dome. The hovels were thatched for the most part, but here and there a square, whitewashed house, with a flat roof, overtopped the rest. Hedges of cactus and prickly-pears walled in the narrow lanes, and now and then a white robe appeared and vanished. Very soon Stretton would turn his back upon Algeria. In the after-time he would remember this afternoon, remember the village as he saw it now, and the yellow streak of desert sand in the distance.

Stretton lay on his back and put together the sentences which he would write that day to Millie. She would get the letter within ten days—easily. He began to hum over to himself the words of the coon song which had once been sung on a summer night in an island of Scotland:

"'Oh, come out, mah love. I'm a-waitin' fo' you heah!
Doan' you keep yuh window shut to-night.
De tree-tops above am a-whisp'rin' to you, deah—'"

And then he stopped suddenly. At last he began to wonder how Millie would receive the letter he was to write.

Yes, there was her point of view to be considered. Stretton was stubborn by nature as few men are. He had convinced himself that the course he had taken was the only course which promised happiness for

Millie and himself, and, impelled by that conviction, he had gone on his way undisturbed by doubts and questions. Now, however, his object was achieved. He could claim exemption from his wife's contempt. His mind had room for other thoughts, and they came that afternoon.

He had left his wife alone, with no explanation of his absence to offer to her friends, without even any knowledge of his whereabouts. There had been no other way, he still believed. But it was hard on Millie—undoubtedly it was hard.

Stretton rose from the ground and set off towards the camp that he might write his letter. But he never wrote it, for as he walked along the lane towards the barracks a man tapped him on the shoulder from behind. He was still humming his song, and he stopped in the middle of it:

"'Jus' look out an' see all de longin' in mah eyes,
An' mah arms is jus' a-pinin' foh to hug you,'"

he said, and turned about on his heel. He saw a stranger in European dress, who at once spoke his name.

"Sir Anthony Stretton?"

Stretton was no longer seeking to evade discovery.

"Yes," he said. The stranger's face became vaguely familiar to him. "I have seen you before, I think."

"Once," replied the other. "My name is Warrisden. You saw me for a few minutes on the deck of a fish-carrier in the North Sea."

"To be sure," he said, slowly. "Yes, to be sure, I did. You were sent to find me by Miss Pamela Mardale."

"She sends me again," replied Warrisden.

Stretton's heart sank in fear. He had disobeyed the summons before. He remembered Pamela's promise to befriend his wife. He remembered her warning that he should not leave his wife.

"She sent you then with an urgent message that I should return home," he said.

"I carry the same message again, only it is a thousand times more urgent."

He drew a letter from his pocket as he spoke and handed it to Stretton. "I was to give you this," he said.

Stretton looked at the handwriting and nodded.

"Thank you," he said, gravely.

He tore open the envelope and read.

XXV

TONY STRETTON BIDS FAREWELL TO THE LEGION

IT was a long letter. Tony read it through slowly, standing in the narrow lane between the high walls of prickly-pear. A look of incredulity came upon his face.

"Is all this true?" he asked, not considering at all of whom he asked the question.

"I know nothing, of course, of what is written there," replied Warrisden; "but I do not doubt its truth. The signature is, I think, sufficient guarantee."

"No doubt, no doubt," said Stretton, absently. Then he asked:

"When did you reach Ain-Sefra?"

"This morning."

"And you came quickly?"

"Yes; I travelled night and day. I came first of all to Ain-Sefra in search of you."

"Thank you," said Stretton.

He did not ask how it was that Warrisden had come first of all to Ain-Sefra; such details held no place in his thoughts. Warrisden *had* found him, *had* brought the letter which Pamela Mardale had written. That letter, with its perplexities and its consequences, obliterated all other speculations.

"You have a camp here?" Stretton asked.

"Yes."

"Let us go to it. The news you have brought has rather stunned me. I should like to sit down and think what I must do."

The incredulity had vanished from his face. Distress had replaced it.

"It is all true, no doubt," he went on, "but for the moment I don't understand it. Will you tell me where your camp is?"

"I will show you the way," said Warrisden

"I think not. It will be better that we should not be seen together," Stretton said, thoughtfully. "Will you give me the direction and go first? I will follow."

Warrisden's camp was pitched among trees a hundred yards from the western borders of the village. It stood in a garden of grass, enclosed with hedges. Thither Stretton found his way by a roundabout road, approaching the camp from the side opposite to Ain-Sefra. There was no one, at the moment, loitering about the spot. He walked into the garden. There were three tents pitched. Half a dozen mules stood picketed in a line, a little Barbary horse lay on the grass, some Algerian muleteers were taking their ease, and outside the chief tent a couple of camp-chairs were placed. Warrisden came forward as Stretton entered the garden.

"Sit down," he said.

"Inside the tent, I think," replied Stretton.

There he read the letter through again. He understood at last what Pamela had meant by the warning which had baffled him. Pamela revealed its meaning now. "Millie is not of those women," she wrote, "who have a vivid remembrance. To hold her, you must be near her. Go away, she will cry her eyes out; stay away for a little while, she will long for your return;

make that little while a longer time, she will grow indifferent whether you return or not; prolong that longer time, she will regard your return as an awkwardness, a disturbance; add yet a little more to that longer time, and you will find another occupying your place in her thoughts." Then followed an account of the growth of that dangerous friendship between Millie and Lionel Callon. A summary of Callon's character rounded the description off. "So come home," she concluded, "at once, for no real harm has been done yet."

Stretton understood what the last sentence meant, and he believed it. Yet his mind revolted against the phrase. Of course, it was Pamela's phrase. Pamela, though frank, was explaining the position in words which could best spare Millie. But it was an unfortunate sentence. It provoked a momentary wave of disgust, which swept over Stretton. There was a postscript: "You yourself are really a good deal to blame." Thus it ran; but Stretton was in no mood to weigh its justice or injustice at the moment. Only this afternoon he had been lying under the palm-trees putting together in his mind the sentences which were to tell Millie of his success, to re-establish him in her esteem, and to prepare her for his return. And now this letter had come. He sat for a time frowning at the letter, turning its pages over, glancing now at one phrase, now at another. Then he folded it up. "Callon," he said, softly; and then again, "Lionel Callon. I will talk with Mr. Callon." For all its softness, his voice sounded to Warrisden the voice of a dangerous man. And after he had spoken in this way he sat in thought, saying nothing, making no movement, and his face gave Warrisden no clew as to what he thought. At the last he stirred in his chair.

"Well?" said Warrisden.

"I shall return at once to England.'

"You can?"

"Yes; I shall start to-night," said Stretton.

"We can go back together, then."

"No; that's impossible."

"Why?" asked Warrisden.

"Because I should be arrested if we did," Stretton replied, calmly.

"Arrested?" Warrisden exclaimed.

"Yes; you see I shall have to desert to-night."

Warrisden started from his chair.

"Surely there is an alternative?"

"None," replied Stretton; and Warrisden slowly resumed his seat. He was astounded; he had never contemplated this possibility. He looked at Stretton in wonder. He could not understand how a man could speak so calmly of such a plan. Why in the world had Stretton ever joined the Legion if he was so ready, at the first summons, to desert? There seemed an inconsistency. But he did not know Tony Stretton.

"You are surprised," said Tony. "More than surprised—you are rather shocked; but there is no choice for me. I wish with all my heart and soul there were," he suddenly exclaimed, with a sort of passion. "I have foreseen this necessity ever since you tapped me on the shoulder in the lane. Because I foresaw it, I would not walk with you to your camp. Were we seen together to-day, the reason of my absence might be the sooner suspected. As it is, I shall get a day's start, for I have a good name in the regiment, and a day's start is all I need."

He spoke sadly and wistfully. He was caught by

an inexorable fate, and knew it. He just had to accept the one course open to him.

"You see," he explained, "I am a soldier of the Legion—that is to say, I enlisted for five years' service in the French colonies. I could not get leave."

"Five years!" cried Warrisden. "You meant to stay five years away?"

"No," replied Stretton. "If things went well with me here, as up till to-day they have done—if, in a word, I did what I enlisted to do—I should have gone to work to buy myself out and get free. That can be done with a little influence and time—only time is the one thing I have not now. I must go home at once, since no harm has yet been done. Therefore I must desert. I am very sorry"—and again the wistfulness became very audible—"for, as I say, I have a good name; among both officers and men I have a good name. I should have liked very much to have left a good name behind me. Sergeant Ohlsen"—and as he uttered the name he smiled. "They speak well of Sergeant Ohlsen in the Legion, Warrisden; and to-morrow they will not. I am very sorry. I have good friends among both officers and men. I shall have lost them all to-morrow. I am sorry. There is only one thing of which I am glad to-day. I am glad that Captain Tavernay is dead."

Warrisden knew nothing at all of Captain Tavernay. Until this moment he had never heard his name. But Stretton was speaking with a simplicity so sincere, and so genuine a sorrow, that Warrisden could not but be deeply moved. He forgot the urgency of his summons; he ceased to think how greatly Stretton's immediate return would help his own fortunes. He cried out upon the impulse:

"Stay, then, until you can get free without—" And he stopped, keeping unspoken the word upon his lips.

"Without disgrace."

Stretton finished the sentence with a smile.

"Say it! Without disgrace. That was the word upon your tongue. I can't avoid disgrace. I have come to such a pass in my life's history that, one way or another, I can't avoid it. I thought just at the first moment that I could let things slide and stay. But there's dishonor in that course, too. Dishonor for myself, dishonor for my name, dishonor for others, too, whom it is my business — yes, my business — to keep from dishonor. That's the position—disgrace if I stay, disgrace if I go. It seems to me there's no rule of conduct which applies. I must judge for myself."

Stretton spoke with some anger in his voice, anger with those who had placed him in so cruel a position, anger, perhaps, in some measure, with himself. For in a little while he said:

"It is quite true that I am myself to blame, too. I want to be just. I was a fool not to have gone into the house the evening I was in London, after I had come back from the North Sea. Yes, I should have gone in then; and yet—I don't know. I had thought my course all out. I don't know."

He had thought his course out, it is true; but he had thought it out in ignorance of his wife's character. That was the trouble, as he clearly saw now.

"Anyhow, I must go to-night," he said, rising from his chair. In an instant he had become the practical man, arranging the means to an end already resolved upon.

"I can borrow money of you?"

"Yes."

"And a mule?"

"Yes."

"Let me choose my mule."

They walked from the tent to where the mules stood picketed. Warrisden pointed to one in the middle of the line.

"That is the strongest."

"I don't want one too strong, too obviously well-fed," said Stretton; and he selected another. "Can I borrow a muleteer for an hour or two?'

"Of course," said Warrisden.

Stretton called a muleteer towards him and gave him orders.

"There is a market to-day," he said. "Go to it and buy." He enumerated the articles he wanted, ticking them off upon his fingers—a few pairs of scissors and some knives, a few gaudy silk handkerchiefs, one or two cheap clocks, some pieces of linen, needles and thread —in fact, a small peddler's pack of wares. In addition, a black jellaba and cap, such as the Jews must wear in Morocco, and a native's underclothes and slippers.

"Bring these things back to the camp at once and speak to no one," said Stretton.

The muleteer loosed a mule to carry the packages, and went off upon his errand. Stretton and Warrisden went back to the tent. Stretton sat down again in his chair, took a black cigarette from a bright-blue packet which he had in his pocket, and lighted it, as though all the arrangements for his journey were now concluded.

"I want you to pack the mule I chose with the things which your muleteer brings back. Add some barley for the mule and some food for me, and bring it with the clothes to the southwest corner of the barrack-

wall at eight. It will be dark then. Don't come before it is dark, and wait for me at the corner. Will
you?"

"Yes," replied Warrisden. "You are going to
tramp to the coast? Surely you can come as one of
my men as far as the rail-head. Then I will go on and
wait for you at Algiers."

"No," said Stretton; "our ways lie altogether apart.
It would be too dangerous for me to tramp through
Algeria. I should certainly be stopped. That's my
way."

He raised his arm and pointed through the tent
door.

The tent door faced the west, and in front there rose
a range of mountains, dark and lofty, ridge overtop-
ping ridge, and wonderfully distinct. In that clear
air the peaks and gaps, and jagged *arêtes* were all sharply defined. The sun was still bright, and the dark
cliffs had a purple bloom of extraordinary softness and
beauty, like the bloom upon a ripe plum. Here and
there the mountains were capped with snow, and the
snow glistened like silver.

"Those mountains are in Morocco," said Stretton.
"That's my way—over them. My only way. We
are on the very edge of Morocco here."

"But, once over the border," Warrisden objected,
"are you safe in Morocco?"

"Safe from recapture."

"But safe in no other sense?"

Stretton shrugged his shoulders.

"It is a bad road, I know—dangerous and difficult.
The ordinary traveller cannot pass along it. But it
has been traversed. Prisoners have escaped that way
to Fez—Escoffier, for instance. Deserters have reach-

ed their homes by following it—some of them, at all events. One must take one's risks."

It was the old lesson learned upon the ketch *Perseverance* which Stretton now repeated; and not vainly learned. Far away to the south, in the afternoon sunlight, there shone that yellow streak of sand beyond which its value had been surely proved. Warrisden's thoughts were carried back on a sudden to that morning of storm and foam and roaring waves when Stretton had stood easily upon the deck of the fish-cutter, with the great seas swinging up behind him, and had, for the first time, uttered it in Warrisden's hearing. Much the same feeling came over Warrisden as that which had then affected him—a feeling almost of inferiority. Stretton was a man of no more than average ability, neither a deep thinker, nor a person of ingenuity and resource; but the mere stubbornness of his character gave to him at times a certain grandeur. In Warrisden's eyes he had that grandeur now. He had come quickly to his determination to desert, but he had come calmly to it. There had been no excitement in his manner, no suggestion of hysteria. He had counted up the cost, he had read his letter, he had held the balance between his sacrifice and Millie's necessity; and he had decided. He had decided, knowing not merely the disgrace, but the difficulties of his journey and the danger of his road among the wild, lawless tribes in that unsettled quarter of Morocco. Again Warrisden was carried away. He forgot even Pamela at Roquebrune waiting for the telegram he was to send from Oran on his return. He cried:

"I will send back my outfit and come with you. If we travel together there will be more safety."

Stretton shook his head.

"Less," said he. "You cannot speak Mogrhebbin. I have a few sentences—not many, but enough. I know something of these tribes, too. For I once marched to the Figuig oasis. Your company would be no protection; rather it would be an extra danger."

Warrisden did not press his proposal. Stretton had so clearly made up his mind.

"Very well," he said. "You have a revolver, I suppose. Or shall I lend you one?"

And, to Warrisden's astonishment, Stretton replied: "I shall carry no weapons."

Warrisden was already placing his arms of defence upon the table so that Stretton might make his choice.

"No weapons!" he exclaimed.

"No. My best chance to get through to Fez is to travel as a Jew peddler. That is why I am borrowing your mule and have sent your muleteer to the market. A Jew can go in Morocco where no Moor can, for he is not suspected; he is merely despised. Besides, he brings things for sale which are needed. He may be robbed and beaten, but he has more chance of reaching his journey's end in some plight or other than any one else."

Thereafter he sat for a while silent, gazing towards the mountains in the west. The snow glittering upon the peaks brought back to his mind the flashing crystals in the great salt lakes. It was at just such a time, on just such an afternoon, when the two companies of the Legion had marched out from the trees of the high plateaux into the open desert, with its gray-green carpet of halfa-grass. Far away the lake had flashed like an arc of silver set in the ground. Stretton could not but remember that expedition and compare it with the one upon which he was now to start; and the comparison was full of bitterness. Then high hopes had reigned. The companies were marching out upon the Legion's special work; even if disaster overtook them, disaster would not be without its glory. Stretton heard the clear, inspiriting music of the bugles, he listened to the steady tramp of feet. Now he was deserting.

"I shall miss the Legion," he said, regretfully. "I had no idea how much I should miss it until this moment."

Its proud past history had grown dear to him. The recklessness of its soldiers, the endless, perplexing variety of their characters, the secrets of their lives, of which every now and then, in a rare moment of carelessness, a glimpse was revealed, as though a curtain were raised and lowered—all these particular qualities of the force had given to it a grip upon his affections of which he felt the full strength now.

"Any other life," he said, "cannot but be a little dull, a little uninteresting afterwards. I shall miss the Legion very much."

Suddenly he put his hand into his pocket and took out of it that letter from the French War Office which his colonel had handed to him. "Look!" and he handed it over to Warrisden. "That is what I joined the Legion to win—a commission; and I have just not won it. In a month or two, perhaps in a week, perhaps even tomorrow, it might have been mine. Very soon I should have been back at home, the life I have dreamed of and worked for ever since I left London might have been mine to live. It was to have been a good life of great happiness"— he had forgotten, it seemed, that he would regret the Legion—"a life without a flaw. Now that life's impossible, and I am a deserter. It's hard lines, isn't it?"

He rose from his chair, and looked for a moment at Warrisden in silence.

"I am feeling sorry that I ever came," said Warrisden.

"Oh no," Stretton answered, with a smile. "It would have been still worse if I had stayed here, ignorant of the news you have brought me, and had come home in my own time. Things would have been much worse — beyond all remedy. Do you know a man named Callon—Lionel Callon?" he asked, abruptly. And before Warrisden could answer the blood rushed into his face and he exclaimed: "Never mind; don't answer! Be at the corner of the barracks with the mule at eight." And he went from the tent, cautiously made his way out of the garden, and returned to his quarters.

A few minutes before eight Warrisden drove the mule, packed with Stretton's purchases, to the southwestern corner of the barracks. The night was dark, no one was abroad, the place without habitations. He remained under the shadow of the high wall, watching this way and that for Stretton's approach; and in a few minutes he was almost startled out of his wits by a heavy body falling from the top of the wall upon the ground at his side. Warrisden, indeed, was so taken by surprise that he uttered a low cry.

"Hush!" said a voice close to the ground. "It's only me."

And Stretton rose to his feet. He had dropped from the summit of the wall.

"Are you hurt?" whispered Warrisden.

"No. Have you the clothes? Thanks!"

Stretton stripped off his uniform, and put on the Jewish dress. He had shaved off his mustache and blackened his hair. As he dressed he gave two or three small packages to Warrisden.

"Place them in the pack; hide them, if possible. That package contains my medals. I shall need them. The other's lamp - black. I shall want that for my hair. Glossy raven locks," he said, with a low laugh, "are not so easily procured in Ain-Sefra as in Bond Street. I have been thinking. You can help me if you will; you can shorten the time of my journey."

"How?" asked Warrisden.

"Go back to Oran as quickly as possible. Take the first boat to Tangier. Hire an outfit there, mules and horses—but good ones, mind!—and travel up at once to Fez. If you are quick you can do it within a fortnight. I shall take a fortnight at the least to reach Fez. I may be three weeks. But if I find you there, ready to start the moment I come to the town, we shall save much time."

"Very well; I will be there."

"If I get through sooner than I expect, I shall go straight on to Tangier, and we will meet on the road. Now let me climb onto your shoulders." Stretton made a bundle of his uniform, climbed onto Warrisden's shoulders, and threw it over the wall into the barrack-yard.

"But that will betray you!" cried Warrisden, in a whisper. "They will find your clothes in the morning —clothes with a sergeant's stripes."

"I cannot help that," replied Stretton, as he jumped to the ground. "I do not intend to be shot as a thief, for that is what may happen when a man deserts and takes his uniform with him. Don't fail me in Fez. Good-bye."

He held out his hand, and, as Warrisden grasped it, he said:

"I have not said much to you in the way of thanks; but I am very grateful, however much I may have seemed to have been made unhappy by your coming. Since things are as they are, I am glad you came. I thank you, too, for that other visit to the North Sea. I will give you better thanks when we meet in Fez."

He cast a glance back to the wall of the barracks, and, in a voice which trembled, so deeply was he moved, he whispered to himself, rather than to Warrisden:

"Oh, but I am glad Tavernay is dead!"

All else that he had said since he dropped from the wall had been said hurriedly and without emotion. These last words were whispered from a heart overcharged with sorrow. They were his farewell to the Legion. He turned away, and, driving the mule before him, vanished into the darkness.

XXVI

BAD NEWS FOR PAMELA

WARRISDEN struck his camp early the next morning, and set out for the rail-head. Thence he travelled to Oran. At Oran he was fortunate enough to find a steamer of the Lambert line in the harbor which was preparing to sail that afternoon for Tangier. Warrisden had three hours to pass in Oran. He went at once to the post-office and dispatched his telegram to Pamela Mardale at the Villa Pontignard. The telegram informed her that Tony Stretton was returning, though his journey might take longer than she would naturally expect; and, secondly, that he himself was sailing that day for Tangier, whither any message should be sent at once to await his arrival at the English post-office. The telegram was couched in vague phrases. Tony Stretton, for instance, was called "The Truant." Pamela became more and more disquieted by the vagueness of its wording. She pondered, and in vain, why in the world Warrisden must be sailing to Tangier. It seemed certain that there were difficulties in the way of Tony's home-coming which she had not foreseen, and at the nature of which she could not conjecture. She sent off a reply to Tangier:

"Bring truant to Roquebrune as soon as possible."

For, on thinking over the new aspect which her problem presented, now that Lionel Callon had come to the Riviera, she had come to the conclusion that this was the safest plan. If Millie Stretton did not come to the south of France, no harm would have been done; whereas, if she did, and Tony went straight home to England, the last chance of saving her would be lost.

This message, however, did little to reassure Pamela. For the more she thought of Warrisden's telegram, the more she was troubled. Tony was returning. Yes, that was something—that was a great thing. But he was going to take a long time in returning, and, to Pamela's apprehension, there was no long time to spare. And the day after she had received the telegram she came upon still stronger reasons for disquietude.

She went down to Monte Carlo in the morning, and again saw Lionel Callon upon the terrace, and again noticed that he was alone. Yet on the whole she was not surprised. Millie Stretton's name figured as yet in no visitors' list, and Pamela was quite sure that if Millie Stretton had come south the name would have been inserted. It was impossible that Millie Stretton could come to Monte Carlo, or to, indeed, any hotel upon the Riviera, under a false name. She could not but meet acquaintances and friends at every step during this season of the year. To assume a name which was not hers would be an act of stupidity too gross. None the less Pamela was relieved. She avoided Callon's notice, and, acting upon a sudden impulse, went out from the garden, hired a carriage, and ordered the coachman to drive along the lower Corniche road in the direction of Beaulieu.

Pamela was growing harassed and anxious. The days were passing and no message had yet come from

Alan Warrisden. She suspected the presence of Lionel Callon on the Riviera more and more. More and more she dreaded the arrival of Millie Stretton. There was nothing now which she could do. She had that hard lot which falls to women, the lot of waiting. But she could not wait with folded hands. She must be doing something; even though that something were altogether trivial and useless, it still helped her through the hours. In this spirit she drove out from Monte Carlo at twelve o'clock, without a thought that her drive was to assist her towards the end on which she had set her heart.

She drove past the back of the big hotel at Eze. Just beyond, a deep gorge runs from the hills straight down to the sea. The road curves round the head of the gorge and bends again to the shore. Pamela drove round the gorge, and, coming again to the shore, went forward by the side of the sea. After a few minutes she bade the driver stop. In front of her the road rose a little, and then on the other side of the crest dipped down a steep hill. On her left a pair of iron gates stood open. From those gates a carriage-drive ran in two zigzags between borders of flowers down to an open gravel space in front of a long, one-storied building. The building faced upon the road, but at a lower level, so that even the flat roof was below Pamela. The building was prettily built, and roses and magnolias climbed against the walls, making it gay. The door in the middle stood open, but there was no sign of life about the house. Pamela sat gazing down into the garden, with its bushes and brightly colored flowers.

Pamela spoke to the driver:

"What place is this?" she asked.

"It was only built last year," the man replied, and

he told her enough for her to know that this was the Réserve at which Lionel Callon was staying.

"Few people come here?" said Pamela.

"It is not known yet," replied the driver. "It is such a little while since it has been opened."

The sun was bright. Beyond the Réserve the Mediterranean rippled and sparkled—here the deepest blue, there breaking into points of golden light. The Réserve itself had the look of a country-house in a rich garden of flowers tended with love. In the noonday the spot was very quiet and still. Yet to Pamela it had the most sinister aspect. It stood in a solitary position, just beneath the road. In its very quietude there was to her harassed thoughts something clandestine.

She knew that Callon was in Monte Carlo. She told her driver to drive down to the door, and at the door she stepped down and walked into the building. A large dining-room opened out before her in which two waiters lounged. There were no visitors. The waiters came forward. ' Would madame take luncheon in the room, or on the terrace at the back over the sea?"

"On the terrace," Pamela replied.

She lunched quite alone on a broad, flagged terrace, with the sea gently breaking at its foot. The greater portion of the building was occupied by the restaurant, but at one end Pamela noticed a couple of French windows. She remarked to the waiter who served her upon the absence of any visitors but herself.

"It is only this season, madame, that the restaurant is open," he replied.

"Can people stay here?" she asked.

"Yes. There are two suites of rooms. One is occupied; but the other is vacant, if madame would care to see it."

Pamela rose and followed him. He opened one of the French windows. A dining-room, furnished with elegance and lightly decorated, a sitting-room, and a bedroom comprised the suite. Pamela came back to the terrace. She was disquieted. It was impossible, of course, that Millie Stretton should stay at the Réserve; but the whole look of the place troubled her.

She mounted into her carriage and drove back. In front of her the great hotel of Eze stood high upon a promontory above the railway. A thought came to Pamela. She drove back round the head of the gorge, and when she came to the hotel she bade the coachman drive in. In the open space in front of the hotel she took tea. She could not see the restaurant itself, but she could see the road rising to the little hill-crest beside it. It was very near, she thought. She went into the hotel, and asked boldly at the office:

"When do you expect Lady Stretton?"

"Lady Stretton?" The clerk in the office looked up his books. "In three weeks, madame," he said. "She has engaged her rooms from the 31st."

"Thank you," said Pamela.

She mounted into her carriage and drove back to Monte Carlo. So Millie Stretton was coming to the Riviera, after all. She had refused to come with Pamela, yet she was coming by herself. She had declared she would not leave England this spring. But she had made that declaration before Lionel Callon had returned from Chile. Now Callon was here, and she was following. Pamela could not doubt that her coming was part of a concerted plan. The very choice of the hotel helped to convince her. It was so near to that at which Callon was staying. Twenty minutes walk at the most would separate them. Moreover, why should Callon choose that lonely restaurant without some particular, nay, some secret object? No one, it seemed, visited it in the day; no one but he slept there at night. Callon was not the man to fall in love with solitude. And if he had wished for solitude he would not have come to the Riviera at all. Besides, he spent his days in Monte Carlo, as Pamela well knew. No, it was not loneliness at which he aimed, but secrecy. That was it—secrecy. Pamela's heart sank within her. She had a momentary thought that she would disclose her presence to Lionel Callon, and dismissed it. The disclosure would alter Callon's plan, that was all; it would not hinder the fulfilment. It would drive Millie and him from the Riviera—it would not prevent them from meeting somewhere else. It would be better, indeed, that, if meet they must, they should meet under her eyes. For some accident might happen, some unforeseen opportunity occur of which she could take advantage to separate them. It was not known to Callon that she was on the spot. After all, that was an advantage. She must meet secrecy with secrecy. She urged her coachman to quicken his pace. She drove straight to the post-office at Monte Carlo. Thence she despatched a second telegram to Alan Warrisden at Tangier.

"Do not fail to arrive by the 31st," she telegraphed; and upon that took the train back to Roquebrune. She could do no more now; but the knowledge that she could do no more only aggravated her fears. Questions which could not be answered thronged upon her mind. "Would the telegram reach Tangier in time? What was Alan Warrisden doing at Tangier

at all? What hindered them coming straight from
Algeria to France?" Well, there were three weeks
still. She sent up her prayer that those three weeks
might bring Tony Stretton back, that Millie might be
saved for him. She walked up the steps from Roquebrune station very slowly. She did not look up as
she climbed. Had she done so she might, perhaps,
have seen a head above the parapet in the little square
where the school-house stood; and she would certainly
have seen that head suddenly withdrawn as her head
was raised. M. Giraud was watching her furtively,
as he had done many a time since she had come to
Roquebrune, taking care that she should not see him.
He watched her now, noticing that she walked with
the same lagging, weary step as when he had last seen
her on that path so many years ago. But as he watched she stopped, and, turning about, looked southward
across the sea, and stood there for an appreciable time.
When she turned again and once more mounted the
steps, it seemed to him that the weariness had gone.
She walked buoyantly, like one full of faith, full of
hope; and he caught a glimpse of her face. It seemed
to him that it had become transfigured, and that the
eyes were looking at some vision which was visible to
her eyes alone. Pamela had come back, indeed, at the
end of all her perplexities and conjectures, to the belief born of her new love, that somehow the world
would right itself, that somehow in a short while she
would hear whispered upon the wind, answered by the
ripples of the sea, and confirmed by the one voice she
longed to hear, the sentinel's cry: "All's well."

The messages which Pamela had sent to Warrisden
reached him at Tangier. He found them both waiting
for him the day after they had been sent. He had

twenty days in front of him. If Tony kept to his time, twenty days would serve. He hired a camp outfit, and the best mules to be obtained in Tangier on that day. The same evening he bought a couple of barbs well recommended to him for speed and endurance.

"They will amble at six miles an hour for ten hours a day," said one whose advice he sought. Warrisden discounted the statement, but bought the barbs. Early the next morning he set out for Fez.

XXVII

"BALAK!"[1]

THERE are two cities of Fez. One is the city of
the narrow, crowded streets, where the cry, "Balak! Balak!" resounds all day. Streets, one terms
them, since they are the main thoroughfares through
which all the merchandise of Morocco passes out to the
four quarters of the compass; but they are no wider
than the alleyways of an English village, and in many
places a man may stand in the centre and touch the
wall on either side. These streets are paved with big
cobble-stones, but the stones are broken and displaced
by the tramp of centuries. If mended at all, they are
mended with a millstone or any chance slab of rock;
but for the most part they are left unmended altogether. For that is the fashion in Morocco. There
they build and make, and they do both things beauti-
fully and well. But they seldom finish; in a house,
dainty with fountains and arabesques and colored tiles,
you will still find a corner uncompleted, a pillar which
lacks the delicate fluting of the other pillars, an embrasure for a clock half ornamented with gold filigree,
and half left plain. And if they seldom finish, they
never by any chance repair. The mansion is built
and decorated within; artists fit the tiles together in a
mosaic of cool colors, and carve and gild and paint the

[1] "Take care!"

little pieces of cedar-wood, and glue them into the light and pointed arches; the rich curtains are hung; and the master enters into his possession. There follows the procession of the generations. The tiles crack, the woodwork of the arches splits and falls, and the walls break and crumble. The householder sits indifferent, and the whole house corrodes. So, in the narrow streets, holes gape, and the water wears a channel where it wills, and the mud lies thick and slippery on the rounded stones; the streets run steeply up and down the hills, wind abruptly round corners, dive into tunnels. Yet men gallop about them on their sure-footed horses, stumbling, slipping, but seldom falling. "Balak!" they cry—"Balak!"—and the man on foot is flung against the wall or jostled out of the way. No one protests or resents.

A file of donkeys, laden with wood or with grain, so fixed upon their backs that the load grazes each street wall, blocks the way. "Balak!" shouts the donkey-driver. And perhaps some nobleman of Fez, soft and fat and indolent, in his blue cloak, who comes pacing on a mule no less fat, preceded by his servants, must turn or huddle himself into an embrasure. There are no social distinctions in the alleyways of Fez. It may be that one of those donkeys will fall then and there beneath his load, and refuse to rise. His load will be taken from his back, and if he still refuse he will be left just where he fell, to die. His owner walks on. It is no one's business to remove the animal. There he lies in the middle of the street, and to him "Balak!" will be called in vain.

A mounted troop of wild Berbers from the hills, with their long, brass-bound guns slung across their backs, and gaudy handkerchiefs about their heads, will ride through the bazaars, ragged of dress and no less ragged in the harness of their horses. "Balak!" Very swiftly way is made for them. "Balak," indeed, is the word most often heard in the streets of Fez.

Those streets wind at times between the walls of gardens, and if the walls are broken, as surely at some point they will be, a plot of grass, a grove of orange-trees hung with ruddy fruit, and a clump of asphodel will shine upon the eyes in that brown and windowless city like a rare jewel. At times, too, they pass beneath some spacious arch into a place of width, or cross a bridge where one of the many streams of the river Fez boils for a moment into the open, and then swirls away again beneath the houses. But, chiefly, they run deep beneath the towering walls of houses, and little of the sunlight visits them; so that you may know a man of Fez, even though he be absent from his town, by the pallor of his face. A householder, moreover, may build over the street, if he can come to an agreement with his neighbor on the opposite side, and then the alleys suddenly become tunnels, and turn upon themselves in the dark. Or the walls so lean together at the top that barely a finger's breadth of sky is visible as from the bottom of a well.

Into this city of dark streets Warrisden came upon an evening of gloom. The night before he had camped on the slope of a hill by the village of Segota. Never had he seen a spot more beautiful. He had looked across the deep valley at his feet to the great buttress of Jebel Zarhon, on a dark shoulder of which mountain one small, round, white town was perched. A long, high range of gray hills—the last barrier between him and Fez—cleft at one point by the road, rose on the far side of the valley; and those hills and the fields beneath, and the solitary crumbling castle which stood in the bottom among the fields, were all magnified and made beautiful by the mists of evening. The stars had come out overhead, behind him the lights shone in his tent, and a cheerful fire crackled in the open near the door. He had come up quickly from Tangier, and without hindrance, in spite of warnings that the road was not safe. The next morning he would be in Fez. It had seemed to him, then, that fortune was on his side. He drew an augury of success from the clean briskness of the air. And that confidence had remained with him in the morning. He had crossed the valley early, and, riding over the long pass on the other side, had seen at last the snow-crowned spur of the Atlas on the farther side of the plain of Fez. He had descended into the plain, which perpetually rose and fell like the billows of an ocean; and in the afternoon, from the summit of one of these billows, he had suddenly seen, not an hour's journey off, the great city of Fez, with its crenellated walls and high minarets, a mass of gray and brown, with here and there a splash of white, and here and there a single palm-tree, straggling formlessly across the green plain. The sky had clouded over; the track was now thronged with caravans of camels and mules and donkeys, and wayfarers on foot going to and coming from the town; and before the Bab Sagma, the great gate looking towards Mikkes, was reached, the rain was falling.

Warrisden had sent on the soldier who had ridden with him from Tangier to deliver a note to the consul, and he waited with his animals and his men for the soldier's return. The man came towards dusk with word that a house had been secured in the town, and Warrisden passed through the gate and down between

the high battlements of the Bugilud into the old town.
And as he passed through the covered bazaars and
the narrow streets, in the gloom of the evening, while
the rain fell drearily from a sullen sky, his confidence
of the morning departed from him, and a great depres-
sion chilled him to the heart. The high, cracked,
bulging walls of the houses, towering up without a window, the shrouded figures of the passers-by, the falling
light, the neglect as of a city of immemorial age crumbling in decay, made of Fez, to him that night, a place
of gloom and forbidding mystery. He was in a mood
to doubt whether ever he would look on Tony Stretton's face again.

In the narrowest of the alleys, where each of his
stirrups touched a wall, his guide stopped. It was almost pitch-dark here. By throwing back his head,
Warrisden could just see, far above him, a little slit of
light. His guide groped his way down a passage on
the right, and at the end opened with a key a ponder-
ous black door. Warrisden stepped over the sill and
found himself in a tiled court of which the roof was
open to the sky. On the first floor there was a gallery,
and on each of the four sides a long, narrow room, lofty,
and closed with great folding-doors, opened onto the
gallery. In one of these rooms Warrisden had his bed
set up. He sat there trying to read by the light of a
single candle, and listening to the drip of the rain.

When he left Tangier he had twenty-one days before he need be at Roquebrune in answer to Pamela's
summons. He had looked up the steamers before he
started. Four of those days would be needed to carry
them from Tangier to Roquebrune. He had reached
Fez in five, and he thus had twelve days left. In other
words, if Stretton came to Fez within a week, there

should still be time, provided, of course, the road to the coast was not for the moment cut by rebellious tribes. That was the danger, as Warrisden's journey had told him. He discounted the timorous statements of his dragoman, Ibrahim, but one who knew had warned him at El Ksar. There was a risk.

The night was cold. Warrisden wrapped himself in a Moorish jellaba of fine white wool, but he could not put on with it the Moorish patience and indifference. The rain dripped upon the tiles of the court. Where was Stretton, he wondered.

He went to bed, and waked up in the middle of the night. He had left the great doors of his bedroom open; the rain had stopped; and in the stillness of the night he heard one loud voice, of an exquisite beauty, vibrating over the roofs of the sleeping city, as though it spoke from heaven itself. Warrisden lay listening to it, and interpreting the words from the modulations of the voice which uttered them. Now it rang out imperious as a summons, dropping down through the open roofs to wake the sleepers in their beds. Now it rose, lyrical and glorious, in a high chant of praise. Now it became wistful, and trembled away pleading, yet with a passion of longing in the plea. Warrisden could look upward from his bed through the open roof. The sky was clear again. Overhead were the bright stars, and this solitary voice, most musical and strange, ringing out through the silence.

It was the mueddhin on the tower of the Karueein Mosque. For five hours before the dawn the praises of Allah are sung from the summit of the mosque's minaret. There are ten mueddhins to whom the service is intrusted, and each sends out his chant above the sleeping city for half an hour. But in the voice of this one of the ten, whom Warrisden heard on the first night when he slept in Fez, there was a particular quality. He listened for it during the nights which followed, expected it, and welcomed its first note as one welcomes the coming of a friend. It seemed to him that all the East was in that cry.

It brought back to him sunsets when his camp was pitched by some little village of tents or thatched mud-houses surrounded by hedges of aloes and prickly-pears — at Karia Ben Ouder, at Djouma — villages where there was no mosque at all, but whence none the less the voice of a priest dispersed its plaintive cry across the empty country of marigolds and asphodels, startling the white cow-birds and the storks.

Warrisden fell to thinking of Tony Stretton. He struck a match and looked at his watch. It was close upon the hour of dawn. Perhaps, just at this moment, by some village in that wild, dark mountain country to the southeast, Stretton stirred in his sleep, and waked to hear some such summons chanted about the village. Perhaps he was even now loading his mule, and setting forth by the glimmer of the starlight upon his dangerous road. Warrisden fell asleep again with that picture in his mind, and woke to find the sunlight pouring through the square opening of the roof. He drank his coffee, and, mounting a little winding stairway of broken steps, came out into that other city of Fez, the city of the roof-tops.

Fez is built upon the slope of a hill, and upon some of the flat roofs Warrisden looked down and through the dark, square holes of the openings; to the parapets of others he looked up. Upon some there were gardens planted—so, he thought, must have looked the hanging gardens of Babylon; on others, linen was strung out to dry, as in some backyard of England; the minarets, here inlaid with white and green tiles, there built simply of bricks and brown plaster, rose high into the limpid air. And on the towers were the great nests of storks.

Warrisden looked abroad, and in the sunlight his hopes revived. It seemed that it must have been into another town that he had entered last night. Nowhere could he see the gash of a street in that plateau of roof-tops—so narrow they were; and no noise rose at all, they were so deep. Here the only sound audible was the chattering of women's voices—for the roofs are the playgrounds of the women, and Warrisden could see them in their colored handkerchiefs and robes clustered together, climbing from one house to another with the help of ladders, visiting their friends. But of all the clamor which must needs be resounding in those crowded streets, not even one stray cry of "Balak!" reached to this upper air. Lower down the hill to the east Warrisden could see the city wall and the gate through which Stretton must pass when he came. And he might come to-day!

That was Warrisden's thought. He went down the stairs, had his horse brought into the dark street before the door, and, accompanied by his *mehazni*, that old soldier who had ridden with him from Tangier, went out of the city over the plain towards Sefru. For through that small town of gardens and fruit at the base of the Atlas spur Stretton would come. But he did not come on that day nor on the next. But, on the other hand, Ibrahim, Warrisden's guide, brought bad news.

He mounted to the roof in the morning, while Warrisden sat there after his breakfast, and crouched down behind the parapet so that he might not be seen. For the men leave the roof-tops to their women folk, and do not trespass there themselves.

"Sir," said he, "the road between Djebel Silfat and Djebel Zarhon is cut. Word has come into Fez this morning. The Z'mur have come down from the hills and sit across the road, stopping and robbing every one."

Warrisden sat up.

"Are you sure?" he asked. He was, as he knew, in a country of liars. Ibrahim, in addition, was a coward in the country districts, though the best of braggarts at Tangier. He had ridden on his mule slung about with weapons—a Spanish rifle on his back, a revolver in his belt, and a Winchester in his hands; while between the fingers of his left hand he carried ready four cartridges—but he was none the less afraid. However, Warrisden remembered that mountain-pass which led from the plain of the Sebou up to Segota. It was very lonely, it was narrow, the road looped perpetually round the bases of the round buttresses of Djebel Silfat. It would certainly be an awkward place wherein to be entrapped.

"Yes, yes, I am sure," replied Ibrahim, "the Z'mur are bad men. They might capture you and hold you to ransom."

Warrisden was inclined to discount Ibrahim's terror of the Z'mur. The lawless deeds of that wild and fanatical tribe had been dinned into his ears ever since he had crossed the Sebou, until he had come to make light of them. But there was no doubt they terrorized the people; in the villages where Warrisden had camped they were spoken of with a dread hardly less than that which Ibrahim betrayed. It would certainly never do to be taken by the Z'mur. They would be released, no doubt; but time would be wasted. They might be kept for weeks in the forest of Marmura. They would reach Roquebrune too late.

Warrisden had brought with him, as a servant, one of the men who had been with him to Ain-Sefra, and descending the stairs he called him, and spoke, bidding Ibrahim interpret.

"Do you remember the mule which I gave away at Ain-Sefra?" he asked. And the man answered, "Yes!"

"You would know it again?"

The man was sure upon that point. He described the marks by which he would recognize the beast.

"Very well," said Warrisden. "Go out to the west of Fez and watch the road to Sefru. If you see a Jew come towards Fez driving the mule lead him at once to this house. Watch all day until the gate is closed."

The man went off upon his errand and Warrisden betook himself to the vice-consulate. On his return he summoned Ibrahim, and said:

"We must travel by Mequinez and Mediyah. A letter will be given to us, passing us on from governor to governor. We can reach Larache, travelling hard, in five days. We may find a steamer there for Gibraltar. If not, we must go on, in one more day, to Tangier."

Ibrahim bowed his head and made no further protest. In the evening Warrisden's servant came back from the gate; his watch had been fruitless. Thus three days had passed. Warrisden became anxious again and restless. The seven days which Tony Stretton could take, and still reach Roquebrune by the date on which Pamela insisted, were now curtailed. Six days formed the limit, and even that limit implied that the journey should be of the swiftest. Of those six days three had gone.

The fourth came and passed. Warrisden rode out upon the track to Sefru in vain. Even the promised letter did not come. Warrisden made inquiries. It would come, he was told. There was no doubt upon that score. But a government letter takes a long time in the writing in Morocco. It was not until the fifth evening that a messenger from the palace knocked upon the door. These were the days when Mulai-el-Hassan ruled in Morocco and was on the march against his rebellious tribes for nine months out of the twelve. Mulai-el-Hassan, at this particular time, was far away to the south in the Sus country, and, therefore, the mountain-pass to the north was dangerous.

Warrisden had his letter, however, sealed with the viceroy's seal. But he gazed out over the city, as it lay, warm and ruddy in the sunset, and wondered whether it would avail at all. His servant had come back from the gate with his familiar answer. No Jew had driven the mule down the road into Fez that day. And there was only one more day.

Warrisden descended the stairs to the gallery on the first floor, and as he came out upon it he heard voices in the court-yard below. He looked over the balustrade and saw a man standing among his muleteers and servants. Warrisden could not see his face. He was dressed in rags, but the rags were the remnants of a black gabardine, and he wore a black skull-cap upon his head.

It is likely that Warrisden would have taken no further notice of the man but that he cringed a little in his manner as though he was afraid. Then he spoke in Arabic, and the voice was timorous and apologetic. Warrisden, however, knew it none the less. He leaned over the balustrade.

"Stretton!" he cried out, in a burst of joy.

The man in the court-yard looked up. Warrisden would never have known him but for his voice. A ragged beard stubbled his cheeks and chin; he was disfigured with dirt and bruises; he was lean with hunger; his face was drawn and hollow from lack of sleep. But there was something more, a wider difference between this ragged Stretton in the court-yard and the Stretton Warrisden had known than mere looks explained. The man who had looked up when he heard his voice loudly and suddenly pronounced had been startled — nay, more than startled. He had raised an arm as though to ward off a blow. He had shrunk back. He had been afraid. Even now, when he looked at Warrisden and knew that he was here in a house of safety, he stood drawing deep breaths, and trembling like one who has received a shock. His appearance told Warrisden much of the dangers of the journey from Ain-Sefra through the hills to Fez.

"Yes," said Tony, "I am here. Am I in time?"

"Just in time," cried Warrisden. "Oh, but I thought you never would come!"

He ran down the steps into the court-yard.

"Balak!" cried Stretton, with a laugh. "Wait till I have had a bath and got these clothes burned."

In such guise Tony Stretton came to Fez. He had gone straight to the vice-consulate, and thence had been directed to Warrisden's house. When, an hour later, he came up onto the gallery and sat down to dinner he was wearing the clothes of a European, and the

"HE HAD RAISED AN ARM AS THOUGH TO WARD OFF A BLOW"

look of fear had gone from his face, the servility from his manner. But Warrisden could not forget either the one or the other. Tony Stretton had come through the mountains — yes. But the way had not been smooth.

XXVIII

HOMEWARD

THE two men smoked together upon the roof-top afterwards.

"I left a man at the gate all day," said Warrisden, "to watch the track from Sefru. I had brought him from Algiers. I do not know how he came to miss you."

"He could not know me," said Tony, "and I spoke to no one."

"But he knew the mule!"

Tony was silent for a little while. Then he said, in a low, grave voice, like a man speaking upon matters which he has no liking to remember,

"The mule was taken from me some days ago in the Ait Yussi country."

And Warrisden upon that said, "You had trouble, then, upon the way, great trouble?"

Again Tony was slow in the reply. He looked out across the city. It was a night of moonlight, so bright that the stars were pale and small as though they were withdrawn; there was no cloud anywhere about the sky, and on such a night, in that clear, translucent air, the city, with its upstanding minarets, had a grace and beauty denied to it by day. There was something of enchantment in its aspect. Tony smoked his pipe in silence for a little while. Then he said:

"Let us not talk about it! I never thought that I

would be sitting here in Fez to-night. Tell me rather when we start!"

"Early to-morrow," replied Warrisden. "We must reach Roquebrune, in the south of France, by the thirty-first."

Stretton suddenly sat back in his chair.

"Roquebrune! France!" he exclaimed. "We must go there? Why?"

"I do not know," Warrisden answered. "A telegram reached me at Tangier. I kept it."

He took the telegram from his pocket and handed it to Stretton, who read it and sat thinking.

"We have time," said Warrisden, "just time enough, I think, if we travel fast."

"Good," said Stretton, as he returned the telegram. "But I was not thinking of the time."

He did not explain what had caused him to start at the mention of Roquebrune; but after sitting for a little while longer in silence he betook himself to bed.

Early the next morning they rode out of the Bab Sagma upon the thronged highway over the plain to Mequinez.

The caravans diminished, striking off into this or that track. Very soon there remained with them only one party of five Jews mounted on small donkeys. They began to ride through high shrubs and bushes of fennel over rolling ground. Stretton talked very little, and as the track twisted and circled across the plain he was continually standing up in his stirrups and searching the horizon.

"There does not seem to be one straight path in Morocco," he exclaimed, impatiently. "Look at this one. There's no reason why it should not run straight. Yet it never does."

Indeed, the track lay across that open plain like some brown monstrous serpent of a legend.

"I do not believe," replied Warrisden, "that there is a straight path anywhere in the world, unless it is one which has been surveyed and made, or unless it runs from gate to gate and both gates are visible. One might think the animals made this track, turning and twisting to avoid the bushes. Only the tracks are no straighter in the desert where there are no bushes at all."

They halted for half an hour at eleven beside a bridge which crossed a stream, broken and ruinous, but still serviceable. And while they sat on the ground under the shadow they suddenly heard a great clatter of hoofs upon the broken cobbles, and looking up saw a body of men ride across the bridge. There were about forty of them, young and old; all were mounted, and in appearance as wild and ragged a set of bandits as could be imagined. As they rode over the bridge they saw Warrisden and Stretton seated on the ground beneath them, and without a word or a shout they halted as one man. Their very silence was an intimidating thing.

"Z'mur," whispered Ibrahim. He was shaking with fear. Warrisden noticed that the two soldiers who accompanied them on this journey to Mequinez quietly mounted their horses. Stretton and Warrisden rose to do likewise. And as they rose a dozen of the mounted Z'mur quietly rode round from the end of the bridge and stood between them and the stream. Then the leader, a big man with a black beard turning gray, began to talk in a quiet and pleasant voice to the soldiers.

"You are bringing Europeans into our country.

Now, why are you doing that? We do not like Europeans."

The soldiers no less pleasantly replied:

"Your country? The Europeans are travelling with a letter from your master and mine, my lord the Sultan, to the governor of Mequinez."

"You will show us, then, the letter?"

"I will do nothing of the kind," the soldier replied, with a smile. The Z'mur did not move; the two soldiers sat upon their horses smiling—it seemed that matters had come to a dead-lock. Meanwhile Warrisden and Stretton got into their saddles. Then the leader of the Z'mur spoke again.

"We passed five Jews riding on donkeys a little while ago. They were kind enough when we stopped them to give us a peseta apiece. We are going to Fez to offer our help to the Sultan, if only he will give us rifles and ammunition. But we shall go home again when we have got them. Perhaps the Europeans would like to give us a peseta apiece as well."

"I do not think they would like it at all," said the soldier. "Salem aleikum!" and he turned his horse, and, followed by Warrisden and Stretton, the terrified Ibrahim, and the train of mules, he rode right through the forty Z'mur and over the bridge.

It was an awkward moment, but the men of Warrisden's party assumed with what skill they could an air of unconcern. Trouble was very near to them. It needed only that one of those wild tribesmen should reach out his hand and seize the bridle of a horse. But no hand was reached out. The Z'mur were caught in a moment of indecision. They sat upon their horses motionless. They let the Europeans pass.

Ibrahim, however, drew no comfort from their attitude.

"It is because they wish rifles and ammunition from the government," he said. "Therefore, they will avoid trouble until they have got them. But with the next party it will not be so."

There are three water-falls in Morocco, and of those three one falls in a great cascade between red cliffs into a dark pool thirty feet below, close by the village of Medhuma. By this water-fall they lunched, the while Ibrahim bared his right arm to the shoulder, stretched himself full length upon the ground, and, to the infinite danger of the by-standers, practised shooting with his revolver. They lunched quickly and rode on. Towards evening, above a grove of trees on a hill, they saw here and there a minaret.

"Mequinez!" exclaimed Ibrahim. "Schoof! Mequinez!"

In a little while fragments of thick wall began to show, scattered here and there about the plain. Brown walls, high and crumbling to ruin, walls that never had been walls of houses, but which began and ended for no reason. They were all that was left of the work of Mulai Ismail, who, in the seventeenth century, had built and planned buildings about this town until death put an end to all his architecture. There was to be a wall across the country, from Fez to Morocco city far away in the south, so that the blind, of which this kingdom still has many, and then was full, might pass from one town to another without a guide. Part of that wall was built, and fragments of it rise among the oleanders and the bushes to this day.

The travellers entered now upon a park. A green, mossy turf spread out soft beneath the feet of their horses, dwarf oaks made everywhere a pleasant shade; Stretton had lost sight now of the minarets, and no sign of Mequinez was visible at all. The ground sloped downward, the track curved round a hill, and suddenly on the opposite side of a valley they saw the royal city, with its high walls and gates, its white houses, and its green-tiled mosques and its old, gray, massive palaces stretch along the hill-side before their eyes.

One of the soldiers rode forward into the town to find the basha and present his letters. A troop of men came out in a little time and led the travellers up the cobbled stones through a gateway into the wide space before the Renegade's Gate, that wonderful monument of Moorish art which neither the wear of the centuries nor the neglect of its possessors has availed to destroy. Its tiles are broken. The rains have discolored it, stones have fallen from their places. Yet the gate rises, majestic yet most delicate, beautiful in color, exquisite in shape, flanked with massive pillars and surmounted by its soaring arch, a piece of embroidery in stone, fine as though the stone were lace. By the side of this arch the camp was pitched just about the time when the horses and mules are brought down to roll in the dust of the square and to drink at the two great fountains beyond the gate.

Later in that evening there came a messenger from the basha with servants bearing bowls of kouss-kouss.

"Fourteen soldiers will ride with you to-morrow," he said, "for the country is not safe. It will be well if you start early, for you have a long way to go."

"The earlier the better," said Stretton.

"It will do if you breakfast at five—half-past five,"

said Ibrahim, to whom punctuality was a thing unknown. "And start at six—half-past six."

"No," said Warrisden. "We will start at five—
half-past five."

That night a company of soldiers kept guard about
the tents, and passed the hours of darkness in calling
to one another and chanting one endless, plaintive
melody. Little sleep was possible to the two Englishmen, and to one of them sleep did not come at all.
Now and then Warrisden dropped off and waked
again; and once or twice he struck a match and lit his
candle. Each time that he did this he saw Stretton
lying quite motionless in his bed on the other side of the
tent. Tony lay with the bedclothes up to his chin
and his arms straight down at his sides, in some un-
canny resemblance to a dead man. But Warrisden
saw that all the while his eyes were open. Tony was
awake with his troubles and perplexities, keeping
them to himself as was his wont, and slowly searching
for an issue. That he would hit upon the issue he did
not doubt. He had these few days for thought, and it
was not the first time that he had had to map out a line
of conduct. His course might be revealed to him at the
very last moment, as it had been on the trawler in the
North Sea. Or it might flash upon him in a second,
as the necessity to desert had flashed upon him amid
the aloes of Ain-Sefra. Meanwhile he lay awake and
thought.

They started early that morning, and, crossing a
valley, mounted on to that high, wide plain Djebel
Zarhon and Djebel Geronan. They left the town of
Mequinez behind them; its minarets dropped out of
sight. They had come into a most empty world. Not
a tent-village stood anywhere beside the track. Far

away to the right, in a deep recess, the white, sacred town of Mulai Idris fell down the dark side of Zarhon like a cascade. A little farther an arch of stone and a few pillars rising from the plain showed where once the Romans had built their town of Volubilis. But when that was passed there was no sign of life anywhere at all. For hours they rode in a desolate, beautiful world. Bushes of asphodel, white with their starry flowers, brushed against them; plants of iris, purple and yellow, stood stirrup-high upon their path; and at times the bushes would cease, and they would ride over a red carpet of marigolds, which would pale away into the gold of the mustard flower. Flowers were about them all that day, but no living things. Even the air above their heads was still. The country seemed too empty even for the birds.

At eleven o'clock they stopped beside a stream which ran prettily between trees across their path.

"We shall find no more water until evening," said Ibrahim. "We will stop here."

Stretton dismounted, and said:

"We can send the mules on and catch them up. It will save time."

The soldiers shook their heads.

"We are in the Berber country," they said. "We must not separate."

Stretton looked around impatiently.

"But there is no one within miles," he exclaimed; and, as if to contradict him, a man walked out from the bushes by the stream and came towards them. He had been robbed on this very track not two hours before by eleven mounted Berbers. He had been driving three mules laden with eggs and food to Mulai Idris, and his mules and their loads had been taken from him. He was walking home, absolutely penniless. His whole fortune had been lost that day; and when once again the travellers started upon their journey he ran at a trot beside their horses for safety's sake.

The road mounted now on to stony and mountainous country. It wound continually, ascending in and out among low, round peaks towards the summit of a great line of hills which ran from east to west opposite to them against the sky.

"Beyond the hills," cried Ibrahim, "is the plain of the Sebou."

A big village crowned the hill just where the track ascended. It had been placed there to protect the road. In a little while they came to the brow of the hill, and suddenly they saw, far below them, the great plain of the Sebou, green and level, dotted with villages and the white tombs of saints and clumps of trees, stretching away as far as the eye could reach. It was afternoon, not a cloud was in the sky, and the sun shone through the clear, golden air beneficently bright. The hill-side fell away to the plain with a descent so sheer, the plain broke so abruptly upon the eyes, that the very beauty of the scene caught the breath away. Both Warrisden and Stretton reined in their horses, and sat looking across the plain as a man might who suddenly, from the crest of some white cliff, sees for the first time the sea. And then Warrisden heard his companion begin to hum a song. He caught some of the words, but not many.

"Oh, come out, mah love, I'm awaitin' foh you heah!" Tony began, and suddenly checked himself with an expression of anger, as though the words had associations which it hurt him to recall.

"Let us ride on," he said, and led the way down the steep, winding track towards the plain.

They pressed on that evening, and camped late in the Beni Hassan country. Stretton slept that night, but he slept fitfully. He had not yet come to the end of his perplexities, and as he rode away from their camping-ground in the morning he said, impulsively:

"It is quite true. I have thought of it. I am to blame. I should have gone into the house that night."

He was endeavoring to be just, and to this criticism of himself he continually recurred. He should have entered his house in Berkeley Square on the night when he contented himself with looking up to the lighted windows. He should have gone in and declared what was in his mind to do. Very likely he would have only made matters worse. Contempt for a visionary would very likely have been added to the contempt for a ne'er-do-weel. Certainly no faith would have been felt by Millie in the success of his plan. He would have been asked, in a lukewarm way, to abandon it and stay at home. Still, he ought to have gone in. He had made a mistake that night.

All that day they rode through the Beni Hassan country westward. The plain was level and monotonous; they passed village after village, each one built in a circle round a great space of open turf into which the cattle were driven at night. For upon the hills, and in the forest of Mamura to the south, close by, the Z'mur lived, and between the Beni Hassan and the Z'mur there is always war. In the afternoon they came to the borders of that forest, and skirting its edge, towards evening reached the caravanserai of El Kantra.

The travellers saw it some while before they came to it—four high, smooth, castellated walls crowning a low hill. It stands upon the road from Fez to Rabat, and close to the road from Rabat to Larache, and a garrison guards it. For you could almost throw a stone from its walls into the trees of Mamura. Stretton and Warrisden rode round the walls to the gate, and as they passed beneath the arch both halted and looked back.

Outside was a quiet country of gray colors; the sun was near to its setting; far away the broken walls of the old Portuguese town of Mediyah stood upon a point of vantage on a hill-side, like some ruined castle of the Tyrol. Inside the caravanserai all was noise and shouting and confusion. In the thickness of the walls there were little rooms or cells, and in these the merchants were making their homes for the night, while about them their servants and muleteers buzzed like a hive of bees. And the whole great square within the walls was one lake of filthy mud wherein camels and mules and donkeys and horses rolled and stamped and fought. A deafening clamor rose to the skies. Every discordant sound that the created world could produce seemed to be brayed from that jostling throng of animals as from some infernal orchestra. And the smell of the place was fetid.

"Let us pitch our camp outside!" said Warrisden. But the captain of the garrison came hurrying up.

"No," he cried, excitedly. "The Z'mur! The Z'mur!"

Stretton shrugged his shoulders.

"I am getting a little bored with the Z'mur," said he.

"They have sent in word to us," the captain continued, "that they mean to attack us to-night."

Stretton looked perplexed.

314

"But why send in word?" he asked.

The captain of the garrison looked astonished at the question.

"So that we may be ready for them, of course," he replied, quite seriously; for life in Morocco has some of the qualities of *opera-bouffe*. "So you must come inside. You have a letter from my lord the basha of Fez, it is true. If the letter said you were to sleep outside the walls of El Kantra, then I would kiss the seal and place it against my forehead, and bring out my five hundred men to guard you, and we should all get killed. But it does not say so."

His five hundred men were really short of fifty. Stretton and Warrisden laughed; but they had to go inside the caravanserai. This was the last day on which they ran any risk. To-morrow they would cross the Sebou at Mediyah, and beyond the Sebou the way was safe.

They rode inside the caravanserai, and were allotted a cell which obtained some privacy from a hurdle fixed in the ground in front of it. The gates of the caravanserai were closed, the sunset flushed the blue sky with a hue of rose; the mueddhin came out upon the minaret which rose from the southern wall, and chanted in a monotone his call to prayer; and then a drummer and a bugler advanced into the crowded square. Suddenly there fell upon Stretton's ears, competing with the mueddhin and the uproar of the animals, the "Last Post."

Stretton started up, amazed, and most deeply moved. An English officer instructed the Moorish troops. What more natural than that he should introduce the English calls and signals? But to Stretton it seemed most wonderful that here, in this Eastern country, while the

Mohammedan priest was chanting from his minaret, he should hear again, after so many years, that familiar tattoo sounded by an Eastern bugle and an Eastern drum. In how many barracks of England, he wondered, would that same "Last Post" ring out to-night? And at once the years slipped away, the hard years of the North Sea and the Sahara. He was carried back among the days when he served in the Coldstream. Then arose in his heart a great longing that something of the happiness of those days might be recaptured still.

Warrisden and Stretton crossed the Sebou the next morning, and rode with the boom of the Atlantic in their ears. Hills upon their left hand hid the sea from their eyes, and it was not until the next day, when they mounted on to a high table-land four hours from Larache, that they saw it rolling lazily towards the shore. They caught a steamer at Larache that night.

XXIX

PAMELA MEETS A STRANGER

MEANWHILE Pamela waited at the Villa Pontignard, swinging from hope to fear, and from fear again to hope. The days chased one another. She watched the arrival of each train from Marseilles at the little station below with an expectant heart; and long after it had departed towards Italy she kept within her vision the pathway up the hill-side to the villa. But the travellers did not return. Expectation and disappointment walked alternately at her elbow all the day, and each day seemed endless. Yet, when the next day came, it had come all too quickly. Every morning it seemed to her, as she turned her calendar, that the days chased one another, racing to the month's end; every evening, tired out with her vigil, she wondered how they could pass so slowly. The thirty-first of the month dawned at last. At some time on this day Millie Stretton would arrive at Eze. She thought of it, as she rose, with a sinking heart, and then thrust thought aside. She dared not confront the possibility that the trains might stop at Roquebrune, and move on to Italy and discharge no passengers upon the platform. She dared not recognize her dread that this day might close and the darkness come as fruitlessly as all the rest. It was her last day of hope. Lionel Callon was waiting. Millie Stretton was arriving. To-morrow Tony might come, but he would come too late.

Pamela lived in suspense. Somehow the morning passed. The afternoon *Rapide* swept through towards Mentone. Pamela saw the smoke of the engine from her terrace, and knew that upon that train had come the passenger from England. Half an hour ago Millie had most likely stepped from her carriage on to the platform at Eze. And still Tony Stretton and Warrisden lingered.

Towards dusk she began to despair. In a little while another train was due. She heard its whistle, saw it stop at the station, and waited with her eyes fixed upon the hill-side path. No one appeared upon it. She turned and went into the house. She thought for a moment of going herself to Eze, thrusting herself upon Millie at the cost of any snub; and while she debated whether the plan could at all avail, the door was opened, a servant spoke some words about a visitor, and a man entered the room. Pamela started to her feet. The man stood in the twilight of the room: his back was against the light of the window. Pamela could not see his face. But it was not Warrisden, so much she knew at once. It could only be Tony Stretton.

"So you have come," she cried. "At last! I had given up hope."

She advanced and held out her hand. And some reserve in Tony's attitude, something of coldness in the manner with which he took her hand, checked and chilled her.

"It is you?" she asked. "I watched the path. The train has gone some while."

"Yes, it is I," he replied. "I had to inquire my way at the village. This is the first time I ever came to Roquebrune."

Still more than the touch of his hand and the reserve

of his manner, the cold reticence of his voice chilled
her. She turned to the servant abruptly.

"Bring lamps," she said. She felt the need to see
Tony Stretton's face. She had looked forward so
eagerly to his coming; she had hoped for it, and de-
spaired of it with so full a heart; and now he had
come, and with him there had come, most unexpectedly, disappointment. She had expected ardor, and
there was only, as it seemed, indifference and stolidity.
She was prepared for a host of questions to be tumbled out upon her in so swift a succession that no time
was given to her for an answer to any one of them; and
he stood before her seemingly cold as stone. Had he
ceased to care for Millie, she wondered.

"You have come as quickly as you could?" she
asked, trying to read his features in the obscurity.

"I have not lost a moment since I received your
letter," he answered.

She caught at the words, "your letter." Perhaps
there lay the reason for his reserve. She had written
frankly, perhaps too frankly she feared at this moment. Had the letter suddenly killed his love for
Millie? Such things, no doubt, could happen—had
happened. Disillusion might have withered it like a
swift shaft of lightning.

"My letter," she said. "You must not exaggerate
its meaning. You read it carefully?"

"Very carefully."

"And I wrote it carefully," she went on, pleading
with his indifference—"very carefully."

"It contains the truth," said Tony; "I did not
doubt that."

"Yes; but it contains all the truth," she urged.
"You must not doubt that, either. Remember, you

319

yourself are to blame. I wrote that, didn't I? I meant it."

"Yes, you wrote that," answered Tony. "I am not denying that you are right. It may well be that I am to blame. It may well be that you, too, are not quite free from blame. Had you told me that morning, when we rode together in the Row, what you had really meant when you said that I ought never to leave my wife—" And at that Pamela interrupted him.

"Would you have stayed if I had explained?" she cried. And Tony for a moment was silent. Then he answered, slowly:

"No; for I should not have believed you." And then he moved for the first time since he had entered the room. "However, it can do neither of us any good to discuss what we might have done had we known then what we know now."

He stopped as the door opened. The lamps were brought in and set upon the tables. Tony waited until the servant had gone out and the door was closed again, then he said:

"You sent a telegram. I am here in answer to it. I was to be at Roquebrune on the thirty-first. This is the thirty-first. Am I in time?"

"Yes," said Pamela.

She could now see Tony clearly; and of one thing she at once was sure. She had been misled by the twilight of the room. Tony, at all events, was not indifferent. He stood before her travel-stained and worn. His face was haggard and thin; his eyes very tired, like the eyes of an old man; there were flecks of gray in his hair and lines about his eyes. These changes she noticed and took them at their true value. They were signs of the hard life he had lived during these years, and of the quick, arduous journey which he had made. But there was more. If Tony had spoken with a measured voice, it was in order that he might control himself the better. If he had stood without gesture or motion, it was because he felt the need to keep himself in hand. So much Pamela clearly saw. Tony was laboring under a strong emotion.

"Yes, you are in time," she cried; and now her heart was glad. "I was so set on saving both your lives, in keeping you and Millie for each other. Of late, since you did not come, my faith faltered a little. But it should not have faltered. You are here! You are here!"

"My wife is here, too?" asked Tony, coldly, and Pamela's enthusiasm again was checked. "Where is she?"

"She arrives in the south of France to-day. She stops at Eze. She should be there now."

She had hoped to see the blood pulse into his face and some look of gladness dawn suddenly in his eyes, some smile of forgiveness alter the stern set of his lips. But again she was disappointed.

Tony seemed to put his wife out of his thoughts.

"And since your message was so urgent," he continued, deliberately, "it follows that Callon comes to-day as well," and he repeated the name in a singularly soft, slow, and almost caressing voice. "Lionel Callon," he said.

And at once Pamela was desperately afraid. It needed just that name uttered in just that way to explain to her completely the emotion which Tony so resolutely controlled. She looked at him aghast. She had planned to bring back Tony to Millie and his home. The Tony Stretton whom she had known of old, the good-natured, kindly man who loved his wife, whom all men liked and none feared. And lo! she had brought back a stranger. And the stranger was dangerous. He was thrilling with anger, he was anticipating his meeting with Lionel Callon with a relish which, to Pamela, was dreadful.

"No," she exclaimed, eagerly. "Mr. Callon has been here all this while, and Millie only comes to-day."

"Callon has been waiting for her, then?" he asked, implacably.

"Oh, I don't know," Pamela exclaimed, in despair. "I have not spoken to him. How should I know?"

"Yet you have no doubts."

"Well, then, no," she said, "I have no doubt that he is waiting here for Millie. But she only arrives to-day. They have not met until to-day. That is why I sent the telegram."

Tony nodded his head.

"So that I might be present at the meeting?"

And Pamela could have cried out aloud. She had not thought, she had not foreseen. She had fixed all her hopes on saving Millie. Set upon that, she had not understood that other and dreadful consequences might ensue. These consequences were vivid enough before her eyes now. All three would meet—Tony, Millie, and Lionel Callon. What would follow? What might not follow? Pamela closed her eyes. Her heart sank; she felt faint at the thought of what she had so blindly brought about.

"Tony!" she exclaimed. She wrung her hands together, pleading with him in short and broken sentences. "Don't think of him! . . . Think of Millie. You can gain her back! . . . I am very sure. . . . I wrote that to you, didn't I? . . . Mr. Callon. . . . It is not worth while. . . . He is of no account. . . . Millie was lonely, that was all. . . . There would be a scandal, at the best. . . . " And Tony laughed harshly.

"Oh, it is not worth while," she cried again, piteous-ly; and yet again, "It is not worth while."

"Yet I am anxious to meet him," said Tony.

Suddenly Pamela looked over his shoulder to the door, and for a moment hope brightened on her face. But Stretton understood the look and replied to it.

"No, Warrisden is not here. I left him behind with our luggage at Monte Carlo."

"Why did he stay?" cried Pamela, as again her hopes fell.

"He could hardly refuse. This is my affair, not his. I claimed to-night. He will come to you, no doubt, to-morrow."

"You meant him to stay behind, then?"

"I meant to see you alone," said Tony; and Pamela dared question him no more, though the questions thronged in her mind and tortured her. Was it only because he wished to see her alone that he left Warris-den behind? Was it not also so that he might not be hampered afterwards? Was it only so that another might not know of the trouble between himself and Millie? Or was it not so that another might not be on hand to hinder him from exacting retribution? Pam-ela was appalled. Tony was angry — yes, that was natural enough. She would not have felt half her present distress if he had shown his passion in tem-pestuous words, if he had threatened, if he had raved. But there was so much deliberation in his anger, he had it so completely in control; it was an instrument which he meant to use, not a fever which might master him for a moment and let him go.

"You are so changed," she cried. "I did not think of that when I wrote to you. But, of course, these years and the Foreign Legion could not but change you."

She moved away, and sat down holding her head between her hands. Stretton did not answer her words in any way. He moved towards her, and asked,

"Is Callon, too, at Eze?"

"No, no," she cried, raising her head, thankful, at last, that here was some small point on which she could attenuate his suspicions. "You are making too much of the trouble."

"Yet you wrote the letter to me. You also sent the telegram. You sent me neither the one nor the other without good reason." And Pamela dropped her eyes again from his face.

"If Callon is not at Eze," he insisted, "he is close by!"

Pamela did not answer. She sat trying to compose her thoughts. Suppose that she refused to answer, Tony would go to Eze. He might find Millie and Callon there. On the other hand, it was unlikely that he would. Pamela had seen that quiet, solitary restaurant by the sea where Callon lodged. It was there that they would be, she had no doubt.

"Where is Callon?" asked Tony. "Where does he stay?"

Pamela closed her ears to the question, working still at the stern problem of her answer. If she refused to tell him what he asked, Millie and Callon might escape for to-night. That was possible. But, then, to-morrow would come. Tony must meet them to-morrow in any case, and to-morrow he might be too late.

"I will tell you," she answered, and she described the place. And in another minute she was alone. She heard the front door close, she heard Tony's step upon the gravel of the garden path, and then all was silent. She sat holding her throbbing temples in her hands. Visions rose before her eyes, and her fear made them extraordinarily luminous and vivid. She saw that broad, quiet terrace over the sea where she had lunched, the lonely restaurant, the windows of that suite of rooms open onto the terrace. A broad column of light streamed out from the window in her vision. She could almost hear voices and the sound of laughter, she imagined the laughter all struck dumb, and thereafter a cry of horror stabbing the night. The very silence of the villa became a torture to her. She rose and walked restlessly about the room. If she could only have reached Warrisden! But she did not even know to which hotel in all the hotels of Monte Carlo he had gone. Tony might have told her that, had she kept her wits about her and put the question with discretion. But she had not. She had no doubt that Stretton had purposely left him behind. Tony wished for no restraining hand when at last he came face to face with Lionel Callon. She sat down and tried to reason out what would happen. Tony would go first to Eze. Would he find Millie there? Perhaps. Most likely he would not. He would go on then to the restaurant on the Corniche road. But he would have wasted some time. It might be only a little time, still, however short it was, what was waste of time to Tony might be gain of time to her—if only she could find a messenger.

Suddenly she stood up. There was a messenger, under her very hand. She scribbled a note to Lionel

Callon, hardly knowing what she wrote. She bade
him go the instant when he received it, go at all costs
without a moment's delay. Then, taking the note in
her hand, she ran from the villa down the road to
Roquebrune.

M. GIRAUD AGAIN

THE dusk was deepening quickly into darkness. As she ran down the open stretch of hill-side between her villa and the little town, she saw the lights blaze out upon the terrace of Monte Carlo. Far below her upon her right they shone like great opals, each with a heart of fire. Pamela stopped for a second to regain her breath before she reached Roquebrune. The sudden brightness of those lights carried her thoughts backward to the years when the height of trouble for her had been the sickness of a favorite horse, and all her life was an eager expectation. On so many evenings she had seen those lights flash out through the gathering night while she had sat talking in her garden with the little school-master whom she was now to revisit. To both of them those lights had been a parable. They had glowed in friendliness and promise — thus she had read the parable — out of a great, bright, gay world of men and women, upon a cool, twilit garden of youth and ignorance. She thought of what had come in place of all that imagined gayety. To the school-master, disappointment and degradation; while, as for herself, she felt very lonely upon this evening. "The world is a place of great sadness." Thus had M. Giraud spoken when Pamela had returned to Roquebrune from her first season in London, and the words now came back to her again.

She ran on through the narrow streets of Roque-brune, her white frock showing in the light from the shops and windows. She wore no hat upon her head, and more than one of the people in the street called to her as she passed and asked her whether she needed help. Help, indeed, she did need, but not from them. She came to the tiny square whence the steps led down to the station. On the west side of the square stood the school-house, and, close by, the little house of the school-master. A light burned in a window of the ground floor. Pamela knocked loudly upon the door. She heard a chair grate upon the floor-boards. She knocked again, and the door was opened. It was the school-master himself who opened it.

"M. Giraud!" she exclaimed, drawing her breath quickly. The school-master leaned forward and stared at the white figure which stood in the darkness just outside his porch; but he made no reply.

"Let me in!" cried Pamela; and he made a movement as though to bar the way. But she slipped quickly past him into the room. He closed the door slowly and followed her.

The room was bare. A deal table, a chair or two, and a few tattered books on a hanging bookshelf made up all its furniture. Pamela leaned against the wall with a hand to her heart. M. Giraud saw her clearly now. She stood only a few feet from him in the light of the room. She was in distress; yet he spoke harshly.

"Why have you come?" he cried; and she answered, piteously, "I want your help."

At that a flame of anger kindled within him. He saw her again, after all this long time of her absence—her whose equal he had never spoken with. Her dark hair, her eyes, the pure outline of her face, her tall, slim figure, the broad forehead—all the delicacy and beauty of her—was a torture to him. The sound of her voice, with its remembered accents, hurt him as he had thought nothing could ever hurt him again.

"Really!" he cried, in exasperation. "You want help, so you come to me. Without that need would you have come? No, indeed. You are a woman. Get your fine friends to help you!"

There were other follies upon his tongue, but he never spoke them. He looked at Pamela, and came to a stop.

Pamela had entered the cottage bent with a single mind upon her purpose—to avert a catastrophe at the little restaurant on the Corniche road. But M. Giraud was before her, face to face with her, as she was face to face with him. She saw him clearly in the light as he saw her; and she was shocked. The curé had prepared her for a change in her old comrade, but not for so complete a disfigurement. The wine-shop had written its sordid story too legibly upon his features. His face was bloated and red, the veins stood out upon the cheeks and the nose like threads of purple; his eyes were yellow and unwholesome. M. Giraud had grown stout in body, too; and his dress was slovenly and in disrepair. He was an image of degradation and neglect. Pamela was shocked, and betrayed the shock. She almost shrank from him at the first; there was almost upon her face an expression of aversion and disgust. But sorrow drove the aversion away, and immediately her eyes were full of pity; and these swift changes M. Giraud saw and understood.

She was still his only window on the outside world. That was the trouble. By her expression he read his own decline more surely than in his mirror. Through

329

her he saw the world; through her, too, he saw what
manner of figure he presented to the world. Never
had he realized how far he had sunk until this moment. He saw, as in a picture, the young school-master
of the other days who had read French with the pupil,
who was more his teacher than his pupil, upon the
garden terrace of the Villa Pontignard — a youth full
of dreams, which were vain, no doubt, but not ignoble.
There was a trifle of achievement, too. For even now
one of the tattered books upon his shelf was a copy of
his brochure on Roquebrune and the Upper Corniche
road. With perseverance, with faith—he understood
it in a flash—he might have found, here, at Roquebrune, a satisfaction for those ambitions which had
so tortured him. There was a field here for the his-
torian had he chosen to seize on it. Fame might
have come to him, though he never visited the great
cities and the crowded streets. So he thought, and
then he realized what he had become. It was true
he had suffered great unhappiness. Yet so had she—
Pamela Mardale; and she had not fallen from her
pedestal. Here shame seized upon him. He lowered
his eyes from her face.

"Help!" he stammered. "You ask me to help
you? Look at me! I can give you no help!"

He suddenly broke off. He sat down at the table,
buried his face in his hands, and burst into tears.
Pamela crossed to him and laid her hand very gently
upon his shoulder. She spoke very gently, too.

"Oh yes, you can," she said.

He drew away from her, but she would not be re-
pulsed.

"You should never have come to me at all," he
sobbed. "Oh, how I hate that you should see me

like this. Why did you come? I did not mean you to see me. You must have known that! You must have known, too, why. It was not kind of you, mademoiselle. No, it was not kind!"

"Yet I am glad that I came," said Pamela. "I came thinking of myself, it is true—my need is so very great; but now I see your need is as great as mine. I ask you to rise up and help me."

"No, leave me alone!" he cried. And she answered, gently, "I will not."

M. Giraud grew quiet. He pressed his handkerchief to his eyes, and stood up.

"Forgive me!" he said. "I have behaved like a child; but you would forgive me if you knew how I have waited and waited for you to come back. But you never did. Each summer I said, 'She will return in the winter!' And the winter came, and I said, 'She will come in the spring.' But neither in winter nor in the spring did you return to Roquebrune. I have needed you so badly all these years."

"I am sorry," replied Pamela; "I am very sorry."

She did not reproach herself at all. She could not see, indeed, that she was to blame. But she was none the less distressed. Giraud's exhibition of grief was so utterly unfamiliar to her that she felt awkward and helpless in face of it. He was yet further disfigured now by the traces of weeping; his eyes were swollen and red. There was something grotesque in the aspect of this drink-swollen face, all convulsed with sorrow. Nothing could well be less in sympathy with Pamela's nature than Giraud's outburst and display of tears; for she was herself reticent and proud. She held her head high as she walked through the world, mistress alike of her sorrows and her joys. But Mr. Mudge had spoken the truth when he had called upon her in Leicestershire. Imagination had come to her of late. She was able to understand the other point of view—to appreciate that there were other characters than hers which must needs fulfil themselves in ways which were not hers. She put herself now in M. Giraud's place. She imagined him waiting and waiting at Roquebrune, with his one window on the outside world closed and shuttered —a man in a darkened room who most passionately desired the air without. She said, with a trace of hesitation:

"You say you have needed me very much?"

"Oh, have I not?" exclaimed Giraud; and the very weariness of his voice would have convinced her, had she needed conviction. It seemed to express the dilatory passage of the years during which he had looked for her coming, and had looked in vain.

"Well, then, listen to me," she went on. "I was once told that to be needed by those whom one needs is a great comfort. I thought of the saying at the time, and I thought that it was a true one. Afterwards"— she began to speak slowly, carefully selecting her words—"it happened that in my own experience I proved it to be true, at all events for me. Is it true for you, also? Think well. If it is not true I will go away as you bade me at the beginning; but if it is true —why, then I may be of some little help to you, and you will be certainly a great help to me, for I need you very surely."

M. Giraud looked at her in silence for a little while. Then he answered her with simplicity, and so, for the first time during this interview, wore the proper dignity of a man.

"Yes, I will help you," he said. "What can I do?"

She held out the letter which she had written to Lionel Callon. She bade him carry it with the best speed he could to its destination.

"Lose no time!" she implored. "I am not sure but it may be that one man's life, and the happiness of a man and a woman besides, all hang upon its quick receipt."

M. Giraud took his hat from the wall and went to the door. At the door he paused, and, standing thus, with an averted face, he said in a whisper, recalling the words she had lately spoken:

"There is one, then, whom you need? You are no longer lonely in your thoughts? I should like to know."

"Yes," Pamela answered, gently; "I am no longer lonely in my thoughts."

"And you are happy?" he continued. "You were not happy when you were at Roquebrune last. I should like to know that you, at all events, are happy now."

"Yes," said Pamela. In the presence of his distress she rather shrank from acknowledging the change which had come over her. It seemed cruel; yet he clearly wished to know. He clearly would be the happier for knowing. "Yes," she said; "I am happy."

"I am very glad," said M. Giraud, in a low voice; "I am very glad." And he went rather quickly out by the door.

XXXI

AT THE RÉSERVE

TONY STRETTON walked quickly down from the Villa Pontignard to the station. There he learned that an hour must elapse before a train to Eze was due. Inaction was at this moment intolerable to him. Even though he should get to Eze not a minute the sooner, he must hurry upon his way. He could not wait upon this platform for an hour, suspense so tortured him. He went out upon the road and began to run. He ran very quickly. The road turned sharply round the shoulder of a hill, and Stretton saw in front of him the lights of Monte Carlo. They were bunched in great white clusters, they were strung in festoons about the square and the streets. They made a golden crescent about the dark, quiet waters of the bay. Looking down from this shoulder of the hill upon the town at such an hour one seems to be looking upon a town of fairy-land; one expects a sweet and delicate music to float upward from its houses and charm the ears. Tony's one thought was that beyond that place of lights lay Eze. He came to an electric tram which was on point of starting. He entered it, and it rattled him quickly down the hill.

At Monte Carlo he sprang into the first carriage which he saw waiting for a fare, and bade the coachman drive him quickly out to Eze. The night had come; above his head the stars shone very brightly from a dark sky of velvet. The carriage passed out of the town; the villas grew more scarce; the open road glimmered ahead of him a riband of white; the sea murmured languorously upon the shore.

At this moment, in the lonely restaurant towards which Tony was driving in such haste, Lionel Callon and Millie Stretton were sitting down to dinner. The table was laid in the small, daintily furnished room which opened onto the terrace. The windows stood wide, and the lazy murmur of the waves entered in. The white cloth shone with silver; a great bowl of roses stood in the centre and delicately perfumed the air. Thither Millie had come in fulfilment of that promise made on a midnight of early spring in Regent's Park. The color burned prettily on her cheeks, she had dressed herself in a pink gown of lace, jewels shone on her arms and at her neck. She was, perhaps, a little feverish in her gayety, her laughter was perhaps a little overloud. Indeed, every now and then her heart sank in fear within her, and she wished herself far away. But here Lionel Callon was at his ease. He knew the methods by which victory was to be won. There was no suggestion of triumph in his manner. He was considerate and most deferential, and with no more than a hint of passion in the deference.

"You have come," he said. His eyes rested upon hers, and he left them to express his gratitude. He raised her hand to his lips and gently took the cloak from her shoulders. "You have had a long journey. But you are not tired." He placed her chair for her at the table and sat opposite. He saw that she was uneasy. He spoke no word which might alarm her.

Meanwhile Tony was drawing nearer. He reached the hotel at Eze, and drove in at the gate at the door.

"Is Lady Stretton in the hotel?" he asked.

"No, sir. Her ladyship went out to dinner nearly an hour ago."

"Thank you," said Tony. "She arrived this afternoon, I think?"

"Yes, sir. What name shall I give when she returns?"

"No name," said Tony. And he ordered his coachman to drive back to the road.

When he had reached it he directed the man again.

"Towards Beaulieu," he said; and in a little while, on his left hand, below the level of the road, he saw the lights of the Réserve. He stopped at the gate, dismissed his carriage, and walked down the winding drive to the door. He walked into the restaurant. It was empty. A waiter came forward to him.

"I wish you to take me at once to Mr. Callon," he said. He spoke in a calm, matter-of-fact voice. But the waiter nevertheless hesitated. Tony wore the clothes in which he had travelled to Roquebrune. He was covered with dust, his face was haggard and stern. He had nothing in common with the dainty little room of lights and flowers and shining silver and the smartly dressed couple who were dining there. The waiter guessed that his irruption would be altogether inconvenient.

"Mr. Callon?" he stammered. "He has gone out."

Tony heard the rattle of a metal cover upon a dish. He looked in the direction whence the sound came— he looked to the right-hand side of the restaurant. A door stood open there, and in the passage beyond the door he saw a waiter pass carrying the dish. Moreover, the man who had spoken to him made yet another mistake. He noticed the direction of Tony's glance, and he made a quick movement as though to bar that passage.

"He is here," said Tony; and he thrust the waiter aside. He crossed the restaurant quickly and entered the passage. The passage ran parallel to the restaurant; and, at the end towards the terrace, there was another door upon the opposite side. The waiter with the dish had his hand upon the door-handle, but he turned at the sound of Stretton's step. He, too, noticed the disorder of Tony's dress. At the same moment the man in the restaurant shouted in a warning voice:

"Jules!"

Jules stood in front of the door.

"Monsieur, this room is private," said he.

"Yet I will take the liberty to intrude," said Tony, quietly.

From behind the door there came the sound of a man's voice which Tony did not know. He had, indeed, never heard it before. Then a woman's laugh rang out; and the sound of it angered Tony beyond endurance. He recognized it beyond the possibility of mistake. It was his wife who was laughing so gayly there behind the closed door. He thought of the years he had spent in the determination to regain his wife's esteem, to free himself from her contempt. For the moment he could have laughed bitterly at his persistence as at some egregious folly. It seemed all waste—waste of time, waste of endeavor, waste of suffering. She was laughing! And with Lionel Callon for her companion! The cold, black nights of the North Sea and its gales; the arid sands of the Sahara, all his long service for her ending in that crowning act of desertion—the story was clear in his mind from beginning to end, detailed and complete. And she was laughing in there with Lionel Callon! Her laughter was to him as some biting epigram epitomizing the way in which she had spent the years of his absence. His anger got the better of his self-control.

"Stand away!" he cried, in a low, savage voice to the waiter. And since the man did not instantly move, he seized him by the shoulders and dragged him from the door.

"Monsieur!" the man cried aloud, in a frightened voice, and the dish which he was carrying fell with a clatter onto the floor. Inside the room the laughter suddenly ceased. Tony listened for a second. He could not hear even a whisper. There was complete silence. He smiled rather grimly to himself; he was thinking that this, at all events, was not the silence of contempt.

Could he have seen through the door into the room he would have been yet more convinced. All the gayety vanished in an instant from Millie's face. She was sitting opposite the door; she sat and stared at it in terror. The blood ebbed from her cheeks, leaving them as white as paper.

"Monsieur!" she repeated, in so low a whisper that even Callon on the other side of the small table hardly heard the word. Her lips were dry, and she moistened them. "Monsieur!" she whispered again, and the whisper was a question. She had no definite suspicion who "Monsieur" was; she did not define him as her husband. She only understood that somehow she was trapped. The sudden clatter of the dish upon the floor, the loudness of the waiter's cry, which was not in mere protest, but also a cry of fear, terrified her; they implied violence. She was trapped. She sat paralyzed upon her chair, staring across the table over Callon's shoulder at the door. Callon meanwhile said not a word. He had been sitting with his back to the door, and he twisted round in his chair. To both of them it seemed ages before the handle was turned. Yet so short was the interval of time that they could hardly have reached the terrace through the open window had they sprung up at the first sound of disturbance.

Thus they were sitting, silent and motionless, when the door was pushed open and Tony stood in the door-way. At the sight of him Millie uttered one loud scream, and clapped her hands over her face. Callon, on the other hand, started up onto his feet. As he did so he upset his wineglass over the table-cloth; it fell and splintered on the polished floor. He turned towards the intruder who so roughly forced his way into the room. The eyes of that intruder took no account of him; they were fixed upon Millie Stretton, as she sat cowering at the table with her hands before her face.

"What do you want?" cried Callon; "you have no right here!"

"I have every right here," said Tony; "that is my wife!"

It was still his wife at whom he looked, not at all towards Callon. Callon was startled out of his wits. Detection he had always feared; he had sought to guard against it by the use of every precaution known to his devious strategy. But it was detection by Pamela Mardale and her friends, who had once already laid him by the heels; the husband had never entered into his calculations. He had accepted without question Millie's version of the husband—he was the man who did not care. In some part of the world he wandered, but where no one knew; cut off from all his friends — indifferent, neglectful, and a fool. Even now he could not believe. This might be some new trick of Pamela Mardale's.

"Your wife!" he exclaimed. "That is not true."

"Not true?" cried Tony, in a terrible voice. He stretched out his arm and pointed towards Millie. "Look!"

Millie flinched as though she feared a blow. She dropped her head yet lower. She held her fingers over her eyelids, closing them tightly. She had looked once at Tony's face, she dared not look again. She sat in darkness, trembling. One question was in her mind. "Would he kill her?" Callon looked at her as he was bidden. Millie was wont to speak of her husband with indifference and a suggestion of scorn. Yet it was her manifest terror which now convinced Callon that the husband was indeed before him. Here the man was, sprung suddenly out of the dark upon him, not neglectful, for he had the look of one who has travelled from afar very quickly, and slept but little on the way; not indifferent, for he was white with anger and his eyes were aflame. Callon cursed the luck which had for a second time brought him into such ill straits. He measured himself with Tony, and knew in the instant he was no match for him. There was a man, tired, no doubt, and worn, but hard as iron, supple of muscle and limb, and finely trained to the last superfluous ounce of flesh; while he himself was soft with luxury and good living. He sought to temporize.

"That is no proof," said he. "Any woman might be startled—" And Tony broke fiercely in upon his stammered argument:

"Go out," he cried, "and wait for me!"

The door was still open. Outside it, in the passage, the waiters were clustered, listening. Inside the room Millie was listening. The order, roughly given, was just one which Callon for very shame could not obey. He would have liked to obey it, for confronting husbands was never to his liking; all his art lay in eluding them.

"Go out!" Tony repeated, and took a step forward. Callon could not cut so poor a figure as to slink from the room like a whipped school - boy. Yet it would have gone better with him had he eaten his look and gone.

"It would not be safe to leave you," he babbled. And suddenly Tony caught him by the throat, drew him forward, and then flung him violently away.

Callon reeled back through the open windows, slipped and fell to his full length upon the terrace. His head struck the stone flags with a horrible sound. He lay quite still in the strong light which poured from the room; his eyes were closed, his face quite bloodless. It was his business, as Mudge had said, to fight among the teacups.

Tony made no further movement towards him. The waiters went out onto the terrace and lifted him up and carried him within. Then Tony turned towards his wife. She had risen up from her chair and overturned it when Tony had flung the interloper from the room. She now crouched shuddering against the wall, with her eyes fixed in terror upon her husband. As he turned towards her she uttered a sob and dropped upon her knees before him. That was the end of all her scorn. She kneeled in deadly fear, admiring him in the very frenzy of her fear. She had no memory for the contemptuous letters which she had written and Tony had carried under his pillow on the North Sea. Her little deceits and plots and trickeries to hoodwink her friends, her little pretence of passion for Lionel Callon—she knew at this moment that it never had been more than a pretence—these were the matters which now she remembered and for which she dreaded punishment. She was wearing jewels that night—jewels which Tony had given her in the good past days when they lived together in the house in Deanery Street. They shook and glittered upon her hair, about her neck, upon her bosom and her arms. She kneeled in her delicate finery of lace and satin in this room of luxury and bright flowers. There was no need for Tony now to work to re-establish himself in her thoughts. She reached out her hands to him in supplication.

"I am not guilty," she moaned. "Tony! Tony!"

XXXII

HUSBAND AND WIFE

THE man who was no good had his triumph then. Only triumph was not at all in his thoughts.

"Oh, please!" he said, very quietly, "get up from your knees; I don't like to see you there. It hurts me."

Millie raised her eyes to him in wonder. He did not mean to kill her, then. All his violence, it seemed, was reserved for that poor warrior of the drawing-rooms who had just been carried away stunned and bleeding from the terrace. When Tony spoke to her his voice was rather that of a man very dispirited and sad. He had, indeed, travelled through the mountains of Morocco hot with anger against Callon, the interloper, but now that he had come face to face again with Millie, now that he had heard her voice with its remembered accents, the interloper seemed of little account, a creature to punish and be done with. The sadness of his voice penetrated to Millie's heart. She rose and stood submissively before him.

In the passage outside the door the waiters were clustered whispering together. Tony closed the door and shut the whispers out. Upon the terrace, outside the window, a man was hesitating whether to enter or no. Tony went to the window.

"Who are you?" he asked. "What do you want?"

"I am Giraud, the school-master of Roquebrune,"

said the man, timidly. "I bring a letter from Mademoiselle Mardale."

"Let me see it," said Tony; and he held out his hand for the letter. He glanced at the superscription and gave it back. "It is not for me," he said, and M. Giraud went away from the terrace. Tony turned back to his wife. His mind was full of a comparison between the ways in which he and she had each spent the years of absence. For him they had been years of endeavor, persisted in through failure and perplexity until success, but for her, was reached. And how had Millie spent them? He looked at her sternly, and she said again, in a faltering voice:

"I am innocent, Tony."

And he replied:

"Could you have said as much to-morrow had I not come back to-night?"

Millie had no answer to that question—she attempted none; and it was even at that moment counted to her credit by her husband. She stood silent for a while, and only the murmur of the sea breaking upon the beach filled the room. A light wind breathed through the open window, cool and fragrant, and made the shaded candles flicker upon the table. Millie had her one poor excuse to offer, and she pleaded it humbly.

"I thought that you had ceased to care what became of me," she said.

Tony looked sharply at her. She was sincere—surely she was sincere.

"You thought that?" he exclaimed; and he replaced her chair at the table. "Sit down here! Let me understand! You thought that I had ceased to care for you? When I ceased to write, I suppose?"

Millie shook her head.

"'OH, PLEASE!' HE SAID, VERY QUIETLY, 'GET UP FROM
YOUR KNEES'"

"Before that?"

Tony dropped into the chair on which Callon had been sitting.

"Before that?" he exclaimed, in perplexity. "When? Tell me!"

Millie sat over against him at the table.

"Do you remember the evening when you first told me that you had made up your mind to go away and make a home for both of us? It was on that evening. You gave your reason for going away. We had begun to quarrel—we were drifting apart."

"I remember," said Tony; "but we had not ceased to care then, neither you nor I. It was just because I feared that at some time we might cease to care that I was resolved to go away."

"Ah," said Millie; "but already the change had begun. Yes, yes! Things which you thought you never could remember without a thrill you remembered already with indifference—you remembered them without being any longer moved or touched by the associations which they once had had. I recollect the very words you used. I sat as still as could be while you spoke them; but I never forgot them, Tony. There was a particular instance which you mentioned —a song—" And, suddenly, Tony laughed; but he laughed harshly, and there was no look of amusement on his face. Millie stared at him in surprise, but he did not explain, and she went on with her argument.

"So, when you ceased to write I was still more convinced that you had ceased to care. When you remained away after your father had died I was yet more sure."

Tony leaned across the white table-cloth with its glittering silver, and fixed his eyes on her.

"I will tell you why I ceased to write. Every letter which you wrote to me when I was in New York was more contemptuous than the letter which had preceded it. I had failed, and you despised me for my failure. I had allowed myself to be tricked out of your money—" And upon that Millie interrupted him.

"Oh no!" she cried; "you must not say that I despised you for that. No! That is not fair. I never thought of the money. I offered you what was left."

Tony had put himself in the wrong here. He recognized his mistake; he accepted Millie's correction.

"Yes, that is true," he said; "you offered me all that was left—but you offered it contemptuously; you had no shadow of belief that I would use it to advantage—you had no faith in me at all. In your eyes I was no good. Mind, I don't blame you. You were justified, no doubt. I had set out to make a home for you, as many a man has done for his wife. Only where they had succeeded I had failed. If I thought anything at all—" he said, with an air of hesitation.

"Well?" asked Millie.

"I thought you might have expressed your contempt with a little less of unkindness, or perhaps have hidden it altogether. You see, I was not having an easy time in New York, and your letters made it very much harder."

"Oh, Tony," she said, in a low voice of self-reproach. She was sitting with her hands clinched in front of her upon the table-cloth, her forehead puckered, and in her eyes a look of great pain.

"Never mind that," he replied, and he resumed his story. "I saw then quite clearly that with each letter which you received from me, each new instalment of my record of failure — for each letter was just that, wasn't it?—your contempt grew. I was determined that if I could help it your contempt should not embitter all our two lives. So I ceased to write. For the same reason I stayed away, even after my father had died. Had I come back then I should have come back a failure, proved and self-confessed. And your scorn would have stayed with you. My business henceforth was to destroy it, to prove to you that after all I was some good—if not at money-making, at something else. I resolved that we should not live together again until I could come to you and say: "You have no right to despise me. Here's the proof."

Millie was learning now, even as Tony had learned a minute ago. All that he said to her was utterly surprising and strange. He had been thinking of her, then, all the time while he was away! Indifference was in no way the reason of his absence.

"Oh, why did you not write this to me?" she cried. "It need not have been a long letter, since you were unwilling to write. But just this you might have written. It would have been better, kinder"—and she paused upon the word, uttering it with hesitation and a shy, deprecating smile, as though aware that she had no claim upon his kindness. "It would have been kinder than just to leave me here, not knowing where you were, and thinking what I did."

"It is true," said Tony, "I might have written. But would you have believed me if I had? No."

"Then you might have come to me," she urged. "Once—just for five minutes—to tell me what you meant to do."

"I might," Tony agreed; "in fact, I very nearly did.

I was under the windows of the house in Berkeley Square one night." And Millie started.

"Yes, you were," she said, slowly.

"You knew that?"

"Yes; I knew it the next day." And she added, "I wish now, I think, that you had come in that night."

"Suppose that I had," said Tony; "suppose that I had told you of my fine plan, you would have had no faith in it. You would merely have thought, 'Here's another folly to be added to the rest.' Your contempt would have been increased, that's all."

It was quite strange to Millie Stretton that there ever could have been a time when she had despised him. She saw him sitting now in front of her, quiet and stern; she remembered her own terror when he burst into the room, when he flung Callon headlong through the windows, when he turned at last towards her.

"We have been strangers to each other."

"Yes," he replied; "I did not know you. I should never have left you—now I understand that. I trusted you very blindly, but I did not know you."

Millie lowered her eyes from his face.

"Nor I you," she answered. "What did you do when you went away that night from Berkeley Square?"

"I enlisted in the Foreign Legion in Algeria."

Millie raised her head again with a start of surprise.

"Soldiering was my trade, you see. It was the one profession where I had just a little of that expert knowledge which is necessary nowadays if you are to make your living."

Something of his life in the Foreign Legion Tony now told her. He spoke deliberately, since a light

348

was beginning dimly to shine through the darkness of his perplexities. Of a set purpose he described to her the arduous perils of active service and the monotony of the cantonments. He was resolved that she should understand in the spirit and in the letter the life which for her sake he had led. He related his expedition to the Figuig oasis, his march into the Sahara under Tavernay. He took from his pocket the medals which he had won and laid them upon the table-cloth before her.

"Look at them," he said; "I earned them. These are mine. I earned them for you; and while I was earning them what were you doing?"

Millie listened and looked. Wonder grew upon her. It was for her that he had labored and endured and succeeded! His story was a revelation to her. Never had she dreamed that a man would so strive for any woman. She had lived so long among the little things of the world—the little emotions, the little passions, the little jealousies and rivalries, the little aims, the little methods of attaining them, that only with great difficulty could she realize a simpler and a wider life. She was overwhelmed now. Pride and humiliation fought within her—pride that Tony had so striven for her in silence and obscurity, humiliation because she had fallen so short of his example. It was her way to feel in superlatives at any crisis of her destiny, but surely she had a justification now.

"I never knew—I never thought! Oh, Tony!" she exclaimed, twisting her hands together as she sat before him.

"I became a sergeant," he said. "Then I brought back the remnants of the geographical expedition to Ouargla." He taxed his memory for the vivid details of that terrible retreat. He compelled her to realize something of the dumb, implacable hostility of the Sahara, to *see*, in the evening against the setting sun, the mounted figures of the Touaregs, and to understand that the day's march had not shaken them off. She seemed to be on the march herself, wondering whether she would live out the day, or, if she survived that, whether she would live out the night.

"But you succeeded!" she cried, clinging to the fact that they were both here in France, with the murmur of the Mediterranean in their ears. "You came back."

"Yes, I came back. One morning I marched my men through the gate of Ouargla—and what were you doing upon that day?"

Talking, perhaps, with Lionel Callon, in one of those unfrequented public places with which London abounds! Millie could not tell. She sat there and compared Lionel Callon with the man who was before her. Memories of the kind of talk she was wont to hold with Lionel Callon recurred to her, filling her with shame. She was glad to think that when Tony led his broken, weary force through the gate of Ouargla Lionel Callon had not been with her—had, indeed, been far away in Chile. She suddenly placed her hands before her face and burst into tears.

"Oh, Tony," she whispered, in an abasement of humiliation. "Oh, Tony."

"By that homeward march," he went on, "I gained my commission. That was what I aimed at all the while, and I had earned it at the last. Look!"

He took from his pocket the letter which his colonel had handed to him at Ain-Sefra. He had carefully treasured it all this while. He held it out to her and made her read.

"You see?" he said. "A commission won from the ranks in the hardest service known to soldiers, won without advantage of name, or friends, or money. Won just by myself. That is what I strove for. If I could win that I could come back to you with a great pride. I should be no longer the man who was no good. You yourself might even be proud of me. I used to dream of that—to dream of something else."

His voice softened a little, and a smile for a moment relaxed the severity of his face.

"Of what?" she asked.

"Out there among the sand hills, under the stars at night, I used to dream that we might perhaps get hold again of the little house in Deanery Street, where we were so happy together once. We might pretend almost that we had lived there all the time."

He spoke in a voice of great longing, and Millie was touched to the heart. She looked at Tony through her tears. There was a great longing astir within her at this moment. Was that little house in Deanery Street still a possibility? She did not presume to hope so much; but she wished that she could have hoped. She pressed the letter which she held against her breast; she would have loved to have held it to her lips, but that again she did not dare to do.

"At all events you did succeed," she said; "I shall be glad to know that. I shall always be glad—whatever happens now."

"But I did not succeed," Tony replied. "I earned the commission, yes!—I never held it. That letter was given to me one Monday by my colonel at Ain-Sefra. You mentioned a song a minute ago, do you remember? . . . I had lost the associations of that song. I laughed when you mentioned it, and you were surprised. I laughed because when I received that letter I took it away with me, and that song, with all that it had ever meant, came back to my mind. I lay beneath the palm-trees, and I looked across the water past the islands and I saw the lights of the yachts in Oban Bay. I was on the dark lawn again, high above the sea, the lighted windows of the house were behind me. I heard your voice. Oh, I had got you altogether back that day," he exclaimed, with a cry. "It was as though I held your hands and looked into your eyes. I went back towards the barracks to write to you, and as I went some one tapped me on the shoulder and brought me news of you to wake me out of my dreams."

Just for a moment Millie wondered who it was who had brought the news; but the next words which Tony spoke drove the question from her mind.

"A few more weeks and I should have held that commission. I might have left the legion, leaving behind me many friends and an honored name. As it was I had to desert—I deserted that night."

He spoke quite simply, but, nevertheless, the words fell with a shock upon Millie. She uttered a low cry. "Oh, Tony!" she said.

"Yes," he said, with a nod of the head, "I incurred that disgrace. I shall be ashamed of it all my life. Had I been caught it might have meant an ignoble death; in any case it would have meant years of prison—and I should have deserved those years of prison."

Millie shut her eyes in horror. Everything else that he had told her—his sufferings, his perils—all seemed of little account beside this crowning risk, this crowning act of sacrifice. It was not merely that he had risked a shameful death or a shameful imprisonment.

Millie was well aware that his whole nature and character must be in revolt against the act itself. Desertion! It implied disloyalty, untruth, deceit, cowardice—just those qualities, indeed, which she knew Tony most to hate, which, perhaps, she had rather despised him for hating. No man would have been more severe in the punishment of a deserter than Tony himself. Yet he had deserted, and upon her account. And he sat there telling her of it quietly, as though it were the most insignificant action in the world. He might have escaped the consequences—he would certainly not have escaped the shame.

But Millie's cup of remorse was not yet full.

"Yet I cannot see that I could do anything else. To-night proves to me that I was right, I think. I have come very quickly, yet I am only just in time." There was a long stain of wine upon the table-cloth beneath his eyes. There Callon had upset his glass upon Tony's entrance.

"Yes, it was time that I returned," he continued. "One way or another a burden of disgrace had to be borne—if I stayed just as certainly as if I came away; I saw that quite clearly. So I came away." He forbore to say that now the disgrace fell only upon his shoulders, that she was saved from it. But Millie understood, and in her heart she thanked him for his forbearance. "But it was hard on me, I think," he said. "You see, even now I am on French soil and subject to French laws."

And Millie, upon that, started up in alarm.

"What do you mean?" she asked, breathlessly.

"There has been a disturbance here to-night, has there not? Suppose that the manager of this restaurant has sent for a gendarme!"

With a swift movement Millie gathered up the medals and held them close in her clinched hands.

"Oh, it does not need those to convict me; my name would be enough. Let my name appear and there's a deserter from the Foreign Legion laid by the heels in France. All the time we have been talking here I have sat expecting that door to open behind me."

Millie caught up a lace wrap whch lay upon a sofa. She had the look of a hunted creature. She spoke quickly and feverishly, in a whisper.

"Oh, why did not you say this at once? Let us go!"

Tony sat stubbornly in his chair.

"No," said he, with his eyes fixed upon her. "I have given you an account of how I have spent the years during which we have been apart. Can you do the same?"

He waited for her answer in suspense. To this question all his words had been steadily leading; for this reason he had dwelt upon his own career. Would she, stung by her remorse, lay before him truthfully and without reserve the story of her years? If she did, why, that dim light which shone amid the darkness of his perplexities might perhaps shine a little brighter. He uttered his question. Millie bowed her head and answered,

"I will."

"Sit down, then, and tell me now."

"Oh no," she exclaimed; "not here! It is not safe. As we go back to Eze I will tell you everything."

A look of relief came upon Tony's face. He rose and touched the bell.

A waiter appeared.

"I will pay the bill," he said.

The waiter brought the bill and Tony discharged it.

"The gentleman—M. Callon," the waiter said. "A doctor has been. He has a concussion. It will be a little time before he is able to be moved."

"Indeed?" said Tony, with indifference. He walked with his wife out of the little, gayly lighted room into the big, silent restaurant. A single light faintly illuminated it. They crossed it to the door and went up the winding drive on to the road. The night was dry and clear and warm. There was no moon. They walked in the pure twilight of the stars round the gorge towards Eze.

XXXIII

MILLIE'S STORY

THEY walked for a while in silence, side by side, yet not so close but that there was an interval between them. Millie every now and then glanced at Tony's face, but she saw only his profile, and with only the glimmer of the starlight to serve her for a reading-lamp she could guess nothing of his expression. But he walked like a man utterly dispirited and tired. The hopes so stoutly cherished during the last few years had all crumbled away to-night. Perpetually his thoughts recurred to that question, which now never could be answered—if he had gone into the house in Berkeley Square on that distant evening, when he had been contented to pace for a little while beneath the windows, would he have averted the trouble which had reached its crisis to-night at the *Réserve?* He thought not—he was not sure; only he was certain that he should have gone in. He stopped and turned back, looking towards the *Réserve*. A semicircle of lights over the doorway was visible, and as he looked those lights were suddenly extinguished. He heard Millie's voice at his side.

"I will tell you now how the time has passed with me." And he saw that she was looking steadfastly into his eyes. "The story will sound very trivial, very contemptible, after what you have told me. It fills me utterly with shame. But I should have told

356

you it none the less had you not asked for it—I rather wish that you had not asked for it; for I think I must have told you of my own accord."

She spoke in a quick, troubled voice, but it did not waver; nor did her eyes once fall from his. The change in her was swift no doubt. But down there in the *Réserve*, where the lights were out and the sea echoed through empty rooms, she had had stern and savage teachers. Terror, humiliation, and the spectacle of violence had torn away a veil from before her eyes. She saw her own life in its true perspective. And that she might see it the more clearly and understand, she had the story of another life wherewith to compare it. It is a quality of big performances, whether in art or life, that while they surprise when first apprehended, they appear upon thought to be so simple that it is astonishing surprise was ever felt. Something of that quality Tony's career possessed. It had come upon Millie as a revelation, yet now she was thinking: "Yes, that is what Tony would do. How is it I never guessed?" She put him side by side with that other man, the warrior of the drawing-rooms, and she was filled with shame that ever she could have preferred the latter even for a moment of madness.

They walked slowly on again. Millie drew her lace wrap more closely about her throat.

"Are you cold?" asked Tony. "You are lightly clothed to be talking here. We had better, perhaps, walk on, and keep what you have to tell me until to-morrow."

"No," she answered, quickly, "I am not cold. And I must tell you what I have to tell you to-night. I want all this bad, foolish part of my life to end to-night, to be extinguished just as those lights were extinguished a minute since. Only there is something I should like to say to you first." Millie's voice wavered now and broke. "If we do not walk along the road together any more," she went on, timidly, "I will still be glad that you came back to-night. I do not know that you will believe that—I do not, indeed, see why you should; but I should very much like you to believe it, for it is the truth. I have learned a good deal, I think, during the last three hours. I would rather go on alone—if it is to be so—in this dim, clear starlight, than ever be back again in the little room with its lights and flowers. Do you understand me?"

"I think so," said Tony.

"At all events, the road is visible ahead," she went on. "One sees it glimmering, one can keep between the banks; while in the little lighted room it is easy to get lost."

And thus to Millie now, as to Pamela when she rode back from her last interview with Warrisden at the village of the three poplars, the ribbon of white road stretching away in the dusk became a parable.

"Yes," said Tony, "perhaps my path was really the easier one to follow. It was direct and plain."

"Ah," said Millie, "it only seems so because you have traversed it and are looking back. I do not think it was so simple and direct while you walked upon it." And Tony, remembering the doubts and perplexities which had besieged him, could not but assent.

"I do not think, too, that it was so easy to discover at the beginning."

There rose before Tony's eyes the picture of a ketch-rigged boat sailing at night over a calm sea. A man leaned over the bulwarks, and the bright glare from a lightship ran across the waves and flashed upon his face. Tony remembered the moment very clearly when he had first hit upon his plan; he remembered the weeks of anxiety of which it was the outcome. No, the road had not been easy to find at the beginning. He was silent for a minute, and then he said, gently:

"I am sorry that I asked you to tell your story—I am sorry that I did not leave the decision to you. But it shall be as though you told it of your own accord."

The sentence was a concession, no less in the manner of its utterance than in the words themselves. Millie took heart, and told him the whole story of her dealings with Lionel Callon, without excuses and without concealments.

"I seemed to mean so much to him, so little to you," she said. "You see, I did not understand you at all. You were away, too, and he was near. I do not defend myself."

She did not spare herself; she taxed her memory for the details of her days; and as she spoke the story seemed more utterly contemptible and small than even she in her abasement had imagined it would be. But she struggled through with it to the end.

"That night when you stood beneath the windows in Berkeley Square," she said, "he was with me. He ran in from Lady Millingham's party and talked with me for half an hour. Yes, at the very time when you were standing on the pavement he was within the house. I know, for you were seen, and on the next day I was told of your presence. I was afraid then. The news was a shock to me. I thought, 'Suppose you had come in!'"

"But, back there, in the room," Tony interrupted, "you told me that you wished I had come in."

"Yes," she answered. "And it is quite true; I wish now that you had come in."

She told him of the drive round Regent's Park and of the consent she gave that night to Lionel Callon.

"I think you know everything now," she said. "I have tried to forget nothing. I want you, whatever you decide to do, to decide knowing everything."

"Thank you," said Tony, simply.

And she added, "I am not the first woman I know who has thrown away the substance for the shadow."

Upon the rest of that walk little was said. They went forward beneath the stars. A great silence lay upon sea and land. The hills rose dark and high upon their left hand, the sea murmured and whispered to them upon the right. Millie walked even more slowly as they neared the hotel at Eze, and Tony turned to her with a question.

"You are tired?"

"No," she answered.

She was thinking that very likely she would never walk again on any road with Tony at her side, and she was minded to prolong this last walk to the last possible moment. For in this one night Tony had re-conquered her. It was not merely that his story had filled her with amazement and pride, but she had seen him that night strong and dominant, as she had never dreamed of seeing him. She loved his very sternness towards herself. Not once had he spoken her name and called her "Millie." She had watched for that and longed for it, and yet because he had not used it she was the nearer to worship. Once she said to him, with a start of anxiety,

"You are not staying here under your own name?"

"No," he replied. "A friend has taken rooms in

Monte Carlo for both of us. Only his name has been given."

"And you will leave France to-morrow?"

"Yes."

"Promise!" she cried.

Tony promised, with a look of curiosity at his wife. Why should she be so eager for his safety? He did not understand. He was wondering what he must do in this crisis of their lives. Was he to come, in spite of all his efforts, to that ordinary compromise which it had been his object to avoid?'

They reached the door of the hotel and there Tony halted.

"Good-night," he said. He did not hold out his hand. He stood confronting Millie with the light from the hall lamp falling full upon his face. Millie hoped that he would say something more—just a little word of kindness or forgiveness—if only she waited long enough without answering him; and she was willing to wait until the morning came. He did, indeed, speak again, and then Millie was sorry that she had waited. For he said the one really cruel thing among all the words he had said that night. He was not aware of its cruelty, he was only conscious of its truth.

"Do you know," he said—and upon his tired face there came a momentary smile—"to-night I miss the legion very much." Again he said "Good-night."

This time Millie answered him, and in an instant he was gone. She could have cried out; she could hardly restrain her voice from calling him back to her. "Was this the end?" she asked. "That one cruel sentence, and then the commonplace good-night, without so much as a touch of the hands. Was this the very end?" A sharp fear stabbed her. For a few moments she heard Tony's footsteps upon the flags in front of the hotel, and then for a few moments upon the gravel of the garden path; and after that she heard only the murmur of the sea. And all at once for her the world was empty. "Was this the end?" she asked herself again most piteously—"this, which might have been the beginning." Slowly she went up to her rooms. Sleep did not visit her that night.

XXXIV

THE NEXT MORNING

THERE was another who kept a vigil all the night. In the Villa Pontignard Pamela Mardale saw from her window the morning break, and wondered in dread what had happened upon that broad terrace by the sea. She dressed and went down into the garden. As yet the world was gray and cool, and something of its quietude entered into her and gave her peace. A light mist hung over the sea, birds sang sweetly in the trees, and from the chimneys of Roquebrune the blue smoke began to coil. In the homely suggestions of that blue smoke Pamela found a comfort. She watched it for a while, and then there came a flush of rose upon the crests of the hills. The mist was swept away from the floor of the sea, shadows and light suddenly ran down the hill-sides, and the waves danced with a sparkle of gold. The sun had risen. Pamela saw a man coming up the open slope from Roquebrune to the villa. It was M. Giraud. She ran to the gate and met him there.

"Well?" she asked. And he answered, sadly:

"I arrived too late."

The color went from Pamela's cheeks. She set a hand upon the gate to steady herself. There was an expression of utter consternation on her face.

"Too late, I mean," the school-master explained, hurriedly, "to help you, to be of any real service to you. But the harm done is perhaps not so great as you fear."

He described to her what he had seen—Lionel Callon lying outstretched and insensible upon the pavement, Tony and Millie Stretton within the room.

"We removed M. Callon to his bedroom," he said. "Then I fetched a doctor. M. Callon will recover—it is a concussion of the brain. He will be ill for a little time, but he will get well."

"And the man and the woman?" Pamela asked eagerly. "The two within the room? What of them?"

"They were standing opposite to each other." The school-master had not seen Millie on her knees. "A chair was overturned, the chair on which she had sat. She was in great distress, and, I think, afraid; but he spoke quietly." He described how he had offered Tony the letter, and how Tony had closed the door of the room upon the waiters.

"The manager did not know what to do, whether to send for help or not. But I did not think that there was any danger to the woman in the room, and I urged him to do nothing."

"Thank you," said Pamela, gratefully. "Indeed, you were in time to help me."

But even then she did not know how much she was indebted to the school-master's advice. She was thinking of the scandal which must have arisen had the police been called in, of the publication of Millie's folly to the world of her acquaintances. That was prevented now. If Tony took back his wife—as with all her heart she hoped he would—he would not, at all events, take back one of whom gossip would be speaking with a slighting tongue. She was not aware that

Tony had deserted from the Legion to keep his tryst upon the 31st of the month. Afterwards, when she did learn this, she was glad that she had not lacked warmth when she had expressed her gratitude to M. Giraud. A look of pleasure came into the school-master's face.

"I am very glad," he said. "When I brought the doctor back the two within the room were talking quietly together; we could hear their voices through the door. So I came away. I walked up to the villa here. But it was already late, and the lights were out—except in one room on an upper floor looking over the sea—that room," and he pointed to a window.

"Yes, that is my room," said Pamela.

"I thought it was likely to be yours, and I hesitated whether I should fling up a stone; but I was not sure that it was your room. So I determined to wait until the morning. I am sorry, for you have been very anxious and have not slept—I can see that. I could have saved you some hours of anxiety."

Pamela laughed in friendliness, and the laugh told him surely that her distress had gone from her.

"That does not matter," she said. "You have brought me very good news. I could well afford to wait for it."

The school-master remained in an awkward hesitation at the gate; it was clear that he had something more to say. It was no less clear that he found the utterance of it very difficult. Pamela guessed what was in his mind, and, after her own fashion, she helped him to speak it. She opened the gate, which up till now had stood closed between them.

"Come in for a little while, won't you?" she said; and she led the way through the garden to that narrow corner on the bluff of the hill which had so many associations for them both. If M. Giraud meant to say what she thought he did, here was the one place where utterance would be easy. Here they had interchanged, in other times, their innermost thoughts, their most sacred confidences. The stone parapet, the bench, the plot of grass, the cedar in the angle of the corner—among these familiar things memories must throb for him even as they did for her. Pamela sat down upon the parapet, and, leaning over, gazed into the torrent far below. She wished him to take his time. She had a thought that even if he had not in his mind that utterance which she hoped to hear, the recollection of those other days, vividly renewed, might suggest it. And in a moment or two he spoke.

"It is true, mademoiselle, that I was of service to you last night?"

"Yes," replied Pamela, gently; "that is quite true."

"I am glad," he continued. "I shall have that to remember. I do not suppose that I shall see you often any more. Very likely you will not come back to Roquebrune—very likely I shall never see you again. And if I do not, I should like you to know that last night will make a difference to me."

He was now speaking with a simple directness. Pamela raised her face towards his. He could see that his words greatly rejoiced her; a very tender smile was upon her lips, and her eyes shone. There were tears in them.

"I am so glad," she said.

"I resented your coming to me at first," he went on. "I was a fool; I am now most grateful that you did come. I learned that you had at last found the happiness which I think you have always deserved. You know I have always thought that it is a bad thing when such a one as you is wasted upon loneliness and misery—the world is not so rich that it can afford such waste. And if only because you told me that a change had come for you, I should be grateful for the visit which you paid me. But there is more. You spoke a very true word last night when you told me it was a help to be needed by those one needs."

"You think that, too?" said Pamela.

"Yes, now I do," he answered. "It will always be a great pride to me that you needed me. I shall never forget that you knocked upon my door one dark night in great distress. I shall never forget your face, as I saw it framed in the light when I came out into the porch. I shall never forget that you stood within my room, and called upon me, in the name of our old comradeship, to rise up and help you. I think my room will be hallowed by that recollection." And he lowered his voice suddenly, and said: "I think I shall see you as I saw you when I opened the door, between myself and the threshold of the wine-shop; that is what I meant to say."

He held out his hand, and, as Pamela took it, he raised her hand to his lips and kissed it.

"Good-bye," he said; and, turning away quickly, he left her up in the place where she had known the best of him, and went down to his school-room in the square of Roquebrune. Very soon the sing-song of the children's voices was droning from the open windows.

Pamela remained upon the terrace. The breaking of old ties is always a melancholy business, and here was one broken to-day. It was very unlikely, she thought, that she would ever see her friend, the little school-master, again. She would be returning to England immediately, and she would not come back to the Villa Pontignard.

She was still in that corner of the garden when another visitor called upon her. She heard his footsteps on the gravel of the path, and, looking up, saw Warrisden approaching her. She rose from the parapet and went forward to meet him. She understood that he had come with his old question, and she spoke first. The question could wait just for a little while.

"You have seen Tony?" she asked.

"Yes; late last night," he replied. "I waited at the hotel for him. He said nothing more than good-night, and went at once to his room."

"And this morning?"

"This morning," said Warrisden, "he has gone. I did not see him. He went away with his luggage before I was up, and he left no message."

Pamela stood thoughtful and silent.

"It is the best thing he could have done," Warrisden continued; "for he is not safe in France."

"Not safe?"

"No. Did he not tell you? He deserted from the French Legion. It was the only way in which he could reach Roquebrune by the date you named."

Pamela was startled, but she was startled into activity.

"Will you wait for me here?" she said. "I will get my hat."

She ran into the villa, and, coming out again, said: "Let us go down to the station."

They hurried down the steep flight of steps. At the station Warrisden asked: "Shall I book to Monte Carlo?"

"No; to Eze," she replied.

She hardly spoke at all during the journey; and Warrisden kept his question in reserve—this was plainly no time to utter it. Pamela walked at once to the hotel.

"Is Lady Stretton in?" she asked; and the porter replied:

"No, madame. She left for England an hour ago."

"Alone?" asked Pamela.

"No. A gentleman came and took her away."

Pamela turned towards Warrisden with a look of great joy upon her face.

"They have gone together," she cried. "He has taken his risks. He has not forgotten that lesson learned on the North Sea. I had a fear this morning that he had."

"And you?" said Warrisden, putting his question, at last.

Pamela moved away from the door until they were out of earshot. Then she said:

"I will take my risks, too." Her eyes dwelt quietly upon her companion, and she added: "And I think the risks are very small."

24

XXXV

THE LITTLE HOUSE IN DEANERY STREET

PAMELA construed the departure of Tony and his wife together according to her hopes. They were united again. She was content with that fact, and looked no further, since her own affairs had become of an engrossing interest. But the last word has not been said about the Truants. It was not, indeed, until the greater part of a year had passed that the section of their history which is related in this book reached any point of finality.

In the early days of January the Truants arrived in London at the close of a long visit to Scotland. They got out upon Euston platform, and, entering their brougham, drove off. They had not driven far before Millie looked out of the window and started forward with her hand upon the check-string. It was dusk, and the evening was not clear. But she saw, nevertheless, that the coachman had turned down to the left among the squares of Bloomsbury, and that is not the way from Euston to Regent's Park. She did not pull the check-string, however. She looked curiously at Tony, who was sitting beside her, and then leaned back in the carriage. With her quick adaptability she had fallen into a habit of not questioning her husband. Since the night in the south of France she had given herself into his hands with a devotion which, to tell the truth, had something of slavishness. It was his wish, apparently, that the recollection of that night should still be a barrier between them, hindering them from anything but an exchange of courtesies. She bowed to the wish without complaint. To-night, however, as they drove through the unaccustomed streets there rose within her mind a hope. She would have stifled it, dreading disappointment; but it was stronger than her will. Moreover, it received each minute fresh encouragement. The brougham crossed Oxford Street, turned down South Audley Street, and traversed thence into Park Street. Millie now sat forward in her seat. She glanced at her husband. Tony, with a face of indifference, was looking out of the window. Yet the wonderful thing, it seemed, was coming to pass—nay, had come to pass. For already the brougham had stopped, and the door at which it stopped was the door of the little house in Deanery Street.

Tony turned to his wife with a smile.

"Home!" he said.

She sat there incredulous, even though the look of the house, the windows, the very pavement were speaking to her memories. There was the blank wall on the north side which her drawing-room window overlooked, there was the sharp curve of the street into Park Lane, there was the end of Dorchester House. Here the happiest years of her life—yes, and of Tony's, too, had been passed. She had known that to be truth for a long while now. She had come of late to think that they were the only really happy years which had fallen to her lot. The memories of them throbbed about her now with a vividness which was poignant.

"Is it true?" she asked, with a catch of her breath. "Is it really true, Tony?"

"Yes, this is our home."

Millie descended from the carriage. Tony looked at her curiously. This sudden arrival at the new home, which was the old, had proved a greater shock to her than he had expected. For a little while after their return to England Millie had dwelt upon the words which Tony had spoken to her in the *Réserve* by the sea. He had dreamed of buying the house in Deanery Street, and of resuming there the life which they had led together in the days when they had been good friends as well as good lovers. That dream for a time she had made her own. She had come to long for its fulfilment as she had never longed for anything else in the world; she had believed that sooner or later Tony would relent, and that it would be fulfilled. But the months had passed, and now, when she had given up hope, unexpectedly it had been fulfilled. She stood upon the pavement, almost dazed.

"You never said a word of what you meant to do," she said, with a smile, as though excusing herself for her unresponsive manner. The door was open. She went into the house, and Tony followed her. They mounted the stairs into the drawing-room.

"As far as I could," Tony said, "I had the house furnished just as it used to be. I could not get all the pictures which we once had, but you see I have done my best."

Millie looked round the room. There was the piano standing just as it used to do; the carpet, the wall-paper were all of the old pattern. It seemed to her that she had never left the house; that the years in Berkeley Square and Regent's Park were a mere night-mare from which she had just awakened. And then she looked at Tony. No, these latter years had been quite real—he bore the marks of them upon his face. The boyishness had gone. No doubt, she thought, it was the same with her.

Tony stood and looked at her with an eagerness which she did not understand.

"Are you glad?" he asked, earnestly. "Millie, are you pleased?"

She stood in front of him with a very serious face. Once a smile brightened it; but it was a smile of doubt, of question.

"I am not sure," she said. "I know that you have been very kind. You have done this to please me. But—" And her voice wavered a little.

"Well?" said Tony.

"But," she went on, with difficulty, "I am not sure that I can endure it, unless things are different from what they have been lately. I shall be reminded every minute of other times, and the comparison between those times and the present will be very painful. I think that I shall be very unhappy, much more unhappy than I have ever been, even lately."

Her voice sank to a whisper at the end. The little house in Deanery Street, even in her dreams, had been no more than a symbol. She had longed for it as the outward and visible sign of the complete reconciliation on which her heart was set. But to have the sign and to know that it signified nothing—she dreaded that possibility now. Only for a very few moments she dreaded it.

"I don't think I can endure it, Tony," she said, sadly. And the next moment his arms were about her, and her head was resting against his breast.

"Millie!" he cried, in a low voice; and again, "Millie!"

373

Her face was white, her eyelids closed over her eyes. Tony thought that she had swooned. But when he moved her hands held him close to her, held him tightly, as though she dreaded to lose him.

"Millie," he said, "do you remember the lights in Oban Bay? And the gulls calling at night above the islands?"

"I am forgiven, then?" she whispered; and he answered only:

"Hush!"

But the one word was enough.

XXXVI

THE END

TONY wished for no mention of the word. He had not brought her to that house that he might forgive her, but because he wanted her there. If forgiveness was in question, there was much to be said upon her side, too. He was to blame, as Pamela had written. He had during the last few months begun to realize the justice of that sentence more clearly than he had done even when the letter was fresh within his thoughts.

"I have learned something," he said to Millie, "which I might have known before, but never did. It is this: Although a man may be content to know that love exists, that is not the case with women. They want the love expressed, continually expressed, not necessarily in words, but in a hundred little ways. I did not think of that. There was the mistake I made: I left you alone to think just what you chose. Well, that's all over now. I bought this house not merely to please you, but as much to please myself; for as soon as I understood that, after all, the compromise which I dreaded need not be our lot—that, after all, the life together of which I used to dream was possible, was within arm's-reach if only one would put out an arm and grasp it — I wanted you here. As soon as I was sure, quite sure, that I had recaptured you, I wanted you here."

He spoke with passion, holding her in his arms. Millie remained quite still for a while, and then she asked:

"Do you miss the Legion? As much as you thought you would—as much as you did that night at Eze?"

He answered, "No"; and spoke the truth. On that night at Eze he had not foreseen the outcome of his swift return, of his irruption into the gayly lighted room murmurous with the sea. On that night he had revealed himself to Millie, and the revelation had been the beginning of love in her rather than its resumption. This he had come to understand, and, understanding, could reply with truth that he did not miss the Legion as he had thought he would. There were moments, no doubt, when the sound of a bugle on a still morning would stir him to a sense of loss, and he would fall to dreaming of Tavernay and Barbier, and his old comrades, and the menacing silence of the Sahara. At times, too, the yapping of dogs in the street would call up vividly before his mind the picture of some tent-village in Morocco where he had camped. Or the wind roaring among trees on a night of storm would set his mind wondering whether the ketch *Perseverance* was heading to the white-crested rollers, close-reefed between the Dogger and the Fisker banks; and for a little while he would feel the savor of the brine sharp upon his lips, and longing would be busy at his heart — for the Ishmaelite cannot easily become a stay-at-home. These, however, were but the passing moods.

Of one other character who took an important if an unobtrusive part in shaping the fortunes of the Truants, a final word may be said. A glimpse of that man, of the real man in him, was vouchsafed to Warrisden two summers later. It happened that Warrisden attended a public dinner which was held in a restaurant in Oxford Street. He left the company before the dinner was over, since he intended to fetch his wife, Pamela, who was on that June evening witnessing a performance of "Rigoletto" at the Opera-House in Covent Garden. Warrisden rose from the table and slipped out, as he thought, at eleven o'clock, but on descending into the hall he found that he had miscalculated the time. It was as yet only a quarter to the hour, and, having fifteen minutes to spare, he determined to walk. The night was hot; he threw his overcoat across his arm, and, turning southward, out of Oxford Street, passed down a narrow road in the neighborhood of Drury Lane. In those days, which were not, after all, so very distant from our own, the great blocks of model dwellings had not been as yet erected; squalid courts and rookeries opened onto ill-lighted passages; the houses had a ruinous and a miserable look. There were few people abroad as Warrisden passed through the quarter, and his breastplate of white shirt-front made him a conspicuous figure. He had come about half the way from Oxford Street when he saw two men suddenly emerge from the mouth of a narrow court a few yards in front of him. The two men were speaking, or rather shouting, at each other; and from the violence of their gestures, no less than from the abusive nature of the language which they used, it was plain that they were quarrelling. Words and gestures led to blows. Warrisden saw one man strike the other and fell him to the ground.

In an instant a little group of people was gathered about the combatants, people intensely silent and interested—the sight-seers of the London streets, who spring from nowhere with inconceivable rapidity, as though they had been waiting in some secret spot hard by for just this particular spectacle in this particular place. Warrisden, indeed, was wondering carelessly at the speed with which the small crowd had gathered when he came abreast of it. He stopped and peered over the shoulders of the men and women in front of him, that he might see the better. The two disputants had relapsed apparently into mere vituperation. Warrisden pressed forward, and those in front parted and made way for him. He did not, however, take advantage of the deference shown to his attire; for at that moment a voice whispered in his ear:

"You had better slip out. This row is got up for you."

Warrisden turned upon his heel. He saw a short, stout, meanly dressed man of an elderly appearance moving away from his side; no doubt it was he who had warned him. Warrisden took the advice, all the more readily because he perceived that the group was, as it were, beginning to reform itself, with him as the new centre. He was, however, still upon the outskirts. He pushed quickly out into the open street, crossed the road, and continued on his way. In front of him he saw the stout, elderly man, and, quickening his pace, he caught him up.

"I have to thank you," he said, "for saving me from an awkward moment."

"Yes," replied the stout man; and Warrisden, as he heard his voice, glanced at him with a sudden curiosity. But his hat was low upon his brow and the street was dark. "It is an old trick, but the old tricks are the tricks which succeed. There was no

Pan

Chittle

Winthill 5-8 19